Illusions of Decency

KEVIN PETTWAY

Cursed Dragon Ship
P U B L I S H I N G

Cursed Dragon Ship Publishing, LLC

6046 FM 2920 Rd, #231, Spring, TX 77379

captwyvern@curseddragonship.com

This books is a work of fiction fresh from the author's imagination. Any resemblance to actual persons or places is mere coincidence.

Cover © 2022 by Lena Shore

Developmental Edit by Kelly Lynn Colby

Proofread by Shannon Winton

ISBN 978-1-951445-25-6

ISBN 978-1-951445-26-3 (ebook)

I dedicate this book to my siblings, Brent and Kristin.
So many siblings grow up in competition,
for the love of a parent, for dominance in a household,
or sometimes just to be noticed.
And while we all grew up in the same crucible,
instead of turning on each other, we used that heat to forge
even stronger bonds. Not just love, but friendship as well.
Thank you for your endless support and belief in me,
whether I deserved it or not.

CONTENTS

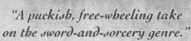

*"A puckish, free-wheeling take
on the sword-and-sorcery genre."*
— KIRKUS REVIEWS

No one wanted to go near Gullhome because of the
demon that rules there, the superstitious idiots.
In the end I turned back because a hoop gull
landed on the bowsprit, and quite sensibly I did not
wish to be marooned and bewitched by sea-fairies.

We were briefly pinned in coastal ice here.
Men came to our aid, but when they were gone,
so were all the sheep we were transporting.
Knowing why they took them, I can only
wish the Norrikmen and their new sheep
the happiest of marriages.

Picked up a dozen crates of shoes in Mirrik.
Raiders make good cobblers, it would seem.
My own pair is both attractive and comfortable.
Later we found out that the shoes were made
from the feet of the last merchant crew.
We were relieved not to have caught
them making coin purses.

Some commotion occurred in Dahut just
ahead of our arrival. Horrifying mercenaries
attacked the town and committed all manner
of depraved and desperate acts.

In fact, if the ill-bred brutes had not
murdered the town guard, we would never
have been able to steal the rest of their food.

Being a ship's captain truly is all
about finding the silver linings.

Our ship was menaced by pirates
coming around the tip of Sedrios.
Instead of fighting we challenged
them to a drinking contest.
Three sailors died, but we kept our cargo
and invented a new dance as well.

Gullhome

Oldguts

Icebits

Spine

Norrik

Raiders
Sea

Vikkan

Summervatn

Krusuvik

Summer

Knarrax

Mirrik

Rousca

Rousland

Arle

Sedrios

The Paradisals

Port Placid

N
E
W
S

laced

enaries

"This is my kind of fantasy."
— ERIC FLINT

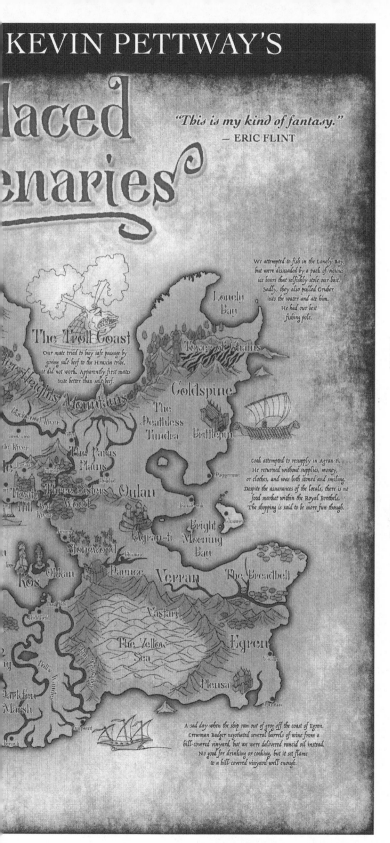

1

I'VE CHANGED MY MIND. I THINK I WILL KILL YOU

SARAH

Sarah rode Apple, an even-tempered bay mare, over the top of a gentle hill and stared down into the Low Wood. She narrowed her eyes against the buzzing mosquitoes. Somewhere in that jungle lurked the demon she hunted: sly, dangerous, and accompanied by vicious mercenaries.

But then, Sarah was not alone either.

The Swift Shields regiment of the King's Swords of Greenshade followed her—fifty men who chafed, stank, and unhappily marched in the warm Arlean weather. The slinking clinks of their mail hauberks fought for attention over their grumbling curses.

They would be only too happy to murder Morholt and *all* his cronies and get the hell out of here. Arlea shared a small slice of border with Greenshade, but it was at the sweaty asscrack end.

Sarah, on the other hand, wanted live captives. She and Falt would have to keep a tight rein on the rest of the troop.

Captain Falt sat straight in his saddle, like an unfortunately mustachioed stick kitted up for battle. The tabard of Greenshade he carried flapped loosely in the morning breeze. His gaze intensified when a pair of green rabbits, the same shade as the grass, jumped into the trees below.

"He's in there all right." Falt nodded toward the wood, not talking about rabbits. "I'm just worried about finding the others. We need to take as many alive as we can. See if they'll talk." His typically pale face stayed blotchy and red in the humid air.

Sarah reached up and behind her head. Her muscular brown arms reflected gold in the early sun as she tightened her dark braids in their leather sleeve. Silver strands ran through the left braid to the wide claw marks on that side of her forehead. "Except Morholt, you mean."

"Of course, except him," Captain Falt replied. "Our orders are quite explicit there."

Slap. She flicked the mosquito's tiny corpse off her finger. Summer in Arlea.

"Why do you want to see Morholt killed?" Sarah asked.

"Well"—Captain Falt ruminated on the question a moment, as if it were a choice stalk of sweetgrass—"I suppose all the murders and raping would be enough." He swallowed, and the knob in his throat, every bit as prominent as his lack of chin, went up and down. "I know they say he's a demon with all the magic and that, but they used to think you were a demon, and you're just a nice lady. Warrior-lady. With army-destroying magic—but on *our* side."

She gave him a level glare. The events on that battlefield still made her stomach churn, and she did not appreciate discussing them.

Falt rolled his eyes and continued, "Anyway, for me, I'd say it was when he burned Hopfield. You know they begged him—*begged* him — to just take everything they had and leave. But he cut down the men in front of the womenfolk, chopped up the women in front of the babies, and then fed the babies to his dogs. I reckon that's what did it for me."

"Hmm." Sarah rolled one broad shoulder and loosened her big sword in its scabbard. Again. "How many people do you think he murdered or raped?"

"The way I hear it," Captain Falt answered, "it must be in the thousands by now. I hear he's giving the old devil Harden Grayspring a run for his money."

"Did you ever meet anyone who got raped by Morholt or his men?" Sarah hopped down from her horse and began to lead it down the slope. "Ever talk to anyone who knew someone who got killed?"

"No," Captain Falt admitted. "But I'm just one man, and Greenshade is a big place. I should know. I've been over every blessed inch of her." He clucked to his own mount, a dapple gray he insisted on calling Fancy Bird, and followed Sarah.

The Swift Shields filed over the hill, row after row of deadly armored ducklings tagging behind their parents.

Sarah's wide lips set in a grim line. "Every blessed inch. Tell me, Renee, where is Hopfield?"

"Well it's in the east, twixt Fenrath and..." Captain Falt paused and put a gloved hand to where a chin would be on a more fully formed man. "No, that's not right. It's in the grasslands, I know that. Maybe north of Old Oak?" He stopped, consideration working through his face. "It can't be as far as Sheaf, can it?" He sighed and shrugged. "Where it is isn't important. What's important is how horrible it was. And it was *horrible.*"

"What if I told you there never was any Hopfield?" Sarah asked him. "What if I were to tell you that as far as I can tell, *no one* has ever known anyone who has been harmed by Morholt or his Free Hand— other than the honor of a few innkeepers' daughters, anyway."

Captain Falt pulled a little ahead. They were halfway down the hillside now and fully in the shadow of it. "I guess I'd say our orders came from the king, and he ought to know better than us."

That thought brought a crooked half smile to Sarah's face. She and Keane, the current king of Greenshade, had been mercenaries together. She loved him more than anyone, but while he was cleverer than most, deep thinking and far-reaching knowledge were not exactly his strengths.

"If we can do it without putting anyone in danger, I'd rather we caught all our quarries alive." The command to catch or kill Morholt and his crew came through Keane, but Sarah felt certain it originated with Finnagel, her untrustworthy sorcerous mentor and Keane's advisor. If they could take the demon alive, she was determined to discover why.

She peered into the brush. What had looked like the shadow of a man through the trees was merely the twist of a vine. "We can take Morholt to the Dovenhouse and bring the rest back to Treaty Hill. Let the Temple of the Sky deal with him."

"You do outrank me," Captain Falt said with another shrug. "Dovenhouse is where they turn demons back to men, right? Seems the right place for him. Then he can be hanged proper, as a man."

It wasn't exactly Sarah's point, but it was a start. The Temple of the Sky would probably kill Morholt anyway. Falt, still riding Fancy Bird, pulled ahead.

She froze in place and grabbed Captain Falt's boot.

He halted Fancy Bird on the spot.

"I smell a campfire," she said. "Someone's cooking breakfast."

"Alir help the dirty demon what's cooking bacon in this wilderness, and I'm here to kill him," one of the soldiers behind Sarah and Captain Falt said. As if laughter were road bread bubbling anxiously in bacon fat before a battle with fifty hungry men, tepid mirth rose around the jokester.

"Shut it," Captain Falt ordered. "If Sarah can smell them, they can most likely hear us."

The smile at the corner of Sarah's mouth pulled a little higher. When she and Keane first met then-Lieutenant Falt, he had been halting and timid, a scrawny squirrel among battle-scarred old wolves.

Those days were gone.

Still thin, Captain Falt now held himself with a rangy strength that kept him erect and looking down on most of his men. His newfound confidence was born of successful leadership in numerous scrapes, including one war. He'd even found a woman willing to overlook his chinlessness and ridiculous mustache enough to marry him and give him three beautiful, normally chinned children.

Some soldiers teased that his head looked like a bottle brush.

Just not to his face.

Sarah shook her head. It had been nine years since they'd met. His confidence was not all that newly found after all.

They tied off their horses at the beginnings of the jungle, and Sarah leaned in to Captain Falt. "We don't kill anyone. The king may have given the order, but it came from Chancellor Finnagel. And I'd like to know why. Morholt may know the answer."

Captain Falt nodded wordlessly. He was not a man who enjoyed equivocation when it came to orders, but a good military man recognized things could change once the field was entered.

As silently as they could, the mass of soldiers moved into the trees and undergrowth. They put away their long swords in favor of dirks to accommodate the densely packed terrain but kept their shields raised. Sarah held a thick-hafted arrow nocked in her troll longbow and scanned the dim greenery.

A growl erupted from behind, and Sarah whirled, the arrow's fletching pulled to her cheek. One of the soldiers grinned, embarrassed, and pointed to his stomach. Everyone could smell the cooking breakfast now.

Knobby tree trunks rose in twisted whorls toward an unseen sky, and the smell of earth and sweet rot layered with cooking pig.

A man's deep and unabashed laughter, loud and joyous, rang out from a glimmer of sunlight just ahead, no doubt at some evil-spirited jest. Sarah raised a hand to stop the Swift Shields and crept ahead. A huge bole grew in a generous slant in front of the tiny clearing, and she scrambled up it as easily as a lord stepped on the backs of his peasants.

Sarah breathed the sorcerous words that allowed her to speak with Keane across the distance from here in Arlea all the way to Greenshade's capital of Treaty Hill. "I found them. I'm going in. Wish me luck."

"Oldam's filthy flint foreskin, Sarah!" Keane shouted, though no one but she could hear him, "Are you trying this alone? You sound like you're alone. I *told* you how dangerous he is."

"Gotta go," she whispered. "Let you know how it turns out." She really did have to cut the conversation off. Sorcerous communication like this was subject to eavesdropping by others if it went on too long, and Sarah was uncomfortably close to Deliah the Unbroken, infamous apprentice to Olandrea, who was turned to glass. She would not have dared the spell at all except Keane made her promise. The worrywart.

Twenty feet up, she spied her quarry: The Free Hand mercenaries, led by the runecrafter Morholt. With weathered green leathers and ginger hair, Morholt passed a plate of food to his sister, Raven. She looked like she could use it. Under her own black mop and black leather armor, she was as thin as a pole snake and reputed to be twice as mean.

Across the fire rested the two big Darrish warriors Mahu and Sabni, some kind of elite fighters from Egren. Their honey-colored armor was oiled and clean despite obvious wear. Keane had spent time with this group, and Sarah knew enough to pay close attention to these two.

The final pair were newcomers, and Sarah did not know much about them. The first was a girl, twenty or so in age, curvy, with a big grin and a headful of strawberry blonde curls. The other was a problem.

Though seated, the northerner next to the girl was massive. He sat shirtless on his folded gambeson armor, and his numerous tattoos and scars rippled across hardened and tanned shoulders. His gold-brown hair and beard were braided down his burly back and chest, and it was he whose laughter boomed through the twilit jungle.

Sarah was definitely sticking an arrow in him first.

Just ahead, a thick branch she had not previously noticed jutted at a perfect angle to hide behind and gave her an excellent field of fire. The Swift Shields would surround the Free Hand and wait for the first cries to come charging in. Once it was obvious how outnumbered the mercenaries were, the fighting would come to a quick end.

Or so Sarah thought just before she fell through that perfect branch, as if she were trying to stand on a column of smoke.

Sarah managed to roll off her shoulder when she hit the knotty roots on the ground. She gasped in pain as thick wooden fingers pounded into her back but partially distributed the hit.

Pink mist billowed from the ground where Sarah struck it and obscured everything, though just before she lost sight of them, the laughing mercenaries blew away, ephemeral as the offensive branch she fell through.

The huge man's laughter rang out from every side.

Horses neighed and stamped close by. The Swift Shields had found the Free Hand's horses and run them off. No sense in taking a chance that one of the Hand might break through to their mounts and escape.

"I'm giving you and your yellowbacks one chance to run away before they get the ass kicking of their lives." The voice floated happily in from somewhere above Sarah. It had to be Morholt.

"Keane told me you were dangerous." Sarah put away her bow and pulled out a thick wooden baton, though she could not see through the pink past the end of it. Shooting arrows off into the obscuring cloud was out of the question. "He didn't tell me you were bad at math. There are six of you and fifty-two of us. I'm not here to kill you—not unless you make me—just bring you back to Green-shade. But you're coming with me either way."

"You'd be kinda cute if I weren't scared of getting my pecker crushed in your butthole." Above her the voice was on the move. "I mean, look at you. That butt is all muscle. I didn't even know women came in that size."

A deep, rumbly voice said, "There are women in Mirrik her size, though none more sturdily built, I'd wager."

This was not good. Sarah could hear the Swift Shields moving into position, but she could also hear their curses and complaints as they encountered the pink fog. Morholt and his crew did not sound as if they had any difficulty seeing her right through it.

No, this was not good at all.

Sarah spun toward a footfall to her right, and her baton arced out in a half-moon of blunt wind. Wind was all it was. She had just enough time to realize that the footfall was yet another trap when she was clubbed in the head from behind. Sarah fell to her knees and tried to make the ground stop trying to pull up sideways.

Though unbelievable just a few seconds ago, Sarah was going to lose this fight. How bad and whether she survived it were the only questions left for her to answer.

The pink-tinged horror that came next assaulted every sense she had. Soldiers from Greenshade screamed and shouted and ran crashing through the brush. Sarah stumbled to her feet, and a cloud of dried pepper went up her nose. It was impossible not to stop and sneeze over and over. If any of the mercenaries were ignorant of her location before, they were not now.

A Swift Shield tumbled to the ground in front of her, a goose-feather fletched arrow stuck out the back of his thigh. No major arteries hit. Either a lucky shot or a skilled one.

Tears and snot from the pepper streamed down Sarah's face as she broke free of the clearing and into the battle—where six people cheerfully thrashed fifty.

Men banged up against her, fell at her feet, and wailed their pain in her ears. Everywhere phantoms of the Free Hand darted in and out of her vision, always just too fast for her to catch them with her baton. She dropped it and drew her wide-bladed sword. At the edge of her vision, a soldier with blood running down his arm and tears in his eyes stumbled past.

In that instant, she flung her wish to bring *any* of the mercenaries home alive to the winds. Sarah heard her Swords being slaughtered all around her, and cold fury filled her arms with a stony strength.

Fuck what Finnagel wants, and fuck why he wants it. I'm killing as many of these demons as I can.

Sarah turned and stepped at the same time Morholt turned to her. He held her gaze with a twinkle in his eye, but whatever he had been about to say was cut off when Sarah, determined not to let the opportunity escape her, rammed her sword through his guts straight to the cross guard.

"Witch's gift, Morholt, she *really* doesn't like you." It was the girl's voice again, but she sounded disturbingly unconcerned.

Morholt's mouth worked in an effort to speak. He clutched Sarah by the shoulder.

"Time to go." The voice of Morholt came from somewhere else in the near distance. "Things are about to get *super* uncomfortable here."

Before her unbelieving eyes, the figure of Morholt turned to smoke and left Captain Falt spitted on her sword, gasping for breath.

"No!" Sarah slid Captain Falt down to the hard, root-covered ground and leaned him up against a tree. "No, no, no, no..."

Captain Falt was unconscious by the time Sarah rested his head on the bark. The pink mist blew away, and she saw she was surrounded by moaning and bloody men—though only one of them had been rendered so by her.

Keane tried to tell her, but she was too intent on the hunt, too excited by the prospect of finally catching the runecrafter, to listen to what he was saying. This was truly all her fault.

She sneezed.

A few soldiers remained unharmed and stumbled dazedly to her. The first, a pretty young man in his early twenties whose name Sarah could not recall, stopped short at Captain Falt.

"Go help those that can be helped." Sarah's gaze narrowed, and her brow pulled down like a cresting tidal wave of anger and grief. "I'm going to kill that evil murdering bastard." She wiped her face with the back of a rock-hard hand. "I'm going to *kill* him."

"I'd say you are." The figure of a person stood next to Sarah with a calm smile on its face, head cocked to one side.

She had first seen it over the battlefield when she killed Valafar, apprentice to the Anger Under the Mountain. It had appeared three more times since then, less and less like a fever dream each time.

"You talk now?" Sarah stepped away from the Shields and watched the figure follow her. She knew from experience that no one else would see it. Holding a lengthy conversation with the air would not help matters. Her rage drained in the face of this long mystery come to resolve itself.

"Your regard has given me strength to appear to you." Its speech was clipped and proper, like real royalty. "The more we interact, the more real I'll become. Rather like flexing a muscle, I suppose." Neither really male or female, it dressed in comfortably worn linens and looked, more than anything else, a little like Sarah herself.

"Are you a ghost?" Sarah asked.

"That's a reasonable question," the figure answered and drew its thumb and forefinger down a smooth brown chin. "I imagine I am a bit. Although conventionally ghosts don't really exist."

"Do you have a name?"

The figure sat noiselessly on a fallen tree trunk. "I've never really needed one before. Do you think I should?"

"How's Gabby sound?" Sarah really needed to get back to the wounded, but thoughts of this *whatever it was* had been distracting her for years. It was hard to just walk away. Especially now that her silent ghost had suddenly become, well, gabby.

"Majestic." It sighed, and the strength faded from it. "I'm afraid that's all I can do for now. I'll see you again when I recover. Be safe, Sarah."

It faded from view.

She stood for a moment and listened before returning to aid her men.

2

THE VICTORY FLEEING
MORHOLT

W e are whole, and the enemy licks their wounds in our tracks." Sabni waved a rangy arm over Morholt's head. The Darrishman stood an entire foot taller than Morholt and was as dark as Morholt was light—except for the ever-present smile that lit up every room he entered. "I count that as victory."

"Then why are we running away?" Raven asked. She sighted along the edge of one of her two long curved daggers. Morholt knew she was checking for nicks in the hard steel. She did it every time she pulled one of them out. Obsessive about it, really.

The captain was dead because Morholt had not noticed when Sarah dropped her baton and drew her sword. He had thought it would be funny when the captain woke up the next day with a creased skull from his own ally. But it really wasn't.

"Because if we stayed back, they'd want to fight some more, and it'd be harder to leave them all alive." Ameli's curly red-blonde hair bounced around her round face with every step through the jungle. She was bouncy all over.

"They weren't all alive," Mahu muttered. Shorter and broader than his battlemate Sabni, Mahu was also generally much less cheerful. He slashed ahead with a heavy-hafted jungle blade.

Morholt wasn't sure what *battlemate* meant in the strictest sense, but for those two it seemed to involve sharing a tent.

"But Mahu, it is as in *The Immortal Queen Nefret and the Fallow Orchard*." Sabni grinned wider. He was always happiest when quoting one of his religious stories.

Mahu rolled his eyes. "The difference between a hero and a corpse is the timing of his retreat. Yes, I've heard." He frowned further. "Are we going to talk about the chinless captain?"

"I'd rather not," Morholt said. In truth, he was rattled. Since the end of the Occupation of Treaty Hill, the northern peoples had taken to calling Sarah "the Hill Fury" and for good reason. She was a sorceress and had killed thousands on that field.

And this time she looked *mad*.

"I bet," Raven said, "Sarah was pissed. She's gonna kill the shit outta you for that."

"Break." Morholt stopped. These idiots weren't helping matters in the least. He needed a wiser ear to talk to.

He walked a short distance from the others and sat in a lonely patch of sunlight amongst the oppressive jungle. Out of his pack, he pulled a rectangle of pasteboard wrapped in a ratty green silk handkerchief. One side was covered in intricate whorls of dull metallic paint, themselves covered in even more impenetrable runes.

On the other side was April.

"Hello, Holt," said the painted image. A thin tongue flickered out and licked one of its round eyes, as glossy and black as its teeth. It curtsied, holding the skirt of yellow dress to either side. "Get tired of your *real* friends?" Her voice and name were those of a girl Morholt knew in school, which was why he rarely called her by her proper name anymore.

"Sure have." He settled amongst the moss and dirt; his faded green leathers matched the surroundings. "Whatcha got for me, Bean?"

Blood red lips pulled back in a leering smile. "A guy goes down to the water to get in his boat and go fishing. Only the boat isn't there. He waits all day for whoever borrowed his boat to come back in, and he gets madder and madder as the sun goes past. Wait, did I say he's a fisherman? That's his job. That's why he's so mad, because he needs that sweet fish money to buy his daughter a new leg or something. I don't think that's important. Where were we?"

"Missing boat. Getting mad. Sun passing by." Morholt rested his chin in one hand and smiled absently. He had constructed April when he was fourteen and given her all the gifts he knew how to give. She had grown in a lot of ways—just not her sense of humor.

"Right! So, the sun goes down, still no boat. Decides the hell with it and goes to the fisher bar to get drunk. He walks in and bam! There's his boat, bellied up to the bar and five sheets to the wind. He says to the boat, 'What the hell are you—' No. Damn. I already said the punchline. Hang on, I'll go again."

Morholt waved a hand. "That's all right. You can get it next time."

Furry gray brows beetled over red-rimmed black eyes.

"It was already really funny," Morholt said. "Please don't tell it again. It feels like I'm jerking off oxen in my ear."

"That's good, right?" April asked.

"The *best*," Morholt answered. "And speaking of the best, how's your local knowledge around here?"

"Are you still headed to Glauth?" the painted creature asked. "She's going to try and take the engine. You know she will."

He flicked his fingers dismissively. "I'm only trying to help her. Besides, taking an engine is twice as hard when you're trying to take it from someone who has one."

April turned her head in a curiously doglike gesture.

"You know what I mean." Smartass painting. "There might be pursuit. Where do we go? We need horses, too." He raised his voice. "Someone tied them right next to the battle site, and we lost *all* of them."

"Sorry," Reinar's deep, rumbly voice boomed back.

"He doesn't sound very sorry," April said.

"I don't think he is." Morholt peered over his shoulder at the others. A veritable giant of a man, Reinar Brokenhilt was the single most impressive warrior Morholt had ever had the terror of seeing. But there was a flaw close to his heart. He seemed attracted to battle and suffered in an unhealthy way like he was trying to punish himself or something. His little friend Ameli had given herself a bigger job than she thought in keeping him alive and out of the bottle.

"I assume we're trying to avoid the Temple of the Sky?" April scratched under her drool-coated chin.

"To the exact same extent we would avoid white-hot shards of glass up our pecker holes," Morholt responded.

"Arlea is out then," she said. "That means no boats to go up the river. Too bad. The Summer Trades would've saved you a week headed north this time of year. Watchpoint is closest, but I suppose walking over the Beacon Sea is out too."

"As always, Bean, your instincts are flawless." Morholt twirled a few strands of his ginger beard.

"That leaves Sheaf." April removed a folded sheet of paper from her flat bodice and opened it. "See here." She pointed at a point on the blank page. The fastest way is to head for the shore and follow the coastline to Shallowhead Bay, where the Low Wood is narrowest, then cut northeast right across to Sheaf." She tapped the page with a taloned finger. "It'd be safer to go straight through the wood. Lot slower though. Sure am glad *I* don't have to trudge through the jungle. I don't like humidity."

"I don't either," Morholt admitted. "What do we have to worry about under the trees?"

April's snout split wide in a black-toothed grin. She loved talking about animals. *Especially* ones that might eat you. "All the cats are south of you in Sedrios. That's dodging the arrow. Nothing north to worry about but rabbit snakes, pole snakes, waxwoods maybe, and a few cast-off gangs of the old Hubrane regime that were no good for anything but murdering and robbing. They live in the jungle now. Smooth sailing." She put her hands on her hips. "Oh, and there's lots of emberflies at night. Super poisonous. Did you bring nets?"

Morholt grimaced and rubbed his temple. "And if we cut through the wood before that and travel along the north edge?"

"How bad off did you leave the Swift Shields?" April asked.

"Bad enough." Morholt felt bleak. He didn't seem to have any good options, just fewer bad ones. Or so he hoped, anyway. "We managed not to kill anyone other than the captain, but the rest are in no shape to come after us." *Except the Hill Fury herself.*

"Are you regretting your decision to try and be one of the good guys?" She smiled and blinked. "I think it's very noble of you to try and be better than that mean old Harden Grayspring was. Leave the world a little better than you came into it. Even if this isn't your world."

That wasn't what caused his change of heart, and April knew it. But he didn't want to talk about the real reason either. "The northern edge?"

"Oh, right." She folded her tiny arms. "If there's no pursuit, there's not much to worry about. You'll be in the Western Marches, and I've heard the new Hubranes aren't quite as gung ho on the temple as the crown is. They might not even know the king is hunting for you. But then again, they might. You could be walking into ten thousand spears. Maybe just eight thousand. I haven't been able to check in a while."

Toad dicks. "You were more useful when you could tell the future," Morholt told the pasteboard card. "Your jokes were funnier too."

"I can still tell the future." April turned her head and pouted. "The future just isn't there anymore. You don't lose the ability to see in an empty room. You're just—bored."

"Sorry, Bean." He really was. About a lot of things. "We'll talk more soon." He wrapped the card in green silk and returned it to his pack.

Morholt disliked taking the Free Hand up the coastline. Tracking would be easier there. He wanted to head north and skirt the wood, but that meant crossing the jungle where it was thickest. Morholt was scared of snakes, but then, he was scared of lots of things.

Right now, he was mostly scared of Sarah.

3

PROLOCUTOR MEANS TALKS TOO MUCH
SARAH

S arah of Levale, the pilgrim handmaiden herself. My eyes are blessed to look upon the favorite of the Alir."

"Uh," Sarah said, uncomfortable at Vancess's ornate address in the middle of the street. "Thanks? Am I supposed to call you Prolocutor or Commander?"

After a week's travel, Sarah had crossed from Arlea to Rousea and managed to make it all the way through the town of Dahnt to the temple complex without being stopped—thanks to a devilishly hot hooded cloak. Once a sleepy fishing town and resupply stop for merchant ships, Dahnt gained instant celebrity when Keane the War King declared the Temple of the Sky officially back in favor. The only remaining temple building in the world was right here.

Now the town was a burgeoning city, and the small temple building with the blue-green facade sat at the center of a sprawling complex of white sandstone buildings. And due to her journey with and tutelage from goddess Magda, the temple adherents had all decided Sarah was some kind of holy figure.

"Call me by whatever name you please, handmaiden." Vancess's armor shone brilliantly in the sunlight. Golden symbols of the temple glittered everywhere on shining steel plates. "Your mere presence fills my soul with light."

"Does that mean you're not going to try and kill me this time?" Both Sarah and Vancess once ran with the mercenary lord marshal Harden Grayspring and his merry band of cutthroats, Wallace's Company. Their parting had not been friendly.

"The gods saved you from my wrath." Vancess bowed again. "And it is with my intense gratitude that they did so. I would be forever saddened to have removed such beauty from the world."

Sarah couldn't make up her mind which thing Vancess had just said was the most offensive. She was not one to become slighted by idiots and typically paid them no mind. But she was here because Dahnt was much closer than Treaty Hill and she needed troops to replace the Swift Shields. This was not how she wanted the conversation to start.

Perhaps no one would mind if she just cut his head off a *little* bit.

A small crowd gathered beneath the high stone archway that let into the temple complex, mostly temple workers in their sky blue and white clothing with their conical wrapped hats but also a few well-dressed clerical types. Sarah heard awed whispers of "pilgrim handmaiden" more than once.

Vancess yelped when Sarah grabbed his arms and frog-marched him through the archway and into the sunny courtyard.

"C'mon, Lowell." She used his first name. "Let's carry this discussion inside. Don't want all your followers seeing you get your ass kicked by a girl."

"I assure you that—*ow!*" He wriggled to no avail. Sarah's fingers were an iron vise. "Leggo. This is no less undignified than—I said *OW*."

Sarah leaned down to whisper into Vancess's ear. "Which of these is the military officers' building?"

He nodded left. "That one with the crest and arrow loops."

They turned left and tromped through the open door. Everything was open. It was too hot for privacy.

A soldier behind a small desk leaped to his feet and saluted Vancess as the pair entered the tiny room. A door and a sky-blue square of cloth with a white arrow pointing up on the wall were the only other adornments. This entrance was obviously for the public and not meant for people like Vancess.

Sarah released Vancess, and he pointed to the outer door.

"Soldier," Vancess ordered, "the pilgrim handmaid and I have matters of fateful import to discuss. Stand outside this door and ensure that no one enters."

"Yes, *sir*," the soldier said and snapped off another salute. He hastened to comply.

After the door shut, Vancess stepped to the desk and turned to face Sarah. "I apologize if I have somehow given you offense, Handmaiden. I don't—"

"That's on me." Sarah frowned and scratched at the scars over her ear. "You *are* offensive. It's up to me to make allowances. It's not like I didn't already know you."

Vancess's eyes widened, and his brow rose, a dawning sun of contrition. But Keane taught her other things to look for in a man's expression, and she noticed that while his eyes begged forgiveness, his jaw tightened in anger.

Sarah sighed and let some of the hardness pass from her pose. "I am hunting demons. One of them trashed my men and killed my captain. There was no time to go back to Treaty Hill for more, so I came here. Can you help me?"

Vancess straightened, and when he smiled, there was no hint of anything hidden away. "There is nothing in this world or the next that would bring me greater happiness and fulfillment, Handmaiden. Such a calling all but guarantees a place in High King Oldam's great army. I have a cohort of noble lads that will be perfect for this. They already have experience and have been trained by me personally. They are the Shepherds of the Blood, temple knights, and we can be underway within the hour."

Irritation prickled across Sarah's shoulders. Vancess was a handsome man. Golden locks, lantern jaw, steely blue eyes. To her, he read like the perfect spoiled rich kid who always got everything he wanted. That might have been his upbringing, but he had taken a dangerous left turn when he joined Wallace's Company. The mercenary life turned an already cracked mind into a violent murderer. Somehow, all the religion just seeped right in through the cracks.

You didn't get into Oldam's great army unless you were dead. That was too much dedication to a god for her.

"Our targets are on foot." Sarah circled the desk and sat in the chair. "We can afford to give me a decent night's sleep. Wait." Her head popped up. "What did you mean by *we* can be underway?"

"Obviously, I meant I will accompany you on this perilous mission." Vancess *gleamed* his pleasure. The heat of his giddy gaze could boil water. "The Shepherds are imperative to this mission. They are specifically skilled in the killing of demons, and I am their commander just as you are our guide to the Alireon in the afterlife. Neither of us is anything less than absolutely essential. Together, we will cleanse the Thirteen Kingdoms of the demon's taint and return our world to the glory intended by the Alir when they created it."

"Great."

"Do you have the demon's name?" Vancess leaned in, eager.

"His name?" Sarah thought Vancess might pop with excitement. "Sure. It's Morholt. He travels with his sister and a small band of mercenaries."

"Wonderful." Vancess stood tall and raised his arms in thanks. "We test ourselves against the foulest creature imaginable, Handmaiden. The Alir recognize our stature and gift us with the rarest opportunity to prove ourselves further. You have brought blessings on all our souls." Vancess lowered his arms and rubbed the edge of his clean-shaven jaw. "This monster has corrupted women across Andos with his filth, teaching them his magics. If he knows you have decided to hunt him, he may well try and alert them. I believe I know where we should begin our search."

During Vancess's speech, Sarah slumped forward and now sat with her head in her hands, elbows forward on the desk. "So, you are actually in *charge* here?" It was a frightening prospect, but, in this one instance, she supposed it might be a help.

"I am Grand Prolocutor of the Army of the Temple of the Sky and Commander of the Holy Noble Order of the Stone Vault. That includes responsibility for the Temple of the Sky's martial forces." Vancess swept into a low bow. "I am yours to command."

Sarah waved a hand at Vancess. "Good. Find me a room with a bed, and be ready to go before dawn. We're going to have a hard ride to catch up to our demons. And we're going to *kill* demons, not clean their taints."

———

A short while later, Sarah lay back on a straw tick mattress and stared at the underside of the bunk above her. There were four in the bare room, and the only light came from a small square hole in a wall that she had stuffed a pillow into. Sarah assumed that the beds' original occupants would be sleeping in chairs tonight. She might even have felt bad about it except Vancess's example probably meant they thought their sacrifices would equate to eternal afterlife.

Religion was weird.

She settled her mind and spoke the words, gathering just enough of the world's ambient energy to open a sorcerous pinprick between herself and Keane. She felt his attention shift to her.

"I've found replacements for Falt and the Shields." She spoke the words to the top bunk. "Has anyone made it back yet?"

"Not yet," Keane said. "Megan and the kids say hi. Oldam's toenail. Bye."

And he was gone.

That was odd. Maybe she caught him in the middle of something? It was difficult to tell much with only a few seconds to judge.

"You look like someone with all the worries of the world on her shoulders."

Sarah closed her eyes and relaxed into the straw. "Hello, Gabby.

I've been wondering how long it was going to take you to show up again. You don't recuperate very fast."

"I'm getting faster." Reassurance and warmth came through that voice. "You've been quite the excellent partner."

She opened one eye to see the blandly attractive face looking down at her. It could have been her brother. Or sister. "How am I your partner? You appear, you disappear. I'm just here."

Gabby sat on the opposite bunk. As before, it neither made noise nor disturbed anything it touched. "What do you know of the origins of this world?"

"The Thirteen Kingdoms?" Sarah spread her hands above her stomach. "I don't know. Egren was the first, I think."

"No, no," Gabby said. "The *world*, not the nations, or even the people."

"Oh." Her arms dropped to her sides. "The Andosh think Oldam made the world, and the Darrish say it was Mother Love. I guess it just depends on who you ask."

Gabby cocked its head to one side. "And what do the Pavinn say?"

"I imagine most of us accept one side or the other," Sarah said. "The world is the world. It was already here when all of us arrived. I suppose someone had to make it."

"History *is* written by the victor." Gabby made a small sound that could have been a chuckle. "Would you like to learn Metzoferran? I mean *really* learn it. Not just mumble a few phrases here and there but *understand* it? Feel the texture of it and what it can do?"

The language of the gods. The true language of magic. Sorcerers used a combination of six other obscure and esoteric languages to make up for the loss of it. Her teacher Finnagel thought Metzoferran was a myth. Sarah knew better.

The goddess Magda taught Sarah the spells she used to decimate two thousand of Tyrrane's Ebon Host at the gates of Treaty Hill and to destroy Angrim's apprentice Valafar. But there had been no time to understand the sorcery itself. This was incredibly dangerous, and Sarah injured herself as a result.

Being unwilling to practice in the aftermath—and with no help

from her instructor Finnagel, who did not trust Magda's spells—
Sarah had long since forgotten how to work any of those deadly
complex magics.

She sat up and kicked her legs over the side of the bunk.

"Now I *really* need to know who you are," she said.

"I suppose you do at that," Gabby said. "This isn't going to work
unless we're honest with one another." It leaned back, hands on its
knees. "In the very beginning, the Consciousness sacrificed itself and
fractured into an infinite number of shards, as limitless divine beings
sometimes will."

"Of course," Sarah said. One side of her mouth went up in a
crooked smile. "Who wouldn't?"

"Indeed," Gabby said, a hesitant smile on its face. "The process
broke some fairly constant universal understandings. The Endless
Provinces were created as a result, and the shards of the Consciousness fell into them. Your world is one of these provinces."

It didn't *sound* drunk. Worse yet, the completely reasonable,
earnest voice encouraged her to believe it. After all, it was not like she
had been there.

"Kill yourself and get a bunch of new worlds." Sarah shook her
head. "But you never even get to see them? That doesn't seem like a
reasonable swap. Especially if it's you who has to go to pieces."

"Don't get ahead of the story." Gabby raised a hand. "You'll get me
telling everything out of order, and I'll have to start over."

"That should encourage me to keep quiet," Sarah responded, one
corner of her mouth playing higher.

Gabby tutted at her. "Very well. So, you may be curious as to what
happened to the shards. Some became gods, most became *real*
demons, and then there was me."

Somehow this did not come as the shock Sarah might have
expected. Even without being aware of the story, Gabby had exactly
the role she knew it would. Perversely, her thoughts flew back to her
time in Wallace's Company. Eating crappy food, drinking crappy beer,
laughing in the stink of a mercenary camp, and, when absolutely

everything else had failed, when there was no further option possible, actually fighting the enemy they had been paid to.

In some ways, her life had changed a lot in the past decade. In other ways, not at all.

She was still fighting.

"All of that, bringer of light and magic, and I suppose it's just a coincidence that you look like my close cousin?" *Except I don't know any cousins*, Sarah thought.

"I'm so sorry." Eyes widened in the brown face. "Is it distracting? I make an effort to appear in a form similar to whoever I'm visiting, but it's been, well, *millennia* I suppose since I've appeared to anyone this side of the universe. I may have overdone it."

"What were you?" Sarah asked.

"I was the strongest shard," Gabby answered. "The biggest shard of the Consciousness to make it to this world. And therefore, I retained more of its personality than the others."

Gabby made a fist of one hand and spun her other hand over it. "I trust Finnagel has taught you the nature of magical energy? Worlds existing within worlds, their spin relative to each other creates a type of friction that sorcerers and gods can access to affect their world."

"We spent a month or two examining the subject." Sarah slumped when she said it, but she had loved the learning. She held an understanding of the way the world worked that very few others did.

"Well, this world was a dud, as it were." Gabby turned its two hands together. "It spun in the exact same direction as the worlds both above and below it. No friction and no magic, whatsoever."

"But we have sorcery now," Sarah said. "You must have done something."

"I did. I sacrificed my own life to change the direction of this province."

Sarah chuckled. "You really *were* the most like your dad. Doesn't look like your death took though."

"I am quite dead, I assure you." Gabby held out a hand. "Go on then."

Sarah reached out to take Gabby's hand. As she had known they would, her fingers closed on nothing.

It became translucent.

"I must go. I'll see you again sooner this time, yes?" It gave her a wide smile.

Before Sarah could say her reply out loud, she was alone.

"I'll be looking forward to it."

4

APPARENTLY, EVERYONE TALKS TO
MADE-UP FRIENDS NOW
SARAH

Most of a week later, Sarah, Prolocutor Vancess, and a thirty-man cohort of the Shepherds of the Blood sailed north into Norrik on the Summer Trades, a collection of rivers that flowed north in the warm months, south in the cold, and, for two weeks in the middle of fall and spring, did nothing at all.

Just a girl and her knights on their way to murder some demons.

The Norrik air was brisk, though not yet bitter, even now in the early summer. They passed field after field of barley, oats, and rye, and saw every type of livestock—though most were a bit more shaggy than normal. As she did most every time she saw a pen of pigs, Sarah wondered whatever might have happened to Gennie, a piglet she and Keane had been obliged to leave in an unknown farmer's yard as the two of them stole out of town in the dead of night.

They had done a lot of sneaking out of places back then.

Thirty-two horses stood aboard a barge that floated two hundred feet behind their shallow-keeled caravel, a two-masted river cruiser with bright blue sails called the *God's Slipper*. Sarah asked around but no one knew which god might wear the vessel on its feet, nor whether it was a right slipper or a left.

The prolocutor stood behind the wheelman and leaned against

the aft rail. He held a cup of silent tea in one hand and gripped the rail with the other. Deep in the grip of the hallucinogenic tea, Vancess shouted at the gods and cringed away whenever they spoke back.

They did not seem to be on friendly terms.

"Think he's really talking to the Alir?" Sarah asked Gabby. The two of them sat on a stack of crates webbed to the deck just ahead of the foremast. Gabby appeared to her daily now and for hours at a time. Her lessons in Metzoferran were going extremely well, and she no longer experienced any discomfort with talking to the face that appeared so much like her own.

"Doesn't seem likely," Gabby replied, and it cast a glance at Vancess. "Though that is how I'd expect him to look if he were. They're not all that pleasant to chat with."

It seemed to Sarah that she should be used to these surreal events in her life. She was a mercenary who went to live in a castle, found out she was a sorceress, *then* took a walking trip across the Paras Plains with a goddess, and now she sat and chatted with one of the creative forces of the universe. *The* creative force of the universe? Everything was fine until Gabby said something like that, and it all fell on her at once.

"You never told me why it was so important that there be magic that you sacrificed yourself for it." Sarah pulled her knees up to her chin and faced into the breeze. It was colder today than it had been yesterday.

Gabby sat cross-legged, hands on knees, and its comfortable linens did not stir in the wind. "Well, the gods were all made to create. It was their only reason for existing. But there was nothing there to work with. The universe was a great yawning void with demons running amok everywhere you looked. Without magic, the gods couldn't create, and that caused all sorts of problems."

It did not seem particularly fair to Sarah. "Couldn't one of them have been the sacrifice? I mean, it seems like sort of a dick move to let you take the hit for all of them."

"I suppose," Gabby said. "Though it would have taken more than a few. Regardless, they were to have revived me once they had the magic. It seems they changed their minds afterward and betrayed me *and* my sacrifice. I returned a shade, and they locked me away in the place they created to house all the demons. As you do."

"The Undergates," Sarah whispered. "You've been in hell for... *forever.*"

"Oh, it's not that bad," Gabby said. "It was at first, but we redecorated. I have lots of friends there."

"Wait." A thought fell uncomfortably into place in Sarah's mind. "You lived in the Undergates when Angrim the giant evil sorcerer fled there from the Alireon? Did you ever *meet* Angrim?"

"Oh yes," Gabby said. The face, so similar to Sarah's own, stared off into the places of legend and terror. "I taught Angrim to use magic."

Sarah's jaw dropped. She wanted to recoil, but what was the point? Where could she go?

Angrim, the Anger Under the Mountain, lived below Dismon, the capital of the aggressively expansionist nation of Tyrrane, north and east of them now. He was a monstrous creature by repute, and Sarah nearly killed herself defeating his apprentice Valafar—and even *that* effort required the help of a goddess. Angrim had in some fashion been behind every one of the worst things that had happened to her, Keane, and all of Greenshade since Wallace's Company was shattered.

And Gabby taught him how to do it.

Sarah did not bother to keep the anger off her face or the betrayal out of her voice. "How could you hand that kind of power to someone so obviously ill-suited to it? He's *evil*. Please tell me you're at least disappointed in what he did with everything you taught him."

Gabby popped up, startled from its reverie. "What? Oh yes. Disappointed, obviously. He was beautiful and charming and clever at the time. But quite mad now. Not to be trusted."

Not to be trusted? Just *who* here did Gabby think couldn't be trusted now?

"I know what you're thinking." Gabby raised a hand and cocked its head to the side. "But you only know this because I told you. I could have kept it to myself, and you'd still trust me. But I didn't because it wasn't honest. I told you the only way this relationship works is if we're both entirely honest with one another. Teaching Angrim was a mistake. Teaching you *might* be a mistake. I'm not perfect, just old. But despite any forces arrayed against us, I will never lie to you, Sarah. Never. That is one thing you may *always* believe."

Dammit. She *did* believe Gabby. There was something about it that was just too similar to herself, and it was not just its face. She would *know* if it lied to her.

Sarah sighed and stared aft. After a moment, she said, "I think he *is* talking to the Alir, and they hate him as much as I do. I mean, how could you not? He's such a... cunt."

Gabby's eyes widened. "*Sarah*. I've never heard you use that word before. I didn't know you had that kind of vocabulary."

"You should meet my friend Keane." She gripped the webbing on top of the crates with her bare toes. "He'll turn your ears blue."

"I've no doubt." Gabby also watched Vancess gesticulate and scream at the air. "You're still worried for him?"

"For Keane? Yeah." Sarah rubbed her legs. She had been sitting still too long. "He hasn't seemed himself for a while. Not since I talked to him in Dahnt."

"Perhaps he's finally growing into his role as king," Gabby offered. "Rising to the responsibility as it were."

Sarah's half grin quirked up. "You haven't met him. Keane doesn't rise to meet challenges. He stays low and chops their feet out from under them. That's one of the reasons we worked so well together."

Gabby nodded.

"Please don't say that," Vancess pleaded. "I didn't mean to—" He flinched as if struck. "You really *are* made of stone! What kind of god hides on top of a mountain while humans fight their—no. Stop. I didn't mean it!"

"I think you might be right," Gabby said to Sarah. "It sure *sounds* like he's talking to the Alir."

5

POLES IN HOLES
MORHOLT

Morholt stalked ahead of the rest of the Free Hand with Ameli and Reinar, scouting northward along the beach. Hoop-gulls laughed and complained to one another against the overcast sky while far above them, their larger cousins, the bonewheels, made lazy blue circles to announce the demise of some poor unfortunate they might find tasty.

The three walked through the shallows. A narrow strip of dirty white beach ran between the water and the jungle to their left, while the vast inland Beacon Sea rested to their right.

Ameli pushed her strawberry blonde hair behind her ears for the thousandth time. "I'm not saying I'm *happy* about it, only that I made my decision, and no matter what happens, I still think it was the right thing to do." The coastal wind immediately blew her hair back into her face. "Witch's gift, I wish I hadn't lost that hair strap."

"And would you still think that trying to kill a royal was a good idea when their pet sorceresses caught up to you and peeled all your skin off in one long strip?" Morholt maintained a low opinion of sorcerous types, generally.

"Tried to kill *one* royal," Ameli corrected. "Did kill *two*." The bubbly sorceress's regicidal past prevented her from ever returning to the Paradisals and her family, the Daughters' Coven. She martyred her happiness and comfort in exchange for what she thought best for the pirate nation.

And if they ever caught her, they would certainly kill her for it.

"There's no way a person could live through having their skin peeled off like that," Reinar interjected. His rumbling baritone rolled like good-natured thunder from his massively muscled chest. "It's not a very efficient way to torture someone."

A low wave glided across their path and forced Morholt to check his footing. Neither the smiling girl nor the giant northerner noticed.

"They can keep you alive while they're killing you." Morholt lifted his green leather leggings higher in his arms against another wave. His shirt stuck out beneath his jerkin and covered up his dangly bits. "Like a surgeon who cuts off a soldier's wounded leg and then sticks it back on so they can keep cutting it off again. Sorcerers really are the rotting horse turds in the ale barrel of life." He glanced over at Ameli. "Present company excepted."

"No, that's fair," she said. Her blue-gray linen pants and vest clung to her ample curves in the wet. "Even the good ones kinda suck."

Reinar yawned and flexed, sending his tattoos rippling across his bare chest and arms. "I thought the Deep Witch promised to strike you dead should you ever enter the waters of sea or ocean again."

As one, all three of them stopped to look at Ameli's feet, unseen beneath the moving current. Neither hurricane nor tentacle seemed immediately threatening.

"That's true," Ameli said. Nothing dragged her to her watery doom. "I guess the sins of my past aren't a big deal anymore?"

"More like your witch disapproves of meeting her end on the edge of Hadral." Reinar patted the sword on his hip. "Have no fear, little Ameli. I will always be here to protect you."

Morholt did not know exactly how Ameli's situation played out or how far anyone out there might take things to pull their revenge out of her hide, but if anything he had been told about the Deep Witch were true, Reinar would have a better chance defending the girl from a mountain falling on her head.

"We were walking in the surf to keep from leaving tracks," Morholt said. "Now you're telling me that we're hanging our butts in the water for a sea goddess with a coral dildo?"

Ameli's smile became a grin. "No, the rest of us are wearing pants."

"Mayhap we should continue our journey along the tree line," Reinar said. "The ground is harder there. We would leave no tracks and be much less likely to suffer abrasive cocks in our assholes as well."

Morholt just stood and stared at Reinar, who gazed back.

"Yeah," Morholt said. "That's a good idea."

The trio put their shoes and pants back on and moved close to the trees, resuming their northward trek. Morholt caught a whiff of decaying animal beneath the musty jungle and salty breeze. A distance ahead of them, bonewheels spiraled closer to the ground.

"How long were the two of you together before you found me?" Morholt asked. He didn't really care, but he also didn't think he'd get an answer if he came out and asked the question he was more interested in.

"We've never been *together* together," Ameli said, "but we were companions for maybe six months when we heard of you and then probably two more before we found you."

"What made you want to be a mercenary?" Morholt stepped across a sweep of roots and imagined himself a sure-footed explorer in an armored-lizard-infested swamp, bravely trekking through the—

"Hey," Morholt said before either could reply to his previous question. "You don't think armored lizards live in this mess, do you?" He craned his neck to look through the trees. "Saw one in the menagerie in Treaty Hill. Those things are creepy. Lizards shouldn't walk around on their hind legs like people."

"Did the bitty card monster say anything about armored lizards?" Ameli asked.

"I don't remember." April's warnings fell right out of his head. He had to think of something else. "Mercenaries. Right. Why mercenaries?"

"Nowhere to go, nowhere to go back *to*." Ameli shrugged. "Can't farm, and the only person who might do anything for me would probably get murdered by the people hunting me as soon as I showed up. There's not much incentive left for doing anything other than killing people for money."

Morholt cut his eyes at her.

"Or *not* killing people for money is what I meant to say." She flashed a now-nervous grin. "Because we don't do that. We're *good* mercenaries."

Reinar boomed laughter.

"I know you two don't get it." Morholt steadied himself with a branch and hopped over a broad hole amongst the roots. "I barely get it myself. It's just... I was at the Country Gate at the end of the occupation. There was *so much* death. Men lay six deep in the streets, frozen together by blood." The smell of dead animal grew stronger, and he could hear the bonewheels now. "Have either of you ever tried to dispose of twenty or thirty thousand corpses? There's literally nothing they're good for. That's why I left town before they started handing out the shovels. But that's what I'm saying. I don't know how much good I can do in the world, but maybe it'd be enough to do a little less bad."

"I was well known in Mirrik." The joviality fell off Reinar's face like the blouse from a two-penny whore. "Favored of king and queen."

"Especially the queen." Ameli aimed high and elbowed Reinar in the ribs.

He tried to smile, but it came off as more of a grimace. "Things happened, and here I am. I chose the mercenary life because swinging a blade is what I'm best at. Just my luck that I've stumbled across the only mercenary captain in the Thirteen Kingdoms who doesn't want me to."

"Hey, you don't have to tell me about it." Morholt spread his hands.

"Good," Reinar answered.

"Just because I'm your captain, and it's probably important that I know how my people are thinking when they go into combat."

"Still good," Reinar said.

"Especially when one of them tends to run into danger like he's looking for a final solution to paying taxes." Morholt frowned. How could he get Reinar to open up?

Ah, toad dicks.

Reinar stood frozen amongst a small stand of stunted saplings—brown, ugly, and limbless—between six and ten feet high. Bark curled up from the rigid poles like scales, and the top of each was adorned with a triangular knob, similar in shape to the head of a snake.

Exactly like the head of a snake.

"What do we do?" Morholt asked Ameli. The two of them were far too close for Morholt's comfort. His dread of snakes and all things creepy and crawly gripped his throat and threatened to drag him into the dark.

She opened her mouth to answer, but even as she did, the pole snakes struck at Reinar. They flashed through the air, bit into his meaty shoulders and arms, and chewed into his flesh.

The Mirrikman went down in a heap, his limbs already jumping from toxins the snakes pumped into him. His body danced in pounding convulsions on the sand, hurling grit and spittle in all directions.

Morholt turned and ran back down the beach.

No more than twenty paces away, he heard Ameli screaming for him to come back and help. Adrenaline roared through his veins and fear controlled his legs. He would rather have tried to bed a crag lion with crotch crickets than even slow his flight one step. Terror sweat flew off him in sheets, and his eyes rolled wide and uncontrolled.

Don't stop. Don't stop.

But he stopped.

Don't look. Don't look.

But he turned around to look.

Ameli waved one hand and then the other toward the snakes who hissed and released their bloody hold on Reinar only to jump back and strike again somewhere else seconds later.

"I don't have anything that'll kill them!" she screamed. "*Do something.*"

The fear melted away as Morholt visualized spinning rings of runes in the air. He reached into the rings and turned his hand palm up to complete the spell with the rune engine he wore on his wrist.

Rats poured out of the jungle, squeaking and screaming. They covered the beach with the smell of their rancid urine.

The pole snakes abandoned their already motionless prey for the flood of leaping rodents. They snapped and struck, but the rats—perhaps more motivated than the already successful snakes—seemed just a bit too fast for the deadly jaws.

The tidal wave of stinking rodents increased, and dozens darted down the holes that still had snakes poking up out of them. The pole snakes erupted out of their holes and wheeled in great slithering circles to squirm in behind the desperate rats.

"*Now,*" Morholt bellowed—though his voice came out as more of a cheeping yelp. He darted forward and grabbed one of Reinar's great wrists and pulled with all his might to no effect.

The cascade of rats petered out from the jungle and turned to skitter up the beach, several more of the big snakes flowing after them.

Ameli grabbed the other arm and Reinar slid several feet through the sand.

"One, two, *three,*" Morholt grunted, and they pulled him another three feet. "One, two, *three.*"

By the time they were twenty feet away from the pole snakes' lair, Morholt's muscles were shaking from exhaustion as much as fright. The rats had already blown away like so much pee-scented smoke, and the snakes glided back up out of their empty holes to find their kill.

This time Morholt added a wide imaginary ring of bright orange runes around the three of them to the other spinning circles. When he pushed his wrist into the place where he pretended the rings existed, a bright fence of illusory flames sprang up around them.

On the other side, snakes hissed their frustration.

"Let one in." Ameli stood crouched over their fallen ally. "Hurry, Reinar doesn't have a lot of time." A short double-edged knife glinted in her hand.

While this action was obviously insane, Morholt's mind was too frazzled to do anything other than what he was told. A section of the flaming wall disappeared, and one of the pole snakes—fifteen feet long if it was an inch—slithered through.

Ameli reached out the hand with the knife to distract the creature, and the instant it reacted, she stomped on it just behind the head.

Loops of muscle and scale flew in twisted gyres, and Morholt tried to grab at it to keep the beast away from Ameli. A high keening wail rose up, which Morholt was not surprised to discover came from him.

Ameli jumped away and left Morholt in a very real wrestling match with a now-headless snake that splashed blood and other less savory fluids all over him.

"Close the gap!" Ameli yelled and pointed to the opening in the fiery wall. Beyond it, more serpents headed their way.

The fingers of Morholt's hand made the rune that finished the wall once more, and the flames closed just in front of a pair of pole snakes who recoiled and slithered backward.

The dying snake shuddered, and Morholt, now coated in gore, shoved it away from him. He fell to his knees beside Reinar and Ameli.

"Is he going to make it?" The Mirrikman did not look good. The only color he had left was green, and even his bushy yellow-brown beard seemed faded. The snakes had taken pieces out of him where they bit, an interrupted dinner torn with inelegant savagery.

"He's already dead," Ameli answered. "Hold out your hand. No, cup it like this." She grasped his hand, turned it, and pressed his fingers together. Then she lifted the snake's head above his hand and squeezed a thin milky liquid from it, run through with lines of bright red blood like some kind of overripe horror-fruit.

Damn. Reinar certainly wasn't the first man Morholt had seen die, far from it. But the Free Hand was already a small group and even sort of controllable. He needed every one of them.

Ameli tossed the squeezed head aside and made flicking motions from her belt of powders and herbs toward Morholt's hand. From prior experience he knew that she was taking pinches of these different items and sorcerously whisking them to wherever she wanted, in this instance into his hand. This ability—added to her extensive knowledge of bodies and toxins—made her a dangerous young woman to contend with but also enabled her to fell opponents without harm when she wished.

The venom in Morholt's hand turned clear with a pinkish tint.

"I knew he was going to kill himself sooner or later," Morholt said. "This kind of guy needs a mother figure to stick his dick in. Tell him he's a good boy."

Ameli continued her work but spared a glance to frown at Morholt.

"If he's already dead, what are we doing?" Morholt added a second hand to contain whatever it was that Ameli was making. "Hey, is it safe for me to be holding this in my hand?"

"Bodies are chemicals." She took Morholt's wrist and held it out over Reinar's broad chest. "Most sorcerers would tell you this is impossible, but the difference between life and death is just a matter of processes. Like baking a cake when the fire goes out. You still have all the goodness in the pan, but it's stopped until you can light the fire again." She turned his wrist and let the liquid fall. But it vanished into a nearly invisible steam before it hit. Even the wet in Morholt's hand evaporated. "As long as you're quick about it."

Reinar went from gray-green to gray-blue as the steam suffused him.

"That will counteract the venom," she said, "but we still need to wake lazybones here up. Here, sit on his stomach and wrap your legs around his arms. We don't want him hurting himself."

"Hurting himself?" Morholt paused his climb atop Reinar. "What are you going to do?"

"Restart some processes." Ameli waited for Morholt to get into position and touched Reinar on the arm. "You've been a very good boy. Hold on."

Ameli made a few more flicking motions, paused, and slammed her fist down on Reinar.

The big man screamed, arched his back, and threw Morholt up over his head and through the circle of flame. Pole snakes on their way back to their holes turned, but Morholt extended the wall of ersatz flame to include him again.

Reinar howled and beat his feet and fists against the sand while Ameli watched, lips pursed and freckled brow tight. All at once he stopped and just lay gasping, covered in a sheen of stinking, dirty sweat.

His breathing slowed, and his bulging arms relaxed.

Voice raw, Reinar said, "Maybe we should continue our journey along the water's edge,"

Ameli laughed.

Reinar cleaned himself in the surf and Ameli used her sorcery to heal his snake bites.

"I hate to be the one to say so," Reinar said as the trio resumed their northward trek, "but pole snakes are not amongst my favorite creatures." He rolled both shoulders forward and stretched his massive arms above his head. "Gods, I feel fantastic. Ameli, what did you do to me?"

"Baked a cake," she said and patted him on one flank. The deep bites were healed, but the scars left faint rosettes in his skin. "I didn't do all that much. The goodness was already in the pan."

Reinar's rich laughter rumbled down the beach, thunder presaging a happy storm.

6

THE MOON DID IT

VOLKER

P rince Volker reached out and took the brass door handle in his eight-year-old hand. An army sounded off on the other side. Orders were given and carried out, followed by banging, grunting, and the sound of flames. Out here in the hall, all was quiet and brightly lit by wide openings high in the rough stone wall just before the ceiling's arch.

At the far end of the hall, Alan, castle guard and appointed body-guard/babysitter, chatted with a pretty scullery maid. He leaned in close and spoke too soft for Volker to make out anything, but the maid smiled and blushed, so it must have been something happy. The pair were sweet on each other, and the plan needed her to distract Alan.

"Ready, boy?" Volker asked the enormous mastiff beside him.

It licked his face, leaving him wet and spluttering.

The boy pushed the door and Moon, who outweighed his master five times over, bounded into the room. An immediate explosion threw a white cloud of flour into the hall, covering Volker and momentarily occluding his vision.

He didn't have to see to visualize the scene once Cook started screaming.

Volker craned his neck and saw Moon on top of the central work-table where Cook and her army of scullions shouted, wailed, and ran hither and thither. Moon delightedly kicked over bowls and slapped staff in the face with his huge tail. The pheasant in his mouth crunched like a fistful of snapping twigs.

In that instant, Cook spied Volker and pointed at him with a bony finger. Her thin face screwed up in anger and turned as red as her tightly bound hair. "Get. Your. *Dog*."

Volker grinned and waved at Moon. "C'mon, boy. Sorry, Cook. It won't happen again."

Moon, bird in mouth, leaped from the table and ran out the door.

On his toes, Volker tried to see through the carnage and exasper-ated staff to the now-empty spot on a cooling rack beside the two big brick ovens. His grin spread wider, and he waved goodbye to Cook.

Cook traced his gaze and screamed, "You get back here this instant!" but it was too late.

Prince Volker of Greenshade—and his dog Moon—sprinted down the hall and past his flustered bodyguard.

7

THE STUMPLEBERRY SNEAK
SHAYLA

S hayla carried the enormous pie in front of her and tried to
ignore the sharp pangs in her belly. Hot and heavy, the smell
of it filled her with deep, unrelenting desire.

And if some of it were in *her* instead of in the pan, wouldn't it be
lighter?

Another corner came up in the busy castle hallway, and she
stepped around it. Seven-year-old legs didn't go all that fast anyway,
and burdened with a warm pastry half her size, she was forced to rely
on guile rather than speed. Cook had dispatched a pair of scullions
after her once the theft was detected, and Shayla's circuitous route
was the only thing keeping her free.

She knew it wouldn't last.

Just ahead a gigantic pile of servant's laundry loomed against one
wall, the servant in question's bedroom door open next to it. Shayla
darted around the pile and knelt down on the other side.

"You see her?" a woman's voice asked.

"No, but I still smell stumpleberries," a second, younger-sounding
woman answered. "She ain't got that much farther."

"I wouldn'ta thought she'da got this far," the first voice said. "We
don't get back fast, Cook'll put *us* inna pie."

Staff rushed past in both directions. Half of them could see Shayla plain as a bear in a sewing box but were far too busy to intervene or, more likely, simply saw no upside to putting themselves in the middle of an altercation involving a member of the royal family.

The younger woman gave a defeated-sounding sigh. "Right then, let's go back. But *I* ain't gonna tell Cook we lost the brat."

Brat? Shayla shrugged. That was probably fair.

After several seconds without any further conversation, Shayla chanced a peek over the edge of the laundry pile. Both scullions, red-faced and sweating, went their sullen way back down the hall.

Shayla grinned, stood, and was dragged backward several feet by the shoulder.

"Oh, no, you don't." Mother Maundy spun Shayla around in a circle and harrumphed. "Did you steal that pie?" The huge woman snatched the pie away with one fat hand and directed her icy blue northern stare through the top of Shayla's skull and into her brain. "Where's Nanny? You run off from her too? That poor woman's like to be beside herself from worry."

"I—"

"Right." Mother Maundy gave Shayla a shove from behind, and the two of them headed back in the direction of the kitchens. "We're taking this straight to the kitchen where you will apologize to Cook for stealing it and then to *me* for wasting my time bringing you here. Honestly, your mother was *never* this much trouble. You've got a double dose of the war king in you, and that's a fact."

Of course. Daddy was the answer here. Shayla would need to be careful though. Mother Maundy was Head Laundress and knew things about the castle that even the spies didn't.

But that was a weakness a clever little girl could exploit too.

Shayla jumped to one side of the bustling hallway and put her back to the green-gray stone wall. "Mother Maundy, I *need* that pie back."

"Is that a fact?" Mother Maundy asked as she pried Shayla off the wall. "Is there a royal pie emergency going on I don't know about?"

The girl squirmed free but stood her ground. "No. It's for the Verranese 'bassador. It's his favorite."

As Shayla spoke, Baroness Tralgar slowed to a stop behind Mother Maundy and watched the little princess.

"There is no chance that King Keane, bless his sword, sent you to steal a pie for the ambassador from Verran." Mother Maundy put her unoccupied fist on one broad hip. A brow went up, and she straightened a bit, her mouth twisted with thought. "Nearly no chance." She clearly grew less convinced the more she thought about Shayla's father.

"The 'bassador is staying in the castle for a coupla' days," Shayla said. "Daddy said to get him a pie so's he feels better. A really *big* one."

Baroness Tralgar pursed her lips and crossed her arms. Her dark blue dress, tightly fitted with a matching hat pinned to her equally tightly bound red and white hair, made her a slice of night sky in the hallway.

The uncertainty vanished from Mother Maundy's face like Volker's dog Moon on bath day. "Now I *know* you're lying to me." The meaty hand fell once more on Shayla's shoulder, and this time there would be no wriggling free. "If the Verranese ambassador were staying the night, there would have been instructions to change the sheets in one of the guest suits from Egren silk to Verranese. As *that* hasn't happened, I'm betting everything else you've said hasn't happened either."

"It's a *secret*," Shayla whispered. "There's 'ssassins in the embassy. They gotta kill 'em all afore the 'bassador can go home. If I don't bring him a really big pie, he'll think Daddy sent the 'ssassins, and there'll be a *war*." Shayla beamed on the inside. That was a *good* one.

Mother Maundy's mouth turned down in befuddlement even as her eyes hardened. Behind her, Baroness Tralgar covered laughter with a silk-gloved hand.

"What's that?" Mother Maundy twisted her bulk to see Baroness Tralgar behind her. "Baroness! What are *you* doing down here? The servants' quarters are no place for a proper lady."

Baroness Tralgar's eyes widened, and she waved away her own mirth. "I'm sorry," she said. "I had no intention of causing anyone discomfort." She pointed to Shayla. "I need that." She pointed to the pie. "And that. I'm sorry but I can't tell you why. Diplomatic intrigue and whatnot. Thank you, Mother."

The baroness took the princess and the pie and left Mother Maundy to her anxious bemusement.

"One of these days, young lady," Baroness Tralgar said, "you are going to have to give up your thieving ways and start acting like a sensible princess." They reached the stairs. "I assume we are headed to the bottom of the spiral stairs beneath the Stone Tower?"

"Oldam's toenail," Shayla said. "How do you always know *everything*?"

A huge smile came over Baroness Tralgar's whole face, though tears stood in her eyes. She leaned down—carefully, with the pie to one side—and collected Shayla in a firm hug. "It's my job, dear." She gripped the princess tighter. "You are *so* much like your father. Has anyone ever told you that?"

"Only all the time." Shayla disentangled herself from the baroness's grasp and took the pie from her. "I'm ready to *go* now."

Baroness Tralgar laughed and smoothed the straight brown hair on top of Shayla's head, causing the princess to wriggle away.

Grown-ups.

8

TAKING YOUR LICKS
VOLKER

In the base of the Stone Tower, Prince Volker sat with his sister Princess Shayla and dog Moon beneath a curving granite stair with a fanciful stone railing and ate their stumpleberry pie. It was hard, as giggles kept coming while they tried to shove the pie down. Quite a bit ended up on their fronts, which Moon, who had already disposed of his third, was excited to help them clean up.

Their tiny corner was a black triangle in a dim room. The occasional servant went by entirely unaware of the little picnic beneath their feet.

"Cook did just what you said," Volker said to his younger sister. "Just azactly. It was 'mazing!"

The pair had the same dark brown hair, though Volker's was curly and Shayla's straight. And while Volker's face could only be described as cherubic, at seven years old, Shayla already bore the air of the smartest person in every room.

"Cook's shtupid," Shayla said while she stuffed pie through a purple-toothed grin. She tried unsuccessfully to interpose her elbow between her mouth and Moon's and lost half her handful of pie. "Unhh."

"Cook's *not* stupid," Volker said. "You're like a *genius*." Moon returned to him. Volker gave up and let the big animal lick him unmolested. It was easier that way.

Shayla shrugged. She never seemed to want to acknowledge what Volker knew. She was *way* smarter than him and smarter than all the grown-ups too. She was probably the smartest person who ever lived.

"I saw Mommy doing it again." Shayla pinned Volker against the stair with her gaze. "Standin' there in her room. Not doin' nuthin'." She pointed at her head. "Like the lantern was out."

Smarter than everyone, Volker thought, *but also stubborner*. She just couldn't let it go. In imitation of Mommy every time she talked to Daddy, Volker rolled his eyes. His whole head described an upward arc for added emphasis.

"She *did*," Shayla said, returning Volker's emphasis with a punch to the arm. "They're both wrong. They talk wrong. It's like... It's like..." Her arms dropped in defeat, her vocabulary failing before what it was like.

Volker had never known Shayla to lie to him, but Mommy said once that Shayla had too much 'magination. That wasn't her fault, was it? Mommy and Daddy were weird, but they'd been weird for a long time. Since the last time Aunt Sarah left.

The final handful of pie rose in Shayla's hand, a slow-moving trebuchet hurling pastry into a bottomless pit. She stopped and stared at the goo and crust. "I wish Cook made cake. Cake's better than pie."

"Easier to eat with your hands," Volker agreed. He tried to scrape away the slime coating Moon left on his face, chest, and stomach. Oldam's nose!

Heavy booted footsteps clomped down the stairs, and all three of them instinctively quieted. The feet came to the floor, but instead of going through the door, they turned and stood before their shadowed hideaway.

"Children."

It was King Keane, their daddy and king of the *whole kingdom* of Greenshade. He was the boss of *everyone*.

Their daddy squatted and looked into their faces, a faint smile on his. Like he was thinking about something else, and he couldn't decide if it was funny or not.

"Nanny and Alan are searching the castle for the two of you, and Cook isn't pleased." He favored one hip in his squat and put down a hand to balance against his bit of paunch. "We'll probably have toad-stools and fish guts for dinner tonight."

"Daddy, you *can't* tell Cook you found us. She'd *kill* us." Shayla used all the girly charms she had. Volker had seen her transform their big strong warrior daddy into a dope this way any number of times. This too had not worked since Aunt Sarah left, but maybe today would be different.

Daddy didn't notice her efforts.

He grabbed Shayla's arm to drag her out from under the stairs. She pulled against him.

"*No,*" she shouted. "Who are you? Where's my *daddy*?" She raised a leg to kick at him, and he shoved her away instead. She rolled backward on the stone floor.

Volker made to jump between them, but the king stopped him with an outthrust hand. Volker fell back on his butt, and his mouth dropped open. *No one* had ever touched him with any kind of violence before, much less his *daddy*. His brain froze up.

The king leaned in and spoke just past Shayla's ear. His voice was full of gravel and menace. "You're being a silly. But your mommy and daddy don't want a silly. They want a good little princess. So, let's *be* a good little princess." He smiled and his voice returned to normal. "Or Daddy will throw you from the tower window."

9

WAIT, HE READS?

KING BRANNOK

In the once-powerful yet perennially frightened nation of Tyrrane, in the central-northern piece of the capital city of Dismon, deep below the Fell Citadel, King Brannok Swifthart the Second—emperor no longer—delved in the bottomless, timeless dark. The big man, his age creeping into his red hair, mail a-jingle beneath his bearskin cloak, ran the fingertips of his left hand across yet another mile of endless tunnel. Most of these didn't even go anywhere, much less to a means of changing his nation's fate.

So why were these corridors even here?

What day was it?

Brannok sneezed. He didn't understand where dust might have come from so far below the busy, dusty world. Mayhap he carried it all down in his sinuses.

Above him, his daughter Jasmayre attended to affairs of state, and his son Jason played at being a soldier. At first Brannok resisted the notion of a woman at the levers of power, but Jasmayre taught him that not only could she excel there, but she far surpassed Brannok's own limited imagination in the role. So enamored he was with her progress, he barely noticed when his own wife, Moru, died of winter fever.

What might other women be able to accomplish? Women other than Moru, obviously.

The thought made him chuckle as he painstakingly dragged the pads of his fingers along the frigid stone wall. Other women were not Jasmayre.

Somewhere in the dark, the lair of Angrim lay in wait, a malevolent spider trap that beckoned him. But he would go to the Anger Under the Mountain when he was ready with a means to end the creature and not a moment before.

Those were the thoughts that swirled through Brannok's mind as he searched for a mythical hidden-weapons room in the bedrock far beneath the citadel. They weren't true, of course, but the situation was both unique and desperate. And how could a mythical weapon that placed the murder of a god in the hands of a king be any more outrageous than a daughter who ran his kingdom more effectively than he could?

Brannok was forced to concede that his position was not what he had allowed himself to believe. With Angrim's apprentice Valafar dead at the Hill Fury's hands, the ancient sorcerer would not lower himself to meet with anyone other than the king, and so Brannok was sent running every time Angrim needed an errand, which was every cursed day.

As long as he was no more than a monster's valet, Brannok felt he could take all the time he wanted to look for an irrecoverable room holding impossible secrets in the dark. It was less emasculating than being king.

How much time had passed since he left the light this trip evaded him? Sometimes he returned to the palace above mere hours after heading down. Sometimes days passed in the black.

Angrim, on the other hand, was equally obsessed with finding and tracking the Hill Fury, who he called "button" for some unfathomable reason. Not that Brannok would have willingly spent an extra moment in the creature's company to ask why, nor would Angrim likely have acknowledged the question.

The Soul of Tyrrane wasn't a sharer.

Today was the first day of the third month of Brannok's search. He would never have thought himself capable of having the patience for it, but the truth was that every day he came down here he was more excited about the possibility than the day before. Angrim had been a hideous shadow over his entire life. The notion of a dawn without that presence breathing down his neck hitched his breath.

The bleak idiocy of it all had been entirely eclipsed by reckless hope.

Brannok raised his right arm and looked at it in the lamplight. A thick-bladed dagger protruded from a metal cap over the end of the arm where a hand should have been. His lantern hung from a wide metal hoop over the blade.

Years ago, he had punched Angrim when the beast seemed in a moment of weakness. His hand shattered, and Angrim had not even noticed. Worse still, the hand refused to heal and made every waking moment a new lesson in misery.

Until Jasmayre returned.

She immediately oversaw the amputation of his hand, swatting aside his most strenuous objections as if he were no more than a child—thank every god who was not Angrim. While he convalesced, she set up dozens of secretive training camps in the countryside and mountains, doing the work of replenishing the fallen numbers of the Ebon Host where Greenshade would never see it.

Even now she dealt with the solidifying bonds forming between Greenshade and Mirrik, but Brannok was not concerned. If the walls of the maze could be tumbled, as the saying went, she was the one to do it. If she could not, likely no one could. Either way, he felt content not to concern himself with it.

A crack.

A seam?

He ran a fingernail in a straight line up the wall and howled in joy. The seam ran seven feet high and six feet left, then returned to the ground. Emotion stole the strength from his legs, and he slid to the ground. This was it. He had found it.

Brannok grinned into the dark.

He wiped the wet from his face and grunted as he pushed himself to his feet again. His knees complained, but Brannok did not care in the least. If it killed him, he was going to give his daughter a world without that old demon snapping at her feet.

And if it *didn't*, he was intent on enjoying that world too.

He pushed on the right side. When he shoved, the left bit pivoted, showing the door affixed at the middle. It swung open, and a quiet mustiness seeped out of the dark. Brannok raised the lantern to see inside.

A large room, dead and forgotten in the black, lay ready to be resurrected by his arrival. Shelves of books covered every inch of every wall, broken only by the doorway Brannok stood in and two other doors in the back and right walls. One was plain wood, and the other was painted a worn green and fitted with heavy bronze rivets. A pair of wide round tables dominated the floorspace, along with a single chair.

He suppressed the immediate disappointment in his warrior's heart at the lack of any fanciful swords or axes on the walls. *No*, he reconsidered, *this is likely far better. The Anger would strike me dead before I ever approached him with something like that. The sword I need is knowledge.*

Brannok held his breath and entered. This was it. One of these books—or perhaps all of them—*was* the weapon he searched for. He entered, placed the lantern on a table, and took a book down from a shelf.

10

MAKING SWORDS FROM TOMATOES

JASMAYRE

Princess Jasmayre sat in the empty stands and watched as her brother destroyed yet another hopeful young soldier trying to make a name for himself on the sporting sand. She pulled a thick braid of dark red hair around in front of her. It contrasted against the crushed velvet gown of deep gold, which fitted her loosely and did not make her look too thin.

Prince Jason was tall, strong, handsome, and devastating with a dulled practice blade and shield. He would have been a perfect prince if his heart were not soft as a boiled tomato.

With a real sword in his hand, he turned to jelly and was barely able to defend himself. It was allegory for his entire life. She sighed even as she clapped for his success.

He had other strengths she would capitalize on.

Jason spied her in the bright sun and gave a big wave. He hopped the wall between the combatants and spectators and bounded up to her, an enthusiastic armored puppy, eager for praise and love.

"Sister!" he shouted unnecessarily. "What are you doing here? I didn't know you liked watching me be remarkable."

"I'm here *trying* to put together a security detail for Father." She waved a hand at the string of dusty and beaten warriors below. "But you've ruined my pool of contenders." She ought to have let someone else do this, but Jasmayre did not like to rely too much on underlings in the running of Tyrrane. Especially not with Brannok's safety outside the citadel. She knew the pride he took in her, and she would not see it wasted.

"I could do it," Jason offered. He looked so hopeful and eager. No sense in letting *that* go on.

"We both know Father would never allow it." She shook her head. "Besides, a bodyguard who can't kill an enemy isn't of much use." His crestfallen face melted her a bit. "Look, if you want to stop being miserable, you'll quit trying to make that man happy and find something you can make *yourself* happy with. At least take up drinking or whoring or something more entertaining than beating the stuffing out of men you don't even detest."

She tried not to think about the fact that until fairly recently she had been in exactly Jason's shoes. But where she had succeeded, she now advised him to give up. It wasn't jealousy or defensiveness or anything like that; her brother was simply hopeless.

Jason sat on the boards with a thump. "I don't really detest anybody. Junior *was* kind of a pig, but he's dead now, so I guess the spot's all freed up."

She sighed again and patted her older brother on the shoulder. "I know dear. You're"—she made a face—"*nice.*"

"You don't have to make it sound like I've got leprosy or something."

Jasmayre tapped a finger against the side of her chin and cast her gaze sideways. "Leprosy would be better. Would you be willing to trade one for the other?"

"Har-de-har," he said. "Have you thought about that *thing* I asked you about?"

"Oh right. That *thing*." She lowered her voice. "That *thing* with the *name*."

"*Don't say her name,*" Jason hissed and pressed his big sweaty hand over Jasmayre's mouth.

She leaned back and laughed, a clear womanly sound of joy and camaraderie. Several young warriors grimaced in her direction. The noble fighters of Tyrrane did not appreciate girlish mirth in their arena of manly endeavor.

"Your secret is safe with me," Jasmayre said. "In point of fact, I happen to know where the *thing* is right now, should you desire an introduction."

The hope and gratitude that rose in Jason's eyes broke her heart. This was no place for a person as good as he was. But the thought made everything else she had to do easier to stomach.

"Let's get you cleaned up, you ox-footed troll spawn. I doubt she'll be impressed with your current decaying-barnyard scent."

He leaped to his feet, and his grin seemed to risk splitting his face entirely in two. "Thank you, Jaz. You're the best sister anyone could ever have."

"That's me."

———

Less than half an hour later, Jasmayre and Jason entered the Soul's Garden behind the Fell Citadel. At their backs, the huge black building dominated. In front, beyond the flowered garden that had been clipped and ordered into utter sterility, the Bitter Heights Mountains sliced lightning-limned wounds in the bellies of flying thunderheads.

Between the bleak citadel and the storming mountains, Lady Wendelin Somay twirled her parasol and aimed a coquettish smile over her shoulder—right at Jason's heart.

The Lady Wendelin, young and pretty with dark hair and pale, translucent skin, was posed as a flower herself, pale green gown in the center of blues, yellows, and pinks. Her pastel attendants fluttered and giggled and stared at Jason from behind white-gloved fingers.

Wendelin *swayed* through the small crowd of hangers-on and strode cheekily to the base of the steps where Jasmayre and Jason waited. She put Jasmayre in mind of a ghost claw hunting after a mouse. Wendelin's stalking stride was exactly the same as the small white cat's, and her claws would be twice as sharp. Jasmayre would not have been a bit surprised if Wendelin practiced in a mirror all day making little snarly noises.

"Prince Jason Swifthart," Jasmayre said, stepping into a curtsey, "I would quite like to introduce you to Lady Wendelin Somay, daughter of Lord Dimas Somay and Lady Miloslava Somay. Wendelin's mother has asked my permission for Wendelin and yourself to enter into a courtship."

Without detaching his gaze from Wendelin's, Jason said, "That would be... remarkable."

Jasmayre patted Jason on the elbow. "Very well then. Off you go, you great plodding nitwit. I have to interview her before I give you my permission. Go. Wait in the family den."

With pleading eyes and a tight, hopeful smile, Jason backed up the stairs. Jasmayre laughed and shooed him away.

No sooner had Jason crested the top of the stone stairs than Wendelin spoke. "So, what do I get?"

"Excuse me?" Jasmayre turned slowly to look down at the young courtesan. This was a relief. Jasmayre would not have to kill Wendelin after all.

Probably.

"Danica Borant said that you gave her two thousand imperials to leave the capital after Prince Jason set his cap for her." Wendelin's head rolled ever so slightly from side to side as she spoke. With her large blue eyes, the effect was mesmerizing.

"Did Danica Borant mention that she made a promise to me never to speak of that arrangement?"

"Yes," Wendelin continued, confident and heedless, "but it doesn't matter. You already know, so it's not like I'm breaking any confidences."

Jasmayre nodded. Her thin face caught the shadows beneath high cheekbones. She twisted to one side and snapped her fingers. A bald man in glasses, black doublet, and hose, and carrying a notepad hurried down the stairs to the princess's side.

"What do you require, My Grace?" he asked at the bottom of his bow.

Her gaze on Wendelin, Jasmayre spoke to the secretary. "Lady Danica Borant, eldest child of Lord Mikolaus Borant. Kill her." It was too late for Danica, but perhaps she could make an impression on the vapid girl in front of her.

The bald man nodded, clicked his heels, and strode back up the stairs.

Wendelin gasped.

Jasmayre narrowed her eyes.

"I'm not killing her because *you* told *me*, you nattering fool. I'm killing her because *she* told *you*."

"But—"

"Shut up," Jasmayre snapped. "I trust you now understand the rules of the agreement you seek with me—and why *you* should keep your lip buttoned. *Do* you understand, Wendelin?"

The girl sniffed, and her bottom lip stuck out of her deep frown. She nodded.

"Very well." Jasmayre smoothed the gold velvet skirt of her gown as she scanned Lady Wendelin's entourage down in the garden below. Every one of them was giggling and darting glances at their lady's back and the princess. "The steward will be in the throne room now. Go to him and ask for a thousand imperials. He will know what it's for. Take it and leave, and never let Jason's eye fall on you again, nor his ears hear your name."

"But," Wendelin said as she controlled her distress and turned it into an almost-believable pout, "Danica got *two* thousand."

Jasmayre leaned her head back and gave Wendelin a hard stare. In less volatile circumstances, Jasmayre could have turned the girl into a formidable ally. With a little time and effort, anyway. "Danica Borant will be long cold and dead by the time you get home. Would you like to have that too?"

Wendelin flinched, squeaked, and then fled to the safety of her frivolous friends and her irrelevant world. A thousand crowns or a hundred thousand, it was a trivial price to pay for Jasmayre to see her

ultimate plans delivered on. And for that, she needed Jason undis-
tracted by vacuous little courtesans whose daddies were looking for a
politically expedient marriage.

A weary sigh escaped Jasmayre. Now she had to think of a reason
why *another* fish had slipped his hook. She should have thought
about this earlier.

After all, she had *much* bigger fish than these to worry about.

11

BEING HEROES AND SAVING WIVES

MORHOLT

The Free Hand rode north into the Grengards, one of the five kingdoms of Norrik. Arlea, the Low Wood, and the shores of the Beacon Sea were well behind them. They had stolen the horses in Sheaf just before entering the Western Marches, so now, according to Morholt's own philosophy of ownership, they were no longer stolen.

If it's been mine for more than two whole days without anyone trying to kill me for taking it, it's just mine.

This philosophy was reinforced in Morholt's mind whenever he stole something that moved faster than a city guardsman.

In the open fields before the Norrik highlands, there was little need for a scout group, so the Free Hand rode in pairs, strung out in a crooked line. The Darrish warriors Mahu and Sabni held the front, then Morholt and his sister Raven with Ameli and Reinar in the rear.

"Because Glauth *hates* me, that's why." Raven scowled into the gorgeous grasslands and crystal clear blue skies ahead of them. "Why would I risk my neck for hers?"

Wind fluttered the ocean of grass and carried the smell of fields and cold. As they climbed both higher and more north, even the summer gave more and more ground. There would be snow on the ground before they got to Morholt's ex-girlfriend.

"No one is asking you to," Morholt answered. "Feel free to sit and watch me walk into my death because you weren't there. I'm sure you and the pommel of your dagger will be very happy together with all the extra privacy."

"You're disgusting." Raven's scowl grew deep enough to collect rainwater.

"I'm not the one traipsing the north with sticky knife handles."

"Look, asshole," Raven said, fixing her brother with a dark-eyed stare, "if you die, there's no one to take us back to our world." She ran a thin hand over the black leather that protected her shoulder and arm. "I don't like it here. It's backward, and everyone wants to kill us. And before you say it, I *know* we only came here because everyone was trying to kill us back home." She returned her gaze to the distant chilly horizon. "But at least the food was better."

"That is true." Morholt nodded ahead. "Company's coming."

"We're not done talking about this."

Morholt flashed a mocking smile at his sister and turned away.

Sabni let his horse, a barely trained roan he called Abet, fall back to ride alongside Morholt. He got a lot more out of the animal than Morholt had thought possible when they grabbed it. Apparently, *everyone* liked the cheery warrior.

"And what would *you* like to climb up my ass about?" Morholt asked. His ginger hair was past his shoulders now, and the wind whipped it against his faded green leather armor.

Sabni chuckled. "I have told you many times, Captain of the Free Hand, you are not my type. I am wondering about our strategy, however."

"Of course I'm your type," Morholt said. "I'm *everyone's* type."

"He's his own type three times a day," Raven interjected.

"My mistake," Sabni replied. "Clearly I was not looking closely enough."

"It's easy to miss," Raven said. Her black hair hung in her too-pale face, but it couldn't hide her wide grin.

"Let's talk about that strategy," Morholt said, his voice raised. "Can't wait to talk about *that*."

"As you will." Sabni assumed a look of unaccustomed solemnity. "The sorcerer Finnagel has sent Sarah the Hill Fury to kill you because you have runecrafting—magic that can be taught to anyone. We ride now to the home of Glauth, the first woman to whom you taught runecrafting."

"Sounds like you have a pretty complete notion of what we're doing." Morholt scratched at his beard. It grew in thin and watery. He found himself jealous—not for the first time—of Mahu and Sabni's carefully cropped black beards.

Was this what grown-ups worried about as they trekked into the unknown with epic murderers at their backs? Beard hair?

"My concern comes from wondering if we are leading the enemy, as it were, straight to what they want." Sabni opened an arm to Morholt, ropy muscles brown in the sun. "I worry we bring death to this woman." He let the arm drop, but his expression of disquiet remained.

"Glauth has been in one place a long time," Morholt answered. He had been thinking about this very thing for a while now. "There doesn't seem much chance that they *don't* already know. Finnagel simply wasn't ready to run us down yet. Maybe he didn't have the men after the occupation, or maybe the stories are true, and his sorcery really has shit out. I don't know any of that."

He twisted the hairs at the end of his chin.

"What I *do* know," Morholt went on, "is that if we *don't* tell her about Finnagel and Sarah, they'll catch her with her pants down and her mouth full of troll cock. And then they absolutely *will* kill her."

"Did she leave you for a troll?" Sabni asked, one brow pricked up inquisitively.

"I thought Glauth said she was going to burn your crotch out from under you until your legs fell off if she ever saw you again," Raven said. She sighted the blade of one of her curved daggers with great care. They were as sharp as an ex-lover's scorn, if not quite as deadly.

The daggers would only kill you.

"There might have been some crotch-burning talk," Morholt answered. "But if everyone who threatened my endowments made good, I'd hardly still be around to threaten, would I?"

"You believe then that this woman will not kill you because no one else has?" Now both of Sabni's brows went up.

Morholt frowned. "Yes?"

"Has not every man or woman who yet lives felt the same?" Sabni did not *appear* to be making fun of Morholt.

"Well, it just sounds stupid when you say it like that," Morholt replied.

"Have you ever heard the *Sermon of Kohoc and the Boy from the Mountain*?" Sabni asked.

"Oh, toad dicks," Morholt said, "no." It didn't matter what he answered, Sabni was going to tell him anyway.

Sabni leaned forward and stroked Abet's ruddy gray neck. "You may evade the Harvester for a thousand days in a row, but he only needs catch you once to end the game. It means—"

"I think I can guess what it means." Morholt closed his eyes and sighed deeply. "Look, I'm doing the best I can. I'm just trying to keep the body count down as much as I can and my dick unburned off. I'm no hero. I'm not like Keane or even Harden. Those guys would have raised an army by now and saved everyone."

"*You* have a short memory," Raven said. "Those guys would have killed everyone. Harden was the meanest bastard I ever met, and the war king is the one who signed off on hunting you down and murdering you in the first place. Those *were* his troops back in the Low Wood, and Sarah is his monster. You like to blame Finnagel but—"

"No." Morholt shook his head. "Keane is a cradle-robbing impostor with delusions of royal cocksmanship, but I won't believe he'd come after us like that. Not after what we did for him."

"I didn't mean *us*," Raven said, rolling her eyes heavenward. "I just said *you*."

In the sky, a flock of crows cawed to one another. There were hundreds of the birds flying toward the Free Hand. When the birds reached the mercenaries, they formed a swiftly swirling mass, a slow-moving tornado of sharp beaks and shiny black feathers.

Morholt lifted his hand against the sun to get a better look. "That's creepy. You'd think that many crows would find something more important to do than try and look down Raven's top. There's nothing to see there anyway." He pulled rings of spinning runes together in his head, ready to send illusory eagles ripping through the dark-winged funnel.

"They are asking for food." Sabni stared up into the sky. "It is considered good luck on merchant caravans to feed a flock of crows so that the death that follows them will pass everyone by. Different flocks ask in different ways, but it all means the same thing."

Abet stamped and snorted, but the other horses seemed oblivious.

Ahead of them, Mahu already had his pack off and was rummaging through it for something to offer. Sabni followed suit.

"Really?" Raven asked.

Morholt shrugged and reached into the pouch on his belt where he kept short sticks of smoked pork.

"Ho, birds," Reinar shouted from behind. He threw the foreleg of an antelope off into the grass which was immediately beset by cawing birds. Ameli tossed a crumbly square of hard tack in the same direction and danced her charcoal gelding around behind Reinar.

With pork in hand, Morholt lifted his arm to toss the treat and was shocked when a very large and glossy black bird landed on his wrist. The crow gazed straight into Morholt's eyes as if trying to communicate something.

Morholt froze, at a loss for what he should do in such a situation. This was a wild animal perched on the end of his arm, with a wild animal's beak and claws.

Morholt was frightened by housecats.

Sabni reached across just past the crow and put his hand on Raven's forearm to push her curved dagger away. "Shh," he said. "We are friends of the flock—until you do that."

"Something I can do for you, you heavy sack of dead mice?" As big as it was, the bird was not all that heavy, but the strain of keeping his arm rigid began to wear on Morholt. "Smoked pork not what you were looking for? Maybe you're hungry for runecrafter eyeballs."

The crow hopped further up Morholt's arm. Its head darted back and forth to look into each of his eyes, as if to decide which would be tastier with a bit of dried meat. It cawed. Morholt jumped, and the bird flapped loudly away, snatching the pork from him as it went.

Morholt's mount whickered and backed up a couple of steps. This was all too close for the gray brindle. Good-natured though she was, great flapping birds on top of her head were outside of her experience, and she did not care for it.

The flock went left toward the thrown food, and Morholt broke forward and to the right, his sister behind him. With a little distance, they stopped and watched the rest of the Hand catch up to them. The crows were already departing, their afternoon snack gone as thoroughly as a Coldspiner daughter's virtue during Bedwinter.

Bedwinter was still Morholt's favorite holiday in the Thirteen Kingdoms.

"What the fuck was that about?" Raven asked. "That thing looked like it was going to peck your face off."

"I guess my good luck is that I still have both of my eyes, eh, Sabni?" Morholt was rattled, but he was only out a short stick of smoked pork. He couldn't get that bird's stare out of his mind though.

"Then we are doubly blessed," the happy Darrish warrior said. "From both the crows and from our commitment to doing better than Harden Grayspring."

"This shit again." Raven glanced up at Morholt through half-lidded eyes. "I'm going to ride with Mahu for a while. I can use the quiet." She flicked the reins of her eager smoky black stallion and flew across the ground to where Mahu reassumed his vanguard.

"Something I said?" Sabni asked.

"Most likely," Morholt answered. "You talk the most, so statistically it's probably you."

"What is statistically?"

"It means it's your fault." That wasn't the particular fault Morholt was thinking about though. His decision to take the leadership of the Free Hand and try to make money without killing had been motivated purely by guilt, and that wasn't an emotion he had a lot of experience with. He was still coming to terms with it.

Why did he even feel guilty? All he had truly done was lived when others died. He did that every day.

Sabni grinned at him. The man lit up any space he was in. "My shoulders are broad enough to take the burden."

They rode for almost a full minute without talking. Long enough to wonder if Sabni were upset at something.

"We are heading toward Gullhome, are we not?" Sabni asked.

"It's across the Summer Trades from the Grim Pines where Glauth lives, but it's not all that far. Maybe three or four days ride." There would be snow by then.

"I am thinking of all the tales told by Harden and Eli about Gullhome," Sabni said. The grin faded. "It is not a place I ever expected to go anywhere near."

Morholt laughed. "Those two old warhorses could talk for *days* about that damned place. You'd think they lost their virginity and got their cocks bitten off there the same day."

"Yes. I feel as if I have lived those horrors alongside them." The lanky Darrishman stared at the horizon. "It is a relief that we do not need to pass through that cursed place."

"Well," Morholt said, sensing a thread in Sabni's psyche that might be fun to pull at, "the truth is we're just trading a blighted beach and coldfire demon for a haunted wood and a runecrafter with, uh, *hot* fire. If you're worried about getting killed, I'm not sure it's all that much of an improvement. Though I suppose being merrily aflame would keep the snow off."

Sabni turned his stare to Morholt and left it there. After a moment, the runecrafter grew uncomfortable.

"It was a *joke*." Morholt pulled himself up straight in the saddle. "You could also just wear a hat."

"Your mother was not kind to you as a child." Sabni tapped a knee against Abet, who wheeled away. "But there is no excuse to take it out on the rest of us."

A hundred responses clogged Morholt's brain and slowed his tongue enough to actually consider Sabni's words. He had never told any of them about why he and Raven fled their home, or the role their parents—their mother in particular—had played in it.

Toad dicks. He *hated* being typical.

"Yeah, well, you're too tall, and your beard is stupid," Morholt yelled after him. "No, no, it's not. I'm sorry, you have a beautiful beard. Can I touch your beard?"

Sabni rode up to Mahu and Raven and did not respond.

Alone between the three in front and Ameli and Reinar behind, Morholt worried about what they *were* riding into. Every runecrafter naturally drifted into a specific form of magic. For Morholt, that had been illusions, and for Glauth, it was fire.

To say their relationship had been tempestuous was a gargantuan understatement. Their arguments were epic, and Glauth burned down two homes right over their heads. Their biggest knot was his refusal to construct a rune engine for her to draw limitless amounts of power for her flames.

He had loved her passionately, but there was no possible world in which giving Glauth an engine was a good idea. Whatever world that might have been would certainly be burned to the dirt.

And the truth was he still loved her. He couldn't let her go without a warning, even if it killed him.

Which he fervently hoped it would not.

12

HI, HONEY—I'M ON FIRE
MORHOLT

S harpened pine boles jutted out of the snow in a circular palisade all around a three-story log tower. Occasional spots of orange torchlight and the cool blue glow of the moon illuminated the snow.

Morholt and Raven stood at the edge of the Grim Pines, which had been cleared in a quarter-mile circle all around the small frozen keep. There would be no sneaking in.

"I want you to sneak in behind me," Morholt told his sister. "Pop me free if things get ugly. If she fries me, go back to camp to collect everyone and then kill 'em all."

"Maybe." Raven wiped her nose.

"Maybe?" Morholt said. "What do you mean, 'maybe?' I'm your only brother. Mom and Dad hate you just as much as they do me. It's not like you can go back and ask them to make you up another one. Dad'd pull out and squirt on the floor just to spite you."

Raven made a fake vomit face. "As beautiful as that imagery is, I just meant that I might not want to risk *my* new mercenary company. Besides, if Glauth doesn't listen to you, the Hill Fury will probably kill her and get all the revenge for me I need."

"That's not wrong." Morholt felt a little bleak. It paired well with the intense cold and thick blanket of snow on the ground.

"Although," Raven said, holding her chin in one hand, "with you out of the way, there'd be nothing left for Glauth and me to fight about. We'd probably be best friends."

Morholt gave his sister a black look. "This is stupid, isn't it?"

"No," Raven replied. "This is *very* stupid. But then you were always stupid where Glauth was concerned. You're sort of like the front half of a baby squirrel trying to climb into the mouth of the wolf that ate your butt just to see if you can find it again. Suicide for a piece of ass."

"I think that's the nicest thing you've ever said about me and Glauth." Morholt put a hand on his sister's shoulder. "But I'm not getting back with Glauth. She tried to murder you. That would be wrong."

They both laughed at that.

"All right, let's go." Morholt created a ring of runes in his mind and set it spinning around his sister's head. Then he created a second ring over that one and an identical ring around the rune engine on his wrist. Seconds after he began his spell, Raven faded from view.

With a heavy sigh, Morholt started out into the snow-covered clearing toward Glauth's keep. Raven, silent as death itself, stepped behind him into his footprints and hid her breath behind his back.

He thought about Glauth and the times they had together. Thankfully, out here in the dark, no one could see how horny he was getting.

———

T he smoky and cramped meeting hall in Glauth's tower was also the smoky and cramped dining hall, and when Morholt was dragged in by rough-handed northerners, the carcasses from the evening meal still lay strewn about the big central table. Hard men looked up from their pipes and their ale and glared at Morholt as if he were a flea-infested mongrel dog trying to hump their legs.

A cheery fire burned with appetite at the far end of the room and reminded Morholt yet again of the danger of bringing Glauth this warning. First loves never really died.

"Hi, Glauth." Morholt gave the tall, dark-haired woman at the head of the table a little wave. Scarred, hatchet-faced, and bitter, she was catnip to Morholt. Her presence dominated the room and left no doubt who was in control.

She leaned forward over the table, and Morholt lifted up on his toes to peek down her shirt. It would probably be all right to get back with her just a little before he left.

"Oldam's spear, look at what the Undergates sloughed off and shat up on our dinner table," Glauth said. Her voice lifted at the end of every sentence, making it sound like a question. She lifted her stein and drank deep.

Morholt grimaced at Glauth's lack of discretion and hoped no one would notice. He did not like to tell people where he and Raven were from. It did not usually go over well.

"I told you she couldn't keep a secret," Raven whispered in his ear.

The faces of the Norrikmen seated around the table did not harden, but then, they were already murderous. It was time to speak up before someone thought to try and put a sword through him.

He took a breath. "Do you remember me telling you about an encounter I had when I first arrived in the Thirteen Kingdoms?"

"With the sorcerer who flattened a farm when he tried to crack you in half with his big magics?" Glauth replied. "It is funny now that the story sounded so over-the-top when first I heard it. Is it not?"

It was a farm market that had been blown up, but that hardly seemed the point. "His name is Finnagel, and he's chancellor to the throne of Greenshade. The king is an idiot and does whatever Finnagel says, and right now, he says to ride out and murder every runecrafter in Andos."

Glauth's expression of distaste did not change, but several of the burly men at the table shifted nervously. One of the women carrying away the remains of the meal put a hand to her mouth and hastened from the room.

"You already know about this," Morholt said. "I guess the yellow-backs've been here already."

"Soldiers from Greenshade have been killing themselves against our walls, haven't they?" Despite the confident language, Glauth appeared rattled. She ran her tongue across her teeth and set down her stein but did not let it go. "We will be very able to handle whatever Greenshade can throw all the way this far, won't we? Especially now that you have brought the engine back here to me, I think."

"What makes you think I'd be stupid enough to bring it in here with me?" Morholt stuck out his chest defiantly—and moved the arm with the engine behind his back.

Glauth rolled her eyes. "Because you'd not come here without Raven, and Raven'd not come without being, ah, *invisible*. And you'd not do that unless you could use the engine—so you can concentrate on our conversation and not on *keeping* her unseen, yes? How am I doing with the guesswork? Quite well, I think."

Solid reasoning. Morholt had never been able to get away with anything when they were together.

Which he felt was a large part of why they were not.

"I asked once for an engine of my own," Glauth said, "and when you said no, I asked how do you make one? And what did you say to me? Do you remember what it was?"

Morholt watched the invisible—to everyone but himself—Raven creep behind Glauth, curved blades high like enormous claws.

"You did not say nothing, did you?" Glauth was close to shouting now. "You crept out of our bed and were gone to Summervatn by the time I was awake, I think."

"My rune engine isn't going to help you against the Hill Fury."

Behind Glauth, the big fire crackled, and a log fell with a muffled *fump*. Raven did not turn.

The Norrikmen went ashen faced at Morholt's words and looked at each other with downturned mouths beneath drooping beards. Glauth's narrowed stare left Morholt disconcerted.

And more than a little aroused. He looked away and tried to think about April telling him a joke instead.

"Warlord Glauth," said one of the seated men, "Sigri and Marin still haven't returned. It *had* to be the Hill Fury. You taught them runecrafting yourself. Yellowbacks could never have taken them."

"It is not the time, now." Glauth's eyes went wide, and she leaned her head back. "I'll thank you to keep your wild theories about Greenshaders in the night to yourself. Sigri and Marin are idiots. They probably fell into a cask of ale and forgot how to stand up, yes?"

"But Glauth, the *fiddler* was with them."

The others went a shade paler, and even Glauth quieted.

"Who's the fiddler?" Getting the subject away from the rune engine seemed an admirable idea to Morholt.

"A warrior I taught runecrafting to." Glauth's response was subdued. "A mute. He played the fiddle. His magic was—"

"Terrifying." The man at the table's eyes shone with fear. "If the Hill Fury took *him*, she can murder us all, and there will be nothing we can do to stop her."

A commotion rose at this point. Men stood and shouted of their fears and their bravery. It lasted until a white-hot flare banged over their heads, cowing the warriors into silence.

Glauth pointed a long finger at Morholt. "*You* have brought the Hill Fury to my house, have you not? You will be our offering, I think, to convince her to return to Treaty Hill and not kill any more Norrik-men. You can—"

A roundish hole opened with a sound like tearing cloth in the air above the table, and a lit torch, linen-wrapped and soaked in oil, dropped through. The flaming oil splattered when it hit the boards and caught the clothing and beards of the gathered warriors alight, to their loud and excited dismay.

The hole vanished, but not until Morholt spied a shadow through it, moving against a night sky with stars.

"That is not a good thing, I think." And Glauth broke for the doors.

13

YOU WERE SUPPOSED TO BRING THE MARSHMALLOWS

SARAH

S arah opened another hole in the air and dropped an oil-soaked torch through it. Gabby had been correct about it being easy, as long as she went slow and steady and visualized the distances and directions from herself. For a thing that was both millennia old *and* dead at the same time, Gabby was all right. Sarah certainly could not complain about the training she was getting. It was faster and more comprehensive than what Finnagel gave her— back when he bothered.

The hole winked out.

The Free Hand had been spotted nearby Glauth's keep, and there was no way they had not come here. She would capture the woman and kill the murderous Morholt, with every bit as much compassion as he had shown Captain Falt. The Shepherds of the Blood, the same temple knights Sarah and Vancess were here with now, took Glauth's runecrafting minions weeks ago.

Beside her, Grand Prolocutor Vancess stared over the wooden rails of a dilapidated fence and across the quarter mile of snowy fields to Glauth's keep. The moon illuminated everything. Already, men yelled and ran, and the glow of uncontrolled firelight sprang up here and there.

He handed her another torch, his movements rendered jittery from his addiction, and she lit it from a taper wedged into the top of a fence post.

"Does not the witch control flame?" he asked. "What prevents her from willing it away with her magics?"

It was a fair question, one Sarah wished she had thought of before. Still, the distant flames only seemed to grow, not diminish.

"I think that she's limited to making things that aren't on fire *be* on fire," she said. "Not the other way around." *I hope so, anyway.*

She said the words in Metzoferran in her head and dropped the torch through the new hole that tore open and blinked out. The idea was to start so many fires in so many corners of the keep that the only alternative would be to run—right into Vancess's temple knights. By this time tomorrow, Glauth would be on her way to the Dovenhouse, where the men she taught waited for her.

And Falt would be avenged.

But what then? Except for flushing Morholt, Sarah had no grudge against his women, even if he had taught them his magic. Would she return to the Forest Castle and let Vancess continue his crusade? Keane had been *off* last time they spoke. Had something happened to him?

Had Finnagel happened to him?

"Vancess," Sarah said, pausing between arsons, "have you ever been to the Dovenhouse?"

"I have," he answered. "I took custody of the lesser demons of Glauth and delivered them there myself."

"What is it?"

"You know the answer to this, Handmaiden. The Dovenhouse is where demons are unmade, and the men they once were are reborn." Vancess turned to her, his face black with shadow and his curly blond locks blue with moonlight reflected from his shining armor.

Sarah shook her head. "Yeah, all right. I do know that. But *how* are the demons—the *runecrafters*—turned back into men? How do they do it?" The only person she had ever seen *after* the Dovenhouse was the uncle of a Rouslander noble who could do nothing more than sit in a chair and drool from one side of his face. The once-handsome man had been reduced to a broken lump of scars and twitches. According to his family, he had never displayed a capacity for demon magic—or any other kind.

"They are given gaffarmord," Vancess said, "a drug that renders their minds pliable. In this state, they can be convinced to give up their evil and return to humanity. The process is long and often ruins the body, but as long as the soul is intact, it is worth it."

"Gaffarmord?" Sarah waved her hand at Vancess's next as-of-yet unlit torch. The keep was burning brightly now. "Never heard of it. Where does *that* come from?"

"Chancellor Finnagel," Vancess replied.

"Of course." Sarah stared at the snow in front of her feet. Finnagel's efforts for peace and stability never failed to include a healthy dose of misery and bloodshed. Sarah knew he had no regard for human life. That callousness was part of who he was. Or *what* he was at any rate. Just the same as it was destined to become a part of her.

"Is everyone who is sent there a demon?" Sarah asked.

"Everyone who is sent there is a threat to the temple."

That lined up with Sarah's understanding. Any other warlord, even Glauth, would simply kill their enemies. Somehow religion, in the name of love and compassion, meant you had to torture them first.

"Handmaiden?" Vancess tilted his head, and Sarah saw his eyes wide and bright, not just from the tea but also with the madness that ran beneath.

He had always been unstable for as long as she had known him. Now was worse.

"Yeah, what?"

"Have you ever been to a temple service?" Vancess's grin showed his teeth, as if he were contemplating biting Sarah.

"No." The Temple of the Sky made Sarah nervous. She didn't understand their fervor, and she never knew how they would react. In her experience, unpredictable people were dangerous, and walking into a big room full of concentrated crazy gave her the willies. Entering their compound at all had been enough of a strain on her nerves. Their capacity for loving torture was only a piece of the puzzle.

"Why not?" Vancess dropped the dripping torch he held back into the bucket of oil.

Unsure of Vancess's motives, Sarah decided to go with an angle of actual truth. "I suppose after you've taken a thousand-mile walk with a goddess while she teaches you the secrets of the universe, spending a day in a stuffy temple listening to an old man rail at me about *his* opinion of what the gods want of you seems a little hollow? Wasteful? Stupid?"

Vancess chuckled and reached out to the wooden fence. His hand trembled. It had been most of a day since his last pot of tea. "I do not think that Messenger Hayké would agree with that. But he is a priest, not a warrior for the Alir as we are. The gods give their truth as they will, and truth on the edge of a blade is for nobility. The words of a man with no knowledge of the true gods on a stone bench in a stone room is how the poor and feckless experience the Alir. We know the gods. Know the *fact* of them. They are not ghosts in the dark for us. The temple is of no use to you and me except as a means to control the rabble."

"Nobility?" Sarah did not remember much about her family, mostly just feelings of happiness. But she did know they had never been rich, or noble, or anything like that, and after their deaths at the hands of a street gang, she had grown up an urchin and a thief beside Keane.

"Surely you are aware the Shepherds of the Blood are all of noble lineage." Vancess licked his lips. "Their fathers are the Holy Order of the Stone Vault and repay their debts to the temple with the noble blood of their sons. How else could they be worthy as the sword arm of the Alir?" He craned his neck at the sound of a nearby steed snorting and stamping in the snow. "Except for the archers. A noble would never kill a man in such a cowardly way."

"I am *so* sorry I asked." At least the temple's misogyny kept them from sending their noble daughters to their deaths along with their sons, though they doubtlessly carried even greater burdens at home. "You should be aware though. In my experience, nobles die just as easy as anyone else. They're just more surprised by it when it happens."

"Men may die, but the Alir do not, nor do their purposes." Vancess lifted his head to the cold sky and closed his eyes. "Just as a drop of water may splash into stream and be gone, but that stream never stops. We are part of a great undertaking that will remake the world. We will become its history, and we will shape the path of the stream.

"For the Alir."

Sarah decided at that very moment that when this was all over and done with, she would kill Vancess. And just as fast, she knew she couldn't. To do so would put her feet on the track envisioned for her by Finnagel, Kadir, and even the goddess Magda. Vancess, too, for that matter.

"The value of people is in being one of them," Sarah said, "not in subjugating them."

"Huh? What?" Vancess lowered his head to stare at Sarah, confused.

Sarah shrugged, sighed, and smiled. "Nothing. Sorceress stuff."

"Oh, sure." Vancess nodded, obviously not understanding.

Across the snow, the first of Glauth's warriors escaped the flaming keep only to fall beneath the attentions of Vancess's ignoble archers.

"No, stop that." Sarah dropped the torch she held into the snow where it hissed out. "Not the archers. They're killing them."

"Hmm?" Vancess raised his head at the Northmen lying bloody in the snow. "Yes. Killing them."

The compassion-impaired prolocutor would be of no help.

"Shepherds of the Blood!" Sarah yelled into the snow and fire-filled night. "Temple knights move forward and intercept the escapees. Archers stand down. No more killing unless it's in defense of your own lives. But if you get a shot at the red-haired demon Morholt—*take it*."

Vancess frowned. "High King Oldam is not going to approve of this. Mercy has no place in combat."

"The next time I give a crap what High King Oldam thinks, I'll let you know." They had agreed on this. Sarah walked away from Vancess to keep herself from tearing his head bodily from his shoulders. Finnagel would not be right about her. Human lives were not for sorcerers to dispense with.

So, where exactly did that leave her with Morholt?

14

NO, KEEP TALKING—I DON'T WANT TO INTERRUPT

MORHOLT

The Free Hand stood at the edge of the Grim Pines and watched Glauth's warriors, who could not make themselves unseen with runecrafting like Morholt, be cut down. The warriors answered the temple knights' offers to surrender with curses and steel, and they paid the price for their pride. The first few Northmen who ran out had been given no such opportunity. As much as he could through his fear for Glauth, Morholt wondered what had changed.

The Hill Fury—Sarah—was probably somewhere on the far side of the cleared field. Her new forces, heavily armored cavalry in the blue-and-white livery of the Temple of the Sky, sat in a wide circle around the inferno.

Morholt could not speak. His throat was too tight. So was his heart.

"Damn." Raven squatted behind a snow-covered bush and peeped over the top. "That bitch is *not* fucking around."

Sabni put a long-fingered hand on Morholt's shoulder. "I am sorry, my friend. I know she must have been dear to you, for you to have risked so much to warn her. We will grieve her properly when we have left this place. Everything and everyone that we experience adds to who we are, even the dead."

Mercifully, he did not attribute the quote.

"I had assumed this *Fury* would have at least made some effort to take prisoners," Reinar rumbled.

"She's the Hill Fury. It's there in the name," Ameli answered. "'Hill Catcher and Fair Trial Giver' just doesn't inspire the same kind of terror."

He would kill her. If Sarah had killed Glauth, then Morholt would kill her back. He could be a good person again after that.

Mahu stepped up beside Morholt and looked to Sabni. "We should go. This isn't safe."

Tension ratcheted up Morholt's spine and legs and made him sway. Sabni kept him upright with a gentle pull. He couldn't leave. Not until he knew for sure.

"Who the arch fuck taught *you* how to be a human being?" Raven asked Mahu. "We'll go when it's done. Save anyone we can. Why don't you go see if you can find some wild animals out there to run away from?"

Mahu frowned and went back to his horse, where he pulled off his bow and strung it. He drew an arrow and nocked it but said nothing.

"So, who's next?" Ameli asked. "I think it's more important now than ever to find all of Morholt's exes and save them. Now that we know what we're really up against."

Morholt tried to answer, but nothing came out. He just couldn't tear his eyes away from the conflagration. Even so, gratitude for Ameli's statement gave him some warmth against the creeping chill in what passed for his soul.

"Um... Selenna, I think." Raven tapped the side of her jaw in thought. "Last we heard, she'd married some minor lord in Hornfield. Between Dismon and the Icewater."

"That's in Tyrrane." Ameli rubbed at her upper arms against the chill.

Raven frowned. "Yeah, so?"

"Nothing." Ameli held out her hands and let them drop. "Just saying it out loud. Oh goodie, we're going to Tyrrane. Hope we don't get murdered."

"I shall protect you." Reinar moved to stand behind her. "As long as the Ebon Host do not choose to attack us with pole snakes."

"I think they use swords and bows and stuff like that." Ameli twisted and patted Reinar on the chest.

The big man put a hand on Hadral's hilt. "Much better."

For the next hour, the group stood and waited and made idle chatter that left Morholt feeling as if he were climbing out of his skin. It required all his concentration to simply keep from exploding.

In the end, the Norrik warriors lay bleeding in the snow, waiting for Sarah and her blackguards to run them through, while the archers retrieved their arrows. Then, with the keep still burning behind them, the temple knights rode south into the wood.

The Free Hand waited another half hour before they moved. Morholt's nerves screamed, but he knew this would be a critical time. Just as Glauth might be dying in the snow somewhere, so might Sarah be waiting behind some stupid tree.

Imaginary rings of circling runes appeared in Morholt's mind as he created an image of himself and stood it close by. If there were an archer out in the trees, there was no sense in risking their own necks finding him. And if there were not, leaving an image of himself behind for the Hill Fury to find might give them the few extra seconds they would need to escape.

Morholt slowed his breathing and increased his attention while he made the next series of tiny rings. He was not certain this next bit would work. It was something he had thought of a while ago and carried around in the back of his mind, and this seemed like the perfect opportunity to give it a try. Morholt forced himself—again— to slow down. This was delicate work and still partly theoretical.

He had surmised that it might be possible to make a very small tightly-controlled rune engine out of the very stuff of illusion itself. This was not taught back in his homeland. Illusion making was a rare talent, and he was pretty sure he would have been reprimanded just for asking about it. There were *lots* of ways this could go catastrophically wrong. He released his mental hold on the construct.

The delicate construct held stable, and the illusion of Morholt scratched its jaw under a scraggly ginger beard. It worked. With just a bit more luck, he could use this to keep Sarah's eyes off him long enough to find Glauth and flee.

"Finely done." Reinar leaned in for a better look at the ersatz Morholt's face which stared back at him. "No less hideous than the original."

"Thank—*yaahh!*" Morholt yelled.

"You should be happier to see me not being dead and all burned away, I think." Glauth stepped out of the shadow a dozen feet away, hands on her skinny hips. "I got out of the keep before the fires really got going, yes? Before things got too hot. Now let's track this Hill Fury down and—" A small thump came from Glauth, and she leaned forward the tiniest amount. "Oh. What is that?"

Glauth coughed. She looked down at the big bodkin arrowhead that stuck out of her left breast. A dark stain spread into her clothing around it.

Then she smiled at Morholt. "That is not a good thing either, I think." And she fell over in the brush.

Ameli rushed to her side as Raven stood and pointed.

"Holt! We're fucked. It's her, and she's running right at us." Raven grabbed her brother's arm. "We gotta *go.*"

An arrow whizzed past Morholt's head from Mahu's bow, but the racing Sarah merely knocked it aside with a flash of her sword. They really did need to go.

Two big imaginary rings spun in opposite directions over Morholt's head while the Hand dove for their horses. The pain of leaving the murdered Glauth behind fell out of the sky toward Morholt's head. The only choice left to him was to be somewhere else when it hit.

Sarah was fifty feet away and running like the wind.

Morholt pulled himself up on Fog's back and squeezed her ribs with his knees. Breath wouldn't enter his lungs. He lifted his arm into the center of the spinning rings and twisted it left.

Sarah was twenty feet away, her wide blade held back and low.

And the Grim Pines exploded into multicolored flame and glowing, shrieking smoke.

15

TAKING OFF THE GLOVES
SARAH

And the Grim Pines exploded into multicolored flame and glowing, shrieking smoke.

Sarah dove sideways and rolled on her shoulder through the snow. "Idiot," she muttered, standing and brushing the crunchy white from her fur cloak. All of this fire and noise would be illusion, and by reacting to it, she had already allowed Morholt the instant it would have taken him to escape her.

Captain Falt would have been disappointed in her. Again.

One brawny hand out in front of her, Sarah crept forward. She felt heat from the explosions and gouts of colored fire. It was as ephemeral as the light which constantly tricked her mind into believing that it illuminated the setting.

But it didn't.

The brilliant display faded away and left dark and shadow behind. Sarah sheathed her sword with more force than was necessary and kicked at the snow. "That murderous red-headed dirtbag is *always* one step ahead of me. I am really starting to hate that guy."

"You skewered the captain," came a voice out of the dark.

A startled leap carried Sarah away from the shadows, and she pointed her sword at the dark shape in the trees.

"*I* didn't kill him. Shoving your guilt off on me isn't going to make you any less of a genocidal harridan. You do make that mail coat work though." The figure stepped out from behind a huge pine bole and into the moonlight.

The blade lowered.

Morholt smirked at her.

"Another illusion." Sarah scanned the woods. "How did he make you? I thought he had to see whatever he was controlling, and I *know* he's not stupid enough to still be around."

"My ways are mysterious and complex, Hill Fury." The illusion of Morholt wandered out of the trees and into the snow-filled field. It put its hands on its hips and stared across at the ruin of Glauth's keep. "I loved her, you know."

That caught Sarah off guard. She was not sure what she expected out of this construct, but that was not it.

"The arrow was meant for you. For him." This was all wrong. "She stepped in front of it after I loosed it. I never even saw her until it was too late."

"You accidentally kill a lot of people. Bet you're a big hit at birthday parties." The fake Morholt dragged a toe through the snow, making a fake furrow of crusty white. "Wonder who you'll blame this one on?"

Sarah did not know what a birthday party was, but she had no intention of spending another instant listening to a person who wasn't even here. The thought sent her mind to Gabby, but she was nearly certain that Gabby was at least *sort of* there when they spoke.

"Can Morholt see me now? Can he hear me through your ears?"

"Of course not." The fake Morholt shook his head. "You really don't know anything about illusions, do you? Telesensory extrusions are a whole different field of runecrafting. Can you remind me why I'm afraid of you again?"

Irritation overwhelmed Sarah's feeling of foolishness at talking to an illusion. She stomped around and placed herself between it and the burning fort. "You're afraid because when I find the *real* you, I'm going to chop you in half and burn the pieces. I'll hunt you down until—"

"You can stop right there, tough tits," he interrupted. "That's not the way this is going to go. I've been doing everything I could not to hurt you. But you killed Glauth. You killed her cold. From behind, and her with a smile on her face." The pale skin and red hair darkened until the illusion was wholly shadow save for its glittering eyes. "If you catch me now, *I* will kill *you*, and I'll be happy to have done it. Your only choice is to fuck off back to Finnagel and stay there. Because I am going to spend the rest of my days on the lookout for giant sword ladies to pitch off a cliff and stab in the head." It turned sideways and held its chin between thumb and forefinger. "That didn't sound right. I'll kill you and let everyone see your underwear. Um, wait. I'll let Mahu and Sabni fill you with arrows and then make a hat rack out of your corpse. That would smell bad after a while though—"

Sarah's punch swung through empty air, but blessedly dispersed the remains of the illusion. She rubbed her temples. The thing had given her a headache, and she already burned with anger at her own allies. Worries about Keane, Finnagel, and the constant stress of dealing with Vancess left her in violent need of control.

Glauth's death had been an accident, but only on her part. Vancess was all too happy to slaughter everyone coming out of the keep, which would never have been necessary without them killing the first men who stepped outside with their archers. They may not have surrendered happily, but they would have done it. When the first man fell dead, negotiations fell with him.

But Glauth. Sarah was not sure how the warlord woman had gotten past Vancess and his temple knights. He was the one with demon-hunting experience. Their intelligence on the woman's abilities whistled with the wind that blew through the holes in it. And one of those holes ended up in Glauth.

Experience or no, Vancess would direct no more battles while Sarah was here. Glauth threatened no one any longer, but the situation with Morholt was so much worse now than just an hour ago.

But was that Vancess's fault? Was she blaming others for her own mistakes like the illusion said? What was she even thinking? Should she have let Glauth go free? Wasn't killing her the better option anyway?

Wasn't she the enemy?

With a sigh, Sarah set off across the snow toward the south end of the field, where her horse—and beyond it, Prolocutor Vancess and his vicious Shepherds of the Blood—waited for her.

16

THE BARON'S RESOLVE

KING BRANNOK

Though Brannok did not much care for entertaining visiting nobles, he was happy enough to sit in on this dinner, if only for an opportunity to spend time with his daughter. His end of the brightly lit table loomed six inches above the rest, allowing him to more easily track all of his guests.

"I have found that the weapon choice of any Mirrikman is less important than the resolve behind my own." To Brannok's left, the young baron from the Sund kingdom of Norrik prattled on. He seemed convinced that the key to winning Jasmayre's heart lay within his ability to talk about fighting. "Have I told you about when two dozen warriors from Norrikborg came charging across the Spiny Oyster River, and there was no one to stop them but myself and my dog?"

The row of servants against the dark stone wall behind him stared ahead as if no foolish nobles were speaking at all while, beside the baron, Queen Tove the Mountain exchanged smoldering glances with Prince Jason across the table.

"Baron Fafnir, really. Your dog defeated two dozen warriors from Norrikborg?" Jasmayre smiled disarmingly at the intense baron. Seated opposite Fafnir, she was every inch the poised and charming princess one might expect. Unless you listened to her carefully enough. Her eyes flashed amusement and wickedness.

"Oh no. That's not what I meant." Fafnir's tone was that of an indulgent uncle correcting an idiot niece. "Pok helped, but 'twas *I* who slew the invaders. But my point was the different types of weapons they carried, against my own spear."

"You didn't kill them with your resolve?"

At Jasmayre's question, even Jason turned his head to hide a laugh.

Smiles popped out on the faces of the court nobility seated around the lengthy table. This looked to be good sport. Tove cut her eyes at Fafnir and shook her head.

Baron Fafnir continued unabated. Brannok remembered dimly what it was like to have that kind of confidence. So certain in your own superiority that you might step into a bear trap, assured that it would not dare snap shut on your leg.

Of course, Jasmayre was far more lethal than any bear trap.

"Well, yes. My resolve, certainly." Fafnir's mighty resolve might be failing him now, though. "But one spear against two dozen—"

"What kind of dog?" Head canted to one side, Jasmayre steepled her hands in front of herself. Brannok could admit she was not the most beautiful woman in the land, but at this moment, she was utterly compelling.

"The dog?" Fafnir could clearly not comprehend why any woman should be more interested in a dog than in a battle against invading Norrikborgers.

This time Jason had to hide his face behind both hands while discreet laughter broke out around the table. Brannok saw Jasmayre and Tove catch each other's attention and grin.

"Pok is a wolfhound." Baron Fafnir straightened in his chair, his dark eyes burning with pride. "I trained him from a pup to defend the Sund. We are as close as any two warriors in the north have ever been."

"The Sund is fortunate to have a mighty defender such as Pok the wolfhound." Jasmayre's expression glittered with warmth. "Just as Pok is fortunate to have your *resolve* so intimately close behind him."

The laughter in the room grew less discreet, and Brannok coughed and looked up into the hanging candelabra over the table. Tove's clear and rich laughter filled the space.

Fafnir's servant stepped up from behind him and whispered something in his ear.

Baron Fafnir grew blotchy and red and stared at his food. He did not speak again.

It had been the correct decision to allow Jasmayre to run Tyrrane while Brannok scoured the contents of the little library below ground. Was she perhaps the smartest woman in the Thirteen Kingdoms? Certainly, her intellect was greater than his and, if he were honest, so was her courage. Even her failures she managed to turn into successes.

He would leave this dank fortress better for her than when his father left it to him. Better for a lack of Angrim beneath it.

Conversation in the hall lifted and grew happy. Almost... unafraid? Yes, the world *was* changing.

Earlier today, Angrim had summoned Brannok into his presence to report on the day's intelligence. The Hill Fury had been spotted in the company of a cohort of temple knights hunting demons in the Grengards. When Angrim heard, he screeched his laughter and said that he knew both where the 'button' would be and when. He ordered Brannok to go and fetch his most elite cavalry and bowmen and put them on the road.

Being treated as some mere messenger filled Brannok with a sense of calm purpose. The books he read deep below did not as yet seem connected, but he could not shake the impression that they were all pieces of a larger puzzle and that he was being somehow changed, *prepared*, just by the act of working through it. Books about runes and books about rings.

He was eager for it.

Brannok awoke from his ruminations when people stood from

the table to move off into a variety of other sitting rooms more suitable for plotting. He saw Jason and Tove leave hand in hand.

The young Baron Fafnir was nowhere in sight.

With a kind smile, Jasmayre pulled her thick braid behind her head and stepped up to her father. "Where have you been, my king?"

Brannok resisted an overwhelming urge to sit his daughter on his knee. She would never do that. He would only look foolish.

"Merely wondering if you ever do plan to marry. Raising heirs is part of the job, you know."

One thin brow went up on Jasmayre's face. This was as close as Brannok had come to telling her he planned on leaving her the kingdom.

She placed a hand on his arm, thin and so elegantly tapered. There was warmth in the gesture, if not in the contact. "I may get around to it someday, but at present, I am far too busy to look after irritating young jackanapes chasing about my skirts."

"You do well enough looking after Jason."

"Yes, Father, but Jason is not trying to marry me and force himself into our royal family."

"And Tove the Mountain? Perhaps she has become tired of being a widow queen?"

Jasmayre's eyes widened a fraction, and her lips drew tight, but her calm demeanor reasserted itself as fast as it had gone. "That situation is progressing well. We need only trust in Prince Jason to be himself, and the rest of the north will fall into our open and waiting pockets."

Of course. His daughter's plans stretched far in advance of Brannok's own sight. Could it be that where he tried for empire and failed so quickly, she might actually succeed?

"Then I withdraw my question. I merely counsel not to tarry overlong in choosing a husband. You will always have whomever you wish; that is also part of the job." He winked at her. "But you will not always be young enough for children without risking your own life."

She rolled her eyes and gripped her father's arm before sliding her hand away. "I must devote all of my attention to steering Tyrrane and supporting you in your great work. When that is over, you can be king again, and I will find a suitable husband."

Brannok nodded. He always suspected she loved him but hearing this admission of loyalty swept away his breath and blew it right off the parapet. To his great shock, he found he believed her completely. The realization left him embarrassed.

Until very recently, he had not been a good father to his only daughter. He had not been nice, nor thoughtful, nor fair. It was not just the books below that were changing him; it was the woman who stood beside him. Did he even deserve her loyalty?

Stunned, Brannok sat back in the tall chair with a thump.

Had he ever, in all his life, even once stopped to consider if he actually *deserved* a thing before he took it?

17

BECAUSE KINGS ALREADY KNOW EVERYTHINGS

SHAYLA

No child, this is a wedding party, not a battle. There will be no need for you to defend yourself with cutlery."

Princess Shayla made a face at her tutor, Miss Thornwhistle, a pale-skinned, gray-haired woman with a big bottom who smelled like dried herbs, and lowered the table knife she held crossed against her brother Volker's. "But no one's getting *married*." She flopped across the place setting in front of her.

"Daddy says kings don't need to learn stuff." Prince Volker sat back in a huff, his small arms crossed. "And I'm gonna be king, so I don't need to learn neither."

"Don't need to learn *either*," Miss Thornwhistle replied with infuriating calmness.

"Oldam's nose." Volker shifted sideways so he couldn't see the tutor.

Meanwhile, Shayla wondered where she might find a frog or a rat or even a snake in the small square schoolroom. She was certain Miss Thornwhistle would run from the surprise introduction of such a creepy-crawly up her skirt. Moon snored in the corner and caused the surface of Shayla's table to vibrate.

He was no help.

The plot was interrupted when scary Chancellor Finnagel stormed into the room. Horrible when he was in a good mood, he was positively terrifying now. Anger boiled behind his dark face, and his malicious glare fastened onto Shayla. He pointed a twisted finger at her.

"Really, Chancellor." Miss Thornwhistle cut off whatever he had been about to say. "This is an important time for the royal children. We simply cannot have interruptions."

Chancellor Finnagel's glower backed the woman up a step. She put a hand to her face and looked down at the floor.

He returned to Shayla.

"You, girl, where is it?" The hate-filled voice promised demons and torments Shayla could not begin to conceive of.

Mommy once told Shayla that Chancellor Finnagel used to be a happy man who smiled and laughed and made her feel warm and safe. But he had an accident that left him mean and bitter, and now it was best to just stay out of his way.

"My pendant, girl. I know you stole it out of my chambers. You brats believe you can get away with whatever you wish because you are *royalty*." He spat the word like a pirate candy filled with dirt. "But your titles won't save you from *me*."

To Shayla's distress, there was nowhere to run. Panic stopped her chest and made it impossible to breathe. He was going to *kill* her.

"You better go away now, or I'll tell the king!" And just like that, Volker stood in between her and the chancellor. He would protect her. He *always* protected her.

"Whatever is missing, Chancellor, I'm certain will wait until after class. The children aren't going anywhere." The tutor's voice failed to match the assuredness of her words.

Chancellor Finnagel paid the quavering Miss Thornwhistle no heed and snatched Volker up off the floor by the front of his shirt. He pulled the boy up into his own snarling face.

And stopped. A low rumble, steady and ominous, filled the classroom.

Moon was no longer asleep in the corner.

The balance of authority in the room shifted, and Shayla grinned.

Chancellor Finnagel's eyes darted between the two children, the dog, and Miss Thornwhistle, doing hard maths in his head and not liking the answer. He set Prince Volker back down on the floor.

Despite his apparent defeat, Shayla was under no pretense that Chancellor Finnagel was giving in because he was afraid of Moon. His wicked eyes held hidden motives.

"This is preposterous. I'll let your parents deal with you." He spun and left, his golden kaftan snapping with the motion.

Then Shayla understood. Chancellor Finnagel told Mommy and Daddy what to do. He would make them punish her and Volker in some way he did not want to be seen doing himself.

That was really not any better.

Stunned silence shrouded the classroom. Shayla traded a nod with Volker and looked up at Miss Thornwhistle. She was white and trembling. Standing up to Chancellor Finnagel had been scary for her too.

Volker made a quick signal to Moon, and the dog jumped up and down, barking like thunder come home for holiday.

Miss Thornwhistle, nerves already frayed, shrieked and dove behind her table.

Shayla and Volker were out the door and sprinting down the corridor long before she opened her eyes.

18

A JAR OF AMBERNUTS

VOLKER

From the back of a stone stag, Volker looked over the wall of the grassy courtyard at the distant blue peaks of the Brighthorn Mountains. In front of him, Shayla stood on her tiptoes to peer at the merchants and messengers a hundred feet below. Hoop-gulls verbally abused each other and tried to steal anything that another gull had already stolen.

The stag's statue family surrounded him—a half dozen does and fawns—but Volker always sat on the stag because it had antlers and could fight. It would be so amazing to have antlers.

"You really made Mister Finnagel mad." Volker swung his legs in unison, brushing the uncut grass. The Deer Garden was tiny and barely anyone ever came, so not as much attention was paid to it as the other courtyards sprinkled about the castle. More importantly, no one had yet caught them in the garden, so neither Alan nor Nanny would ever think to look for them here.

"*Chance-ler* Finnagel." Shayla drooped in an exaggerated sigh. "And he always looks scary at me. He's mean."

"He looks scary at everyone." Volker shakily got to his feet and stood on the stag's gray back, arms outstretched. "Look at me! I'm a

stupid grownup who loses his stupid pengant and blames little kids."
He wanted to make his sister feel better. She was quiet. Nervous.

Shayla smiled and giggled a little.

Pleased with himself, Volker tried to take a bow and had to grab
hold of the antlers to keep from falling off.

Shayla guffawed laughter.

Well, that *had* been the point.

Volker slid to the ground. "Why d'you think he got so mad at you
about it?"

"I dunno."

Shayla was an excellent liar. She could talk her way past any
grownup in the castle, Daddy included, and *he* was the best. But she
could never quite manage it with Volker.

"You *did* steal the pengant!"

At this height, cool breezes blew away the hot air but carried the
gulls' combative squawking closer.

"Pendant." Shayla rarely missed an opportunity to correct her
older brother. Volker didn't mind though. She was making his brain
smarter, like Mommy's.

With a secret smile, Shayla slowly withdrew a glossy yellow stone,
shaped like a teardrop and run through with white veins, from her
pocket. A black leather loop hung through a hole in the pointy end.
She passed it to her brother.

Pretty, but not special as stones went. Volker frowned at it. "I
wonder why he's so mad about it. Maybe he got it from a monster or
something."

"I heard him tell Mommy he doesn't amember where it came
from. He's super old. Maybe even older than Daddy."

That did not seem likely. Daddy was *wise*, and that was the same
as old. But then if Mister Finnagel had forgotten who gave him a
pengant—*pendant*—maybe he was even wiser than Daddy?

He returned the pendant to Shayla.

"You better hide it." Volker looked around for someplace good. A
hole in the mortar of the wall or beneath a loose flagstone. At the
outside corner of the courtyard, a round peak-roofed watch station

jutted into the air and kept an impassive eye on the active city. He climbed the few steps into it and sat on the circular stone bench in the middle. "If he finds it in your pocket, it won't matter how good you lie."

Shayla's smile turned into a scowl, and she placed the leather loop over the head and neck of her favorite doe which she had named Petal. She had named them all, but Volker only amembered Petal and Valiant, his big stag.

"You can't hide it there." While almost no one came up here, that was not exactly the same as saying no one *ever* came up here.

Shayla's fists went to her hips. "I'm *not* hiding it. I took it for Petal. She likes it."

There did not seem to be any argument for that. Volker shrugged. The pendant did look good around Petal's neck.

"Do you think Mister Finnagel did something to Mommy and Daddy?" This question had burned a pocket into Volker's tummy and rumbled around and made him feel sick any time he thought about it. This time he asked it without thinking, so the question wouldn't have time to get him. Though he expected it to hit him at once, all he felt was relief.

"Yes."

And now he felt sick again.

On hands and feet, Shayla climbed the steps and sat beside her brother. Out of the open-sided watch station, Volker, alarmed, saw a white-cheeked hawk pluck a soaring hoop-gull right out of the sky.

The shouting gulls went silent. Volker did not mention it to Shayla.

"Mommy and Daddy are diff'rent." Her voice was soft. Contemplative. It was her Big-Plans voice. "They been diff'rent since Aunt Sarah left, but now they're mean because they do everything Chancellor Finnagel says, and Chancellor Finnagel is mean. He's getting angrier. I think his fingers are in their brains."

"What?" Volker did not always understand everything Shayla said. Like now. "How would he do that?"

"I think he's *magic*," Shayla whispered the last word.

Though his first reaction was a strong "Nuh-*uh*," given that the notion came from Shayla, he was obligated to give it some consideration first. Mister Finnagel being magic *would* explain a lot.

"How're we gonna save Mommy and Daddy then? We're not magic." There was no doubt that they would rescue their parents and fast. Well, right after lunch. He was getting pretty hungry.

"I dunno yet." Shayla shook her head, and her brown hair curtained her face in a straight fall. She brushed it aside. "But when I do, we'll have the cat-chucker's ambernuts in a jar."

"Daddy just says nuts."

"*Unh!*" Shayla slipped off the bench and stomped her foot. "I like *ambernuts!*"

19

NO PLAN EVER SURVIVES CONTACT WITH ANYONE

JASMAYRE

A sharp pull smoothed the wrinkles in front of Jasmayre's gold velvet dress and straightened the neckline. The heavy garment was designed to add a little bulk to her whip-thin frame and to ward off the ever-present chill of the citadel.

She peered into the looking glass at the far end of her dressing room and rubbed her teeth. A row of similarly styled dresses, most of which she had never worn, covered the length of the left wall, while shoes covered the right. Jasmayre understood why her late mother gifted her with all these things, even though they were of almost no use. The woman had simply not known what else to do.

Jasmayre was not nervous, not exactly, anyway. But this meeting represented a culmination. All of her efforts for the past few years, the trips to Norrik—everything really—could be decided in the next hour. That parts of this relied on the actions of others was not ideal but also not an unwarranted risk. She was certain they could be guided into playing the roles she laid out for them. It was, after all, her most accomplished skill.

Also, she held deep affection for the woman who had come to meet her. That was rare enough to make the occasion special.

Her father had found the library deep in the bedrock below the

Fell Citadel and even now studied the books there to find the answer to Tyrrane's greatest strength and most formidable threat. Once Angrim was eliminated, it would be on her efforts, here and now, that the nation either stood or fell.

Long clever fingers picked a silver hairpin out of her armoire and tucked it in at her temple. The white-petaled flower set off well against her dark red hair. She pulled her heavy braid in front of her like an armored vest and set out for combat.

―――――

"Finally, a ray of sunshine in this bleak place." Queen Tove the Mountain, ruler of the Grengards, raised long muscular arms out of her wolf-fur cloak and strode across the small meeting chamber, her thick boots muted on the ornamental rug. The tall Norrikwoman engulfed Jasmayre in a powerful hug as though she were a child.

"I have missed you in my court," Tove said, holding Jasmayre out at arm's length. "As have the young men of Gullhome." Like everything else about the Mountain, her smile was extraordinary. Seeing that smile given to Jasmayre, one might never suspect that just ten years ago King Brannok had employed mercenaries to attack the Grengards's capital city of Gullhome and kill their sorcerer.

Queen Tove was a stunning woman. Her father was from the wild tribes of the Troll Coast and had gifted her with a river of rich black hair and large dancing eyes. She stood out anywhere but most especially in a graying court full of dour-faced Norrikmen.

This close to Tove, Jasmayre was an unattractive stick poking out of a frozen mud field. The thought brought no end of amusement to her. She was not interested in any of the prizes beauty might offer anyway.

Jasmayre knew what real power was and where to find it. An ample bust and a pretty face were entirely beside the point.

Mostly beside the point.

"I understand you bring good news." Jasmayre walked past the table, loaded with roasted birds and vegetables, to stand close to the fire. Tove was right; the Fell Citadel enveloped its occupants in bleakness. Even in this room of elegant chairs and welcoming art, the low ceilings and black walls of the citadel found a way to oppress its occupants.

Maybe she and her father would tear it down and build something more pleasant. *That* would be a legacy worth remembering.

"I do at that." If anything, Tove's brilliant smile grew more radiant. "My daughter, Princess Línhildur, has married Prince Yngvi, son of King Stigr Manybeards of Kingsdal. Stigr will be the father to Línhildur she never had."

"And a wealthy one at that." Jasmayre nodded appreciatively to Tove. Kingsdal was the richest of all five kingdoms of Norrik. Such an alliance could only benefit Queen Tove.

"Fat coffers never hurt a relationship." Tove reached over and picked up a goblet of deep red wine. She lifted it. "To fat, happy, and monetarily secure grandbabies."

But now Princess Línhildur would be the queen of Kingsdal, which meant that Tove needed another heir. While Tove was older than Jason, in Jasmayre's estimation, the woman could produce a few more children without endangering herself if she moved fast enough. How fortunate Jasmayre held a solution in her hand.

Jasmayre laughed and found a glass of her own. The sole servant in the room jumped forward and filled it before retiring to his darkened corner. The flavor was rich and sweet—the taste of too much money mixed with flowers and overripe cherries. She rarely drank in diplomatic engagements, but she was feeling celebratory.

It lit a little fire in her stomach.

"I hear that Horrikvik has found funding for a raiding fleet of longships as well," Jasmayre said. A flush rose in her cheeks and she stroked her thick braid of hair.

Queen Tove's eyes narrowed the smallest bit, though her wide smile never faltered. "They have, though I might wonder how *you* discovered it. King Stigr only agreed to give them the money two days ago. I didn't find out until I'd arrived here in Dismon."

"That's hardly important," Jasmayre said. In fact, she had been the one to suggest to Stigr that he offer to fund Horrikvik's fleet in return for half their profits, just as she had prodded Stigr to push his daughter into marrying Tove's son. "The important thing now is that Kingsdal and Horrikvik are bound together, as are Kingsdal and the Grengards. That's three of the five kingdoms of Norrik allied at once. And you know *what* that means."

The smile finally fell off Tove's face. She sighed. "It means war with the other two." She set down the goblet and fell into a padded chair, her arms on the cushioned armrests. "I'm happy for Línhildur. My daughter deserves whatever satisfaction she can take out of life. She is sadly not the smartest woman in the north, certainly not compared to *you*." She nodded to Jasmayre, whose blush increased. "But, with Hedra's blessings, she'll make a good wife, and she'll support Stigr's son Yngvi. Turn him into a responsible monarch for Kingsdal's throne."

Jasmayre said nothing and let Tove talk herself out. The rest of her glass turned the flame in her stomach into a cozy campfire that made her feel as if she could see the future. She knew exactly what Tove was going to say and where she would end up.

She set her glass down on the table and waved the servant away when he tried to refill it.

"Every time three of the kingdoms reach an accord, the other two ally themselves to attack the weakest of the three, and the whole thing falls apart. The Alir know I've even done it. No one wants to be the last one out, and everyone's so stubborn they won't join if they see any hint of threat in it. And there's *always* threat in it." Her brows drew in. "What's so funny?"

The laughter spilled out of Jasmayre. "I'm sorry," she said. "It's just listening to you complain about the other rulers being stubborn—"

"I know." Tove waved an alabaster hand. The woman's skin positively glowed. "Stubborn is *my* thing. That's why I'm *the Mountain*." She leaned to one side and placed her chin in the palm of her hand.

An ache tightened Jasmayre's chest. What was it? This was not a convenient time to come over ill. She was not one to be sick at any rate. It didn't feel like—oh no.

No.

It was longing. That was so much worse. That did not work at *all*.

Jasmayre spun to face the table, away from Tove. Her cheeks burned with fierce heat. Why this, and why now? Obviously, she had been attracted to the woman; who wouldn't be? But over the last year, she had spent *months* in Tove's court in Gullhome without this kind of addle-brained reaction—though the two of them had never been alone.

Like they were now.

She glanced at the servant, who stared at the floor. "Leave us."

Sending the man away was part of Jasmayre's plan, but having feelings for the queen of the Grengards certainly was not. None of what she had put in place was about *her*. It was about Tyrrane. About securing the future of her country and her family.

Her fingers twisted into her braid and released it. She ran her hand down the ropy coils, trying to sooth her nerves.

That was it then. She would ignore these fanciful yearnings for the childish distractions they were and proceed with the business of state. Jasmayre forced a smile on her face and returned her attention to Tove.

Issta's Gates, she knows. She can see right through me. What am I doing?

Tove the Mountain leaned on an armrest and supported her head with a single finger against her temple. A lazy smile crawled up one side of her face.

"I once witnessed a man get his leg chopped off at the knee by a salt-blood giant up on the Troll Coast," Tove said. "He had the exact same expression on his face as you do right now."

"I was only thinking that Stigr's idea of paying for Horrikvik's raiding fleet means that your daughter's marriage was a waste." Jasmayre winced inside. This manipulation had seemed so easy mere minutes ago. "You can't afford to be allied to Stigr now, not unless you're willing to go to war."

Tove erupted from her chair with a sudden violence that made Jasmayre flinch.

"If Norrikborg and the Sund want to make war on the Grengards, *or* Horrikvik, *or* Kingsdal, I will be waiting with my blade in my hand and their blood in my teeth. Are you all right?"

Jasmayre had quite forgotten to breathe during Tove's vehement display. "I am..." Jasmayre's hand went to her chest. "I am well. I only forgot your... passion." What was the next thing she was supposed to say? All of her planning and work could not be blown away on the heated gales of some stupid crush.

A big hand, sinew rippling beneath ivory-hot skin, took Jasmayre by the forearm. She had to close her eyes to keep from being over-whelmed by the contact.

"Will Tyrrane come to our aid if we need it?" Tove asked.

Ah, there it was.

Jasmayre's eyes flitted back open, and a sly smile spread on her lips. The Mountain had led her back to the plan after all.

Only now Jasmayre hated the idea of it.

"Of *course* Tyrrane will be there for you," Jasmayre answered. Tove smelled like winter winds and cooking fires. Maybe a little bit of horse. "Perhaps the mere threat of our involvement would be enough to forestall the Sund or Norrikborg from beginning an assault at all?"

"If only that were true." Tove neither sat back down nor lessened her grip from Jasmayre's arm. Instead she lifted the heavy braid of dark red hair in her other hand and moved it behind Jasmayre's back, leaving her front thrillingly exposed and vulnerable. "Krysuvik is still under siege from Mirrik, so the Sund is irrelevant, but neither they nor Norrikborg would believe a mere declaration of alliance. It would require something much more substantial than that. Northmen make a habit of suspicion. It comes from centuries of warfare, backbiting, and generally treacherous behavior."

A soft knock came from the chamber door. Tove released Jasmayre's arm and stepped backward.

"Enter." Jasmayre coughed to cover the crack in her voice.

Jason poked his head in the door. "Hey, Jaz. I was told to stop in and pay my respects to..." His voice trailed off when he saw Tove, as Jasmayre had known it would. Also, as she had known would happen —though she held considerably less enthusiasm for it now than she had when she entered the room herself—Tove's attention fastened onto Jasmayre's young, beautiful, and romantically simple brother like a circling bonewheel on a dying calf.

"Queen Tove the Mountain, widowed ruler of the Grengards of Norrik, you have already met Prince Jason Swifthart of Tyrrane." Jasmayre forced the words out. This was not about what she wanted. And it wouldn't matter if it was because *this* was what she wanted.

Sure it was.

Tove stepped up and lifted her hand, which Jason sprang forth and took it in his. He bowed and kissed the back of Tove's fingers.

Tove turned her head and looked at Jasmayre out of the side of one eye. "Princess Jasmayre. I believe I have a possible solution to establishing a *very* public alliance between the Grendals and Tyrrane. With your kind permission, I'd like to extend my stay to explore its possibilities."

Though the very notion was absurd, Jasmayre was certain she heard her own heart crack at Tove's words. Jasmayre had known the queen for years, and yes, they had become close over the past few months, but this sudden infatuation was so foolish and so *inconvenient*.

"Of course you may, Your Grace." Jasmayre was unable to be informal. It hurt. "We'll have a suite of rooms set aside for your use. Meals and activities will be set up to facilitate your exploration." All of this Jasmayre said through clenched teeth, though it did not matter. Tove gave all of her attention to Jason.

"I wish you the very best of fortunes," Jasmayre said.

Just as she had known she would.

20

LUNCH ON THE ROOF—NO JUMPING
JASMAYRE

Tove the Mountain swept across the rooftop of the Fell Citadel, a shining flame in ermine and white silk beneath a brilliant noonday sun. She approached the luncheon table and curtsied to Jasmayre and Jason. Behind Tove, the Blackwood River flowed around Dismon's outskirts toward Greenshade under a cloudless blue sky.

Until recently it had been Jasmayre's favorite vista from the high table.

Something between a giggle and a scream clamored for release from Jasmayre's throat. As the sibling in charge, it was her duty to chaperone the two royal suitors, which she had done for three days now. While excited that her plan to unify Norrik behind Tyrrane was succeeding—and more excited that Tove would always be close by—Jasmayre was tortured beyond words to have watched Tove fall for her *brother* and to see firsthand the affection she gave to him.

It had been three days. Why couldn't she let it go?

"Your Royal Highness," Jason said with a bow.

"*Your* Royal Highness," Tove returned.

Everyone forgot Jasmayre, herself included.

The trio sat, Jason opposite Jasmayre and Tove to her left in the informal style. Servants buzzed around the table filling glasses, adjusting napkins, and presenting trays of fresh fruit to begin the meal. Jasmayre spooned from a small bowl of berries and set them to one side.

"And what do you have planned for us today, Princess?" Tove asked. She pinned Jasmayre to her chair with a glance.

"Well," Jasmayre said, mouth dry, "I thought you'd appreciate seeing Jason in action." At her brother's wide-eyed gaze, she clarified, "That is, I know you've heard of his skill on the practice sand. I've taken the liberty of arranging a series of duels with some of your protectors for us to observe."

Tove blanched, no mean feat given the paleness of her skin. "With whom *specifically* did you arrange this demonstration?"

"I was told that Torfi Two-Foes and Valiant the Burned were your most impressive warriors." Jasmayre picked up her napkin, unfolded it, refolded it, and set it on the other side of her plate. "They agreed to battle our young prince here on the pitch."

"That is... not a good idea." Tove sat straight and regal, a statue of a woman carved by a god. "Those men are berserkers. They used to fight beside Reinar Brokenhilt."

"Mirrikmen?" Jason leaned in, a tight and eager smile on his face. "Did they really serve with Brokenhilt? How did they end up working for you?"

"That's not really the point," Tove said. "Those two have seen more real war than High King Oldam himself. They are legends in Norrik and Mirrik and simply can't be controlled in battle. Pick other men to test yourself against. *Any* other men."

Jasmayre and Jason exchanged a knowing glance.

"You almost make it sound like I shouldn't have arranged for him to fight them both at once," Jasmayre said.

Jason laughed.

"I will *not* be mocked," Tove said in a low growl. "There won't be an alliance between Norrik and Tyrrane if my suitor is murdered."

"Everyone will be armored," Jasmayre said. "And the weapons

will be practice swords without points or edges. No one will be murdered."

Tove took a deep breath—which Jasmayre averted her gaze from —and stroked the side of Jason's face. "Then I will serve as nursemaid to your broken body after the duels and, with Hedra's blessing, get to know you in your bed." She winked at him.

Fork clattered to plate when, below the table, Tove rested her other hand on Jasmayre's knee.

"C'mon, Jaz." Jason's grin claimed his whole face. "If we're going to get married, my bed is where everything is headed anyway."

Jasmayre coughed. Tove's hand felt hot and soft even through the velvet skirt. She needed to escape, but there was nowhere to go. And she didn't want to even if there had been.

"Don't be a lout," Jasmayre admonished her brother. "You're not Junior. Let's just relax and enjoy the view and *try* not to be idiots about this. I was referring of course to the prince, Your Majesty." Jasmayre nodded to Tove and, out of sight, placed her own hand atop the queen's.

Her breath came too fast and hot. A thrilling rush of blood and heady euphoria assaulted Jasmayre and tried to wash her off the rooftop. She had never felt anything like it.

A tiny whimper escaped her when Tove gave her the same wink she had just given Jason.

———

J asmayre and Tove sat together in the short stands that surrounded the sporting sands, hand in hand, and watched Jason defeat one of Tove's protectors. The young prince had insisted on warming up with a few individual rounds before the main event. Under the curved wooden awning that bordered the back half of the oval practice pitch, Torfi Two-Foes and Valiant the Burned watched with narrowed eyes and whispered to one other.

Despite the chill air, Jasmayre was hot, fevered. Her skin pulled on her bones, tight and restrictive. She forced herself to sit still beside the larger woman. The queen pulled one of Jasmayre's hands across her lap, and her other arm held Jasmayre tight beneath her wolfskin cloak, which she had covered both of them in.

"What are we doing here?" Jasmayre asked. "I can't, I mean that I've never—we have an alliance to think of."

"Both of us know what you want," Tove said breathily into Jasmayre's ear, which started a red flare up the side of Jasmayre's neck. "Other than that, we are simply two women sitting on a bench in the sun while the mighty prince makes my retinue look foolish."

No. Just—no.

"I will be your friend," Jasmayre said, "and I will be your sister when you and Jason have wed. But I will not be your mistress, and I won't make my own brother a cuckold. That would break him. We should have thought of this before I introduced the two of you. It's just too late now."

The hardest thing she had ever said was also the biggest relief. The iron bands constricting her chest fell away, and a light happiness welled up from her stomach.

Tove turned toward Jason and nodded, a slight frown on her lips. "Very well. I suppose I'll take what I can get." She pulled Jasmayre tighter against her. "The very least you can do is help keep me warm, my friend."

Whether or not this represented an improved state of affairs fell to the wayside as Jason's opponent was dragged from the sporting sand. Jason stood and shook his sword hand. He had taken a sharp knock to the knuckles through the thick leather gauntlet in the last bout, and it obviously smarted. The combatants were instructed to strike only on armor and, even then, not to put all their power behind a serious lunge. A long piece of hardened steel did not require a needle's point to cause damage.

Torfi and Valiant entered the pitch and strode to opposite sides, leaving Jason between them. He looked up, yanked the armored glove tighter, and motioned for his squire to hand him a practice blade.

Both Northmen stood half a head taller than Jason, with hard faces and flinty eyes. Torfi was thin and rangy, while Valiant bulged with fire-scarred muscle. They raised their swords in salute, as did Jason.

Then everyone ran at once.

The Northmen charged the middle while Jason ran at Valiant. The burned man roared, and Jason dove for his legs, curling into a ball as he flew through the air.

A scream and a crack exploded from Valiant when Jason's shoulder hit his knee at precisely the wrong angle, and the big warrior slammed forward into the sand, the end of his tongue flying bloodily from his mouth.

To his credit, Valiant rolled over and swung a wild attack at Jason, who nimbly dodged aside and dented the side of the Northman's helm in return, knocking him unconscious.

And then Torfi was there.

Jason jumped back again and again, narrowly avoiding blow after furious blow. Torfi's face was a blank mask of impersonal hatred, his sword strokes hammering at Jason, fast and hard. Very real and deadly skill lay inside this battle-crazed berserker. Would he stop if he won?

Despite the heat of her contact with Tove, Jasmayre shivered. It would be fine. Jason never lost as long as he wasn't expected to actually kill anyone. He wouldn't lose today either.

Jasmayre's gaze flickered above the contest, and she went rigid.

Across the sporting sand, between the stands on the other side, King Brannok, her father, stood and stared into her. He saw Jason in battle with an obvious killer while she sat and looked on, curled up against the queen of the Grengards.

His expression was not happy.

She opened her mouth to call to him, but he turned and stalked off, mail clinking beneath his furry bearskin.

Beside Jasmayre, Tove tensed and squeezed her hand. Jasmayre whipped her attention back to the sand to see Jason bent backward over Torfi's thigh, with the square shouldered berserker about to plunge the practice sword through the prince's guts.

No blunted tip would prevent that from being a killing blow.

Jasmayre screamed.

Torfi coughed and Jason slid off his leg. The berserker dropped his blade, still lifted over his head. He fell to his knees and twisted sideways, so Jasmayre could see her brother's sword sticking out of his throat.

Dust rose when Torfi went down, and just beyond him Jason, on his hands and knees, spat mud into the sand.

"Issta's Gates," Jasmayre said. Instead of feeling thrilled for Jason's success, she was frightened and embarrassed for having created the situation to begin with. She got up and ran to the short gate and knelt beside Jason, one hand on his back. "Are you all right?"

That happy grin turned to her in a dirt-covered face and morphed to round-eyed fear. Somewhere a woman shouted.

Pain jolted her ribs, and Jasmayre flew through the air. She landed on her wrist, which crunched beneath her and stole her breath. Men yelled and roared angrily.

Jasmayre rolled to her side and saw Valiant the Burned, both of his hands on Jason's throat, swing the young prince in violent jerks as Tyrranean lordlings beat his scarred flesh and tried to pry his hands apart. Eventually someone found a blacksmith's hammer and stove the Northman's head in.

A creamy white hand floated in front of Jasmayre's face. She took it and lifted herself to her feet.

"How bad are you hurt?" Tove asked.

"I can't see Jason." Jasmayre tried to look around Tove. She knew she was responsible for all of this. She had been trying to impress Tove with her brother's ability on the sand. If she had been able to think at all instead of worrying what the Mountain thought of her, the alliance would already have been wrapped up and not about to collapse on her head. And who knew *what* her father was thinking.

No, she probably knew.

Tove turned so that Jasmayre could see Jason sitting up and swishing red-tinged water through his mouth, surrounded by laughing and back-slapping young nobles. He grinned again and waved at her, though he winced when he did it.

"I'm sorry," Jasmayre said to Tove. "I've cost you two of your best protectors, just to make an impression. Ow." Her ribs hurt when she inhaled too deeply, and the throb in her wrist was picking up. "Just don't leave yet. We can figure a way out of this."

"Leave?" Tove shook her head. "I have a job playing nursemaid to that young man, or did you forget? Did you *see* him in there? He was magnificent."

"Yeah," Jasmayre said. Jason had never managed to deliver more than a few broken bones before. Now two deadly fighters lay unmoving in pools of their own blood, and he just sat there grinning and laughing.

"He was."

21

GRIEF, CHICKENS, AND UNHYGIENIC MASTURBATORY PRACTICES

MORHOLT

W hy aren't there any temple guys in Tyrrane?" Ameli asked, her voice raised above the sounds of the swiftly running stream. "They all worship the Alir, don't they?" She still wore the blue-gray linen vest and pants of the Daughters' Coven. Morholt couldn't imagine why. They were supposed to all hate her now.

The better part of a week had passed since that frightening night in the Grim Pines, and the Free Hand had stopped to rest and water the horses at a stream. The cold snow melt flowed down the western tip of the Bitter Heights Mountains and marked a dividing line from Norrik into Tyrrane.

Morholt concentrated on the crystal water and tried to ignore the conversation. To his left, the mountain peaks glowered down at him in no better a humor than he was.

"There is only room for the Anger Under the Mountain in this black country." Reinar's answer rumbled out of him, a distant thunderhead considering its next stroke of lightening. "This place has already been claimed by its share of evil. Look around. The grass is gray, and the rabbits are starved. The scrub is... scrubbier. Even Khanah's egg couldn't see through these iron clouds."

Mood worsening the more Reinar complained, Morholt pulled his woolen cloak around himself. He had yet to figure out how rescuing Selenna was going to go any better than Glauth should Sarah and her temple warriors show up. Raven was pissed, and Morholt hadn't put any coin in his company's hands for more than a month now.

Strangely, none of them seemed to mind. But then they all had their own reasons for being here.

Everyone stretched their legs and backs and stamped their feet on the dry grass. They were not here to make camp, just to take a little rest from their saddles.

"Sorry," Ameli said, a wide smile stealing across her freckled face, "I grew up with Pavinn gods, remember? What's a Khanah?"

A cold Tyrranean summer wind blew at Reinar's dark blond braids, and he squinted into the sky. "Sort of a god chicken?"

"A what?" Despite himself, Morholt's thoughts were lifted away from his guilt by the idea of this chicken of the Alir.

Reinar laughed. "Monster that lays eggs? The beast is a famous mischief-maker."

At the edge of the water and through a stand of scrub bushes, Sabni turned his head and smiled, a question in his eyes. To either side of him, Raven and Mahu filled their water skins, incurious to tales of monster hens.

"Every morning," Reinar continued, shifting his quilted armor on his broad shoulders, "Hedra sets fire to one of Khanah's eggs and rolls it across the blue dome of the Alireon. This is what you are looking at when you watch the sun rolling across the sky. The mighty egg cools when it hits the ocean in the west and is ready to be eaten by all the gods as breakfast the next morning."

"If I'd wanted religious instruction," Morholt said with a sour expression, "I'd have stabbed myself in the brain and let the gods tell me themselves. It would have been less painful than getting it from Sabni and Reinar at the same time." He considered the notion of listening to the rangy Darrishman's parables for the rest of the trip.

"Maybe I'll just give myself up to the temple. They only want to kill me, not educate me. That'd have to be easier."

Mahu, Sabni, and Raven walked their animals back from the stream to rejoin the rest of the group.

Glauth's grinning face popped up *again* in Morholt's imagination. Nighttime. Woods. Moonlight. Struck by Sarah's arrow. But somehow, it was *his* heart that felt the pain.

Again and again.

He turned his face from the rest and walked with his horse to a lone tree. More like a natty bush on a short and skinny stalk. He could hear the Hand converse, but no one asked him to join in. He would have thanked them for ignoring him if he had been capable.

Fog, Morholt's gray brindle mare, nosed around the base of the tree and snacked on whatever it was she found there.

"Do we think the temple will send anyone in after us?" Ameli asked. "Into Tyrrane, I mean. Are they welcome here? Won't the Anger Under the Mountain get, well, angry?"

"Angrim may well resent the intrusion of temple forces," Sabni answered, "but he works through his own armies and agents, and he has precious few of those left. The Hill Fury saw to that."

"Then why wouldn't they kill her if she followed us here? That's what I'd do, you know, if she didn't kill me first." Ameli's curly red-blonde hair caught the meager afternoon light and returned it with an extra touch of fire.

Morholt used to find it pretty. He used to enjoy a lot of things.

"Because they're scared of her, just like Angrim is." Mahu's blunt assessment put a cap on everyone's hopes that Sarah might quit her pursuit at the border. There was silence for several moments.

"At any rate, while the Temple of the Sky holds no property nor directs troops inside of Tyrrane as far as I am aware," Sabni said, a wry smile on his ebon face, "I have been told they are the newest and best funded loaners of coin here. Indeed, over all of the Thirteen Kingdoms. If you are of noble blood, that is."

"Why would you give money to your enemies?" Reinar asked.

"This is not a tactically sound strategy. They are apt to return to you with that same money turned into infantry and spears."

Though Reinar asked the question of Sabni, Morholt noted that he never took his gaze from Raven. He was a big, dopey puppy where she was concerned. A big, dopey, horrifying killer puppy. Morholt sighed. She could handle it. He'd learned long ago not to get involved in his sister's catastrophic love life.

"Because these puckered old shitholes are loaning to the people in power and then taking their sons and daughters as collateral against the loans." Raven's smoky black stallion snorted as if to punctuate her statement and pawed the ground beside her. "That's right, Nightwind." She patted the side of his neck. "Our friends here can't help being so stupid, can they? No, sir."

"Oh, I get it." Ameli nodded to Raven and grinned. "They control political power through the money they lend to the nobles, and the nobility can't do anything about it because the temple has their kids. Does it strike anyone else as kinda backward that those are supposed to be the good guys while *we're* evil for trying to save Morholt's exes?"

"Every fucking day." Raven left the group and walked Nightwind over to Morholt and Fog.

"Hey, Holt." Her thin frame twisted side to side, wrapped in black leather and the hilts of knives. A beautiful, too-pale face frowned beneath short wind-whipped black hair. "You look like shit."

"Thanks," he replied. "You gonna do something about Reinar? That kinda saddle sniffing can destabilize a group. I wouldn't care except it's my group." He did not want to be talking about this, but at least it distracted him from thoughts of...

Glauth. Moonlight. An arrow.

"Reinar!" Raven shouted.

The big warrior whipped around, eyes wide, a half-committed smile on his bearded face. Hope and fear warred on that face, neither securing a reliable beachhead.

Raven let him totter for a while. "Please stab yourself in the stomach, stick your cock in the hole, and do sit-ups until you fuck yourself to death. Nothing personal, but I'm not looking for a boyfriend, and you take a hint about as well as you shit gold coins."

Sabni's brows went up, and Ameli gasped. Reinar's smile stayed fixed, but beneath it, hopelessness mounted a brutal offensive against his hope *and* his fear and swept them both into the ocean.

Mahu adjusted the saddle belt on the old chestnut mare he called Horse. "Unsanitary," he said.

"Witches gift." Ameli looked from Raven to Reinar. "That was brutal."

Next to Morholt and Raven, Nightwind tried to brush up against Fog, who warned him off with a no-nonsense chuff. Raven reinforced the message by poking her scowl between the two. The stallion found an interesting patch of grass in the other direction.

"That was pretty shitty, sis," Morholt said. He wiped his runny nose and rubbed his hand on the leg of his faded green armor. "He doesn't know your history. He's not—"

"You can shut the fuck up, too." Raven's frown intensified. "Unless you were about to tell me that you're ready to go home."

"None of the reasons we left have solved themselves while we were gone." Morholt hated this conversation. If Raven were capable of returning to the Undergates without him, he would have let her go. "We shoved the whole oxcart up Mom and Dad's asses. They may not be in charge anymore, but they're still rich, and they still want us dead."

"You're such a Khanah." Raven leaned toward her brother to emphasize her words. "That means you're a *chicken*."

"I deciphered your clever insult." To his shock, Morholt felt less miserable. Sparring with Raven lifted his mood. "Be sure to save some of that for Dad's degenerate soldier slaves. I'm sure they'll crap themselves running away from your razored wit."

"We don't have to go *home*-home." For just an instant, Raven looked as bleak as Morholt felt. "Mom and Dad don't have any pull in the Reaves." She fiddled with the buckle of her saddlebag.

"There aren't any humans in the Reaves. You know that. We'd be dinner for one of Issta's pets as soon as we stepped off the Crying

Road." Morholt embraced his frustration with Raven and armored himself in it against his grief.

"Then we kill our parents before they can kill us." Raven folded her angular arms and leaned against Nightwind's middle. The horse turned to look at her sidelong and nuzzled her shoulder.

"That would be fun," Morholt admitted. They certainly deserved it. "But it isn't possible. Not now." He studied his sister's face. "Is there any chance you could just be happy here?"

"You promised me."

"Ah, toad dicks." He *had* promised her, to get her to leave their home in the first place, fifteen hard years ago. This conversation always ended in the same place. Here. And he had to admit he was tired of dodging it.

Maybe it was *him* who couldn't be happy in the Thirteen Kingdoms.

"When we've warned them all and they're safe, then we'll go. I won't argue with you any more about it."

"All right," Raven replied at length. "But none of those women are going to be any happier to see you than *she* was. I just hate seeing you get the shit kicked out of you over and over again, jackoff."

"Thanks for that, tramp," he replied.

Through the edges of his vision, Morholt saw Raven's flash of a smile, gone as fast as it appeared.

22

GROUNDHOG EX

MORHOLT

Morholt climbed the worn wooden steps to the front door of the abandoned clapboard home and let himself in out of the harsh light. He put his hands on his hips and addressed the Free Hand. "Everything is good here, crapsnackers. She doesn't need our help. We can leave for the next one now." It was quite a relief.

"Un-*fucking*-believable," Raven said from the dusty floor. The group had been eating a lunch of smoked venison and stolen stone fruit. "Three times in a row."

"Why does he keep calling us crapsnackers?" Ameli sat cross-legged next to Reinar and cut the yellow fruits into wedges. "Is *she* telling him to say it? She doesn't even know us."

Sabni stood and stretched. Spots of sunlight that fell from the holes in the roof ran around his shoulders and arms and shone where it hit the honey-colored armor. "I believe it is time, my good friend, for us to change our tactics." He placed a hand on Morholt's shoulder. "Close your eyes and let go, or this tree will be the death of you."

"What?" Morholt regretted asking the instant the question left his lips.

Raven groaned.

"From *The Cow and the Tick.*" Sabni's warm smile reinforced the calm pressure of his hand. "The tick climbed too high in his tree and was unable to see the cows in the field below him. Every time he talked himself into falling free and gaining his next meal, the cow below convinces him that he would miss and be dashed on the rocky ground." Sabni lifted his hand from Morholt's shoulder and tapped the side of his nose. "But Immortal Queen Nefret counseled the tick. 'If you let go and release your fate to the gods, you may die, or you may live strong and happy. But if you remain, you will surely wither and perish.' You are the tick, and Lady Selenna is the cow. Every time you go to her, she uses her runecrafting to convince you to return here to us. It is time to be bolder. We have been here most of the day already. The Hill Fury and her temple knights cannot be far behind."

"So that makes you Nefret?" Dammit. Morholt knew better than to ask follow-up questions.

Mahu came to his rescue. "That story ends with the tick jumping onto the cow and the cow eating the tick. It's not a complete success."

"Wait. Selenna tongued my brain and sent me back to you crapsnackers?" Morholt's thoughts were a jumble, but he was latching on to a few irritating memories.

"He did it again," Ameli said. "Witches gift, why is she telling him to call us that?"

Morholt wrinkled his nose. "She's not. I just can't stand the smell of Reinar's deer jerky."

"Brother Sabni," Reinar said, chewing on a piece of venison, "please tell us, what do your parables say about ungrateful mercenary leaders who turn up their noses at healthy food, freely offered, and feed instead on their own sourness?"

Sabni opened his mouth to reply, but Morholt held up a hand and shook his head no.

With a shrug, Sabni returned to the circle of mercenaries on the floor.

"Apparently Nefret says, 'know when to shut the fuck up,'" Raven offered.

Boulders rolled down a stony hill within Reinar's infectious laughter. Even Sabni joined in, nodding.

Raven side-eyed Reinar sourly.

"Did I give offense?"

"Stop laughing at my jokes." She no longer sounded funny at all.

"I only wish to enjoy your company." Reinar's face grew bleak, and Morholt found himself wishing to be elsewhere. "Although perhaps I wish you to enjoy mine as well."

"I'm not interested in what you wish, assmeat." Her face was blank. Unfeeling. "I've told you a dozen times to fuck off, and you're not taking the hint. I don't want your company, I don't want your stupid, sad face sniffing around my crack, and I *definitely* don't want your giant oafish dick poking me in the back when you think I'm asleep. I'm *never* that asleep."

That was precisely the kind of information Morholt did not feel was necessary for him to know.

Stricken, Reinar stumbled to his feet and clambered out the front door.

"It was an accident," he mumbled as he let the door fall shut behind him.

"It's just... he lost... well, he lost everything back in Mirrik." Ameli stood to follow Reinar and stopped at the door. "They even think he's a coward, but he's not. He just needs a—"

Raven held up a hand to Ameli. "I'm going to stop you right there, Sprinkles. I could not possibly give less of a shit about what that man *needs* if he were a cow turd in your sleeping bag. So just shut up about it, shut up about Reinar, and shut the ever-loving fuck up about who you think I ought to let between my legs so they can get over their goddamn trauma."

"I'm going out back." Morholt pulled the green handkerchief from his pack. "See if April has any ideas." A protective, big-brotherly part of him wanted to confront the huge Mirrikman and poke a finger in his chest to make sure the message was received this time. But he knew that Raven would not appreciate it, that Reinar had understood completely, and that he didn't want to chance getting his finger broken off at the elbow.

He also wanted to tell his sister to lighten up. But he had suggested she make herself plain to Reinar in the first place, and if he reversed himself, he also invited all her ire up his own ass.

"Um, I'll just go find Reinar, and we'll scout around," Ameli called out after him. "We won't get close enough to talk to Selenna and get convinced to become bakers or anything. I just want to see if we can figure out a way to do this without confronting her."

"Please be bakers and stay here forever," Raven said.

Morholt walked around the circle of fighters and stepped over the debris of previous owners and animal squatters. The house boasted three rooms, all well-ventilated by missing sections of wall, and an empty doorway in the rearmost one that led to an overgrown garden.

The back steps provided a perfect spot to sit and chat with a pasteboard painting.

As he withdrew the card from its cloth, Morholt cast a quick look around. This house moldered at the far end on the main street between the town of Hornfield and its outlying farms. On the back stoop, he was invisible to either side.

"Knock, knock," said the two-dimensional imp.

"Who goes there?" Morholt answered.

"Butter."

"Butter who?"

"Butter get the door because someone's knocking and—wait, no. You butter not knock... That's not it either. Hang on. I know this one."

Morholt waited for a full minute before the gray-and-red dog girl gave up and sat down inside the card. She puffed her cheeks and blew a raspberry.

"Hi, Holt."

"Hi, Bean." He tried to smile but couldn't quite get there. "What've you been thinking about?"

"That stupid joke, for one." She frowned, which was a terrifying sight to those unused to furry imps in pretty yellow dresses. "I wish you had painted some paper and a quill when you made me. You know, for making joke notes."

"Who knew you would turn out to be such a comedienne? You're so much more exceptional than I thought you'd be when I designed you."

April's frown changed into a blushing grin that stretched across her whole face, revealing shiny black teeth set in bright red gums.

Morholt felt a little better.

"Whatcha got for me? More lady problems?"

"Obviously." A bird caught Morholt's attention, and he watched it fly away, exactly the way he could not. "We're in Hornfield."

"Selenna." April tapped a clawed finger against her snout. "I take it she thinks she can handle anything coming for her?"

"She does." Morholt sat, chin in one hand, April's card extended at the length of his other arm. "And every time I try to convince her otherwise—"

"She uses the brain whammy and convinces you that *you're* wrong."

"She's a thistle up the poophole, that's for sure." Brow furrowed, Morholt ran a finger along the edge of April's card. "She's paranoid and controlling. Her runecrafting abilities are either the most perfect or most horrible she could have learned." He blew a sigh. "This would be so much easier if we could get a blindfold on her or a gag. Or even just a bag over her head. Her magic doesn't work if she can't talk or can't see her victims."

"I think we're all lucky she's not more ambitious than she is," April agreed, nodding. "Of course, *someone* said you shouldn't have taught her anything at the *time*."

"That's piss in the road now." Morholt blew out his cheeks and sighed.

"You mean water under the bridge?"

"No."

April giggled, then turned serious. "I know you're worried that if you can't convince Selenna to run, the same thing will happen to her that happened to Glauth. But that's not going to happen. We're going to get her out of here, even if you don't like her as much as the others."

"I like your attitude, Bean, but how do we make it happen?"

"Selenna is married to the local lord here, right?" April stood and paced back and forth across the surface of the card. "That's how you're going to get her out. First you have to—do you hear that?"

Alarmed, Morholt jumped to his feet and pressed his back against the rundown home.

23

THE ART OF CONVERSATION

SARAH

Sarah rode at the head of the Shepherds of the Blood alongside Prolocutor Vancess. Her intention had been to keep the eager knights from murdering everyone in Hornfield, but her mere presence was enough to scatter all the civilians. Small Tyrranean towns were not thrilled to see the Hill Fury riding up the main thoroughfare.

She was always surprised to be recognized at all, but enough Tyrranean soldiers had fled the Country Gate Offensive in Treaty Hill that she imagined there must be ex-Host everywhere in Tyrrane who knew her face. Or maybe everyone was on the lookout for a six-foot-two Pavinn warrior woman with clawed scars across her forehead that ran up into the white streaks in her hair.

Yeah. That might be it too.

"Does everyone understand what's expected of them?" Sarah squinted against the reflected sunlight in the bright street. Rows of businesses and houses huddled fearfully to either side of the street as the whole place held its breath.

"Indeed, Handmaiden." Vancess held himself erect in the saddle as he spoke. "We are here to capture, not kill."

"Unless we see Morholt." Sarah did not believe Vancess had any real thought to keeping his word, but just in case, she also did not want anyone missing an opportunity to take that evil bastard out.

"I pray that we do." Vancess met Sarah's gaze, and mad fire burned behind his eyes. He looked stoned, but Sarah was certain he had not been drinking his tea. Not in days, maybe weeks.

"He no longer requires the tea to hear the voices of gods in his head." Gabby walked beside Sarah's horse, its calm, cultured voice soothing Sarah's nerves. "Look there. That's a tavern. You should nip in for a bit before you get to the end of the street."

Sarah widened her eyes questioningly at Gabby.

"Yes, do." Its face, so much like her own, smiled up at her. "You'll thank me for it. I promise."

With a shrug, Sarah held up a closed fist, and the twin lines of knights halted behind her.

"Everyone wait right here. I've got to—um—I'll be right back." She handed the reins of her mount to Vancess and slid off the other side.

"Deftly done. I daresay none of them will suspect a thing."

"You *just* promised me it would be worth it," Sarah whispered. "You're going to make fun of me about it *now*? Are they watching me?"

"Only if you mean the prolocutor and his thirty armored noble knights." Gabby glanced around. "But really, what else is there to look at? This place truly is dreadful."

Sarah did not care much about finding and capturing the demon Morholt's women or the other demons they might have taught, but she felt certain it was the best way to uncover Morholt himself. That he was the sort of person to come riding to the rescue of others was not a thought she preferred to dwell on.

The door swung more easily than Sarah expected and banged against the wall. A half dozen sets of eyes snapped to her and just as quickly jumped away.

"See anything familiar?"

Sarah frowned. "No." The shabby and stale little room housed a bar against the left side and a pair of round tables in the floor. Too many chairs crowded the rest of the space. A pall of smoke hung low and did not hide the stains of age on everything, including the weathered patrons.

"Look more carefully." In front of her, Gabby extended his arm as if presenting Sarah the tavern as a gift.

Chairs scraped on the floor as Sarah pushed past them. She knew what she was looking for now.

"Little Sarah?" An old man with a scruffy white beard and an unlikely hat looked up at her and favored her with a gap-toothed grin. A man who ran away from Wallace's Company when she was little more than a girl, taking Lord Marshal Harden Grayspring's favorite hat with him. The hat he wore even now.

The white beard widened from the mirth within it. "All growed up. Look atcha."

"Hi, Marbles." Sarah sat at the table, now vacated of dusty and terrified street toughs.

"What brings ya to Hornfield?" One side of Marbles's jaw worked up and down in constant motion. He did not appear to be in control of it. "Lose a bet?" He pushed the hat back on his head. Its wide brim swooped dramatically on one side, and sweat stains painted intricate designs around the brim.

"Marbles," one of the men who had fled the table said, his floppy black cap in his hands, "that's the Hill Fury!"

"Nonsense." Marbles's good-natured grin grew. "This here's little Sarah. We used to run together in my bad old days. She could outfight any man I ever met by the time she were fifteen." He met her gaze with a yellowing eye. "Where's that boy you used ta run with? You two were stuck together like rusty old knives. What was his name?"

"His name was Keane. And if you don't already know what happened to him, I doubt you'd believe my telling of it." She meant Keane's ascension to the monarchy of Greenshade, but in truth, she could not stop worrying if something more sinister had happened to him.

Gabby sat unnoticed next to Marbles and studied the old man.

"I have some business with Lady Selenna." The bar was to Sarah's back and with it the other tavern patrons. She watched Marbles's face and listened to the rest.

"There's temple knights in the street," one of them said.

"Best not go out there just yet." Sarah gave a nod in the man's direction. "They're good people, but they're excitable and well-armed. Also, they're not very good people."

Marbles laughed and slapped the table. "Can I get a couple ales over here fer me and my dear old friend?"

Some motion and pouring from behind.

"So then," Marbles said, "what business you got with my lady and a buncha temple bruisers?"

"Your lady?" Sarah's crooked half smile popped up despite herself. She did not recall all that much about Marbles from the old days, other than he was funny and unreliable.

"I got me a job running Lady Selenna's crew. I'm in charge of security in this pisspot little town." Marbles beamed. "Been here ten years now."

"Really?" Sarah leaned in a fraction of an inch. "What's *that* like?"

The barkeep brought two leatherjacks of ale and left them on the table. Marbles attacked his with gusto. As he did, Sarah examined his coat: dusty but fine and dark blue with gold buttons.

She scratched at the scars under her scalp.

"Mm. Well, I got the job under the old lord here, Lord Hornsy. He fell outta favor with the royals, and they gave it to a fella name of Talon. Think he were a retired Major in the Host or some such. He weren't around for too long. Got recruited into some diplomatic post I think. Lord Goodfern came next, and Lady Selenna were with him, bless her shoes. She's the one what really runs the town. Lord Goodfern's more of a—whatchacallit—figgerhead."

"I can see why Harden wanted this hat back." Gabby gave a crooked half smile, so like Sarah's own. "It's splendid."

Sarah flicked an annoyed glance at Gabby and returned to her interrogation.

"Ever have any real trouble here?" Sarah pulled her ale closer. "You must have a unit of Ebon Host in case things get exciting."

"No, no Host here." He took another pull from the jack, already half empty. "It's fifty miles to the Icewater and another two hundred to the Paras Plains, fuck High King Ivarr very much."

This made Sarah smile into her ale. Ivarr had been very successful on his campaign to reclaim the plains over the last seven or eight years.

"We's closest to Greenshade 'cept for the Brighthorn Mountains betwixt us." He hunkered over the table, and his voice quieted to a conspiratorial whisper. "Besides, I don't need the Host here, do I? I got my own squad of the hardest sonofabitches you ever saw. Real mean motherfuckers. Brought 'em in meself. Some of them is *runecrafters*. Lady Selenna taught them. Brannok's little war in Greenshade drained most of the able-bodied men outta the country, now didn't it?"

His grin faded. "Now I know you expect to ride in here and take Lady Selenna like she were a bittersweet candy on some old lady's bedside table, but it ain't gonner be that way. We gotcha outmanned, and we got magic, too."

"And you're telling me this because?" Sarah leaned back and pushed her chair away from the table. Despite the shift in tone, she still did not detect any menace from the old mercenary.

He chuckled. "Because of old times, girl. I don't wanna be the one to put you inna dirt. We was friends."

Sarah slid the leatherjack across the table to Marbles. "Stay in this tavern. Stay in that chair. No one will come in here, and no one will kill you. That's the best I can do. My business with Selenna isn't personal, and I have no reason to see her harmed." *We won't have another accident. Not like Glauth.*

Marbles opened his hands and spread his arms wide. "Sorry, girl. I got a job, and old times'll only carry you so far." He looked over her shoulder. "Boys."

A stony fist sent Marbles's head spinning sideways and thumping to the tabletop. His fancy hat flew up and onto the boards beside him.

Sarah's sudden violence alerted the hired toughs behind her, three of whom drew knives while a fourth ran out the door.

"Think about your next move, *boys*." Sarah stood and faced them across the room's other table. "You know who I am, and I'm offering to let you go free."

A scream came from outside.

The three men exchanged glances and placed their knives on the table. Sarah nodded to them, and the middle thug nodded back to her. She twisted to look at Marbles's unconscious form, sprawled across his own table.

"And I'm taking Harden's hat back, you old thief." She snatched it off the table and stalked outside.

24

RING MY BELL

SARAH

That's not a good idea." Vancess swayed in the dusty street, brows drawn together to regard Sarah. His gaze flickered around her as if tracking things no one else could see.

She liked him less and less these days, though she never liked him enough for that to mean much. Vancess had always been off, and he had never shied away from using his religious fervor to justify any act of brutality or depravity. Well enough when Harden had been holding the leash, but who held him back now?

"It's my decision." Sarah put a hand against the door of the country manor house that sat at the end of the main street. A wind blew grit between all the buildings of Hornfield and scratched against the armor of thirty knights standing in the sun. "I'm going in there, and all of you tin soldiers are going to wait out here. There might be a fight, but you're going to stay here anyway. Does everyone understand?"

If there was any chance of doing this without further bloodshed, she would take it. She had enough red on her hands.

As one, the temple knights stamped a foot and stood straight, signaling their assent. Vancess's frowning face relaxed, and a lazy smile spread across it.

This hat really keeps the sun out of your eyes. If I ever see Harden again, he may have to fight me for it.

"As you command, Handmaiden."

"Great." Sarah turned her back on Vancess and entered the home of Selenna, demon runecrafter, alone.

Sarah stepped into the well-appointed home just in time to hear a door slam at the rear. She vaulted over an elegant velvet upholstered footstool and knocked over a rosewood bookstand in her rush to reach the back door. A surprised and shrieking cook grabbed a carving knife when Sarah barged into a kitchen full of light and savory smells, and then she was through the doorway into the back garden.

Whoops.

A woman in an ornate dress of scalloped overlays and iridescent bows stood on the grass with one brow raised, light brown hair piled up on her head. Her expression was that of a woman discovering mouse prints in the butter.

That one would be Lady Selenna. The threat.

Behind the runecrafter, a blandly handsome man in fine green merchant's clothes pulled at her to flee through the garden gate at the far end, which she ignored. In his other hand, he held a number of carpet bags with clothing spilling out.

He must be Lord Goodfern, the husband. No threat at all.

To Sarah's right were a pair she had seen once before during the battle that killed Captain Falt: Ameli of the Daughters' Coven and Reinar, disgraced hero of Mirrik.

Slago's fishy breath. This got out of hand in a hurry.

"Is Marbles still alive?" Lady Selenna squinted against the sun.

"What?"

"You are wearing his hat." The runecrafter indicated Sarah's new acquisition. "Did you kill him?"

"No." Entering the house alone had been a mistake. "And it wasn't his hat."

"Please ring that bell." Lady Selenna waved Ameli toward an iron bell on a tall post amongst the flowers and squash. The young sorceress happily flounced off to do as she was bid.

The runecrafter locked eyes with Sarah.

"Go to sleep."

A wave of drowsiness smothered Sarah's thinking, and she stumbled sideways to catch her fall on a tasteful pedestal of mortared stones. She yawned wide and got her feet back underneath her.

"I didn't expect that to work against you, but I had to try." Lady Selenna yanked her arm away from Lord Goodfern and straightened her posture, preparing herself.

Goodfern cringed away from her.

"Lady Selenna"—Sarah took a step forward and did not draw her sword—"let's stop this now."

Deep percussive notes, clear and loud, rang out from the bell Ameli enthusiastically yanked on.

Sarah winced. "You can't win this fight. I've got thirty temple knights—Shepherds of the Blood—standing in front of this house. The only way for you to live is to give up."

"Don't look at me." Reinar crossed his arms and shook his head at Lady Selenna's questioning glance. "That's the Hill Fury. I am not fighting her. And don't think your tricks will—"

"Put her down."

"All right then." Reinar whipped an ancient sword from its leather sheath and grabbed the shield off his back. He advanced on Sarah, calm and deadly.

Selenna and Goodfern ran for it, leaving a trail of undergarments and hosiery.

This was exactly what Sarah did *not* want to happen. She drew her own broad blade and circled left into the garden. Shouts from several directions rang out over the stone wall surrounding them, even over Ameli's continued ringing. Sarah would have to finish this fast and get out there.

She swept a blast of sorcerous wind at Reinar's legs, but the big man crouched and caught it on his shield.

He leapt forward and filled the air with edged steel.

Sarah bent her efforts toward simply staying alive. Reinar pressed her from every side at once. He was just as strong as she was but longer limbed and, if possible, even faster. The Mirrikman barely seemed human.

He banged aside Sarah's sword with the steel rim of his shield, reversing direction with it instantly to thud into her shoulder. She spun and pushed off the trunk of a skinny apple tree just in time to keep from being cut in half.

The tree was less lucky.

"She just said to put me down." Sarah's words came out as grunts. "Are you sure she didn't mean for you to say something insulting about my mother?"

She slid her blade against his downstroke to halt it against her cross guard, but Reinar's blow broke the guard from Sarah's sword and cracked into the knuckles of her first two fingers, leaving them flayed open with sheared bone and flesh exposed.

A white light flashed in Sarah's brain, and her sword fell to the dirt.

"I would never say anything about someone's mother." Reinar swung at Sarah's head, and she fell out of the way. "I suppose that's not true. But I wouldn't say anything about *your* mother. It's unseemly. You're a woman."

The next blow would have been a killing one had Sarah not managed to clear her head enough to dive out of the way. She rolled to her feet, her bloody mess of a hand held against her chest screaming its pain, and ran not for the gate, but just beside it.

Reinar spotted her objective an instant later and pumped his enormous legs to catch her before she got there.

But he was not fast enough.

Sarah turned sideways and let herself crash into the stone wall, even as she gripped the largest stone that would fit in her good hand from a neat pile in front of it. Reinar, moving full speed, raised his shield in front of his face, which was exactly what Sarah was hoping for.

The fieldstone flew like an arrow into Reinar's raised knee. The crack was thunderous.

Not as thunderous as Reinar's roar of pain, however. His raised shield, backed up by seven feet of thick-bodied muscle flying at a full sprint, crushed her against the wall. They fell through it and collapsed a ten-foot-wide section of it on Reinar's back.

Sarah'd already lost her hat.

For several moments, no one said a thing.

Reinar groaned. "I can't move." For certain the giant Mirrikman *wasn't* moving. "Can you move?" Another pause. "Are you alive?"

"Ow." Sarah hurt far too much to be dead. "Can you get her to stop ringing that bell? I feel like she's knocking the clapper on my skull."

Reinar turned his head and another stone shifted off and fell onto Sarah's already broken nose. She bit back a scream.

"Ameli? *Ameli.*" He couldn't quite yell, but the ringing slowed. "I think you're done there, girl. I'm sure whoever was supposed to hear that bell already has."

And then Ameli was above them. She pulled at the stones covering their bodies, revealing blood and bruises. Sarah shrieked when one of the rocks knocked against the hilt of Reinar's old sword which she had not realized went all the way through her side. The garden faded a bit, and Sarah gripped the broken wall to push the shock away.

"Now *that* counts as putting a person down." Ameli helped Reinar roll off Sarah without hurting her any more than she already was. She inspected the sword that jutted from Sarah's abdomen.

"Normally doesn't... ah *shit*... hurt *me* so much when I do it." Reinar winced and blew air through clenched teeth. Gripping his crushed knee in both hands, he pushed himself to a sitting position with an elbow. His face, where it was not covered in powdered mortar and blood, hung white as death.

"We can't cut your mail open because, you know, it's *mail*, and we can't lift it over your head with that big pin through it." Ameli frowned at Sarah's reddening wound. "Let's get you in a little less pain first."

Sarah wanted to run away, but none of her limbs were responding to her wishes. These people were only *just* trying to kill her. Now they could finish the job, and she would not be able to do anything to stop them. She used to rely on Keane to have her back in situations like this.

It seemed like forever ago.

"Why are you helping me?" Sarah's voice came out strained and husky. A dry creek bed choked of water.

Ameli's round face cocked to one side, sending a tumble of strawberry blonde curls tumbling. She smiled. "Because I'm *trying* to convince you we're not your enemies. We didn't want to attack you here; we were just all puppetized or whatever by Selenna. Now, if you die, then the temple knights just keep coming until they finally get us. But if you *live* because we saved you, then maybe everyone gets to go home and not be killed at all. See?"

Fine powders flew from Ameli's fingertips and vanished on contact with Sarah's skin. According to Vancess, the pretty girl was a former member of the Daughters' Coven of the Paradisals, an actual daughter of the Deep Witch herself, cast out for some grave sin against the pirate nation. Probably not saying *yar* enough.

The Daughter raised an eyebrow and gave a slight smile when Sarah sighed in relief. Numbness radiated out from the blade, and Sarah slumped against the stones as her body relaxed. At that moment, she might have been all right with it if Ameli had decided to cut her throat.

Which was the same moment that Ameli slid Reinar's sword out of Sarah.

Sarah's back arched, supported by the top of her head and her butt, and she screamed without sound. Blood ran from both sides of the wound, and she dropped back to the rocky ground. The motion pounded pain against the insides of her broken nose.

In an instant, Ameli lifted the mail hauberk and Sarah's shirt beneath it and ran her fingers inside Sarah's injury. Sarah grabbed at the Daughter, prompting a cry from Ameli.

"Reinar! Hold her down. I have to find out what's been punctured. Witch's *gift*, she's strong."

"I know." The big warrior leaned over on one hip and gripped Sarah's arms. "Better hurry." His voice was quiet and raspy. "Shattered knee here. I can't hold her for long."

"Hush up, you." Ameli scattered more colors into the air that settled into Sarah.

Sarah relaxed once more. She did not want to relax. She wanted to shout and fight and possibly even run away. Finnagel had done very little to prepare her for battling other sorcerers. Even Gabby's training was still mostly theory at this point. Nothing she could use to—

It was weird to feel someone else's fingers wiggling around in your insides.

Sarah laughed.

Her nose ached.

"Might have overdone the reedy-red powder." Ameli withdrew her blood-stained hand. "Most people don't find a bisected descending colon all that funny."

"Could..." Reinar's breathing hitched, shallow and inconsistent. His eyes rolled back in his head. "Could I have some?"

Ameli rolled her eyes. "Fine." She flickered her clean hand over Reinar's knee, and a dry red mist appeared and disappeared in the space between breaths. "Although you're neither bleeding out nor fouling your insides from your own sword attack."

It was possible they were no longer trying to kill her. Sarah watched Reinar's eyes close and a relieved smile creep across his face.

"I know it sounds like I'm just being a jerk at this point, but this next part is going to hurt." Ameli lifted both hands above Sarah.

"Thank... you." The pain from Sarah's nose paralyzed her face, and the whisper was as much noise as she could make.

The Daughter nodded and moved her arms in a rapid dialect of Ghost Hand that Sarah had never seen before. Ameli had been right about one thing, Sarah thought as her insides scoured, rearranged, and knit themselves back together.

It hurt like hell.

————

When Ameli fell across Sarah's middle, exhausted and flushed, a slight pain—almost a phantom—flitted up. Curious, she felt her face. Plenty of blood but no swelling and no hurt. Fully healed, her nose bent slightly left, then forward again. No one had thought to pull it straight while they were saving her life.

A reasonable oversight.

Sarah sat up and lifted Ameli to her knees. The freckle-faced girl smiled at her, eyes half lidded.

"You need to look after Reinar." Sarah did not want the Mirrik-man's death on her. Not after being rescued by his companion.

Ameli raised an arm and waved it at the now-slumbering giant. "He'll be fine. I'll take care of him before he wakes up. I gotta get a little rest first. You shouldn't have let him bang you around so much."

"I'm flattered you think I had any say in it." Sarah needed to get out of there. Go find Lady Selenna and Lord Goodfern. But she needed to understand something first.

"You say you want to leave in peace, but Morholt is still trying to kill me. What's the truth here? Are you defecting?"

Ameli's hand slid over to Sarah's knee. Warm, soft. So young for a girl involved in horrible matters. "Holt is a good man. All this time, he's just been trying to save lives. Even yours. Well, he *was* trying to save yours before Glauth. That rabbit's already in the pot now, I suppose. But I'm sure Reinar and I could convince him to just leave well enough alone."

"No." This sounded like so much fantasy and smoke to Sarah. "The Morholt I've seen is none of those things. Even if every ghastly rumor about the man is contrivance, he's still responsible for..." She trailed off before she could say Captain Falt's name.

"We're not all good people. But he's trying to make us better." Ameli glanced away but returned her gaze to Sarah. "Your man in the woods, the captain, he was an accident. It wasn't supposed to happen that way. Holt thought you were still carrying that baton."

What was Sarah supposed to make of all this? If Captain Falt's death was not Morholt's fault, it could only be... her own.

"We're going now." Ameli gripped Sarah's knee, intense now. "We're getting up and walking away and hoping we never see you again. I guess whether or not that happens is up to you. I've done what I could to show you we're not who you think we are. You're fully healed. It's your choice."

A strong breeze blew the leaves of the few fruit trees in the garden and carried a woman's scream from what sounded like the front of the house.

Unsure what her next words might even be, Sarah opened her mouth to speak.

"Hello, Hill Bitch." Morholt's voice rolled in from all around them. "Mahu and Sabni here are going to fill you up with arrow shafts, and I'm going to do my birthday dance on your face to make sure you're dead. You've murdered the last of my ex-girlfriends. I never even did that, and I *lived* with them."

Even as her eyes rolled and her wide mouth turned down, Ameli faded from view, along with Reinar.

Ameli's words rang in Sarah's ears. A good man. *A good man*?

She couldn't help but shout at the empty space around her. "The biggest illusions you have are of being a decent human being. All this crap about not killing people is just that: crap. You murdered Captain Falt as sure as if you slid the sword in yourself."

Morholt's answer rode the wind in circles. "Keep telling yourself that if it helps you sleep, Man Hands. I reckon you're two or three thousand ahead of me if we're counting."

"You could have made him look like anyone! It didn't have to be *you!*"

"Sorry if I assumed you *weren't* trying to murder me!"

"Stop it," shouted Ameli. "Let's just go."

Morholt's voice grated as he spoke. "Sabni, Mahu, fill her up with arrow shafts, and we'll leave. I *did* just promise."

"This does not seem sporting." A pleasant-sounding Egren voice came from somewhere nearby, an orator's voice. "Kohoc the Harvester does not suffer men to take up his mantle."

"Allz's wounds, Sabni." Another Egren man, this one irritated. "Can we not simply kill the woman now and recriminate later? She *is* dangerous, you know."

"No! Stop this!" Still seated next to Sarah, though now invisible, Ameli shouted at her companions. "She's going to let us go. It's all over with." A breathy whisper spoke into Sarah's ear. "You *are* gonna let us go here, right?"

"Not sure it's my call anymore." Sarah frowned into empty air and got to her feet. "Maybe you should have double-checked with good demon Morholt before making deals with me."

"Dammit," Ameli said.

Although Morholt's runecrafting hid their actual locations, it made the most sense for them to be through the broken section of wall. Sarah should have heard them if they had crept into the garden. Probably. Or they could be at the gate. Could Morholt make them inaudible too? She prepared to Blow Out the Candle to spoil the archers' aim.

If only she knew which way to point it.

Loud shouting erupted anew from outside the wall from both the left and the right.

"Boys." A woman's voice this time. That one had to be Raven. It was a voice with some force behind it, though it sounded a little farther away. "The Shepherds have nabbed Selenna and her boy toy, and there's a shitstorm on the way. Never mind, here it is."

From her position half in and half out of the wall, Sarah saw a band of temple knights churning around the outer corner from the right and a group of Marbles's mercenaries running in from the left. She snatched up the hat and legged it for the back of the house.

This time the cook was waiting for her, and Sarah ducked the carving knife that came at her head. She jumped to the doorway on the far side of the room and pulled a cabinet full of ceramic plates and bowls over to block her retreat.

The cook howled and waved her knife.

Sarah spun and jumped back over both footstool and toppled bookstand on her way to the front door. She jammed Harden's hat back on her head and flung the door open, eyes narrowed against the glare.

Out in the street between the rundown buildings of the tiny strip of town, three temple knights battled four rough-and-tumble mercenaries. To the side, Lady Selenna and her husband Lord Goodfern struggled against the ropes that bound them back-to-back. Selenna's head thrashed within a burlap sack tied under her chin.

The knights moved as a unit, keeping each other's backs safe and striking out with precision. They danced together, choreography made perfect by endless training and repetition, and brought death to their partners.

Or they should have. Sarah realized in seconds that the Shepherds were going to lose. She bore down toward the fight, knowing she would not make it there in time.

Every time one of the young knights struck, the mercenary would vanish and switch places with another of their number—a powerful woman, thick bodied and broad shouldered, who would take the blow with a chilly grin. A loud *pop* accompanied each one of these transferences. At the back, a short, skinny man with lank brown hair orchestrated the movements with broad gesticulations.

Sarah ran toward that one, magic on her lips.

A fast pair of pops whisked two of the knights from where they stood and put them with their backs to the two remaining mercenaries.

At the same time Sarah used Blow Out the Candle on the skinny guy and sent him flying into the side of a chandler's shop, a handsome mercenary with a rakish smile punched the back of a knight's armored head with such force that he sent it spinning off the man's shoulders, dented and spewing blood, through the wall of Lord Goodfern's manor house.

Nary an instant later, the last of the four mercenaries, an older woman with straggly hair, a pinched face, and rosy cheeks and nose that spoke of a long and intimate history with the bottle, laid her hand on the shoulder of a knight who stood with his back suddenly to her.

The armor plates on his back glowed orange, and her hand fell through them as they melted away.

His horrified scream provided speed to Sarah's legs. She did not like these men, these knights. But she was almost among the attackers, runecrafters trained by Lady Selenna, and she would not watch another of her allies murdered in front of her.

The broad-shouldered woman took the final knight's sword blow and stabbed him in the neck with a short triangular-bladed dirk.

Well, *damn*.

Sarah smacked the wine-and-acid-smelling older woman in the side of the head with an elbow as she ran in, which crumpled her to the ground. The pretty-faced man who punched the knight's head off grinned wide at her and shot off the ground, leaping a good forty feet straight up. Sarah ran right through the space where he had been and collided with the big woman who was yanking her dirk free of the dead knight's armored neck.

Sarah bounced off and fell backward.

The woman jerked the knife free, and Sarah kicked, sweeping her legs out from beneath her. Behind, Sarah heard the pretty-faced man land and come running. She spun and rolled sideways just in time to avoid a smashing fist that left a small crater in the hardpacked dirt.

Soundlessly, Sarah's blade came out of its sheath.

"That's not gonna help you, honey." The woman spat and wiped straight black hair out of her face. She maneuvered just in front of her pretty companion, whose smile Sarah was finding less and less charming.

With her blade high and left, Sarah jumped forward and punched the big woman in the forehead. Her head snapped back at just the right angle to crunch into the pretty face of her companion, and while she appeared unhurt, *he* went down bloody and unconscious.

The woman lifted her dirk—and stopped. Sarah gripped the knife wrist in one hand and, dropping her own sword, pulled the small blade from the purpling fingers.

"You can't... hurt me."

Sarah did not respond. She turned the woman around and wrenched the arm upward until it gave a soft cracking noise.

The woman gasped, went white, and fell to her knees. Whatever rune magic protected her did not seem to go all the way through.

Motion at the far end of the street caught Sarah's attention. Lady Selenna, bag over her head and hands still bound behind her, fled, wailing, out of town.

Her husband, left behind and still bound hand and foot, tumbled over and landed on his face.

The rest of the knights filtered back into the street from behind Lord Goodfern's manor, none the worse for wear. Captain Vancess ignored the fallen knights in the street.

Sarah picked up her sword, wiped it, and sheathed it. She straightened Harden's—*her*—hat and sighed.

Vancess stared at the dwindling Lady Selenna. "She cannot cloud the minds of men she cannot see. We are safe until she manages to remove that bag."

"She'll run into a tree before that happens." Sarah walked off in the direction of the horses. "Get these four in chains. I'll go fetch Lady Selenna. What happened to the Free Hand?"

"We battled the trash protecting the demon, but I never saw Morholt or his miscreant soldiers. Doubtless they fled for their lives when they saw us."

Vancess's certitude never failed to make Sarah wonder if she was doing the right thing.

"Doubtless."

25

WATCH ME SNEAK

SARAH

I must say, this really is quite brilliant." Gabby stood in the center of the clearing, next to the bound Lady Selenna with the bag still over her head, beneath gnarled oak branches. "Oh look, here comes Morholt now."

These woods, miles from Hornfield and thick with brush, were perfect for an ambush. Morholt would be on his guard but unable to resist the opportunity. Especially when he discovered Sarah's mistake.

In the distance, the sounds of fighting began. The plan was working exactly the way Sarah intended.

A quarter mile away, a temple knight sat bagged and bound and garbed in Lady Selenna's ornate dress next to the browbeaten Lord Goodfern—a ruse Sarah knew would never fool the mercenaries. Vancess and the temple knights kept watch over him while the real Lady Selenna sat here in her smallclothes, guarded by Sarah. The distraction attack by the Free Hand on the temple camp had begun while Morholt, on his own, crept into this clearing to be the hero and rescue the real Lady Selenna.

Keane was not the only one who could read people.

"You're very good at this." Gabby beamed at Sarah, who tried to ignore it and concentrate on the footprints stalking toward Lady Selenna. At least Sarah was the only one who could see the ghost god. She pushed the hat up to scratch at her scars, then pulled it back down. After years they still itched. That was not normal, especially for her.

A pair of creeping footprints stole into the edge of the clearing and halted, waiting.

With any luck, Morholt also could not see Sarah. The sky dwindled to a darkish purple, and Sarah lay as still as possible beneath a thick pack of tiny-leaved shrubs. It was the darkest corner of this little tableau she could find.

The footprints halted in front of Selenna, pointed away from Sarah. One corner of the burlap bag lifted.

Sarah sprang forward and grabbed with her left hand for aim, then swung her right fist. A dull *ponk* announced Morholt's appearance, and the runecrafter twirled to the dirt.

Gabby bent down to observe the unconscious Morholt.

"*Quite* brilliant."

———

S arah walked into the battle zone leading Selenna by the rope around her wrists and holding Morholt high in front of her with her other arm.

"Free Hand mercenaries, stop fighting and get lost." She shook the unconscious runecrafter in the air to make her point. "You failed. Morholt failed. No use throwing bad lives after bad."

Everything paused in the dark. The sky cleared of whizzing arrows. Vancess and the Shepherds peered over their hastily made fortifications of bush and deadwood. Nothing could be heard across the broad expanse of pebbled stone and grass except the oblivious babble of a stream and the very distant howl of a wolf.

Gabby vanished when Sarah stepped into the open. It never could maintain interest in events around Sarah for long. Not the smaller things anyway—things like the lives and violent deaths of the people around it as well as Sarah's own brushes with mortality.

A voice rang out from the dense trees nearby. "How do we know you won't kill him?" *That would be Sabni again*, Sarah thought. The one who did not want to kill her in cold blood.

She answered the trees. "I'd kind of like to. To be honest, the only reason I haven't is the mercy you bunch showed me back at Hornfield." Sarah lowered Morholt's limp form. "Doesn't mean I won't if you get in my way, though."

"We shall retreat for now. I cannot promise that we won't try and retrieve our friend in the future. As in the tale of *The Opal Woman*, 'How can I do less than everything I can to save the man who values my soul more than his own?'"

Walking into the knights' enclosure, Sarah handed Selenna off and dropped Morholt on the ground where two of the knights set about tying him and his fingers into awkward knots to make runecrafting impossible.

"I think we're talking about two different people." Sarah addressed a tall, lanky figure she could just make out in the trees. "But if it's that important to you, we can tie you up with him, and you can both go to the Dovenhouse."

"Hurt him, and you'll never sleep a restful moment again!" That powerful voice was Raven. "I'll be in every shadow you pass. I'll be behind you for the rest of your short and frightened life, waiting to stick a knife right up your ass. I'll—"

"I know, I know." Sarah signaled to Vancess to break camp and get on the road. "You'll be in every chamber pot I pee in, in every sandwich I eat, and up the hole of every—"

The knife that flew out of the black trees came so close to impaling Sarah right through her eye that she shut up and ran a little way to stand behind a dense pile of brush. That was too close. If she had not been a sorceress, with a sorceress's senses and speed, she would be entirely dead right now.

"Keep back and he'll be fine. Throw another dagger at me and..." She had nothing. "Please don't throw any more daggers at me."

Sarah and the knights ran to their horses and galloped away, leaving only one of their archers behind them, dead from Egren bows.

The trees were silent.

26

SCARIER THAN THOU

MORHOLT

The Furious Hill Cow tied a heavy rope around Morholt's wrists with bruising tightness. The knights were breaking camp, and only the sight of Selenna and her hapless husband similarly bound kept him from crafting illusions that would have the armored lot of them at each other's throats within minutes.

Not that he couldn't sow suspicion other ways as well.

"Sarah? May I call you Sarah?"

She ignored him while she tied the other end of the rope around her own waist.

Morholt took that as a yes. "Sarah it is. You know, I don't require my hands to cast spells. Or even the ability to speak."

Sarah glanced up at him and went back to her knots.

"They make it easier, faster, but I can do it all in my head." This was all true. "I want you to understand before we begin, that from here on out, every step you take might be into a hundred-foot chasm. Every person you talk to could be an angry bear with a hankering for sorceress face. And every bite of food you put into your mouth is almost certainly going to be rabbit poop. A person who can't see the real world can kill themselves in more ways than you've ever imagined."

Rope in hand, Sarah crossed to Morholt and tested his knots.

"Ow. Watch it, ox legs. I'm just saying you can avoid a lot of trouble by letting us go." That was as plain as he could make it. No need to mention that he'd try and find a way to kill her later. She had excepted herself from his resolution to become a better man.

That project had turned out to be harder than expected.

He found himself staring up into Sarah's brown eyes. The claw marks across her face and her bent nose—was that new?—spoke volumes to him about the levels of violence she was accustomed to.

She held up the rope that linked them.

"This isn't to keep you from running away." She yanked him even closer. "This is in case any aspect of my world turns out to not be exactly as I expect it to be. If that happens, I'm going to close my eyes, pull myself to the other end of this rope, and beat whatever I find there to death with my bare hands."

Sarah dropped the rope and lifted herself into the saddle of her horse.

"Keep up."

"Yeah." Morholt's hands shook, and his palms had gone cold and clammy. He stumbled behind on fear-numbed feet. That woman was *terrifying*. "I'll keep up. Been thinking about getting some exercise anyway." He hoped she did not see the three illusory temple knights who blew away in the breeze. His half-baked scheme to dupe the Hill Fury with shouting knights while he and Selenna ran into the woods fell apart under the scrutiny of lethal pummeling.

Maybe he'd wait until they got to wherever they were going and escape then.

———

The trees grew right up to the edge of the Greenshade River. Rather than being cut out of it, the small Tyrranean settlement of Zagan's Rest nestled among the woods. A wide bayou slowed the flow of water here and created the perfect spot for resupplying and repairing river craft, even if only smaller and flatter keeled vessels could make use of it. Greenshade proper lay on the other side of the river, and places like this would provide goods and service to either side without comment.

A dozen times or more along their two-day journey here, Morholt had devised foolproof plans to mislead Sarah and the temple knights and just as many times abandoned them. The fear that he might not succeed before Sarah sussed him out and murdered him kept him in line. Selenna too. His life was not the only one on the line.

He really couldn't give a shit what happened to Goodfern and the other runecrafters.

The thing that kept him glancing furtively ahead at Sarah and left his mouth dry was that she had taken April from him. She had looked at the card and tossed it in her own pack without even rewrapping it in the ratty handkerchief. He just knew it would come back out bent and misshapen, paint cracked and magic spoiled.

Dead.

Raven and the rest of the Free Hand would be tracking them. Morholt hoped they kept their distance. The people of Zagan's Rest certainly did. Aside from a few pulled-aside curtains and fleeing women, not so much as a rat turd would have rattled in this hamlet if you lifted it over your head and shook it.

The Hill Fury was well known on the border. No place in Tyrrane, neutral or not, would rest easy with the slayer of thousands of Ebon Host in its borders.

After the minute it took to walk through town, Sarah and Captain Vancess rode their horses onto a wide and well-maintained dock that jutted into the Greenshade River and up to a single boat tied off there. Twelve feet with a tiny mast and square sail, it was entirely insufficient to carry the knights and their prisoners.

"Get in the boat." Sarah pointed at the flat-bottomed vessel and nodded at Morholt.

He got in the boat.

"Vancess, bring Selenna over here. I'm taking the demons to Treaty Hill." She unspooled the line from the dock cleat. "Commandeer the first boat that'll fit everyone, and take it to Kos. Main island, northernmost point. I'll meet you there. Our next target has an olive farm nearby. With luck, we can grab the rest of the Hand there."

Sarah was not telling Vancess anything he did not already know; in fact, it had been he who first told her about the women that Morholt taught runecrafting to. The Temple of the Sky tracked Morholt for years before now and had been ready when Sarah walked in looking for troops to help. It felt as if she were merely part of someone else's plans, already in motion.

Vancess gazed at Sarah through lidded eyes. "I serve at your pleasure, Handmaiden." There had been more than enough strange behavior from the batshit captain to make Morholt glad he was not coming along.

"You should know, however," Vancess said, "that High King Oldam has ordered me to kill you. He says you will be the ruin of the Alir."

Coiled rope in her hand, Sarah stared at Vancess. "The King of Gods wants you to kill me. Is that what's about to happen here?"

The temperature on the dock fell several degrees. Morholt felt the chill, at any rate.

"You have been blessed by goddess Magda. Walked her path." Vancess bowed and extended an open hand to Sarah. "But Magda is an enemy to High King Oldam. Perhaps the ruin of the Alir was her aim all along. I cannot know these things. What then does a servant of all the Alir do?"

Morholt would have kept his damn mouth shut about it.

"Servant of all the Alir better consider his next words very carefully." Sarah held no weapons, nor even looked concerned, but those temple knights close by walked at top speed to back up their prolocutor.

"I told High King Oldam to bend over and fuck himself in the eye." Vancess showed his teeth. He probably thought he was smiling. "He is quite unhappy."

"I bet. Go, Vancess. Kos."

With shining armored fists, Vancess shoved Goodfern away from

Selenna and into the arms of his knights. The idiot jumped into the air and called out to his idiot wife.

Selenna, her head still in the sack, paid no heed to being separated from Goodfern. She was far too concerned for herself.

Vancess stepped up, clubbed Goodfern on the head, and dragged him away.

Morholt turned away to hide his smile. His feelings toward Selenna were not as unresolved as those for Glauth had been, but it never hurt to see the new boyfriend get clobbered.

Plus, Vancess was moving in the opposite direction. The guy made Morholt's skin crawl.

Morholt scooted to one side when Selenna was pushed on the two-seater middle thwart beside him, facing aft. Selenna cried to herself, breath hitching.

It did not surprise Morholt to see Selenna demonstrate no affection for her husband, yet cry for herself. She was selfish and entitled but also lazy and cowardly. For a more motivated woman of Selenna's talents, a man like Goodfern would have been a mere steppingstone. But Morholt reckoned that climbing any further up the ladder of Tyrrane's nobility represented too much effort for her as well as a risk of exposure.

How many things were there in the world he liked better than Selenna? Sandwiches? Well-cooked fish? He liked his boots.

"Like your hat." Morholt squinted up at Sarah. "Impressive clothes are a good substitute for a personality and moral fiber." Fear pushed the words out of his mouth. Fear of showing just how goddamn afraid he really was.

"Please be quiet." The words from beneath Selenna's sack stuttered and sniffled. She need not have concerned herself. Sarah paid him no mind and dropped her pack into the aft of the boat.

Morholt winced, worried for April. He would not risk telling his captor how much the card meant to him.

Back on land, Vancess shoved Goodfern, now bleeding from his forgettably good-looking face, to his knights and stalked back to the boat. He held a large silver flask high and climbed into the bow of the boat behind Morholt. As the man settled, Morholt felt the hairs on the back of his neck prickle.

Sarah stood on the dock with her hands on her hips and watched Vancess. "Fine. Why don't you come too, Prolocutor?" She stepped into the aft and pushed off with one well-muscled leg. The boat glided into the bayou, and Sarah unfurled the sail.

"I did not wish to." Vancess shook his head and looked put-upon. "I have been ordered. Someone *still* wishes me to kill you." He pointed toward the sky.

If Sarah heard him, she gave no indication of it.

From behind, Vancess tied Morholt and Selenna to their seats.

"Wonder whose boat this is?" Morholt watched the knights throw Goodfern over the back of Sarah's horse. They would have no need of the lord of Hornfield now. Would they kill him or maybe press him into some kind of service to the temple in return for Selenna's life?

"Are we friends now?" Sarah's gaze was flat. She gave nothing away. "Would you like to chat? I thought you wanted your men to fill me up with arrow shafts so you could leave."

"You tried to kill me first." *Don't think about Glauth.* "And to be fair, that was when I was invisible and had archers. We might as well chat. There's not much else to do now."

Sarah snorted and shook her head. She tied off the sail and sat down, the tiller firm in her hand. The boat turned southwest and picked up speed. Soon they passed into the far edge of the bayou where the water ran fast and from there into the river.

"You can take the sack off my head." Selenna spoke clearly with no hint of her earlier upset. "I won't spell you. We're already underway."

"Sure." Though his hands were tied together, Morholt took hold of the pull cord that cinched the sack around Selenna's neck. "Because the eternal and immutable laws of the universe that govern runecrafting all go on vacation with sexy costumes and a gallon of pig oil when you're *on a boat*. Come on, Selenna. At least do me the favor of *trying* not to make me look stupid for having taught you magic."

Sarah reached for her sword when Morholt took hold of the cord but relaxed when he pulled it tighter.

"*She's* not the one to blame if you feel stupid," Sarah said, "considering your criteria for who you teach."

Selenna shrugged. "Sorry, Holt. It's hard *not* to make you look dumb."

Mountains and woodland skirted past at speed. They stopped at no ports, and they returned greetings from no passersby. A warm breeze blew in from the east, smelling of someone's cookfire.

Sarah yawned. "Vancess, take the tiller. I'm going to try and get some rest."

Still in his full and shiny plate armor, save the helm, Vancess nodded and stepped over Morholt on his way to the stern. Sarah crossed again to the bow and curled up in front of the mast behind Morholt and Selenna.

Sarah carried the length of rope that tied her to Morholt with her.

Captain Vancess stared at the two of them, his once-handsome eyes bloodshot, blond stubble standing out on his chin. Rich blond hair stuck dank and greasy to his skull.

Selenna, beneath her sack, sat straight and stiff. She smelled like old sweat.

"The gods do not care for you, Morholt Demonkin." Vancess's rasping voice caught Morholt's attention in a *jump-out-of-the-way-of-that-charging-bull* sort of fashion. He needed to establish some sort of common ground with this man. Something that might temper whatever inferno raged behind those hate-filled eyes.

Fast.

"If you'd be willing to teach me about the gods, I'd love to listen." Morholt would rather go fishing for spunt with his tongue than listen to a sermon on the Andosh gods, but he would also rather live, so instead, he did his best to act interested. "I admit to—Oh shit. No. Don't—OW!"

Still tied to the thwart he sat on, Vancess's mailed punch to Morholt's face knocked his torso back and thumped his head against the bottom boards. But his ass stayed put.

The world spun away from Morholt and left him with crystal sound and fuzzy colored shapes. Pain from his face and the back of his head went abruptly numb, as if afraid he wasn't ready to experience it.

He blinked, searching for something to focus on other than the tilting of the wood he lay on.

A muffled scream and panicked breathing came out of Selenna's sack, but she did not speak. He could have chuckled if doing so would not have caused his skull to fly into bits. Had Morholt known that tying a stinky cloth bag and threatening Selenna's life was all it took to keep her quiet, well, it probably would not have changed the trajectory of their relationship, but he might not have let her put him through so much misery. Theirs had been the most unpleasant of his breakups.

He hooked the toe of his boot into an oarlock and pulled himself into a sitting position. There the pain was. Blood ran down into one eye. With the other, he watched Vancess.

The armored fanatic smiled and put a single finger over his lips. "Shhh."

Then he looked up into the sky and scowled. "What do you want now?"

By reflex Morholt turned and looked up and saw something even more frightening than anything his imagination could conjure.

Nothing but clouds.

There was no illusion that Morholt could think of that might fool a man who was already seeing things that weren't there into untying him and Selenna from the thwart *and* getting the rope off him that bound him to Sarah.

Ah, toad dicks.

"She is a symbol of your supremacy. How do you think it would look if I did that?" Vancess's brow tightened. His lips pulled down, and his jaw bunched. "I already told her. She knows your plans."

He recoiled. "No, *you're* a fucking worm."

Behind Morholt, Sarah snored loudly. Had she heard so many of these one-sided conversations with the air that they were no longer noteworthy?

Vancess turned away and stared at his feet. "I hate you so much."

Even his imagination is against him. Morholt wondered what exactly it was the sack of broken marbles in the shape of an asshole saw above them.

"I *am* important!"

"On this boat? Are you mad or simply stupid?"

Was Vancess accusing his imaginary playmate of being crazy?

"No. I *will* kill her but not today. That isn't what you are truly asking me to do."

Wait. What? Kill? Kill who? At least it was a her and not a him. Still, it didn't seem to be a good direction conversationally. Beside Morholt, Selenna sat rigid and still.

"I will display your authority to the world. I will kill Morholt Demonkin and his cow and hang their corpses from the Country Gate. All who witness will know the cost of heresy to the Alir and to you, Oldam, High King of Gods." Vancess closed his eyes and smiled. The tension went out of his body.

This was not good.

"*Yes.* And *then* I'll kill Sarah." Vancess peeked up, and a trace of irritation crept back into his voice. "You're so single-minded."

Morholt could wake up Sarah and tell her what he had just witnessed, but she already knew and felt comfortable sleeping in front of the man anyway. And then Vancess would still kill him and Selenna first chance he got. He could try an illusion, but if he did and Sarah realized what he had done, which she certainly *would*, then *she* would kill him.

That only left the stupidest option. Morholt steeled himself against the next punch and opened his mouth. "Grand Prolocutor Vancess, may I be allowed to speak?"

"Last words are customary." There was a pause as Vancess glared into the empty sky. "Why not? I allow *you* to speak."

"What do you want now, Morholt Demonkin?" Vancess turned

his head to one side and the sunlight left deep hollows around his eyes. He did not look well.

"Am I to understand that High King Oldam himself wishes me dead?" At the moment, Morholt wished High King Oldam no small amount of harm, so it was probably fair.

Vancess's gaze flickered up. "He does, but that is not special. Oldam is not a kind god."

"I don't mean to sound suspicious"—Morholt inhaled and plunged ahead—"but are we really certain it's him?" His spine was a rigid curve, and every muscle in his stomach was a knotted and angry snake.

Again the flicker. Whatever Vancess saw was probably talking.

"It's just, well, if I'm going to be killed, it'd be a relief to know that the god who ordered it was genuine."

"What do you mean?" Vancess leaned forward, eyes narrowed. "Do you think I have taken leave of my senses and now converse with empty air?" He winced and glowered up with renewed passion.

"Um, no. Of course not? I mean, you know I can make illusions, right?"

Those hollow eyes slid back down to Morholt. "And thus you must be contained. Or destroyed."

Morholt had to remind himself to breathe. "Ah, sure. All right. Let's skip over that for a minute. The point is that if I can make you see and hear things, maybe someone else can too. Maybe someone else is doing it right now."

Vancess's head went up, and his brows went even further down. He gripped the aft thwart and turned his knuckles white. "Who would do this?"

Though not certain to whom the question had been directed, Morholt answered, "I don't know. The temple has taken the kids of a lot of powerful people. And what about Finnagel? You know he wouldn't want you getting too powerful."

"The sorcerer of Greenshade. The Father of the Temple Renewed." Vancess was whispering to himself now. "Is he afraid I will take the temple from him?" Vancess jerked back as if struck, his face pale.

Whatever the apparition, Morholt had hit a nerve. "I bet Oldam's starting to sound desperate, isn't he?"

Vancess pulled back into himself but never dropped his stare. "He is at that." And then he relaxed, sat up straight, and smoothed the front of his sky-blue temple tabard. "An honor?" He spoke to the sky. "An honor to be berated and cajoled by figments of gods? Chosen to be a pawn? A plaything? *Fuck* you."

Apparently Vancess's feelings about speaking to the Alir were more complicated than Morholt would have thought.

"And now he is gone. Interesting." Vancess turned his head to one side and shrugged.

"Sure." Morholt tried to stay upright. His body wanted to faint from relief. "You were getting too close, so it buggered off." His shirt was soaked with his sweat. "I could really use a beer."

"And now I have only to decide whether or not to kill you."

"No. No, you don't have to do that now. You don't need to kill me." Morholt could not quite get a hold of what he was trying to say. He thought this was over. "That's not the plan. Sarah's taking me to Treaty Hill."

With a nod, Vancess relented. "Yes. To Treaty Hill and to Finnagel. Very well. We shall follow this path for now.

"But we shall not walk in the pilgrim handmaiden's footsteps forever."

———

The Cattle Streets were a series of artificial canals that ran between the port community of Fish Hill, where the quartet landed, and Treaty Hill, the capital of Greenshade. Polemen pushed barges laden with sacks, crates, barrels, and livestock up and down the waterways in a boisterous, stinking celebration of commerce.

Instead of sending word to Finnagel or the king when they

arrived, Sarah strode with her head down and her cowl up and took pains to avoid meeting anyone's gaze. Curiosity blazed in Morholt's brain, wanting to know why the skulking about, but he was not entirely confident of not getting his brains dashed out for asking overly probing questions.

To the east side of the canals, Sarah and Morholt walked toward the castle on the hill, with Vancess and Selenna far enough behind to be out of earshot. The morning sun hung low, already warming the day and promising clear skies and sweat.

"What are you expecting in return for this information?" Sarah's long legs ate the distance on the cobbled road and forced Morholt to trot to keep up.

"I was hoping you'd set me free and convince the king you'd ensorcelled me into a very nonthreatening kind of rodent. Or maybe a dove. Something he wouldn't have to kill."

Sarah snorted. "That doesn't seem very likely, does it?"

"Not with that attitude." Morholt kicked at a dried horse turd and sent it skittering off the road to bounce off a shack. A man selling meat pies cast an angry glance his way. "Just don't turn me into a pet. I don't want to have to watch my owners masturbate all the time."

"You've told me that Vancess is plotting against me." Sarah yanked on the rope and forced Morholt to run just to keep from tripping to the stones. "That's not new or useful information."

"What about the talking to imaginary gods?" Morholt was having a hard time accepting Sarah's unconcern. "How does that not bother you?"

"How do you know they're imaginary?"

Morholt shook his head and pushed dirty red locks out of his eyes. "To begin with, he was talking to Oldam himself. The one that's supposed to be turned to stone on the path to the Alireon."

Sarah shot Morholt a sidelong look. "And you know so much about gods and how they talk to their people?"

Morholt frowned. "Why are you defending that crapstick? He as much as told me he's going to murder you. Personally, I'd be grumpy about it. Possibly even crabby."

Sarah said nothing but increased their speed.

"Hang on." Morholt ran alongside her. "You traveled with that goddess. Magda, right? Is she still talking to you? Is that why you're all weird about this?"

"You don't know me, and you're still my prisoner." Sarah stopped and yanked Morholt around so they were face-to-face. "You've told me about Vancess, and I thank you. Unfortunately for you, he told me the same thing himself. Now shut up and walk quietly to your imprisonment and/or death."

Morholt grinned. "You've got a god in your head too. Maybe more than one? You have big head orgies every night, don't you?"

Sarah made an inarticulate noise of frustration and resumed their walk.

"Just how big is a god's dick, anyway? I wonder if they can do tricks with them."

A lengthy pause went by without either of them speaking. Morholt assumed she was considering whether or not to throw him in the canal.

"Ameli told me you thought I was still holding the baton." She spoke slowly, eyes on the ground ahead of her. "She said that Falt's death was an accident. Is that true?"

He sucked his teeth and made a small noise as he considered. "Yes, though I'd thank Ameli in the future to keep her comments to herself. The only solace I've had after Glauth's murder was knowing you thought I killed Falt on purpose. At least that way, we were even."

The big woman nodded fast. The wind flapped at her cloak and hood. She still did not look up. "We're still even. I told the illusion you left that night in the woods that I was aiming for you. She was hidden when I let go of the arrow and stepped in front of it while it was still in the air."

Morholt stopped on the wooden planking. "So where does that leave us?"

Boots scuffed as Sarah turned to face him. She held her arms out to her side. "Here? I don't think anything has changed. But I'm willing to tell the king that Falt wasn't deliberate."

"That ought to help." A thought came to him. "Can I ask a favor? The card you took from me? With the painting of the imp on it? Can you at least wrap it back up? It's old and it's delicate, and it is very special."

A distant smile touched one corner of Sarah's mouth. She unslung her pack and opened it on the ground. She withdrew a smallish brown book and let it fall open where April's card, wrapped in its tatty silk handkerchief, rested. "Safe as castles."

The lightness of relief lifted Morholt's own smile.

With the book back in the pack, Sarah once more led Morholt to the Forest Castle and his certain-to-be-stinking cell within. At least until they executed him.

"You were about to tell me about all the gods you talk to in your head?" The more he could get her to open up, the more likely he might convince her to let him go.

"Yeah." She shrugged. "We can talk about that. There's just one god I've seen that no one else can." The hand that Sarah held the rope in was loose. Relaxed. "It teaches me sorcery. Languages. It's… magic."

Morholt gave a low whistle. "It makes sense. There are tales where I come from about heroes who are guided by gods. Whenever it happens, there's always other gods who get involved and start talking to other people in the story. Usually trying to kill the heroes."

"Are there stories where you come from about a dead god who looks sort of like the person it visits, and it teaches them the god tongue of magic?"

The cobblestones suddenly became very interesting to Morholt. The place he was from had a legend exactly like that. In fact, the runecrafting Morholt practiced was learned from teachings handed down by the Dead God.

The Dead God who ruled the Undergates.

"Nope. Never heard of that." The *last* thing he wanted was to involve himself in affairs with forces of creation. His life was complicated enough as it was.

Sarah frowned ahead. "I guess I'm not surprised."

"I'm not one to judge other people's crazy." Morholt couldn't help but see Sarah differently. It was not a welcome revelation, seeing as she was still leading him to his doom. "And if I did, Raven'd be way ahead of you in line."

"Keep it to yourself, and I'll do what I can for you." Secrecy stole all the little pieces of an expression from her face. "I'm not sure what good I can actually be to you. It probably depends on whether or not I can manage to see Keane without Finn being in the castle."

Ah, Morholt thought, *that's why we're sneaking. She doesn't trust the bastard any more than I do.*

"The last time I talked to Keane—the last few times—there was something different about him. I need to see him for myself. I need to know if Finn has done anything to him."

The big woman glanced around and turned her head against a pair of Swords walking toward them. "I'm not promising I can save your life, Morholt, but I'll try. Maybe the Dovenhouse is better than a rope."

"A fistful of silver dukes and a horse is also better than a rope," Morholt said. "You know, if you're taking suggestions."

27

DO YOU NEED TO PEE?

VOLKER

Plance. I can't... you're going to *die*. Just... *please*."

Alan, a member of Sergeant Stath's special contingent of castle guards dubbed the "King's Elbows," pleaded at the edge of a short wall, arms outstretched and tears in his eyes. Looking down on him, far out on the gnarled branch of a wide oak, sat Prince Volker. The youthful guardsman had been assigned the royal children to keep them out of trouble.

Now, here in the Tall Garden, the tiny forest that grew atop the Stone Tower, Volker kicked his legs out over the city hundreds of feet below and laughed. The tree grew over the side of the tower, and Volker knew—because Shayla had told him—that the much bigger man would neither climb after him for fear of breaking the limb, nor call for help for fear of frightening Volker and escalating the situation.

"Why would I die?" Volker saw a boy running after a man on a horse below him on the Quarter Road. What was the boy after? Volker decided the man on the horse was his grandfather, and the boy was chasing him for a candy treat.

"No one's going to die." Alan breathed deep and slow. "You're going to come down right now, and no one is ever going to know that this happened."

Volker looked around. Moon sat next to Alan, panting and drooling.

"All right." Volker slid around and got one foot beneath him. He grinned as the color drained from Alan's face when he walked along the branch to the trunk.

Big hands gripped Volker under his arms and pried him off the tree.

"Hey, I was comin' down."

Alan knelt in front of Volker, his hands cupping the boy's head. "I know you think you can't die, but you can. If you fell out of that tree, you would be gone, and your mother would go mad with grief. And then I'd be gone because I was supposed to be watching you. Do you want me to be gone?"

"No, sir." Volker struggled to keep a straight face. "I promise never to climb the tree again."

"Not good enough." Alan's dark eyebrows pulled together. "I know how you two operate. I get you to promise not to climb *that tree*, and the next thing I know, you'll be up every tree *but* that one. I want you to promise not to climb any trees—wait, no, any*thing*—unless an adult says it's all right."

"Where's Shayla?" Volker made a show of looking around. "I thought you were s'posed to be watching her too." Nanny had taken a much deserved but all too rare day off.

"Hagrim's forge, I'm a dead man." Alan spun around. Nothing but tastefully manicured trees, bushes, and an empty stone bench looked back at him. "Where is she?"

"She likes to try and pet the chipmunks." Volker pointed toward the far eastern wall of the tower top to their right. "Sometimes they bite her though."

"Sonofa... fiddle." Alan stood and gripped Volker's shoulder. "Follow me. And no more climbing."

Alan ran right.

Volker ran left.

Two children and a huge white dog crowded into the narrow servants' corridor between the hallway and Mister Finnagel's private chamber. Volker had discovered the hidden entryway months ago, and Shayla had reasoned that even if anyone knew about it, no one would dare use it. Who would want to walk in on Mister Finnagel unannounced? They huddled up against a barred and nailed-shut door, listening. They could not have entered the rooms beyond if they had wanted to.

Discovered failed to capture the extent to which Volker went to find this particular corridor. A loose key found its way into his pocket during a daring sandwich theft in the chamberlain's office, and a week frittered itself away searching for the door that belonged to it. Eventually Shayla reasoned that being by itself—at the bottom of a locked drawer beneath a stack of heavy books because you never knew where you might find a sandwich—instead of on the chamberlain's ring, meant it paired with an unused door. Volker recognized it as a servant's key. From there they decided that Mister Finnagel's servants' corridor was most likely to be unused... and here they were.

"Moon's breath is stinky," Shayla whispered.

It wasn't Moon's fault, but it was true.

"Do you think Mister Finnagel is in there?" They were here to spy on the mean old man, but they could hardly do that if he was outside being mean to someone else.

As if in answer, a thump came from the other side of the wall, followed by the sounds of dragging furniture. Both children fell silent, and Moon lay on the stone floor.

A sing-song voice came from inside, but the words did not make sense. Volker pressed his ear against the door. He could hear clearly enough, it was just blah-blah talk.

"He's singing in a *language*." Volker could just barely make out Shayla's subdued words.

The singing stopped, and the tiny corridor filled with the smell of sitting by a fire on a winter morning. The scent was strong enough to completely cover the dog breath.

"Hail, Fee Lay, watcher in the dark and bringer of everlasting night." Mister Finnagel sounded strange. Respectful?

"*What do you want, Finn? Dani and I* were *on a date.*" The voice was deep and resonant. It vibrated through Volker's chest and made him need to pee. "*If this is another show murder, I'm going to leave* your *skin spiked to the horse's ass.*"

"Here is the covenant, and here is your offering. I need a powerful individual bargained with. Someone you may know." Mister Finnagel was being sneaky. Volker could hear it in his voice.

"*No offense, Peanut, but it doesn't matter what you need. Nice offering though. You know I like redheads.*"

"I told you not to call me that."

Shayla shifted. "I have to pee."

"*Nicknames aren't your problem, Peanut. The Boss is out of pocket, and that means no jobs topside until He comes home. I am not getting involved in your bullshit and running the risk of crossing wires with whatever He has going on.*"

"But he can't leave there." Now Mister Finnagel was scared.

What could frighten *him*? The thought made Volker want to throw up.

"He can't even be summoned. When did he leave? My senses haven't returned to me. They're always the last thing to come back after I die. I can't even *hear* any better than a human."

Something about that statement raised Volker's brow, though uncertainty as to what exactly it was kept his mouth closed about it.

"*Hah. The only thing less likely than me signing that contract is me spilling on the Boss. And* you *couldn't sense Him anyway. Nothing personal, but I think this has gone about as far as it can. Things change, we'll talk. Otherwise, go step on a rusty nail.*"

Volker put a small hand against the wooden door.

"*But I'm taking that dead girl. Dani'll love it. Bye.*"

A *whump* pushed the air around them and hurt Volker's ears. Moon whined.

"What? Who is that? Show yourselves!"

Both kids fled as a grinding screech filled the corridor, though neither moved as fast as Moon. Volker hit the hidden escape at the same instant that the door into Mister Finnagel's chambers blew off hinges, nails, and a pair of bolted iron bars and slammed into the stone wall opposite it.

The three of them raced down the castle hallway away from Mister Finnagel's diminishing shouts, raising eyebrows but no comment among the pedestrian servants and functionaries.

They didn't like Mister Finnagel either.

———

B ack in the schoolroom, Volker, Shayla, and Moon huddled beneath Miss Thornwhistle's large desk. It was literally the last place anyone in the castle might look for them.

"Who do we tell?" Volker reached out to brush cobwebs out of Shayla's hair. He himself was liberally coated in dirt and wooden shards from the exploding door.

Shayla gazed up at the underside of the desk. She tapped the side of her chin with a forefinger. "Mommy and Daddy won't help us. Daddy might even do somethin' bad if we tell him. This doesn't help us at *all*."

"What do we do if Daddy is against us?" Volker's tummy hurt. "We can't even tell the other grown-ups."

"No, we can't." Shayla scrutinized the desk legs. "Even if they b'lieved us—which they wouldn't because they're grown-ups, and grown-ups are *stupid*—Daddy might still do somethin' bad to them."

"If we knew what Mister Finnagel did to Mommy and Daddy, maybe we could stop it."

"Well, *I* don't know," Shayla put a hand on the chest of her dirty dress, "and that means *you* don't know either." Harsh, but true. "And 'cause we can't tell, that means we have to figure it out ourselfs."

"Oldam's nose."

She moved her hand to Volker's knee. "Don't worry, big brother. We'll figger it out. Well, I will."

Moon lay his head in Volker's lap. Dejected, he petted the dog's massive head. "I wish Aunt Sarah were here. She'd believe us, and Daddy wouldn't dare do nothin' to her."

28

LOSING A SON, BUT GAINING A MOUNTAIN

KING BRANNOK

K ing Brannok stared at his daughter. Disappointment and embarrassment wheeled through his head. He sat in the secret library's sole chair, while she stood with her head down just outside the hidden entrance. Her big braid twisted in one nervous hand, while her other arm hung splinted in a sling.

"You place all of Tyrrane in jeopardy with your actions." His voice struggled against his control, and his face flushed with heat.

"Yes, sire."

"I expected this kind of thing from Despin. Even Tobin. But not *you*. Were you aware I had convinced myself that *you* were my most capable child? *You*?" He lifted the small red book from the tabletop— perhaps to throw it—and set it back down.

"No, sire."

"You endangered your brother's life." Brannok's good hand flexed. Tendons stood out along his arm, making the freckles and thick red hair there rise and flatten. "You endangered the alliance with the Grengards and all of Norrik besides." He glared at her broken wrist. "You even endangered *yourself*. And for what? So that you could sit close to a pretty woman in the cold?" He swallowed hard on the question he most abhorred asking.

"Did you intend for Jason to survive that fight?"

Jasmayre's head jolted up, her thin face wet with tears. "Yes, sire." Even now, she held to decorum. Even now she stood a princess first.

"Then why?" Would an explanation help? Had he ever allowed explanations of anyone else?

"I arranged the fight with Queen Tove's men to impress her with Jason's ability. To advance the marriage." Jasmayre's voice cracked, but she never stopped. "I should have allowed her to pick the men."

"You're fucking right you should have." Brannok took a deep breath and eased it out. "Or perhaps not risked him at all? Was this even necessary?"

"No, sire." She released the braid. "I don't believe it would have made a difference if I had suggested Jason play a game of draughts instead. He and Tove were already inseparable."

Arranging this stupidity for the reason of diplomacy aligned more closely with Jasmayre's character than to further a crush—other than the inane foolishness involved.

Brannok cleared his throat. "You'll have to excuse me. I am unaccustomed to hearing my children tell me the truth."

"I understand, sire."

And still Jasmayre had not scraped and simpered and offered endless apologies as might any other in her position. She stated what Brannok already knew to be the facts and kept her dignity. His flinty heart warmed, dangerously close to the unfamiliar sensation of forgiveness.

"What of the queen?"

"As for Tove and me, I have no justification. I allowed myself to become... infatuated with her, and she with me." She picked her way through the thorny account and did her best not to step on the hedgehogs, as befit a professional royal. "I have already put a stop to it. Tove has agreed it is for the best."

Brow furrowed, Brannok held fast to his scowl while his anger vanished. The problem, as he reasoned it, was that though Jasmayre had been unwise, she would learn from the experience and was certain never to repeat it. Given his other children, Brannok had no means to deal with this.

"If you were one of your brothers, I'd give you a lecture about shortening your leash and duty to Tyrrane and perhaps box your ears." He relaxed and gave a weary sigh. Perhaps this was what other men meant when they spoke of the bond between father and daughter. Brannok was not sure he deserved the right to that bond... yet. "But we don't have the time, and I lack the strength. At least your brother finally managed to kill someone."

Jasmayre's eyes widened at Brannok's admission.

Brannok stood and gestured to the bookcase behind him. "We will discuss this again when my mission is finished. But for now, you haven't seen the weapons yet."

Jasmayre made a slow circuit of the secret library. Of all his children, living and dead, only she would truly appreciate the potential of what he had discovered here. Her misstep had not been fatal, and she would be a better ruler for having made it, especially with him teaching her from the throne.

"Some of these works are ancient." She ran a long thin finger over a half dozen spines on the cramped bookshelf. In the lanternlight that lit her well but failed to touch the further reaches of the room, Jasmayre *glowed*—pale skin, blazing red braid, her gold and russet velvet dress. Yet, none of it compared to the brilliance of her intellect.

Brannok rode the inevitability of her queendom. She *was* the future of Tyrrane.

"They all point to possibilities. Suggestions. Past failures. Lessons learned." Brannok was not at the edge of this chasm. He leaped off and thrilled to fall into its darkness. He had barely eaten in the past few weeks, his excitement and passion keeping him moving. His mail hauberk hung loose on his shoulders, a drooping sack of clinking metal. "I am nearly there."

"How can I help?" Her hand rested on his cloak which Brannok had pinned over the worn green door with nails stuck between the door and its stone frame. The only source of any color in the room, Brannok did not like the door. The bottom of his cloak hung eighteen inches off the ground, and the green peeked out underneath, sullen and resentful.

Brannok smiled. "Do not fuck your brother's fiancé. Other than that, tell me of the world above." Jasmayre smelled of fresh breezes and rare opened windows. A refreshing contrast to the twisting tunnels and long-ago-hidden libraries of Brannok's current life.

She leaned against his cloak, her shoulder lost in the thick bear fur. Brannok turned the chair to face her and sat back down. His knees had hurt ever since coming down here.

"Tyrrane has formally abandoned Mirrik," she said this without emotion. "King Wagnersen might have expected us to continue the pretense of alliance as long as he conducted his campaigns against us indirectly, but I have no patience for it. As well, we have gained allies for having made our position official."

With a nod, Brannok bade her continue.

"As you already know, Jason is to be wed to Tove the Mountain. Somewhat shockingly, these two actions have resulted in a united Norrik for the first time in, well, ever." Jasmayre shrugged, as if the accomplishment were not the most astounding feat of politics in history. "Once the Norrikmen collectively set their sights south to Mirrik, there will be *six* kingdoms of Norrik, with Jason and Tove as High King and Queen."

Emotion rose to the surface, but with practiced savagery, Brannok clawed it back down. In that glimmer of sentiment ran the fruition of his life's work, represented by a daughter who had overcome the prejudice and rigidity of an entire nation and, moreover, that of her *father* to earn the crown. With the combined might of Tyrrane, Norrik, *and* a conquered Mirrik, she would be able to take whatever she wanted from this world.

Even if that were nothing at all.

After the heat of his anger, Brannok was unprepared for these emotions. Where did they go? How did lesser people deal with seeing their life's ambitions realized? How might an ordinary man process pride in his children?

Jasmayre demurely turned away to allow her father to wipe the weakness from his face. In this too, she had his gratitude.

"Has the sorcerer continued to call on you?" she asked after a moment.

"Not since he ordered me to send cavalry and archers to the midst of nowhere. Our most elite troops, on holiday." It still rankled him. He clung to this bit of stray anger that jutted out of the turbulent sea of his emotions. "Since then, the old beast seems to have forgotten I exist. I've found I do not mind. More time for me to plot his extinction."

"Time well spent." She pushed away from the door and turned to face it. "What's behind these two doors?"

Brannok stood and indicated the rightmost with his blade hand. The green paint was both faded and well-worn, indicating it had once seen considerable use. Diamond-shaped bronze rivets below the bearskin cloak held ages of bluish patina. "That one cannot be opened. I ruined that axe on it without making a scratch. It offended me, so I covered it instead." He pointed left. "But that one. Let me show you."

The hinges screeched when Brannok pulled at the unremarkable door, and he hooked the lantern on his blade hand and stepped inside.

The space itself was gray, fifteen-foot square, and mostly feature-less except for a tall cabinet standing open and empty against the left wall. At second glance, the straight flatness of the walls, floor, and ceiling drew their own attention, being so perfect as to question if they were created by human hands.

But set perfectly flush into the stone floor was a copper ring a foot wide and ten feet across, burnished as brightly as the day it had been made. Into the mirrored surface were inscribed bizarre symbols and pictograms.

"This is... what is it?" Without touching the ring, Jasmayre bent down to examine it. She frowned in concentration.

"I have been reading about a kind of magic that does not require sorcery." Brannok's heart quickened at the telling as it had upon his

initial discovery. "It requires only knowledge of runes and the imagination to use them. These are some of those runes."

"What do they do?"

"I'm not fully certain yet." Brannok had not realized how much he
wanted another human being to share with. "It was built by someone
who didn't get any further than this. But I *am* sure it has something to
do with killing Angrim."

"Father. My King." Jasmayre spoke softly, slowly. "You will be the
one to create a new age for Tyrrane, an age of freedom from that
thing, and an age of freedom from fear."

"Not just for Tyrrane, daughter." Brannok gripped her shoulder in
his good hand. "For the world. The whole of the Thirteen Kingdoms
will rejoice at the fall of the Anger Under the Mountain. But I won't
be king forever, and soon it won't be my name they cheer.

"It will be yours."

———

Much later, after Jasmayre had left, taking her vague guilt
and scents of the daylight world with her, Brannok
reached the end of the small red book. He jumped from
his chair and paced the room, face in the leatherbound pages, or as
much of it as he could pace within the lantern's light. Laughter
bubbled out of his chest, and he smacked the table with his fist twice.

This was it.

The book was a diary of sorts of a king of Tyrrane. His name was
not written, but from clues of the time and particulars of the man's
life, Brannok felt it had to be one of the Evalds. That family had been
known to be esoteric and mysterious.

The first page of the entry had been torn out, but the rest detailed
a ritual using the copper ring in the next room as a step to killing the
great beast Angrim. The author had lost his nerve and never
completed his plans—it was not for the faint of heart—but he had
been confident that a more capable man than he would succeed.

Capable or not, Brannok would have to fill the role.

That was a strange thought. Five years ago, it would not even have occurred to him that he might not be the only man in the Thirteen Kingdoms to do this. Now, he felt worry that he could fail, and yet he continued anyway. Where had *that* come from?

The contents of that missing first page bothered him, but the ritual itself as well as its effects were complete. Brannok closed his eyes and considered a Tyrrane without the Anger. He had never known such a thing. No one had. Angrim was as much a piece of Tyrrane as the trees or the dirt or the evil rotten soul that begat cruelty and murder in its every corner. Being rid of Angrim would mean being rid of the dirty wickedness that suffused his nation.

Brannok raised his head and stared at the red book. There would be no place for him in the new Tyrrane he was making. He was too much a part of the thing he was trying to kill. He hated it, but he had grown in it, been formed by it.

A new kind of ruler would be required. Smarter and more agile than he. A smile formed on his face as he saw the blocks that had always been falling into place in his mind. He had thought to remain on the throne until he was too weary to be there, and hand it down to a thoroughly trained Jasmayre then. But that would not do.

No, instead he would abdicate as soon as Angrim was gone and be her advisor. A monarch for a new Tyrrane.

She would be magnificent.

29

SEEING STARS

SARAH

"Good day, milady." Secreed gave Sarah a stiff bow in the doorway of her quarters. The elder master butler and chamberlain somehow divined her presence in the Forest Castle and, by just standing there, threatened to expose her.

She grabbed him by the arm. "Get in here."

He hopped when she yanked him into the darkened room, and Sarah eased the door shut behind him. She wore the stolen uniform of a castle guard, her new hat pulled low to shadow her face. The conical helmets the guards typically wore left her face too exposed. She pushed the hat up on her forehead. Time pressed against her. Vancess would have already taken Selenna and Morholt to the dungeons, and it could only be a matter of hours before word rose to the top of the castle. Possibly much less.

"Who else knows I'm here?"

Unruffled, Secreed smoothed his gray hair back and straightened the yellow sash with the green tree of Greenshade over the front of his livery. "I assumed by your furtive movements since your arrival that you wished no one to know you were here. Therefore, no one does."

After a moment to process Secreed's words, Sarah relaxed,

grinned, and hugged him. "Thank you, Secreed. I should never have doubted you."

"My." He remained rigid but did close his arms around her at the very end of the embrace.

Sarah sat on the sturdy bed and indicated the lone leather chair for Secreed. He did not sit.

"I need to get to Keane and Megan but without Finnagel around." She glanced around herself. Just enough light crept through the cracks in the shutters for a normal person to make out shapes and figures, but Sarah's sorcerer eyes picked out the room clearly. "Can you find out when he's going to be in meetings or whatever?"

Secreed's presence solved some problems for her. Without an agent working for her, any means she might have employed to contact Keane ran a huge risk of tipping off Finnagel. If any chance existed that the old sorcerer was not the villain she thought he was, Sarah could only find out without him in the room. If he *was* as bad as she suspected, running across him before she was ready would be catastrophic. Either way, she needed to see Keane and Megan and the kids and make certain everyone was all right.

"The lord chancellor has an appointment with the newest head of the Capital Merchant's Guild in two hours. He is not expected to be overly long, but he will be out of the castle. You should have at least an hour."

"That ought to be enough time to make contact and find out what the hell Keane's been thinking. Or *if* he has."

"Indeed."

That was the closest Sarah had ever heard Secreed come to expressing a negative opinion on any royal in Greenshade. "Secreed, before you agree to this, sneaking around behind Finnagel's back is going to be dangerous. I'll be honest, I think Keane lied to me about some fairly important stuff, and I want to know why. Having my back'll mean exposing your own."

The return answer was both immediate and firm. "Milady, I do not serve Greenshade's lord chancellor. I serve her *throne*. Curious things are afoot in the castle, and someone needs to get to the bottom of it. I have done what I can, but other than saying that I believe His Majesty and Her Grace are behaving bizarrely, I seem to be at my limit. I know you to be both honest and competent, and I therefore put my faith in you."

"I get what Baroness Roselle sees in you." Sarah chuckled in the dark. "You're quite a man, Chamberlain."

Secreed's eyes widened for an instant before he returned to his typically stoic self. "She is quite the woman herself. We are... yes."

Sarah clapped a hand over her mouth to keep from gasping. Secreed had just admitted to his secret affair with the baroness, which Sarah knew had begun *years* before her rightful husband's death. They really were connecting here.

"I think we're best friends now." Sarah bounced just a bit on the heavy down mattress. "Would you like to hear about all the boys I met in Arlea and Norrik?"

"Ah, if I am to keep up this pretense, I should attend to my other duties." Secreed backed toward the door. "Perhaps another time."

Sarah stood. "Relax. It was a joke. Pretty much everyone I met was an ass, and most of them are dead. You're safe from girl talk." A thought occurred to her. "You said the *newest* head of the Capital Merchant's Guild. What happened to whatsername? The one after Barnabus?"

"There have been three guild masters of the chief guild since you left a year ago." Secreed was dry and to the point. "The other major guilds have had at least as many changes in leadership. They displeased the crown."

"What?" Even Sarah knew this wasn't how things were supposed to run. "The king doesn't have that authority. The guilds determine their own leaders. What's the Great Council saying about all this?"

"His Majesty is the War King now. He has placed the Great Council on indefinite recess." Secreed picked a speck of lint that only he could see off his sleeve. "Several of them have met sticky ends."

"Slago's teeth." Sarah shook her head. Things here were so much worse than she thought. "Don't worry. I'll get to the bottom of this. And then that's where I'll stab it."

He nodded to her. "Very good then. I'll take my leave. Fortune to you."

"You too, buddy."

Sarah closed the door and turned to face the room.

"How long have you been there?"

"Not long." Gabby walked to the wall just past the end of the bed and sat in the chair Secreed had refused. The leather made no sound. "Well, long enough to hear that you've got a little time on your hands. I thought you might be interested in a lesson."

"Now?" She tightened her hair in its leather sleeve behind her head and pushed the wooden pin back through it. "It hardly seems the time. Finnagel is still in the castle. What if he senses us? Or you? What if they find out Morholt is below?"

"The sorcerer of Greenshade remains blind, for now." Gabby cocked its head to one side. "It's been barely five years since he died, and as I understand it, he died quite a lot. He'd be doing well to sense a frog on the end of his nose. And as for your runecrafters, Selenna and Morholt are safely ensconced in their own flea-ridden chambers in the dungeons, and Prolocutor Vancess is off in search of a cup of tea. The only person who knows anything is the jailor, and I daresay he doesn't know what he knows." Gabby looked at her, clearly expecting a response. "That is to say, he is aware that there is a woman in one of his cells and a man in another, but he is unaware of who they are or what they represent. He won't be telling anyone anything."

"All right then. I guess I'd just be pacing in the dark here anyway." She leaned back against the door. "What do you want to teach me?"

"Here, you take the chair." Gabby stood and stepped aside for Sarah, who creaked loudly into the piece of furniture. "If you are to prevail against sorcerous allies, it is vitally important that you be able to understand the conditions on the ground, magically speaking, and that you be able to do so without resorting to sorcery that might draw attention to yourself."

"You mean look around for magic without screaming, 'I'm a sorcerer, explode here.'" She pointed at her own head.

"Yes. Quite." Gabby smiled, a fetching expression on its strangely asexual face. "Very droll. Now lean your head back against the wall, and close your eyes."

She tossed the hat on the bed and did as she was asked. "I hope every sorcerous duel comes with a chair and a headrest."

"Be quiet. Very few sorcerers will wither away beneath an onslaught of clever banter. Now, I want you to picture your conscious-ness as a point of light in a vast universe of nothingness, extending forever in every direction."

"Can there be ale in the universe?" One side of Sarah's mouth quirked up.

"No, there is no ale." Amused patience settled within Gabby's voice. "Everything is nothing except for you. The most important thing you can learn is how to see. Perceiving and understanding your enemy is the key to defeating him, whether by sword, spell, or diplomacy."

"This is a dumb universe." She settled into the experience, letting her attention to her body fade. "Oh yeah, this is kinda nice. I feel floaty."

"That was fast." A pause. "I want you to slow down though. This is not easy, or all the gods and sorcerers would be doing it. You need to listen to me. I never even taught this to Angrim. All right, let other images slowly take form, but don't guide them. Let them happen on their own. They will also appear as lights but different shapes and colors. For instance—"

"They're all over the place," Sarah interrupted. She jerked in the chair before relaxing again. "It's so huge." Unlike an afterimage behind lidded eyes, the spots and clouds Sarah saw fixed themselves into place. When she turned her head to look more carefully, they stayed put.

"What? No, don't make up things. Your brain will trick you into seeing things that aren't there." Gabby tutted at her. "I should have explained. What I am attempting to teach you is beyond the ability of all but the most knowledgeable gods and is extremely difficult. You can't just close your eyes and *poof*, master this ability."

"It's a map." Gabby's voice was fading as the new reality lay on top of the old. A deep blue numbness glowed dully from the ocean and seas, which helped Sarah find her bearings along the coastline. That coast filled in and up and out, becoming all of Andos.

"Oh. Well perhaps you can," Gabby said. "I'll take it as testament to your being instructed by the most knowledgeable god, though I do wish I understood how you figured it out so quickly."

"What am I looking at?" Eyes shut, Sarah turned and twisted in her seat.

"You're so smart; you tell me."

To the north, a powerful throb like the blood rushing painfully to her head radiated out of Dismon. A dim red light that hurt to look at directly glowed in Agran-ti. There were other points, some too small and weak to pick out at this distance, that fell among the vision of the continent.

The Forest Castle, where Sarah was now, stabbed at her—a bright green toothache inside her brain.

"Nope. Done with that." She jumped out of the chair, shook her arms, and paced the floor. The pains of her vision receded. "Those were places of power?"

"Yes, they were. You saw much more than I expected you to." Gabby put its hands on its hips. "And with much greater strength. At best, I expected you to see Finnagel's place. You are going to be a sorceress out of legend."

"There were two places." Sarah tried to figure out how to say what she had seen. "In the mountains. One in the Bitter Heights and one in the Little Gods. They were there but not, like they didn't want me to see them."

Gabby's eyes went round, and it blinked once. "Indeed, they did not. I suspect you already know or at least suspect this, but those were the homes of the gods. The Alerion in the Bitter Heights and the House of Gods in the Little Gods Mountains. This is really quite extraordinary. The Alir and the P'tak have hidden their refuges from, well, from everyone for millennia. And you spotted them on your first try."

Sarah pressed on her skull to massage away the muffled pounding. "Where are the Pavinn gods? Don't they get a house of headaches too?"

"The Pavinn gods are a special case." It leaned against one of the tall bedposts. "They are legion and spend most of their time in a separate space. You'd know it as the Untamed Paradise. It touches Andos in places but remains distinct."

"Like the Undergates."

"Yes. Quite like that." Gabby cocked its head again. "I need to impress upon you, Sarah, no other sorcerer can perceive in this manner. It is not as easy as you made it look, and they will want to know how you did it if they understand what you are about. There are much deeper implications to this I will need to show you, and no one else can know about it."

"Top secret, tell no one, murder everyone who finds out. I got it."

"I'm serious, Sarah. This is not a game."

"I need a new sword." Sarah unsheathed hers and lifted it up. The hand guard had been entirely sheared off on one side. "Reinar broke mine."

"I can see five suitable blades from where I'm standing. You should get ready. More time has passed than it appeared. I hope you'll be able to help your friends. I think they'll need it."

And then it faded away.

"Hunh," Sarah said as she went to the door. "Goodbye."

30

LIKE A MOTH TO THE GUILLOTINE
SARAH

Sarah slipped into the Red Room, the royal sitting room that adjoined the king and queen's private chambers. Sergeant Stath of the King's Guard stood outside with another of his men, relieved.

A gasp escaped her when she looked up at Keane and Megan.

Megan sat in a small rocking chair and knitted, her tiny hands working the needles with speed and precision. But her attention was gone. Loose brown curls fell tangled over her shoulders, and big brown eyes stared vacantly out of her pale face. Her nose bent slightly to the right where she had broken it during the Country Gate Offensive.

A ten-inch-wide strip a hundred feet long of knitted cloth sprawled in a pile at her feet, punctuated by knots where she had switched spools of thin yarn.

Keane drew a knife blade, sharpened almost out of existence, across a long whetstone that lay over the top of an anvil. To his right, a selection of daggers rested in a neat row across a tabletop, and to his left, a scatter of pommels and broken bits of ground steel blades decorated the stone floor. His normally rich brown skin had grown grayish and clammy.

But none of that was what had elicited the gasp from Sarah.

"Hello?" Keane placed the knife he had been working on atop the whetstone. "Do you have an appoint—" His head fell to one side, as if something off-balance inside his skull had tumbled over. A wide grin that did not reach his eyes spread across his off-color face.

"Sarah!" Keane stood and raised his arms. He had grown thicker in the middle over the past few years, but it suited his role as king. "Oldam's slithery sandworm, woman, you're early. What are you doing back in town already?"

Without recognition, Megan looked up from her knitting.

Keane stepped around the anvil and limped to Sarah, arms wide for a big hug. Swallowing her revulsion, she took off her hat and opened her arms to him. As he leaned in, the two-foot-long demonic insect that was controlling his actions curled tightly over his head. Sarah once watched Finnagel use these creatures, called dominance moths, to take over a tribe of trolls. No one but sorcerers could see them.

The likelihood that Finnagel's goals were truly for the good of Greenshade—as he had claimed—slipped ever closer to the open window, poised and ready to leap to its death.

As she hugged Keane, the egg-sized eyes of the moth, blue-black and bulbous, stared right into her own less than an inch away. It shifted and bit down on Keane's skull for purchase.

Not leaping away or drawing her sword or screaming for every guard in the castle took all of her will. The moths did not fully exist in this world and were only a physical threat if they unfurled their fiery wings. But they were *so gross*.

And so was Keane. He stank of old sweat and crotch.

With relief, Sarah restored her hat and released Keane, who grabbed a walking stick and put his weight on it. He carried his own wounds from that final battle against Tyrrane and her allies. It seemed that the moths only forced their thralls to obey Finnagel's commands. It did not know what Keane knew.

That she was a sorceress and could see it, for instance.

"It's so good to see you." Keane leaned on his stick with both hands. That was new. "There's all kinds of exciting news."

Good. Sarah came here intending to grill Keane about the *real* reasons she had been sent after Morholt and the runecrafters. They might be dangerous individually, but they were hardly the huge evil she was sold. And the temple? Why was the crown supporting that? If anything, the Temple of the Sky seemed worse in this new incarnation than it was back when King Eggan Rance the First originally decimated it over two hundred years ago.

"Really?" Sarah took an extra step backward. An eighteen-inch brick-red bug curled around Megan's face and hung there, washing its own eyes with moisture stolen from Megan's. "Uh, what news is that?"

"I have fashioned the tip of my spear."

"Your what now?" She forced her hands away from her weapons. "We're talking about your penis, aren't we?"

"No, Sarah, nothing so impressive as *that*." Keane shook his head. "This'll be a letdown in comparison, but I have chosen and trained one hundred of the hardest bastards in the Thirteen Kingdoms to be the vanguard of my new army. I am going to lead the invasion of Tyrrane!"

Several things occurred to Sarah simultaneously. First, this plan had obviously come from Finnagel. Second, Finnagel intended to sacrifice Keane on Tyrranean swords and make him a martyr at the same stroke, and third—and this one was the real kicker—Finnagel was well and truly her enemy. The only way this could all end was with his death.

"That's really... great." Sarah tried to smile while four sets of eyes stared at her.

"Hey," Keane's diffuse smile grew more so, "I recognize that hat. Is that Harden's old hat? The one Marbles stole? How did you get that?"

"I ran into Marbles. He was happy to give it to me."

"No shit? Harden really wanted to kill him for that." The moth plucked at the skin of Keane's face. "If you ever get tired of it, I'd love to burn it. Looks good on you though."

"Thanks? I thought you and Harden were good with one another these days." Sarah needed to get out of here.

"Oh, we are." He sat back down and picked up another blade to drag to its death across the whetstone.

"Some habits are just hard to break."

———

S arah ran to the dungeons, heedless that she might be spotted. Finnagel should still be out of the castle, and no one else would challenge her. Time poured through her fingers.

In the top level of cells where there was actual light and occasional air, Sarah entered a fifty-foot hall with barred cells cut into either side. At the left end sat Selenna, slumped against the far wall, her dress torn, dirt-stained, and bloody and her head still covered by the filthy cloth sack. The cell across from her lay barren, and sleeping figures filled the rest.

The bars of the abandoned cell felt cold in Sarah's hands, and the whole of the hallway smelled of old hay and eye-watering human waste.

Kind of like a mercenary camp. Same crowd, at any rate.

"I want to tell you first how sorry I am for Glauth's death." She only felt slightly silly addressing an empty cell. "I know it doesn't really help my case here that I was aiming for *you*, but you should know that if things had gone the way I'd wanted, Glauth would still be alive."

One of the bleary-eyed prisoners raised his head with some difficulty to glare at Sarah but dropped it again to the dirty straw.

"I have been... taken advantage of by my mentor." That was hard to say. "I let myself believe him when he told me you were dangerous." That wasn't the whole truth. "No, I let that be my excuse. When you killed—when Captain Falt *died*—I pretended what Finn said was true. But I knew it wasn't. I'm sorry. I'm so, so sorry."

Silence from the empty cell. Sarah wondered if she had misjudged the situation.

She lowered her voice. "Now the king and queen are under the control of dominance moths placed by Finnagel. He's using the moths to control them, run them like marionettes. I think I can remove the things, but while they're normally invisible, Finn will be able to see that they're gone. My only plan is to grab Keane and Megan and run. And the kids. But I'll have to do it before Finn gets back. If he's recovered his powers at all, I won't be able to confront him, and if he's summoning demons—"

Morholt stood a few feet from the bars, his dusty green leathers grimy with mud. Though she expected his sudden appearance, Sarah couldn't help but jump.

"That's a relief. I was pretty sure I was talking to some straw and a bucket."

"I can help you." Morholt's eyes narrowed, and he spoke in a whisper. "But both of us walk. Me *and* Selenna."

"If I had a dog in this fight, it's dead now." That much was true, but there was still more to bargain for. Sarah did not see anyone else obviously trying to listen in, but that did not mean much. Hopefully, they would all be gone before it mattered. "Before we start braiding flowers into each other's hair, I want to know that you'll stop trying to kill me. I'm over it. I'll never bother you again. I just want to be sure we're together here."

Morholt smiled. "Yeah, we're both on the same barmaid. For as long as we're dodging Finnagel, anyway. The orgy's over as soon as you change your mind and go crawling back to Mister Short, Dark, and Genocidal."

"I think you're safe on that score." Sarah fitted the key she had stolen from the dungeon keeper in the lock. "As soon as Finn figures out what we're doing, he's much more likely to make a kite out of my guts than give me a pat on the head."

She handed him his knife back, which she had taken when she grabbed the keys, and he slid it back into its waiting sheath.

"A guts kite sounds neat." Morholt stepped out of the cell and crossed to stand next to Selenna's. "What do you make the string out of?"

———

"I hate this plan." Sarah's voice came from the air in front of a woven depiction of a family of nobles on holiday. A relatively upbeat piece for castle art, there was barely anyone getting killed in it at all.

Sarah and Morholt stood in a tall and dimly lit ballroom surrounded by tapestries along with Volker and Shayla. The two adults had come—invisibly—to the remote chamber to be far away from prying eyes and had been overheard bickering by the children, who would not be dissuaded from following their Aunt Sarah. Morholt released the spell that hid them, and both children clapped.

Selenna was still in her cell for now. Neither Sarah nor Morholt trusted her out and about in the castle.

"The boy wants to help; let him help. It's his dad." Morholt glanced around at the life-sized figures stitched into the artwork. "I know now why you chose this place. It is *way* too creepy for normal people to want to hang out in. Unless you just like people watching you." He leered suggestively at Sarah. "You kinky thing, you."

She ignored his taunt. "I have a special affinity for this room. This was the site of the very first attempt on my life in the castle."

"I'm impressed." Morholt put his hands on his hips. "You're not kinky; you're richly bent. If I didn't hate you, I'd love you."

"Here." Sarah gave Morholt back the pasteboard card wrapped in the green silk handkerchief.

He took it without comment and slid it into his own pack.

Shayla pulled on Morholt's hand. "What's kinky mean?"

Sarah winced, and Morholt knelt next to Shayla and looked her in the eye.

"It's when a mommy and daddy love each other very much. And sometimes they love each other from behind, or with horses and fruit, or even with ladders and ropes and about a dozen maids—"

"Here." Shayla twisted and tossed something that glinted in the flickering candlelight to her brother.

"Get away from my sister, pervert." Volker held Morholt's knife, unwavering as a Darrishman's disdain, in a straight line pointed at the runecrafter's right eye.

Sarah's mouth fell open. Laughter threatened and she tried to cover a grin with one hand. "Better do what he says. Remember who his parents are."

Hands in the air and a thoughtful expression on his face, Morholt stood and stepped back. "This kinda proves my point. These two can obviously take care of themselves. And we're just asking them to bring Keane back here. No reason it should be dangerous at all."

"No, there's a better way." Sarah paced to the other side of the room and came face-to-face with a depiction of Varrinn Hubrane, the first Hubrane duke and the man who lost the crown of Greenshade back to the Rances. In doing so, he had avoided a civil war that would have torn the nation to pieces.

How would a man like *that* have handled this?

"What if we went to Finnagel disguised with your illusions?" This didn't seem like a good idea either, but she wanted to see if it led anywhere. Too bad she couldn't ask Keane.

"Possible." Morholt's hushed voice was swallowed by the hanging stitchwork. "But who would we be? And what would we say to him? 'Hey, Finn. Howzabout we cancel the big kill-all-the-runecrafters dance and you sit on the end of this broadsword?'"

"I don't know." Sarah turned her back to the first Hubrane duke, raising her arms and letting them fall again. "Maybe we could disguise ourselves *as* Keane and Megan, and then we—where's Volker?"

Shayla stood, arms crossed and eyes narrow, a general in the field with her troops sent away to battle the enemy. Secretive wheels turned behind her eyes.

"Oh, him?" Morholt grinned sheepishly. "He took off to get the king the second your back was turned. I figured it was safer to just let him go. What with the knife and all." His eyes went wide, and he shrank against the wall as Sarah stalked across the dark room.

"You figured wrong."

———

Three-quarters of an hour later, the heavy wooden door creaked open.

"C'mon, Daddy." Volker pulled a disheveled Keane into the room by the hand. "Shayla says she's gonna tell Aunt Sarah that Mister Finnagel did magic stuff to your brain. We gotta stop her."

Keane limped into the room and peered into the gloom. "Shayla, are you in here, girl? We're taking a little trip to the top of the tower now."

Quietly, Sarah cast one of her *tiny portals* directly in front of Keane's head. The dominance moth reared up, agitated by the unseen magic.

"Hey, King Cradle Robber, remember me?" A green blaze flared and lit Morholt's face and shoulders with a touch more drama than was necessary. He chuckled.

Keane raised his walking stick and slid a thin sword out of it. He spun left to face the runecrafter. The moth jerked but not enough to prevent part of it from passing into the *portal.*

Sarah snapped it shut.

Half of the dominance moth bounced off Keane's shoulder on its way to the ground, while the other half fell in front of Sarah.

Morholt startled. Apparently, the things became visible when you murdered them.

"Wow. *That's* what those little monsters look like?" Morholt scrunched up his face and turned his head. "No wonder you look like shit, Your Roach-Nest-ness. Hey, was *your* roach kissing *her* roach when you and Megan were—"

"Ow." Keane gripped his head. "Oldam's gritty sharts, my head feels like it's full of rusty dagger blades. What's going on? Am I in the castle? Sarah, is that you?"

"Daddy!" Both children ran to Keane and hugged his legs. Keane leaned down and hugged them back, careful not to stab anyone with the sword cane.

"Shayla, I assume it was your idea for your brother to run off like that?" Sarah placed her arms behind her back and tried to look stern.

"Yes, ma'am." She tried to hide behind her daddy. "Mister Finnagel's fingers were in Daddy's brains telling him what to do ever since you left us. The only way to make Daddy come here was to say we figgered it all out." She hid a smile behind Keane's leg. "And I did."

"It worked, and it was smart." Sarah scowled. "Don't ever do it again."

"Yes, ma'am."

With one hand massaging his injured hip, Keane stood straight. "And I return to 'what's going on?' What the fuck is—sorry kids, don't say that word—what is *that* thing?" He pointed at the portion of dominance moth that lay at his feet. "And why do I feel like a prize hog the morning after slaughtering day?"

"Daddy said a bad word." Volker was laughing and beaming up at his father.

"When are we getting Mommy?" Shayla stood by the door and peeked into the hall outside.

"Just a moment, Little Pie." Sarah turned to Keane. "What was the last thing you remember?"

"I'm trying not to think about it, but my children were shorter."

That was what Shayla meant. Sarah left Treaty Hill just over a year ago. Had Keane and Megan been Finnagel's pawns for that long?

Sarah shook her head as she tried to take in everything Finnagel was up to. "There's more to the story than this, but the short of it is that Finn has his powers back, or most of them anyway. You know he was resurrecting the Temple of the Sky, but now we know it wasn't to let people pray again. He's using it to solidify power across all of Andos. He's not just controlling the masses; he's using money and loans to take the children of the richest families and control the wealth in all Thirteen Kingdoms." She took a deep breath.

"Also, he intends to invade Tyrrane and get you killed in the process."

"And he put a bug in your brain." Morholt leaned against a

tapestry and crossed his legs. "It made you stupid and mean." He smiled. "I don't think anybody noticed."

"At least Morholt is still invisible and silent," Keane said, glancing askance at the not-at-all-invisible Morholt, "since no one here wants to listen to his bullshit." He raised his sword cane menacingly.

White teeth showed through Morholt's ginger beard. "Give a guy a little power and a job in management, and he loses all sense of humor. Hey Sarah, was he this sensitive when he was a mercenary?"

Volker laughed louder. "Daddy said another bad word."

"Mommy's gonna be mad," Shayla joined in. "We should get her now."

"I agree." Keane picked up the cane portion of his walking stick and sheathed the blade inside it. "On a scale of everything's rosy to fucking typical, how screwed are we?"

Despite herself, Sarah chuckled. "Definitely on the typical end of the scale. Megan's still got one of those things on her skull, and I've got to go rescue some runecrafters from Finn's crazy temple dogs. We need to fix you and her without Finn realizing, and then you need to stop the Tyrranean attack and not die in the process." She looked at Morholt. "Did I forget anything?"

"I didn't hear anything about fabulous riches for the handsome and well-hung ginger-haired hero."

"You're getting ex-wives and girlfriends for Oldam Reave." Sarah raised an eyebrow. "If you don't like your present, you can always give it to someone else."

"That holiday is always such a letdown." Morholt twirled a curl of red hair around his finger. "I *wanted* a wagon. With a prostitute in it. Speaking of, we should go grab Selenna out of the dungeon before we flee."

"What's the next step?" Keane asked. "I assume no one can see the brain bugs. We just have to make sure Megan and I keep acting the same."

"Finn'll be able to see." Sarah's crooked half smile returned. "But Morholt here has an idea for that."

"Sit down, bughead." Morholt stepped forward and shooed

Volker and Shayla away. "Scoot, kiddies. It's time for the *grown-ups* to do something stupid."

"Did you kill Marbles?" Keane sat and raised an eyebrow at Sarah.

"What?"

In answer to Sarah's question, Keane pointed at his own head to indicate the hat on hers.

"He's not dead, just a little dented. I already told you we'd talk about it later."

"Can everyone please sit still and shut the hell up?" Morholt stood behind Keane and gripped him by the shoulders. As soon as the king settled down, Morholt began crafting his runes.

Sarah knew the idea of what Morholt was doing, but watching him *do* it was both fascinating and bewildering. She heard snatches of her language lessons with Gabby fly past, and following a hunch, she closed her eyes and observed the casting in the manner Gabby taught her when searching for places of power.

Letters of glowing gold and silver swirled in circles through the air, creating larger and more complex patterns. A silent symphony of fire.

She could now *see* the magic.

Watching nothing more real than Morholt's imagination, three bands of differing thicknesses and widths appeared in the air in front of him. Runic letters glowed on the bands in godly Metzoferran as well as its dark sister language, Kirrokoan. A fourth band held all of them in place and governed their rotations relative to each other.

This would be the engine that kept the scam running without Morholt. If it worked.

He placed a fist through the middle of the four rings, twisted it a half turn and, with a flare that Sarah could only see in her mind, started all of them spinning. But that was not completely correct. The power had not come from Morholt but from something beneath his shirtsleeve.

She would ask about that another time.

Almost imperceptible rings appeared above the first four, no thicker than hair. She could not even tell how many there were. They were a cloud. And then they were a dominance moth.

"Ew." Keane wrinkled his nose.

"Now." Morholt reached out.

"Right." She drew her dagger and made a shallow cut across the heel of her left hand. She pressed the wound against Morholt's outstretched hand.

He waved it in a circle over the ersatz dominance moth, which followed his movements with its head.

"Where'd it go?" From the floor, Keane had watched the entire procedure, though Sarah could only imagine what it must have looked like from his perspective. "Is it invisible now?"

"Theoretically, the moth is now only visible to sorcerers." Morholt stood back. "Hill Fury? You still see it?"

"I do. Let's get it on his head and find Megan."

"All right." Morholt made a few more motions and attached the unreal assemblage to the top of Keane's head. To Sarah, it looked like the dead dominance moth had resurrected and crawled on Keane's skull. "Let's hope the blood part really does make it visible to all sorcerers and not just you. Oh, wait."

He made a motion as if tightening a shoelace, and the evil-looking moth hunkered down close to Keane's head, gripping his scalp. "Less chance of him fouling the spell if it's low profile," Morholt said.

"I don't like it on Daddy's head." Shayla, frowning, turned her head away.

Sarah, Keane, and Morholt exchanged looks.

Keane's brow shot up. "How...?"

"We'll unpack that later," Sarah said. "Right now, we need to find Megan and bring her back here. Finnagel has got to be back in the castle already."

"I'll go." Keane clambered awkwardly to his feet, favoring his good hip. "Ow. No one will question me."

"First, no." Morholt shook his head. "That thing on your head, which you cannot discern in any way, is incredibly fragile. I need to explain all the ways you'll wreck it before... There, you've already destroyed it. Sarah, I'll need more blood."

In the end, Volker collected his mother much the same way he had his father, though with Moon by his side and Sarah skulking in the shadows behind him to make sure everything went as planned.

"I understand," Megan said soon afterward as she pulled greasy strands of hair out of her face. Dominance moths were not big on the personal hygiene of their hosts. "Don't let anything touch our heads. Don't scratch. No hats. Should be easy enough... *Keane*."

"Sorry." He lowered his hand from his hair.

Morholt held out his arm to Sarah again. "More blood."

After yet another casting, Sarah sat cross-legged on the floor in front of Volker and Shayla. "I'm headed out on a secret mission, you understand? *No one* can know about it. No one at all."

"We know," Volker answered.

"We're not *babies*," Shayla added.

Sarah smiled. "Good. That's good. Because I'll be coming back with two whole crates of pirate candy, and if I find out that anyone ratted me out, I'll eat it all myself."

Volker stood straight and puffed out his little chest. "We'll be good, Aunt Sarah."

She tousled his hair. "Don't make promises you can't keep. Just don't tell anyone I was here."

"I'll watch him." Shayla's cunning eyes were serious, her gaze level and flat. She never joked about pirate candy.

"See that you do." Sarah gathered both kids in a big hug. As always when she held Keane's children, she felt her being expand to encompass them as if they were part of her physically—as if they were her heart.

Moon licked her in the face.

"I love you, Aunt Sarah." Shayla kissed her on one cheek, followed seconds later by Volker on the opposite side.

"I love you guys too." She released them. "Now lemme go. We all have lives to save."

On Sarah's way out, Megan pulled her aside.

"Thank you for doing this. The kids, they've been alone all this time. I can't imagine what might have happened to them while we were... whatever we were."

Sarah watched the illusion of Megan's dominance moth walk in a circle around the top of her head like a tiny dog before settling into her hair. "I think it might be more appropriate to worry about what *they* might have happened *to*. They've been insufficiently supervised for what, a year now? And neither of them are exactly trouble free."

"I think I'll just be happy that no one is dead and the castle is still standing." Megan blew at an errant strand of hair. "Now that I can't, all I want to do is scratch my head. I can't even bathe without giving away the ruse."

"We'll figure it out." In reality, Sarah had no clear path ahead. Finnagel was not a beatable foe. She would have to find something he wanted.

Or something he was scared of.

31

IT WAS A JOLLY CHICKEN, THEN WE COOKED IT

MORHOLT

lthough Selenna's mouth was gagged and her hands bound behind her back, Morholt couldn't help glancing over his shoulder at her every chance he got. Out here on the streets of Treaty Hill, she could cause him untold pain in his hole with a simple raised word, and he might not even realize it was happening.

It wasn't so much her power that shifted Morholt to the terrified side of caution, it was her pique. While Sarah and the temple knights had technically burned down her life, he had not managed to help that much, and it was his fault she had been in that position to begin with.

And now here he was working *with* Sarah.

They were disguised by Morholt's illusions as three nondescript pedestrians, though Morholt entertained himself by turning Sarah into a burly, overweight man.

The dirty river of humanity passed them by, and buildings, older as they went, hung over the street, casting shade from the afternoon sun.

"That was an amazing use of magic back there," Sarah said to

Morholt. "I could never have done anything so delicate. I'm not even sure Finnagel could have done anything like that. How did you do it?"

Morholt considered the question. Knowing how he did what he did wouldn't really help her, and he found himself wanting to extend this feeling of the two of them not wanting to murder each other. "Sorcerers pull ambient energy from their surroundings, right?"

"Right." Sarah nodded. "It's the frictional energy between universes that gets suffused everywhere. That's what makes magic possible."

"Yeah, but the ability to pull that energy is something only sorcerers can do." Morholt held up his hands and mimed clawing unseen energy out of the air. "It's what makes you special."

"Then how do you use magic at all?" One brow, the one without the old claw mark through it, went up on Sarah's forehead.

"Think about it like this." Morholt tapped a finger against his chin. "Sorcerers are born in a pond. They live in the pond. Anytime they want water, they just lean down and grab a drink."

"That's convenient."

Selenna made a *mrphr* kind of sound and rolled her eyes.

"Sure. If you're one of the happy few who get to live in the pond and drink the water they pee in."

"Wait." Sarah grabbed Morholt's shoulder and stopped him in the street. "I get the pond is the ambient magic, but what's the pee? Why is there pee in the water?"

Morholt smirked. "The pee is your place of power. It accumulates around you and makes your water nasty to any other sorcerers who come to call. You love it though."

"I feel like this metaphor may have biased undertones." Sarah released Morholt, and they resumed their walk.

Nearby, an argument broke out over what sounded to Morholt like the price versus quality of baby rats. Were these people intentionally raising rats as food?

On second thought, he was kinda hungry.

"Now people who were not lucky enough to sit in stinky pools and drink their own piss all day have to figure out a way to get their own water." He checked on Selenna again. She did not look happy, but Morholt did not think she wanted to murder him. "So runecrafters make a tunnel that bypasses the sorcerers' pissy ponds and goes straight to the river where all the clean water comes from. Every time I cast a spell, the first part of it is to make a new tunnel to the river, or specifically, the space between universes where the metaphysical friction that powers all magic is created."

"*Mmrrph.*"

"Does that mean runecrafters aren't affected by sorcerers' places of power?" Sarah's tone was light, but it was an obvious ruse.

"Yeesss…" Morholt had not intended to be that literal, but he had been, and Sarah picked up on it. "A place of power calcifies ambient magic, but runecrafters don't use ambient magic, so it doesn't much matter. Sorcerers are still more powerful overall because runecrafters tend to specialize. We're able to craft more delicate magics, but the trade-off is that we can't handle as much raw power."

"What about the illusions back at the castle? How did you keep them going after we left?"

"That was an experiment." He had not wanted to admit it at the time, but it hardly mattered now. "I created a self-sustaining tunnel out of illusions to power the spells indefinitely—or until the king stuffs his head in the dog's ass and destroys them."

"But illusions aren't real." Sarah's brows knit together. "How can you make a construct that pulls power like that out of something that doesn't exist? It doesn't make sense."

"Nope. This seems to be a quirk of illusory magic. Illusions are made of my imagination, just like the runes all runecrafters use." Morholt rubbed his flat stomach. "But I am hungry now, and imagining food in my belly is not going to help."

"We're almost there." Sarah stood straight and scanned the milling crowds of people on the street, all in a hurry to get somewhere. "That's Magda's Cross. The Jolly Chicken is right around the corner." Sarah's crooked smile returned. "Of all the places in Treaty

Hill for the Free Hand to pick as a rendezvous spot, you picked the one place that the king and I both frequent. That's some spectacularly bad planning, that is."

"I didn't pick it." Morholt stepped around a fruit cart ambling across the cobbles and narrowly avoided a scattered pile of horse dung. "This was Harden's choice, back when he ran the Free Hand. He knew the owner or something. I never took the time to change it."

The warming day lifted the baked-in smells off the street, which did little to improve Morholt's mood. Say what you would about the Undergates and the country of Savach within it where the humans lived, at least it was cleaner than up here.

Of course, no one was trying to kill him in the surface world. Morholt stopped that thought and chuckled. *Lots* of people were trying to kill him in the surface world. It was just easier not to take it personally since none of them were related to him. Trying to kill his exes, on the other hand, hit closer to home.

He couldn't believe Raven wanted to go back.

They settled in, and Morholt ordered for himself and Selenna. The menu was mostly fish, which Morholt thought disreputable for a place named the Jolly Chicken. Across the table, Sarah glanced at a loud patron sitting alone with several empty ale tankards in front of him who yelled at the barkeep for more. His disheveled gray hair, beard, and threadbare clothes along with a bit of flab painted a picture of a career tavern seat-warmer. Sarah's eyes narrowed, and her jaw clenched ever so slightly, betraying her own feelings.

"Man Hands, I want you to know something." Morholt drummed his fingers on the worn tabletop. "I have had firsthand experience with Finnagel which I very nearly did not survive. Although I'd still like to knock you in the teeth with a rusty crowbar—and I can't *believe* I'm going to say this—I understand how you could have done what you did to Glauth."

"*Mmrrrmmph.*"

"And Selenna."

One of Sarah's brows lifted. "How are you going to let her eat?"

"Move the gag up over her eyes." Morholt shrugged. "She has to be able to see her victims as well as communicate with them."

Sarah did so, placing her hand over Selenna's eyes until the transfer was complete.

"Now there's spit all over my face." Selenna's mouth went down until it looked as if she might cry. "I hate you both so much."

Conversation dwindled when their plates arrived. Morholt found himself astounded at the not-awfulness of the food. The fish was not even overcooked and was liberally slathered in some kind of salty orange butter that he could not get enough of.

"Vancess and I are heading to Kos next to capture a woman named Romi," Sarah said to Morholt after the food disappeared. "I have to keep up appearances as long as I can. If we can't figure out a way to deal with Finn before Vancess sniffs us out, we'll have the whole Temple of the Sky down on our heads." The big woman took a drink of her ale and placed the jack back on the table. "I know you knew this Romi. She meant something to you. Sorry. That was creepy, but the temple has been keeping tabs on you for a long time. I'll do everything I can to slow us down so you get there first. Maybe I can put them on the wrong trail altogether. If I can't, don't attack. We'll work out a different plan. Even with me helping, I don't think the entire Free Hand could beat Vancess and his knights." She pushed back her chair.

"Before you go"—Morholt reached out and put a hand on her forearm, stopping her—"thanks for helping us."

"Thanks for helping me." Sarah smiled and pulled the tall hat with the wide brim back down. "Together we have a chance to stop Finnagel before he kills all your exes—or whatever it is they do to people at the Dovenhouse—and takes over. He has a really bad attitude toward normal people."

"Yeah, thanks." Selenna sat stiff-backed, facing straight ahead. None of the other patrons saw the blindfold. "I really appreciate the two of you coming in and burning my life down."

A plump woman in a baggy, stained blouse and a dirty skirt entered and called excitedly out to the gray-headed seat-warmer, whose face lit up at the sight of her. She ran to him, and the pair embraced with obvious affection. She sat next to him.

Sarah's eyes widened, surprised, before her face settled into sadness, as she watched the couple talk, smile, and gaze happily at one another.

To Morholt, Sarah's expression betrayed longing. Maybe she was not the hard-assed monster the stories made her out to be. Maybe she was just like anyone, doing the best she could, wanting to love and be loved. Although now that they were working together, a hard-assed monster was more what Morholt needed.

"What about Catlia?" Morholt released Sarah's arm, surprised by the warmth and hardness of it. "Have you heard anything?"

Sarah refocused on Morholt. "She was the first captured. She's been in the Dovenhouse for months now. Let's get Romi out of harm's way, and then I'll help you get Catlia back. If I can't, Dovenhouse is in Arlea, north of Sejent."

"You know, I actually married her." The memories made him feel warm and ashamed all at once. "She was always scared. Broken even. Teaching her runecrafting was supposed to help, but it didn't."

"I'm sorry. But that's not today's problem. For now, we're focused on saving people. Right?" One side of Sarah's mouth played upward in a cockeyed smile. "I've been wanting to ask, now that we're friends, what's with the card? What's that weird dog thing painted on it?"

"Would you believe she Sees the future?" Morholt pulled April out of his pack and smiled at the ratty silk that wrapped the card. "Or she used to before *someone* broke the future off from the world. Now she mostly tells bad jokes."

"Sorry."

"That's all right. See you in Kos, and good luck."

As he watched her leave, Morholt thought about the women whose lives he had imperiled by teaching them runecrafting: Catlia, secretive and fearful; Glauth, brash and passionate; Selenna, distrustful and girlish; and Romi, perhaps the only woman who loved him back the way he loved her, before he ran away.

He picked the cloth-wrapped card up off the table and slid it into his shirt. The rest of the Free Hand would be here soon, and then they would fetch Romi in Kos before heading to the Dovenhouse for Catlia and what's his name, Selenna's husband.

Morholt was a coward, and he knew it, but there would be no more running away.

32

NEVER BARGAIN WITH A DEMON KING
KING BRANNOK

Brannok read the final words aloud... and nothing happened. He glared at the small pages but knew the problem was in his visualizations, not his pronunciations.

The copper and silver rings in the floor of the small stone room made one-third of the spell. The second part was a ring of runes that Brannok was to hold in his imagination, spinning them slightly. This was the part that kept tripping him up.

Reading one set of words in an unknown language while picturing another set in your mind was trickier than he thought.

He returned to the outer library and sat down at the table. Cold and the smell of dust both pulled at him, leaching his body of warmth and moisture.

When cast correctly, the spell would summon a demon from the Undergates into the copper ring. Brannok would enter the ring and kill the demon with a blade, which would soak up the demon's blood. Thus prepared, Brannok would be able to kill Angrim with the bloodied knife.

Or that's how everything should have worked if Brannok had been able to do the damn ritual properly.

He cut a piece of cheese and poured himself another glass of pale-yellow wine. There was no need to get angry. Indeed, he was uncharacteristically calm. He had time here. This was a matter of practice and discipline, things he was well acquainted with.

Brannok held the wine glass up to the candlelight and turned it slowly in his flesh hand. In the yellow glow, he could see rings of runes, glowing with their own fire.

Of course. How simple.

He stood and walked away from the table, leaving the red leather-bound book behind. He had been too distracted trying to read the words, physically *seeing* the words, to hold the image in his mind.

With confidence born of inspiration and two bottles of wine, Brannok brought the image to bear, set it alight, and began to speak. The words spilled out of him as the image grew more defined and burned all the brighter. He shouted the last lines, squinting against a glow that was not there, and bellowed laughter into the tiny space. Heat buffeted him, and the intermingled smells of honey and rotten meat filled his nostrils.

Three sets of eyes blinked back at him.

"Hey guys, look at the newest suicide." The demon who spoke was taller than the other two, nearly Brannok's height, with stony gray skin and a huge beak like a vulture's. It flexed oversized taloned hands.

"I gets tha feet. I said it first." This was from a creature the size and rough shape of an ale barrel with a tooth-ringed mouth that could have swallowed a fully grown doe whole. "Lookit. It keeps 'em in boots. Soft and squishy feet. Them's the best."

The third thing, humanoid but no more than two-and-a-half feet tall, creased its already evilly disposed face and sighed. "I never asked to be part of a triumvirate being. And if I had, I never would have signed on with a fuckwit like *you*."

The barrel's mouth did something that might have been a frown or a horrifying leer. Brannok could not tell. Whichever, it interjected another winning smell of decay into the room, presumably the thing's breath.

"Hush, boys." Vulture had not taken its eyes off Brannok once.

"No need to bicker. Not when lunch has so kindly called us to eat it. Brambleknot, you didn't want the feet anyway."

"I thought there was only one demon." Brannok frowned at his three new guests.

"Nice." Brambleknot reached behind himself and began a long scratching session in the crack of its ass that left its eyes closed and a smile on its face. "This jackass is gonna tell *us* the rules."

"You can't believe *you're* the first king in Tyrrane to try and kill the Anger." Vulture's face twisted into a maniacal grin, impressive for a monster with a beak for a mouth. "I've eaten a dozen like you. Proud, stupid men who think they control the world. You don't even know what the world *is*. C'mon. Get it over with. Let us put you out of all of our miseries."

The little leather tome warned against listening to the lies of demons. It even referred to several other volumes in the library with more extensive information on them.

On its hands—and knees?—the barrel scooted forward to the edge of the rings and extended half a dozen red ropy tongues to lick at the floor.

Brannok turned and strode from the room. There was something he needed upstairs.

"Nice going, dickface," Brambleknot said to Vulture, causing Brannok to pause in the library to overhear. "You scared it off. Now we have to wait until the next asshole finds this place just because you thought it'd be funny to make this one fill his pants before you ate him. Ten thousand years I've had you growing on my ass like a carbuncle, and I *still* don't understand your tastes."

Twenty minutes later, Brannok returned with a heavy hunting crossbow in his good hand and a quiver of bolts slung over the wrist of his other.

"This is new." Vulture's attention lazed over Brannok and his weapon.

Thunk.

Hit dead center, the barrel squealed and ran in circles around the inside of the ring, ejecting pink foam from its wound, its mouth, and its hindquarters. As it ran and spewed, it deflated until it could no longer support itself. It fell over, pawed the ground weakly, and died.

The acrid smell of exploded weasel lay heavy in the room.

"You candy-cunted smear of nut cheese!" Brambleknot's mouth distended as he screamed, revealing rows of stumpy crushing teeth. His shoulders bulked, and he grew to almost four feet. "Silver-tipped bolts? Where'd a shit-covered cretin like *you* learn about *that*?"

"Books."

Having an actual head, Brambleknot gave Brannok a much better target to aim at than the barrel did. He cocked the weapon against the ground, loaded it, and raised it.

Thunk.

The creature shot backward, its skull a crumpled sheet of burning tissue folding in on itself. *This is going even better than I thought it would.*

"Poor Brambleknot. Poor Donker. I won't miss either of them." Vulture dragged a hand across its bony chest, making scraping noises with its lengthening talons. "But it won't help you. I know the spell in that little red book. You have to kill *me* with your blade, and to do that, you have to come in *here*. Use that"—it pointed at the crossbow —"and all your trouble will have been for nothing."

Though he could not tell what it was, something between Vulture's legs was growing. There was a wicked barb on the end, and the liquid it dripped onto the floor wisped away in whirls of steam that left pits in the stone.

That did not seem pleasant.

Brannok stood in the crossbow's stirrup and pulled the cocking lever that slid the cord into place. He was not listening, but he did acknowledge that the creature talked too much. Most of his thoughts roiled with the closeness of his objectives. Giddiness surprised him.

"What's your point, here?" Vulture's voice went up an octave. "You can't have summoned us just to shoot us. You get nothing from that. Hey, I can make other kinds of deals, too, y'know. Any ladies you've had your eye on? I hear that daughter of yours is quite the force of nature, if you know what I mean."

Brannok lifted the crossbow and rested it between his forearm and his hip. He fitted another bolt into the groove. His hand and blade shook with excitement.

"I know what Angrim's really afraid of, huh?" It held its talons out in front of itself as if to ward Brannok away. The Dead God. Hey, you ever hear of that? Go look for it in those books. You'll find it. I'll wait."

It would be a world without Angrim.

Thunk.

"*Aaaagh!*" Vulture, the thick haft of a silver-tipped bolt protruding from its crotch, screamed and grabbed at the shaft, eliciting more cries of pain.

Brannok threw the crossbow aside as he plunged forward and planted his bladed hand into Vulture's chest again and again. Black blood splattered them both.

The creature clutched at Brannok's arm, lacerating it shoulder to wrist with its filthy talons, but it might as well have been trying to hold back a storm.

Vulture's legs gave way, and Brannok drove the blade a final time, riding the demon to the ground. He left it in Vulture's chest, standing over the foul body.

How long does this part take? "Oh."

All around Brannok's blade, the demon fell away, turning to dust as he watched. The squat dagger at the end of his arm grew heavier, and more and more of Vulture vanished. In seconds, the creature was nothing more than a bloodless pile of filth on the floor.

Brannok stood and stared at the dagger at the end of his arm. Dark brown along the straight edge, the blade faded to a deep orange like the breast of an orven. It practically *sang* with death.

"I shall call you Happiness," Brannok said to his blade. "The killer of Anger."

A smile spread across Brannok's lips, and a chuckle escaped its prison deep in his chest. He tried to regain his composure, but a wild titter flew out of him and would not stop. It turned to uncontrollable, full-throated laughter, and why not? He gave up trying to shove this expression of the only real joy he ever experienced back inside himself as the tears rolled down his blotchy face.

Gasps hitched under his ribs, and Brannok fell to the floor and went over into the pile of demon dust, coating his mail and naked arms. A lifetime of suppressed elation threatened to break him in half. His laughter became screams, and he arched off the stone, unable to breathe.

It would make a certain kind of sense, he decided, as he coughed air out but could not draw it back in, that after everything he had suffered, jubilation would be the thing to do him in. But even while spots covered his vision, he exulted. Jasmayre could still carry the blade. And she would be *free*.

Finally, he calmed.

Brannok pulled himself against the wall next to the empty cabinet and rested there. He pulled in long, slow breaths of cold catacomb air, the smile still on his face. He felt cleansed. Renewed. Purposeful.

Deadly.

33

WELL, LOOK AT YOU
MORHOLT

That's not it." The imp in the card fidgeted and stared upward. "Don't go, I've almost got it."

"Little pressed for time here, Bean." Morholt stood on a wide and dusty path between twisty broad-trunked olive trees festooned with white and yellow flowers. "Kos is the smallest country in the Thirteen Kingdoms, and we already know we're close. We just need a direction."

Yet more flowers in purples and golds grew on the sunlit ground between the trees, soaking up the warm yellow light and waving hello in the cool breeze.

It was as far from a snow-covered night in in the Grim Pines as Morholt could imagine. A bit further behind, the rest of the Free Hand waited in the shade while he communed with April.

"No. Wait! I've got it." April hopped from foot to foot. "Right. Why did the farmer and his daughter take *two* carriages to market?"

Morholt couldn't help but smile. "I don't know, Bean. Why *did* the farmer and his daughter take two carriages to market?"

"Because one of them was a—did I say carriages? I meant wagons." April's tiny black eyes scrunched as she thought. "That's not the way it goes. I'll try again."

"Let's think on that one and get back to it next time. All right?"

"All right," April agreed. "Keep going down this road and turn south for about a mile. Everything that way belongs to Romi. You can't miss it."

"Why are you smiling, you scamp?" Morholt made April to be good-natured, but she seemed especially happy this particular afternoon.

"I just like Romi, is all." April swayed side to side as she said this, like an eager yet shy six-year-old. "She was really nice to me. I miss her."

"You'll see her soon. I promise." Morholt wrapped the card and placed it in his new pack. It was a lighter leather than his old one, and he didn't think it matched the faded green of his armor as well. He stood and waved to his friends—when had he started thinking of them that way?—and waited for them to catch up.

———

"This may be the best thing I have ever seen." Reinar stood with his hands on his hips, staring out at the dozen or so field hands pulling vines off the trunks of much smaller olive trees. "And I've seen Queen Maarika naked."

"Does King Wagnersen know you were spying on his wife?" Ameli poked Reinar in the ribs.

"She was five and I was four." Reinar's brilliant white teeth gleamed out of his beard. "I doubt it would bother His Majesty overmuch. Trust me when I tell you this is much better."

Raven tilted her head to one side, observing the hands at work. "Why are they so much more... muscly?"

"And tan." Selenna crossed her arms and cocked a hip. "It's a very good look. Despite the raw material." She had stitched her inappropriately fine dress and refused to replace it with anything they might purchase on the road. So far, she honored her oath not to subvert the wills of any of the mercenaries.

"You people are a riot." Morholt scowled and pointed down the hill at the big house amongst the trees. Rolling hills of rich green grass surrounded the big single story, and it faced a wood across a wide front garden, just beginning to turn yellow in the oncoming summer. "She's down there. I'm sure you'll have plenty of time to ogle later."

"Morholt?" Sabni jogged up to walk next to Morholt as they descended the hill. "I thought I understood your telling of the Lady Romi's abilities, but now that I have seen them for myself, I find I am confused again."

"She makes people." Morholt let out a sigh. Of all his exes, this was the one he least—and most—wanted to see. "Anyone she has seen, able to do anything she has witnessed them doing. Or just anything *she* knows how to do. Apparently, she thinks it's funny to have me tending her olive orchards."

"And this is my confusion." Sabni's forehead wrinkled up. "These men in the fields, they do not look like you. They *do* look like you, but they are not thin and pale. They are healthy."

Morholt directed a flat look at Sabni. "She must've made these a while ago. They just look like people who've been working in the fields a while. It's not a mystery."

"They look like Holt would if he'd ever done a day's work in his life." Raven laughed and danced away down the hill. "So, you know, a fantasy."

"They can accomplish any feat your Romi has seen you do?" Sabni phrased the question without bias, but his eyes went wide for a fraction of a second. The thought frightened him. "They can use your magics?"

"No, runecrafting happens mostly in your head. You can't actually see it." Morholt patted the Darrishman on the shoulder, feeling awkward. "Also, her copies don't have much thinking power. They just do whatever she tells them. You need to be able to think to runecraft."

"Then why make copies of you to tend fields?" Ameli raised a brow and waved a hand to indicate the entire orchard. "Sure, it's funny, because you're, y'know, *you*. Not exactly prime farmhand material. But if it were my farm, I'd pick guys who were already big and strong, like Reinar here, not a weedy little twig man I'd have to train up. It's just not practical." Her eyes slid sideways to Morholt. "No offense."

"None taken." Morholt shrugged. "Given that her creations replicate physical performance, I'd imagine that farming was a secondary consideration."

"Huh?" Ameli's brow went higher.

"He's talking about the size of his dick," Raven said. She pushed her unruly black hair out of her face, darker even than the black leathers she wore.

"Oh." Ameli's puzzled expression faded. An instant later, she wrinkled her freckled nose in revulsion. "*Oh.* That was more than I needed to know."

Reinar's laughter rolled over the fading green hills.

Ten minutes later, Morholt stood on Romi's broad porch and stared at her door. Behind him, the Free Hand stood in the sunshine and laughed behind their hands.

All he had to do was knock. Why was *that* so hard? Glauth had wanted him dead, and talking to her was easy. Of course, he had been hoping she might decide to forgive him and fuck him, but he had always known it wasn't likely.

He glanced over his shoulder.

Selenna was the prettiest of his exes but also the shallowest. Walking in and yanking her out of her cushy life just seemed the most humane thing to do. Really it was unfair *not* to rescue her when he was going to so much trouble for everyone else.

Acknowledging what a dick he was to Selenna did nothing to help him knock on the door in front of him.

And then there was poor Catlia, languishing in whatever horrors the Dovenhouse held even as he stood here. She had always been fragile, frightened. Morholt thought that giving her runecrafting would give her confidence enough to be happy. But her abilities were too strong. They scared her more. And the fear she always carried turned inward.

Romi's door remained. A planter hung to one side with blue-eyed red flowers spilling out of it.

"Knock on the fucking door!" Raven, ever helpful, shouted from the yard.

Morholt lifted his fist.

The door opened, and there stood Romi. Almond-shaped Pavinn eyes narrowed and thin Andosh lips set, her straight brown hair streaked by the sun. She looked older than he remembered but in the best possible way, still lean and ropy but wise now, too.

"C'mere, asshole." Romi reached out and grabbed Morholt by the collar to pull him to her. She held him fast. He melted inside. Eventually, he held her back.

She pushed him away and held him out at arm's length. Happy tears ran down her smiling face. "You look like shit. Do you ever stop anywhere long enough to eat?"

At least now he understood why he had been so scared to knock. He had not still been in love with any of the others. Even his feelings for Glauth had been rooted in sex and... well, sex. He had cared deeply for her but nothing like this.

"Romi, you've got to gather your things. I'm here to—"

"You're here to rescue me from the temple knights that are on their way here to kill or capture me. Don't stare at me like an idiot. I hear things."

Morholt closed his mouth. "Uh, yeah. I guess."

She leaned over and lifted the strap of a canvas bag onto her shoulder. A straw hat to keep the sun off went on her head.

"Ready."

————

The Free Hand walked in a wide line up the grassy hill, the sun now on a downward slope to their left. Each tried to be close enough to overhear Morholt and Romi's conversation except for Selenna, who walked behind and sighed loudly. She cast her gaze around her, bored and tired.

She had yet to express any concern for her husband, Lord What-shisname, who they left in the hands of Prolocutor Vancess and his temple knights. Morholt regretted breaking up with Selenna least, which was to say not at all.

"After Catlia stopped writing me, I sent a letter to her uncle." Romi's voice was a little lower than Morholt remembered it, a little rougher. He had missed so much of her life. "He told me she'd been snatched by the Temple of the Sky. I wrote Glauth next and never got any response at all. That seemed bad enough for me to get prepared. When word got to me that you and the rest of your vagabonds had arrived on the island, I knew it was time."

"You never wrote *me*." Selenna's lower lip protruded.

"Selenna, you're a spoiled twat who thinks she shits gold, and it smells like roast beef." Romi spoke over her shoulder at the pouting woman. "But I'd never let you go hang in the wind. I *did* write you; you were just too self-important to read my damn letters."

Selenna looked up into the sky, avoiding Romi's gaze.

"You were in contact with Catlia?" Morholt found the notion unsettling. "And Glauth? Glauth wrote you back?" It did not fit with his idea of the fiery tempered and impatient Northwoman.

"Glauth was an excellent correspondent." Romi climbed the hill-side as easily as she might pick an olive off a tree. "My favorite. She knew you better than the others, I can say that much. That woman goes through life with her eyes open."

"Glauth is dead, Romi. The, uh, the temple got her." Morholt hoped that no one, mostly Raven, would correct him.

"Damn." Romi frowned. "That's just not right. She was a good woman. She was my friend."

"What are those trees?" Reinar pointed west toward the distant forest. Individual trees towered hundreds of feet above the rest. Morholt was thankful for the change of topic.

"Dendro." Romi raised her head and favored the huge Mirrik warrior with a thin smile. "They're a variety of olive tree if you can believe it. The trunks are three boles that grow together and spiral all the way to the top. You can walk right up 'em. Lots of things do.

Some things you wouldn't want to walk up on way the hell up a tree."

"And what are those?" Reinar pointed east at a tall hill ringed with rows of grapevines twined about man-sized wooden crosses. A pack of small animals scurried up and down the slope. There had to be thirty or forty of them.

The creatures looked a little like small pigs with round hanging bellies, except that they ran on their knuckles and climbed the crosses with nimble fingers on their hands and feet. And they *really* liked grapes.

"Pests." Romi squeezed her fist but didn't stop climbing. "They're called hossos, and they eat everything. They're a plague here in farm..." She went silent and halted her climb. "They're spooked. There's something over there."

One of the hossos sat atop a cross and made low honks to its brethren, who scattered. That one leapt from its perch, swung from the crossbeam of another cross, and vanished into the orchard.

Mahu and Sabni both had their bows out and strung, and Raven held a curved blade in either hand.

"I'll go and see." Reinar stepped forward and drew his sword, Hadral, even as he slid his other arm through the straps of his shield. "Perhaps I might spook whatever *it* is."

"Might just be a crag lion." Romi gazed intently at the hillside. "Some farmers build houses for them in their fields to control the hossos. But they're still very rare this far away from the cliffs. More likely it's—"

A woman's shout came over the hill just before the danger did. "*Morholt, look out!*"

Arrows arced from the grape stands through the sky, falling where the Free Hand stood just before Sarah's bellowed warning.

Rather than charge the hill, Reinar stood in front of Ameli and protected her with his body and his shield.

From the north and the south, mounted temple knights pounded around the big hill, lances lowered and armor shining in the sunlight.

Sarah raced behind the northern contingent, a red-faced and screaming Vancess on her heels.

The Shepherds of the Blood had arrived.

Fear covered Morholt in sweat, and he became acutely aware of the tiny blister that had risen on the ankle of his left foot and the salty smell of his armor that had been too long without a good cleaning.

These are distractions. Do *something.*

A spinning ring of runes appeared in his mind that split and twisted, then did it again, so that three rings spun madly on differing axes. The rune engine on his arm flared when he thrust it into the rings, and a solid wall of flame sprang up in front of the knights, stretching across the entire base of the hill.

He did not expect to fool the men, but he hoped he might at least stall the horses.

He did not. The flawlessly trained animals ran through the flames as if they were not even there, which of course they were not. But the instant in which the riders could not see them allowed Morholt just enough time.

When the knights looked up once more, the Free Hand was gone.

"Have I told you how much I enjoy this trick? Mind the arrows, everyone." Though Morholt could see Sabni's broad grin as he spoke, the archers among the grape stands could not. Everyone moved again, and more arrows fell ineffectually to the ground.

"Shit my dick." Raven stared into the thunder of the oncoming cavalry. "Any more bright ideas, anyone?"

The knights had extended their line and now all charged up the smaller hill together. Thirty riders wide, there was no time for the mercenaries and exes to run out of the way.

"Get down!" Morholt yelled. He crouched and saw someone else crouched down, hidden in the tall grass ahead of him. Several someones.

The knights were less than thirty feet away when three Reinars leapt shrieking out of the grass onto the heads of three horses, surprising and unbalancing the beasts. With no regard for their own safety, two of the Reinars twisted the animals' heads and brought them down in a huge tangle of flailing legs, screaming horse and men, and crunching armor.

The third Reinar was unable to pull down his target horse and was both kicked in the stomach and stabbed in the face before mount and rider collided with the charger next to them, and that whole side of the line was forced to peel away.

Morholt ran straight through the temple knights' line, mercenaries and exes behind him. Fleeing was a thing he was very good at. He turned toward Sarah, now unhorsed, and Vancess, who clung to his mount against the gouts of wind she threw at him.

At the same time that Morholt made Sarah invisible, Romi made another Reinar to catch Vancess by the ankle and drag him from his horse. Morholt winced at the loud crack when Vancess's horse planted both rear hooves in Reinar's chest and sent the huge man flying.

"Must you continue to get me killed right in front of me?" The real Reinar looked sick. "It is disquieting in the extreme."

"Sorry." Romi shrugged as they ran. "You're the biggest person I've ever seen. Size matters."

Vancess came to his feet just in time to get hammered in the chest by a now invisible Sarah. He shouted in pain and went down on his ass, chest plate dented and cracked.

"Everybody run!" Sarah shouted. The knights were regrouping, and Morholt remembered Sarah's assessment that the Hand would likely not be able to defeat them in a prolonged battle.

"Just a second." Morholt created a version of the self-sustaining illusory rune engine he had made to power the king and queen's disguises and set it within a twenty foot in diameter ring that held several smaller rings spinning in its broad band. He pointed, and the ring sped off, seeming to all eyes and ears to push aside grass and argue with itself as it fled the scene.

Moments later, the knights were on the trail, never quite able to catch up to the speeding illusion. The archers followed from behind the hill on their lighter, faster mounts.

"Al-Dagos hold your souls. Thank you." Sarah approached Morholt, one hand out.

Though the Free Hand knew what had transpired between Morholt and Sarah in the Forest Castle, only Sabni appeared unbothered by her presence now. Morholt clasped her hand.

"I am not traveling with that bitch." Raven twirled a blade around her finger and pointed it at Sarah. "No way. I don't care if you think she's changed. She killed Glauth, and she's trying to kill the rest, too. She only let you out to track down Romi here."

"Let us discuss this after we have run away." Sabni held his arms to one side, palms up.

"Yes, please." Ameli held up a hand. "I'd like a good running away also."

Raven vibrated with anger. She looked from face to face, settling on Mahu. The broad-shouldered Darrish warrior nodded.

"Fine." Raven spoke with her teeth clenched together. "I can kill you later." She turned and stalked away.

"She's touchy," Sarah said. "You did explain the whole thing with Glauth was an accident?"

"I did." Morholt set off after his sister. "But at the risk of repeating myself, you *were* trying to kill *me*. That doesn't get you any extra points."

"I just yelled 'look out' before the archers started loosing arrows at you. I'm basically a villain now as far as Greenshade is concerned."

"Sarah Hill Fury, are you familiar with the parable of *The Opal Woman*?" Sabni asked.

Morholt gave a slight involuntary groan.

"Just say yes," Mahu said.

Sarah's forehead wrinkled and one brow went up. "No?"

"It is about a man named Bahnesk whose best friend, who is also his brother, has entered into a contest with the Opal Woman with the intent of bedding her if he wins. He loses and is taken by her terrible white hounds to be killed."

"That was not a good deal." Sarah scratched at the scars on her forehead.

Slowly shaking his head, Sabni continued. "It was not. But Bahnesk pleads with the Opal Woman for his brother's life. 'What do you have to offer me in return for your brother?' she asks him. 'For the love of a true friend, I would throw my soul into the pits of the Undergates. But for the love of my only brother, I would throw in everyone's soul,' is his reply."

"What's the point, Sabni?" Morholt found himself more irritated than usual at the Darrishman's stories.

"Passions for family run deep." The rangy warrior gave a faint smile. "Perhaps it is best if we give Raven time to cool off and accept the woman who tried to kill her brother on her own time."

"Oh, sure." Sarah walked on a few more yards. "Is there some reason you couldn't've just said *that*?"

"Because then you wouldn't know how much time he's spent memorizing all these depthless sermons and stories to make himself look smarter." Mahu said this with no particular expression at all.

"Mahu." Sabni's mouth fell open. "I only seek wisdom—"

"You had a crush on High Priest Te-nal, and you were trying to impress him. That is the *only* reason you even know all of this drivel."

"*Mahu.*" Ameli stepped in front of the squat fighter and stood still, her hands on her hips. "You apologize to Sabni this instant. He has done nothing to deserve that from you."

Sabni began to laugh, and Mahu followed close behind.

"No, he is right," Sabni agreed. "I was smitten and now do not wish to waste the wisdom, so I pass it on where I can. But we really need to keep running now."

Sarah spared a backward glance at the hoodwinked knights as the mercenaries crested the hill. "I thought it was a good story."

This time everyone groaned but Sabni, who just grinned.

34

PLANNING FOR THE FUTURE

BRANNOK

I have been there before. It is not a pleasant place. Are you certain you're ready?" Was he trying to give his daughter an out or make himself feel better by appearing brave? "There won't be any turning around once we go down those stairs."

Jasmayre put a cold-fingered hand on Brannok's forearm and gave a light squeeze. By the light of her candle, her eyes were serene, her face relaxed. "Be of good cheer, My King, my father. It's almost over. You enter this place of death and disease a one-handed king, but you will leave it the liberator of Tyrrane for the rest of history. Who else is bold enough to make such plans for our future?"

He brought her with him not for support, but because he felt that the new monarch of Tyrrane should be present at the nation's most important event since its birth. She would need to tell people about what happened down here. Those stories would shape the character of the country that would follow, and all mistakes, even recent ones, would be forgotten.

With his gloved hand, he squeezed her arm back. "Let's go kill the old fuck."

They crept into the cylindrical room and made their way around the railed balcony. At the far side, black stone steps curled down along the inside of the wall.

Beneath the two royals lay the broken remains of a wooden table and shards of white glass, their previous contents crusted on the floor and wall. Brannok took the first step, and the second, his fear heightening with every footfall.

Halfway down, they could see an archway in the wall behind them below where they first stepped on the stair. No light escaped it, though Brannok made out a small scraping noise.

He froze. Frigid sweat broke out on his face and soaked into the padding of his mail. His feet wouldn't work. Everything smelled of decay.

Again, that slight hand gripped him, this time on his shoulder, so full of strength and reassurance. How could he be less than that to her? He would not fail his daughter.

He took another step.

"*Brave mote.*" The voice from the black scraped a rusted razor over Brannok's soul. "*You are not invited into my home.*"

Jasmayre's hand still held his shoulder. "You are king," she whispered in his ear. "You require no invitation anywhere in Tyrrane." She coughed and cleared her throat. "Although I suppose a bit of caution would not go amiss."

Together, they finished the stair and entered the next room. Small and square, the space stank with piles of bones and other things Brannok had no desire to identify scattered here and there. A corroded mirror hung on the left wall, and two more open doorways showed nothing but dark ahead of them.

"*Do not stand on ceremony now, King of Motes. Enter. Enter and be seen.*"

Being seen bobbed to the top of Brannok's mind as the most frightening thing imaginable. But instead of listening to his feet, he took Jasmayre's hand in his, and together they entered the parlor of the Anger Under the Mountain.

Brannok saw the stone bench against the far wall before he noticed the man cut in half on the floor in front of it. He startled when the man, mouth sewn shut and tears in his eyes, looked up and raised his arms beseechingly. Brannok turned away only to find a woman roped facedown to a stone table with metal cords, her back cut open and the skin peeled away. She cried and moaned in pain, her mouth also sewn closed.

Both of them had rings of runes cut into or painted onto their flesh of the kinds Brannok read about in his secret library.

Jasmayre's grip became icy stone, and she gasped aloud.

"*They were gods once.*" Clad in soiled black robes that covered his face, Angrim fluttered into view. "*Not important gods. No one alive is likely to have heard their names. Still, they have made entertaining playthings for the past thousand years and resilient subjects for my more speculative musings. Something I have at length perfected.*" It directed a glare at Brannok that pressed against his heart. "*You sent the cavalry and the archers to the place I instructed.*" Not even a question. Just a statement.

"I did." Brannok's voice sounded small and human amidst the other, harsher presences in the domed room. "For whatever reason you wanted it. Do you think you'll get to see if they succeed in their mission?"

The dark figure did not move, only continued to stare out of its black cowl at Brannok.

"I know you aren't afraid of me or any man." Brannok could barely hear his own words over the pounding of blood in his ears. Everything rode on getting this right.

Everything.

"But I know what you *are* afraid of." Brannok swallowed. Jasmayre's hand tensed. "The Dead God speaks to me."

In an eyeblink, Angrim roared forward to occlude Brannok's view of anything else. Within the twisted folds of the blood-stiffened robes, Brannok saw the outlines of Angrim's white, hairless, and tragically beautiful face snarling in rage. Terror flowed through the king, a mad flooded river snapping off the twigs and branches of Brannok's reason.

But still, he held his daughter's hand. Still, he would not disappoint her.

Brannok *had* looked up the Dead God in the library as the vulture-faced demon suggested. He had not found much, only a reference or two, but enough to suggest there might be some truth to the idea.

"*What does the Dead God tell you, mote?*"

"The only way for you to save yourself from him is to flee back into the Undergates, hide yourself in the pits where you won't be found, and never return." Brannok's voice cracked as he spoke.

Angrim took a step away, pitched his head back, and roared laughter that flaked away the sense that Brannok might ever feel safe again. "*You know nothing of the Dead God. The Dead God IS the Undergates!*"

Jasmayre's hand fell to her side when Brannok slipped away.

He flowed forward, and his world spun down as he went. His feet rolled across the stone and launched him toward the monster. Happiness, blade stained orange by the blood of the demon, sang in Brannok's mind for Angrim's neck.

All was slow serenity. All was calm. He understood the sacrifice that was being asked of him in this moment, and he was at peace with it.

The hood of the beast moved back as it followed Brannok's trajectory, and the light of Jasmayre's candle fell fully on it. There was no fear on that horrible, corrupt, and perfectly beautiful face. No malice. No Judgment. No—

"Father, *no!*"

Time spun to a stop, and Brannok's awareness expanded. At the far end of the room, a door stood open, a door with worn green paint and diamond-shaped bronze rivets. On the floor below it lay Brannok's bearskin cloak and beyond that, the shape of a bookcase.

Angrim's brows drew together in an evil, angry grin.

At once, Brannok, still hanging in the air, understood. It was all a trap. The legends, the library, the red book, and the demons, they were all a trap to catch disloyal kings who would plot against the Soul of Tyrrane.

But he pushed the blade forward through calcified air because—
what else could he do now?

With a snap, Brannok's Happiness vanished into Angrim's chest,
rushing in to the depth of his wrist. For the space of a thought,
Brannok let himself believe that he had won. That they were free.

Angrim lifted Brannok from the ground with one long white arm.
The blade refused to dislodge, and Brannok felt his shoulder wrench.
With a laugh, Angrim pinched Brannok's bladed arm off at the
shoulder.

Jasmayre screamed again.

She leapt in and tried to wrench Brannok out of Angrim's grip,
but the sorcerer broke Brannok's other arm from his body and
swatted her to the ground with it.

Numbness and light filled Brannok's head. Angrim yanked him
back to consciousness.

"You are not finished yet, mote." Angrim swung the king about as he
spoke, and the fear curdling in Brannok's guts came heaving out. *"You
are the tenth king of Tyrrane to find my trap, though you are the first to
survive the summoning ritual. You may feel pride in that."*

Brannok felt horrified laughter crack open his mind. He felt
nausea, and he felt shame. Not only had he failed, he had failed
Jasmayre, and now she would suffer the consequences. His ribs and
spine crunched beneath Angrim's grip, but still he did not die.

The one thing he did not feel was pride.

*"The button severed Andos from its future and cast everything into the
unknown. I was nearly undone. But I have recovered, and I understand
what is needed."* It looked into Brannok's eyes, and the king responded
with screeching barks of blood-frothed laughter.

*"Such a simple solution, and one I would never have been able to accomplish
had the button not cast off this world from the destiny it was meant to have. I
could not have disposed of Andos's future myself. But now the deed is done, I can
make a new future and yoke our world to it. A future with me at its end."*

The fevered laughter deserted him, and between Angrim's words,
Brannok heard Jasmayre's labored sobs.

She was still alive and awake.

Run!

Angrim tossed Brannok aside, and he rolled facing into a wall. He tried to move, but too much of him had been crushed and ripped, and he lacked arms to push himself over. With Angrim's sorcery sustaining him, he could not even die.

"Ah, the daughter. I have such plans for you. Plans for the future. What a weapon you will make!"

Why did Jasmayre not run? Death came for her, and it was all Brannok's fault. Would Angrim turn Jasmayre into his newest plaything, cut open on a table? *No.* The beast said he had perfected something with the bodies of gods. Perfected what?

Brannok could not save her, nor even cry out his grief and rage in the face of his horror. He could do nothing at all except for lie there and listen to Jasmayre's raw-throated screams as Angrim slowly broke his daughter into the pieces for his weapon.

35

AN OLD FRIEND

MORHOLT

After sailing the length of the Beacon Sea and entering the Sedrian Channel, Morholt finally worked up the courage to be honest with Romi. For all the good it did him.

She tried, and failed, to suppress a snort of laughter. "I'm sorry." Romi mastered herself. They stood on the aft castle of a converted Oulani hulk that now carried large cargoes and livestock all over the inner coast of Andos. On the deck below them, their horses whickered nervously and stamped their hooves. "Why would you think I'd want to get back together with you?"

"Uh..." Morholt had somehow thought that she would jump at the chance. He didn't have an argument ready. "Well, all those versions of me at the farm, and you seemed so happy to see me. You don't have another man in your life. It just seemed..." He did not know how to finish his thought.

"It just seemed like I'd jump back into your arms, and everything would be sunshine and rainbows again? No." Romi smiled, not unkindly, into Morholt's face. The dying sun highlighted her dark weather-beaten face in deep shades of orange. She took his pale hand in hers. "I do love you, Holt, and I suppose I always will. And it *is* good to see you again. I've even forgiven you for the way you left me

—I got more than enough return for the pain. But that doesn't mean I'm ready to let you do it to me again."

"Aren't you willing to at least give it a try?" Morholt felt his brain push up against a wall. In front of him, the second mate called instructions to the sailors up in the rigging and pretended not to hear their conversation. Morholt knew that everything he said would be common knowledge to each man, woman, and rat on the ship within minutes, but he did not care. "Things are different now."

"They certainly are. I'm happy on my own now." Romi stroked Morholt's cheek. "And you've promised Raven to take her back to the Undergates when all of this is over. Were you planning on breaking my heart again or hers?"

"Toad dicks."

"Hey"—Romi slapped Morholt on the shoulder—"let's talk to April. Maybe the little shit can cheer you up with a funny joke."

If April ever told a genuine joke, Morholt might keel over on the spot, but it seemed like a welcome distraction. He flicked a single finger to set a tiny ring of imagination spinning behind his head, and a small light, no brighter than a candle, caught the air. It shone steady despite the wet breeze.

"Hello, Bean. Got any jokes for me and Romi today?"

April sat facing away from Morholt, the blue and white flowers standing out on her sun-yellow dress. She shook her gray-furred head, broad ears flopping with the motion.

"April, honey, it's Romi. You wanna tell me what's wrong?"

The imp turned and watched Romi with one shiny little eye. "I can See again."

A huge grin split Morholt's face. "That's great. That's exactly what we need right now. Thanks, Bean, you really came through for us when... All right. I'm clearly missing something. Why is this bad news?"

"What do you See, little girl?" Romi leaned over the card with Morholt. Close. Touching. The heat of their bodies made him flush.

"Nothing." April lowered her head.

"I'm confused." Morholt ran a hand through his reddish hair as if that might massage his brain into activity. "Can you See again or not?"

"I can See." April turned so she was facing them. "There's just nothing there."

They sat in silence for several heartbeats.

"What does that mean?" Romi asked the question Morholt thought he should already know the answer to but didn't.

"When the Hill Fury cast Andos off from its future, there was nothing left to See." April drooped as she spoke. Her eyes were swollen from crying, and she moved in a listless, apathetic manner. "Something has made a new future and put it in place of the old one. But the new future... there's nothing there. No flowers, no happies, no *life*. We should find a cliff, a really tall one. The future can't get us if we're already dead."

Romi lifted her gaze to Morholt and raised an eyebrow at him.

He shrugged. "Obviously, I do *not* agree with this assessment. And even if it were real, which it is *not*, it doesn't affect us. We're headed to the Dovenhouse to rescue Catlia whether the world shits itself to death afterward or not. Besides, the Hill Fury is on *our* side this time. We can't fail."

Romi rolled her eyes, and April sighed. Morholt took a chance and kissed Romi on the lips.

To his happy surprise, she kissed him back. Heat spread out from his chest and into his crotch. He drew the worn silk handkerchief over the card in his hand.

"I thought you didn't want to get back together." Morholt slipped April into his pack.

A warm Beacon Sea breeze picked up and blew Romi's hair back over her shoulders.

"I don't." Romi turned and pressed herself up against him. "But if the world's gonna end, I think it's forgivable to spend one of your last nights with someone you care about."

Morholt would have argued with her about the world ending, but it was working out well for him in the moment.

————

Morholt and Romi woke to the morning bells. They smiled and dressed without any conversation, lost in their thoughts. As she opened the door to the passenger cabin, Morholt spoke up.

"I'm never going to get over you, you know."

"I know." She gave him a wink. "But you'll be happier if you try."

Above decks, the city of Sejent was visible in the distance. Once there, they would lay in supplies and travel north to the Dovenhouse. It wasn't far now, and that thought made Morholt queasy. He had been scared since this whole mess began, but nothing had frightened him as much as their current destination.

He was not the only one.

Ameli stood next to Reinar, who leaned against the mast and gazed thoughtfully into the distance. He did not care for arguments or plans. He was a weapon, a giant arrow to be pointed and released.

Selenna sat on a crate behind them, quiet and alone.

Gesturing to Raven, who stared back intently at her, Ameli asked the same question Morholt ruminated on. "Why are we going to the *very* place that the temple knights have been trying to drag us to? It doesn't make any sense. Witch's gift, we should be headed as far away as we can. We're doing their work for them."

"Catlia deserves to be rescued as much as Romi did and a lot more than Selenna." Raven gave Morholt and Romi the side-eye. "You two fuck bunnies have a good time keeping the rest of us awake before the big caper?"

"Slept like a baby." Romi straightened her straw hat. "Eventually."

Reinar rumbled his low laughter.

"If we're all through discussing *The Adventures of Morholt's Giant Cock*"—Morholt furrowed his brow to try and appear stern—"Ameli, you don't have to come. I understand if you're chicken. I mean cowardly. Sorry. That came out wrong. I meant a big, whiney, baby sorceress."

She laughed and threw a mock punch at his face. "Don't be a jerk-hole, jerkhole. You know what I meant."

"I do." Morholt sat on a crate lashed to the deck with netting. "But think about it. We just need to free a couple of prisoners, and we become as unstoppable as a stampede of horny bulls running over naked milkmaids in there. Every runecrafter we release turns into another soldier for our side. All we have to do is be careful and stick to the plan." He held up a hand as Ameli's mouth opened. "Which I will figure out as soon as we can actually *see* the place."

"I'd be keen to get a little payback," Romi added.

"That might not work." From behind Morholt, Sarah stepped out onto the main deck. "Vancess told me about a drug Finnagel has been using on the runecrafters to keep them quiet. Something called gaffarmord. They might be too out of it to help us."

"Gaffarmord?" Ameli's brows drew together. "That's from the Undergates. Mind control stuff. It's made from demon moths or something. I wouldn't count on help from anyone taking that kinda junk. No time soon, anyway."

"Even so"—Morholt tapped nervous fingers on the top of the crate, visions of dominance moths being ground into powder behind his eyes—"we still need them for what comes next. After we take our friends back, we'll need to carry the attack to Finnagel. It's going to take everyone we can muster to push that turd back up his daddy's ass."

"I can probably help them even if they're drugged." Free of snark, Morholt almost did not recognize Selenna's voice. "They won't be the *most* effective, but they'll be on our side."

"Thank you, Selenna." Morholt rewarded her rare display of helpfulness with his own even more rare display of magnanimity. "That may make all the difference."

Selenna nodded and watched the oncoming city.

At Sarah's request, Morholt broke off from the group and followed her to the forecastle. They took seats next to one another just behind the prow.

"What's up?"

"I tried to contact Keane this morning." The big Pavinn woman chewed her lower lip and bounced one leg. "There was no response."

"Worried Finnagel discovered our ruse and put a new dominance moth on him?"

"I think that might be the best-case scenario." Sarah glanced back at the rest of the group as Mahu and Sabni joined the others. "The worst case is that Keane and Megan are dead, and we're walking into a trap."

"That does sound worse." Morholt shrugged. "But if it were true, Finnagel would probably have already killed us. I think we're safe assuming that the plan is still working, and Keane and Megan are distracting Finnagel like they're supposed to. Why, do we have a better idea?"

"I'll let you know if I think of one. But as long as Finnagel is drawing breath, we're all in danger."

"Oh, hey." Morholt held up a finger. "In case it's important, April says that someone made a shitty new future for the world, and now we're all going to drown in pigshit. Or you know, words to that effect."

Sarah blinked. "Thank you?"

"Just passing it along." He leaned back and crossed his legs. "I don't want to be one of those dicks who knows something important and keeps it to himself like he's hoarding women's undergarments, and everyone *almost* dies because he doesn't mention it until it's *almost* too late. So I'll just say it now." He nodded at her. "Not that I hoard women's undergarments."

She blinked again. "Thank you. I'm going to check on the horses now." She headed toward the stairs.

"Um, you couldn't just snap us off from that new sucky future like you did the old one, could you?"

"I didn't understand what I was doing even when I *could* remember how I did it." Sarah did not slow her pace.

"Good enough." He waved at her retreating back. "I'll just sit here and not be a dick then."

———

The Free Hand peered out of the huge bushes that surrounded the Dovenhouse's front lawn. To the right was a small farm that probably fed the inhabitants, a field of various vegetables and a few animal pens. On the left, the woods approached to within a dozen feet of the main building. A small barracks outbuilding with a low fieldstone wall around it squatted on the lawn, big enough for ten men. A single guard in a blue and white temple tabard stood watch at the front door, and another circled the yard.

Sabni gave a low whistle. "That is a big place."

"According to April, this used to be the Inquisitorial House of Arlea." Though the imp saw nothing but bleakness in the future, she remembered everything she knew of the past well enough. "It's made of white marble from Sedrios, though it's stained and crappy now."

Sabni shaded his eyes with a rope-muscled hand. "There are bars in all the windows."

"It's the front door for us. You'd never fit in one of those windows anyway." Morholt shifted to look behind himself. "Sarah? Any luck?"

She shook her head. "Keane still doesn't answer. We have to assume the worst."

"All right." Ice water filled his guts, but Morholt took the lead anyway. "Free Hand, Romi, Selenna, we think that the sorcerer Finnagel knows what we're up to and has sent a thousand yellowbacks to stomp our faces into paste."

Ameli raised a hand. "Yellowbacks?"

"King's Swords," Raven said. "Yellow tabards?"

"Oh, right."

"Anyway, the point is that we have a time limit." Morholt sneezed. Springtime in Arlea was playing hell with his sinuses. "We get in, grab our people, and get the hell out. Catlia is first priority. Everyone else is just dingleberries on her butt—we'll take them if they can hang on. Any questions?" Real vengeance for Glauth rose up in front of him. Today he took aim at the forces behind Sarah's misguided and mistaken attack.

"I don't want to do this." Selenna stared with wide eyes and breathed too fast. But she sat in one place, not running. "Maybe we could look for Lord Goodfern?"

"That's the husband? All right. If he's convenient." Morholt frowned. "Anyone else?"

Mahu held up his arm. "How do we get in?"

"Sarah and I are the distraction." Morholt shared a nod with the warrior woman. "You bunch get to the door invisibly, and we'll follow you in. Circle around behind to the left corner where the trees are closest, and we'll do our thing when you're in place."

"I'm coming with you." Raven pulled out a curved knife and sighted along the sharpened edge. "You'll need someone around in case you get into a fight with a chicken or something."

"You're going to protect Romi." Morholt gripped his sister by the shoulder. "I've got the Hill Fury with me. I'm good."

Romi took Raven's hand and pulled her away from Morholt. "She's mine now, you just said. Get your own."

Morholt and Sarah ran behind the trees toward the farm. She put a hand on his shoulder.

"This isn't really a plan." Sarah's voice was quiet but urgent. "This is run in and hope for the best. I've been a part of a lot of really sketchy plans, and this has all the hallmarks."

"Will it matter if Finnagel runs a company of Swords down our throats?" Morholt's frustration trickled out. "Or more likely, given how close we are to Dahnt, about a thousand more temple knights. We're out of options."

"I wish Keane were here." She released his shoulder. "He's always been the planner. And he's one of the sneakiest bastards I know."

"Harden was the sneakiest bastard you knew, and he snuck off, never to return." Morholt wished someone else were there to tell him what to do as well. He hated sticking his own neck out, and being the leader meant he stuck everyone else's necks out too. It was no fit place for a coward. "But as neither of them are here, you're stuck with me. You have a better idea? I'd love to shit on it."

"All right then." Sarah nodded. "Let's do the stupid thing the best we can. That pen looks perfect."

Under the cover of Morholt's magic, he and Sarah approached a pen of swine. Most were huge, a few were smaller, but the undisputed queen of the sounder was a colossal sow, patched with pink and black.

"It can't be."

"What can't be what?" Morholt looked around for anyone paying attention, but the only person in sight was a farmer picking weeds.

"I know that pig." Sarah pointed to the sow. "The markings are exactly the same."

"How do you know a pig? Does hill-furying give time off for swiney relationships?" He gasped. "Are you a pig lesbian?"

Without taking her eyes off the sow, Sarah said, "Call me 'Hill Fury' again, and the pig's next meal is asshole runecrafter."

"Damn. Try to have an open mind, and get your head bit off." Morholt whistled to himself. "But look at her. How much do you think that thing weighs? She's going to be perfect."

Sarah opened the gate of the pen, and one of the younger pigs ran out. The big sow lifted her massive head and grunted. Chastised, the smaller pig returned to the pen.

"Huh." That sow was the key to this. Morholt twirled up the illusion of a ripe pumpkin and rolled it in front of the animal's snout. She hauled herself to her feet and trotted after it, warning off the rest of her brood with deep snorts. Snouts raised, they followed her through the gate, around the pen, and into the small vegetable field.

Obligingly, the farmer screamed bloody murder.

Both the guard at the door and the one circuiting the grounds ran for the field, as well as another half dozen blue-and-whites from the barracks. They milled into the field, trying to surround the rooting and happily eating animals.

Behind the guards, the rest of the Free Hand slipped into the front door of the Dovenhouse.

"Wow." Morholt put his hands on his hips. "That went amazingly.

No *plan*. I look forward to all the ways you might make your short-sighted insults up to me."

The pair went up the short flight of stairs to the door which flew open, knocking Morholt to the ground and spoiling his and Sarah's invisibility. He bounced to the base of the steps with Sarah beneath him. At the top, blade drawn and teeth bared, a guard with a generous splatter of blood across his front snarled and ran down the stairs.

Both Morholt and Sarah tried to move at the same time, which resulted in a tangle of limbs that Morholt thought might tear his leg off. The guard reached the ground and lifted his blade, a wild cry on his lips.

Morholt swallowed the pain in his leg and brought a fiery ring of runes to mind. Even as he did it, he knew it was too little, too late. In his mind, he already saw a Temple of the Sky sword sticking out of his guts, and by accidental reflex, he incorporated it into the illusion.

For an instant, the temple guard hesitated, confused, at the long blade piercing his target.

A low rumble became a hard pounding, and the guard flew left, carried and then churned underfoot by the thousand-pound sow. He screamed once before his shattered ribs were ground into his lungs.

"My leg."

"Oh, sorry." Sarah straightened her leg and released Morholt's. With a small cry of relief, he rolled off her and to the right, away from the monster pig.

Sarah sat up. The sow went to her, snuffling and grunting. She hugged its broad head and scratched behind its jowls.

"Hiya, Gennie," Sarah said. "How's life been treating you?"

"Knew you were a pig lesbian." Morholt pushed himself up and limped to the stair. The marble doorframe was covered in runes he did not recognize. "Let's go. They'll have made a mess of everything by now."

36

THE DOVENHOUSE
MORHOLT

They stepped into music and blood. White marble walls and floors offset garish crimson splashes, and the notes of a melancholy fiddle haunted the air.

No more than fifteen feet across, the foyer stretched three stories in height with a spiral stair rotating up a wide iron pole. Beneath it stood Reinar, sword in hand, holding himself up against the wall, bleeding from a dozen cuts. Behind him, Ameli lay on the bright red and white floor, eyes closed and breath shallow. Three bodies of temple knights lay on the floor around them.

The shouts of more came from above. From a hallway to Morholt's left, despairing wails carried on still, crushing air as well as the smells of unwashed bodies, decay, and the insides of men.

"What... how?" Morholt did not even know how to ask the question. A sense of despondency washed over him. He was alone here, cut off.

The music played with him, spoke to him, told him of terrors in the dark places. He should run. They all should. Before those wailing cries were their own.

"Vancess and his bastard temple knights were already here."

Reinar winced and leaned his head back against the stone wall. I don't understand how they beat us here, but they did."

"Is Ameli...?" Sarah stepped toward the curly-haired girl. A shallow cut in her scalp left half her face covered in red.

"Unconscious. I must stay by her side and watch over her." The huge Mirrikman slipped a few inches and caught himself. Blood seeped out of his quilted gambeson armor and plastered his golden-brown hair to the side of his head. "You have to find the others. Get them out of here."

The music knew Morholt was here. It hungered for him.

"Yeah. Sure." Morholt's arms swung front to back, keeping time with his fear. "That's a thing I want to do. Toad dicks, toad dicks, toad dicks." He stared at the wall under the stair so as not to look at all the blood. It was white, run through with large-grained veins of gray and black, oppressive, sterile, and uncaring stone.

"You'll be fine." Sarah took him by the shoulders and held his gaze. The brim of her fancy hat bumped his forehead. "Make us invisible. They'll never even know we were here."

Relief flooded Morholt as he brought up the images of the rings in his imagination. He inserted the rune engine, twist and flare... and nothing happened.

He did it again.

Nothing.

"*Toad dicks!*" Rings, twist, flare. Rings, twist, flare. "Why won't it work?" The rune engine still had power, but Morholt was unable to use it.

A scrawny man, naked and grimy, his dark hair wild, stumbled out of the left hall. He broke for it and ran at the front door. His feet slapped the marble as he went, and he bashed into the door. Sunlight flooded the room as he fell out of it.

All Morholt could think about was the hellish music that screwed its way into his ears. The music knew why his runecrafting had deserted him. A sweeping note vibrated through his spine. The music knew, but it was not telling.

Sarah spoke unfamiliar words and twisted her fingers to no

obvious effect. "This is a place of power. But I can't see it. It's not natural. And it's total."

"Stupid sorcerer *bullshit*." Morholt kicked at the bottom step of the spiral stair. What was this place? None of this made any sense. He did not want to die. He wanted to go, run far from here where no one would ever find him again. But he could not bring himself to leave his friends—certainly not Romi and *never* Raven.

Selenna he could probably leave.

"Come on," he said to Sarah. He forced his feet to move in the direction of further danger. "Maybe if they think we're all already here, they won't be looking over their shoulders."

Fiddle notes bound up the cries of the hopeless and tickled them up Morholt's back.

"There is one more thing you should know." Reinar's voice was strained, rasping. "The other runecrafters are not sleeping. They fight for the Dovenhouse. And their magic works very well."

Morholt glared at Sarah, his panicked heart pounding.

She shrugged. "It was *your* plan."

They moved through a second-floor corridor toward the sound of fighting. Shiny black doors stood to either side every fifteen feet, and a tall barred window adorned the far wall. A temple knight burst through one of the doors as they passed, a bloody horror show on the bed behind him. Sarah swung for his throat, and he knocked her blow above his head and jabbed her in the arm with the butt of his own sword.

Testing blows were exchanged as Sarah and the skilled knight circled each other, while Morholt tried to look for more combatants in every direction at once. He retched when the stench from the desecrated room hit him.

Sarah came in high with an overhand slash, distracting the knight from dodging the solid kick she planted in the middle of his chest.

The knight flew backward and crunched into the wall behind him, and Sarah's heavy blade punched through plate and mail and pinned him to it.

He dropped his sword and coughed.

Sarah put her other hand on his chest and yanked the sword out, spilling blood down his front. He fell to the floor and gurgled, his fingers looking for purchase on the cold marble.

Fresh blood and urine added to the smells of the Dovenhouse.

Morholt picked the dying man's sword up and stepped over him. He needed to focus on something else. "So how does this place of power affect *me*? And whose is it? I thought they were more spread out than this, not just a single building." He whispered as they crept, though part of him wanted to scream. Go ahead and bring the knights to kill him where he stood. Anything to stop the music from laughing at his weakness.

"I'm sure I could figure it out if we had time, but it's obviously part of the cage that makes this place." Sarah slithered along one wall, her sword held in front of her. She turned her head away from a doorway across the hall.

Before he could stop himself, Morholt looked into it. A metal table lay on its side, surrounded by corroded knives and stained-glass vials on shelves or broken on the floor. Something human-sized but with the wrong number of limbs, all of them stumps, flopped along the filthy marble.

He couldn't breathe. They were here to rescue Catlia, but where was Raven? His sister should be here at his side.

Another woman's scream came from ahead, and the music, knowing secrets they did not, laughed.

"I think it's also making me feel, I don't know, hopeless? I didn't feel this way before we walked in, and there's no real reason for it, but I can't shake it." Sarah looked back over her shoulder. "Get against the wall. You're less of a target that way."

Morholt froze, terrified that everyone knew where he was and could see him walking down the center of the hall. By reflex, he began an illusion but abandoned it and scooted behind Sarah. What was that she just said about feeling hopeless? Whatever it was, *he* certainly did.

This was no place for a coward.

"They're behind that door." Sarah counted backward from three on her free hand, then rushed across the hall and kicked it in.

A tall, skinny Northman with a white beard and gray pants and shirt fell into the wall when the door banged into him. Against the far corner of the room, lit by a wide window with teethlike bars, a rickety bed lay on its side, hiding someone. Spatters of blood decorated the walls behind it, and the powerful smell of people's innards made Morholt's stomach spasm and his throat close. He couldn't decide if he wanted Raven to be behind that bed or not.

The Northman spun on Sarah, who jumped out of the range of his long arms and knife. He grinned, teeth red from smacking his face into the wall, and jabbed at Sarah, who jumped as if hit, though the knife arced through air several feet away. She grunted and pressed her hand to her side.

The hand came away wet and red.

Laughter sprayed droplets of the Northman's blood over his lips as he surveyed Sarah's reaction just before she lowered her head and ran at him.

That was the last Morholt saw of that fight. A woman, just shorter than him but far broader and more powerfully built and dressed in gray like the Northman, clouted him in the temple with a bare fist. The next one hit him in the mouth and snapped his head around.

This woman worked for Selenna before Sarah beat her and sent her here.

The world went sideways, and Morholt tottered to the wall with the window. He managed to spin enough to get the blade up, but the woman let it stab her in the stomach and then punched Morholt in the chest for his trouble.

His lungs exploded in pain, and he gasped for air that would not come.

"*Danica*, stop that this instant." Was that Selenna standing behind the bed? A long dark arm with ropy muscles reached up and yanked Selenna back down. "*Ow*."

The thick-bodied woman named Danica pulled the long blade

out of her stomach, and it came away clean. "You can't hurt me, ginger. But I can sure as hell hurt—*urgh*."

Sarah lifted Danica by her hair and the waistband of her pants and shoved her head through the bars of the window with a loud *clang*. With one knee in the woman's back, Sarah gripped the bars and pulled.

Her muscles bunched and iron cables in her neck stood rigid and tense. Sarah made a noise somewhere between a grunt and a hum, and a loud wrenching sound came from the window. The marble cracked along the top when the bars' frame pulled out of shape, and Danica screamed and pounded against the wall.

Morholt pushed himself along the floor away from the crazy lady with her head stuck in the window. His world still spun, and his breath came in hitches and starts.

But he was alive.

A meandering series of fiddle notes found the idea amusing and promised *much* worse to come.

Sarah pulled down the bed to reveal Sabni covered in shallow cuts, Mahu unconscious or dead in his arms, and an unharmed Selenna, proving that the gods of Andos *did* appreciate a sense of bloody and undeserved whimsy.

Hopelessness dragged Morholt away and down. He wanted out of here *so much*.

"How bad is he hurt?" Sarah knelt beside Sabni and put a hand on Mahu's forehead.

"He still breathes." Sabni's red-rimmed eyes watered over his turned-down mouth. "But I do not know for how much longer. Have you seen Ameli? She can heal him if we can get him to her soon."

Sarah looked into Sabni's eyes for a moment without speaking. "Downstairs. Unconscious. We'll get you there."

Sabni nodded once. "Raven and Romi fled upstairs. Everyone was running. The Shepherds split us up. I don't know where they went." He held Mahu up as best he could and dragged him back down the corridor, leaving a trail of red on the floor. Sarah led, and Morholt brought up the rear with a jittery Selenna.

Mahu flopped like the dead. Sarah bled from her side. Sabni stared ahead, eyes wide and hopeless. And below, Ameli lay, probably dead herself.

One jittery hand on the wall, Morholt followed, pointing his stolen sword in every direction he thought he heard a noise which, with the fiddling, was everywhere. They passed bodies of inmates and knights, some dead, some less so. One pair of captives writhed on the floor and splashed in a pool of their own fluids. Morholt was unable to look close enough to tell if they were screwing each other, eating each other, or both.

"I knew you would rescue me." Selenna, beyond Morholt's belief, not only smiled but winked at him. Did she not understand how earthshakingly fucked they all were? "You may not say it, but I know I was your favorite." She stepped closer to him.

For an instant, Morholt snapped back to normal. "Please shut up, Selenna. It doesn't mean you're my favorite when you're on the way to rescuing people I *do* care about." The anger felt good. It distracted him from the music, the blood, and the unearthly stench.

She jerked away as if slapped. "I... Don't leave me here." Her bottom lip trembled and threatened to give way to a tidal wave of sobbing. The come-hither looks were an attempt to make herself feel better, keep a hand on the tiller of her own survival. He knew that. "I don't deserve this place. You taught me runecrafting. It should be *you* in here."

Selenna's crumble gave Morholt back a further measure of self-control. And she made a point. At no time in their tumultuous relationship did she volunteer for anything like this.

"I hope you die here." She spat on his green leather boots.

On his *boots*.

He started then stopped an illusion of a slavering bear designed to chase an entitled idiot ex-girlfriend down the hall and over the railing of the stair at the end. It would not have worked anyway. *Relax, it's always good to have one person to throw to the sharks while everyone else swims away. Hopefully, sharks and mind-controlled runecrafters operate by the same rules.*

He moved to the other side of the hallway, away from a broken hole in the marble wall. Who knew what might have been on the other side?

Sword held up front, Morholt hoped no one would mistake him for knowing how to use the thing and make a target out of him. Yet he could not quite put it down. Didn't they say that inexperienced swordsmen made the deadliest fighters because you never knew what they were going to do? That didn't make any sense. If it were true, no one would ever bother to learn, and everyone would be the deadliest.

From somewhere ahead, a wail turned into a raw-throated scream and cut off with a splutter.

He looked again at the sword in his hand, swallowed, and continued back up the hall.

The music agreed. The sword would be of no use against what was coming for him. The music ran the taste of his own blood through Morholt's mouth and tittered. He could not have said how he knew the taste was him.

"We're not going fast enough." Selenna's hands shook. Her gaze twitched in every direction, and she jumped at every sound. "They're going to find us."

"Selenna, we're just being careful." Morholt heard his voice as if it were someone else speaking. "Sarah will get us out of this. She knows what she's doing."

A long bass note reminded him that Sarah killed Glauth. How would *she* feel about his expedition with her murderer? The Dovenhouse held him, trapped and withering, his enemies at every turn.

You know Sarah is going to kill you too.

Selenna rounded on Morholt like a surprised rabbit snake. "*That* is the bitch who wanted to throw me in here to begin with. Fuck her and fuck *you*. I'm getting the *fuck* out of here right now." With that, Selenna ran up the hallway at top speed, light brown hair and ratty dress flying behind her.

Alarmed, Sarah watched her shoot past, though she made no effort to stop the terrified woman.

As Selenna breached the double doors at the end and set her foot on the spiral stair, a handsome bearded man in the gray uniform of the Dovenhouse jumped down from the stairs above her and punched. A boom echoed down the corridor.

Selenna's head detonated in an expanding cloud of red mist and brains.

An evil leer on his face, the handsome man launched himself through the air, leaping at Sarah with his fist cocked back, before Morholt had time to inhale for a scream.

His arm covered in Selenna's brains to the elbow, the man fell against Sarah and off her to the marble with one of Sabni's arrows through his throat.

Sabni knelt beside Mahu, whom he had dropped on the floor.

The handsome man had been another of Selenna's runecrafters, and he killed his former mistress in an eyeblink.

Morholt felt nothing.

"Sarah." Morholt pointed to the double doors. A short man with greasy hair and a pinch-faced woman with a pink nose and cheeks—the last of the runecrafters Sarah captured in Hornfield—stepped into the hallway, flanked by four temple knights. Greasy Hair moved his hands in a swirling ring, and with a loud *pop*, Sarah suddenly stood in the midst of them.

It was too much. Fright overrode all of Morholt's reasoning and crystallized into an insane anger. He ran wailing up the hall, sword held high while the fiddle music laughed.

A harsh orange glow, unclean and caustic, grew from the pinch-faced woman's hands. She reached for Sarah, who grabbed her wrists and threw her into a knight. The man screamed as the hands passed through his armor and into his chest.

The smell of potash overpowered everything.

"This is for Selenna, you bastards!" The other knights raised weapons just as Morholt collided into them and sent two to the ground. Greasy Hair swept his arms again, and just before the pop, Morholt grabbed him by the ankle. He did not know where Greasy Hair intended to send him, but he was not going alone.

The two runecrafters were transported to the ceiling of the foyer thirty feet above the blood-slickened marble floor.

They fell.

Greasy Hair screamed and circled his arms in a mad attempt to transport himself. Morholt released him, twisting his own body to try and grab the railing of the spiral stair. He bruised his fingers when the tips smacked the rail, but he only succeeded in making himself spin as he plummeted.

I'm sorry, Raven. I tried. We should have left when you asked the first time.

At the same instant that Greasy Hair cracked against the stone, Morholt hit Reinar's arms. The Mirrikman fell under the blow, and Morholt panicked, thinking that either his, Reinar's, or both of their necks had broken.

Whimpering bravely with the effort, Morholt hauled himself to his feet. He leaned on the railing, listening to sounds of fighting, fiddling, and despair. His legs tingled, and he could only drag them in the direction he wanted to go. Reinar, maybe dead, lay in front of him where he had caught Morholt out of the sky, and Ameli lay where they'd left her. The two unmoving and gore-covered knights were recent additions, however.

Reinar had not been idle.

Beyond checking that both still breathed, Morholt did not know what to do for his friends. But those upstairs, he might still be of use to.

"Gotta go. Gotta go." One step at a time, Morholt pushed his feet up the stairs. As he climbed, feeling spread back into his legs. He was almost to the second-story landing when Sarah stuck her head out.

"Morholt. Al-Dagos's eyes, you really saved my life. How did you disappear that guy?" Sarah had an angry red welt on her shoulder in the shape of a human hand that burned through her mail as well as a half dozen other scrapes and cuts, but she acted as if it were all perfectly normal. Maybe for her it was. "I can't pull any sorcerous energy at all."

The pieces clunked into place in Morholt's head. *He* had access to power, but this place kept him from runecrafting.

"Why are you grinning?" Sarah arched an eyebrow.

A strong voice rang out from above. "Sarah, Pilgrim Handmaiden, Hill Fury to the Tyrraneans and eternal disappointment to the Holy Alir of the Andosh, I, Prolocutor Vancess of the Temple of the Sky, hereby condemn you to death." Temple archers ran out onto the top landing around Vancess, arrows nocked and bowstrings pulled.

"Aim."

The fiddle playing grew terrifyingly loud. The despondent wails held their breath.

"It's going to be a lot." Morholt held Sarah by the arm, preventing her from diving back into the temporary safety of the hallway behind her. He pushed the rune engine over her muscular hand. "Use it fast, control it later."

Sarah's eyes shot open, and white light blazed from them and from the silver streaks in her hair.

Vancess's face shifted from calm detached cruelty to alarm. "*Fire!*"

A wind more powerful than any hurricane blasted out of Sarah. It turned the arrows in flight, blew the archers, Vancess, the marble landing, and the top quarter of the spiral stair into and *through* the ceiling of the Dovenhouse, sending them flying like broken dolls above the countryside.

At least I was right about one thing in all of this, Morholt thought.

The fiddling drew down, sonorous and low. The laughter in it withered. Only menace and the promise of horrific violence remained. Above them, despite the sunlight pouring in the newly opened roof, darkness seeped out of the top floor hall. It coated the white walls and turned them gray, and it choked the air until the sunlight fell to it, fluttering to the floor. The despair that stalked them since they walked into this place redoubled. Spasms of sadness bore down on him, *into* him. It wanted his life.

From above and below, sobs turned to screams. Angry gnashing pulled against restraints as the denizens of the Dovenhouse poured their violence and sadness into the halls.

"Take care of the others." Sarah spoke to Morholt, but her eyes were fixed above her. She had gained control over the rune engine's channeled power quickly. The white glow faded. "I'm going to go take care of that shit with the fiddle." Sarah opened her mouth to say more but shut it and rolled her eyes instead.

"I don't know his name," Morholt said, "but they talked about him in Glauth's keep. Everyone was terrified of him, and that was before he turned all evil. Just be careful. And please bring Raven and Romi back safe."

"And Catlia?"

Damn. Things were so out of hand, he had forgotten why they were here. "Yeah. And Catlia."

One side of Sarah's mouth turned up in a crooked half smile.

"You be careful too."

She ran up the stair and jumped where it ended, catching the broken landing and pulling herself up. Then she was gone.

Morholt and Sabni half carried, half dragged Mahu down the stair. His honey-gold leather armor was slippery with his blood, and he continued to leak more down both heavily muscled legs. At the bottom, they lay him on the ground next to Reinar.

Sabni ran to Ameli. "Awaken, little sister. We have desperate need of you." He lifted her in his arms and brushed the strawberry blonde curls and blood out of her face. "Please." A tear dripped from the end of Sabni's nose and splashed between Ameli's eyes. She jerked.

Angry notes hung in every corner, pulling darkness firmly around them. Morholt made light from a tiny spinning ring of his imagination. He remembered it could not work here and then realized it had. Whatever spell, runes, or ritual the Dovenhouse used to smother his runecrafting must have been spoiled when Sarah blew the roof off.

Ameli coughed and pulled herself against Sabni. He held her tight until she recovered.

"Mahu is gravely wounded. We need you." Sabni lifted himself and the Deep Witch's daughter to their feet and helped her to Mahu. She cried out when she put any weight on her right foot and again when she saw Reinar.

"*No.* How long has he been like this?" She stumbled onto the huge warrior. Reinar's skin was ashen. "*How long has he been dead?*"

Morholt's mind recoiled. Reinar was alive the last time he checked on him. How long ago was that? Morholt carried the blame for all of this. These were the hallmarks of a bad plan.

"Ameli, *please.*" Sabni went down on his knees beside her. "You must heal Mahu. I will die without him."

She wiped the tears from her face and placed a hand on both men's chests. A silent moment passed. "It's been too long. I can only bring one of them back. I'm not even sure I can do that, but I'll try."

Sabni said nothing, and Morholt closed his eyes. Ameli could have healed them both with the power of the rune engine he had just given to Sarah, but then they'd all be dead when the fiddler found them.

"They're both my friends." Ameli spoke to Sabni, but her voice broke Morholt's wicked heart. "I owe Reinar my life more times than I can count, but Mahu *is* your life." Ameli and Sabni embraced. Released. "Holt," Ameli said, "what do I do?"

He opened his eyes. Ameli and Sabni both sat staring at him, hand in hand, grief shining in their faces. Somewhere above, the music turned violent and the darkness in the tall room absolute. They sat in a tiny bubble of light, just the three of them, with Mahu and Reinar's cooling bodies and the sobs of distant men and women floating in the air, suspended snowflakes of sadness.

Don't ask me this. Why would you ask me this? How can you hate me so much that you would make me live with this decision for the rest of my life?

That may not be too long, the fiddle music reminded him.

"Heal Mahu." Morholt's voice cracked when he said it, just like the remains of his soul.

Ameli wept, but she began work regardless. Sabni pulled one of Mahu's arms to him and pressed his forehead against Mahu's hand.

"He's badly damaged inside." She unbuckled Mahu's armor and pulled the chest piece off to cut the underpadding away. He had been run through a dozen times over by the Northman's long knife. "I'll have to repair as much as I can before I can wake him without him dying again and ruining everyone's day." She cast a glance at Reinar when she said this but continued working.

Powders flickered into the air, mixed, and vanished while Mahu grew more and more waxen. Ameli gasped and fell forward, and Sabni took her by the shoulders and set her right.

A numbness enveloped Morholt. What were you supposed to do in this sort of situation? Had *anybody* ever been in this sort of situation before? He gave out a soft moan and, in doing so, realized that the cries he heard were not a cacophony; they were a *chorus*. And he was a part of it.

"I'm all right." Ameli swayed a bit. "Sure. I'm fine. The room is spinning for you guys too, right?" She placed both hands on Mahu's broad chest and closed her eyes, mouthing silent words.

This time Sabni caught her when she fell.

The music hitched, stuttered, then ran with renewed force.

Raven. Morholt shook his head. Nothing he could do. He would have to trust Sarah.

He really did *not* trust Sarah.

"Nope, s'all good." Ameli slurred the words together. Her head drooped. "C'mon, you. Wake up."

Ameli lay down on Mahu's chest and fell asleep. As she did, Mahu's eyes fluttered open. He lifted his head.

"Why's this girl asleep on me? Everything she's lying on hurts."

Sabni grabbed Mahu's face and covered it in kisses. "Foolish man. Mother Love does not approve of her followers allowing themselves to be killed."

"Ow."

A noise that sounded like tearing stone crackled through the air, and the ground lurched and trembled beneath them. Patterned fractures appeared in the floor. One screeching note faded out, and the fiddling stopped for good.

"Time to go." Morholt hauled Ameli off Mahu, eliciting a groan of pain from him. "Sabni, you get Mahu. I think the door is this way."

"What about Reinar? We can't leave him here." Blood coated the left half of Ameli's face and made that eye shine white and blue.

"Run now, cry later." The darkness drained away, filling the cracks and corners of the room. Morholt pointed right of where he had been crawling. "There's the door."

Together they clambered out the doorway, down the steps, and into the yard, just in time to see the third story front fall off the Dovenhouse with a thunderous crash that lifted all of them off the grass.

Above and to their right, Raven and Romi, carrying an unconscious Catlia between them, stepped off the building and were guided by steady winds safely to the ground. Sarah waved down to Morholt and vanished.

"Guess I'm not getting my rune engine back."

37

ROAD TRIP!

SARAH

S arah entered the darkening hallway while Morholt ran down the metal stairway behind her. Though she promised him she'd rescue the three remaining women and 'take care of that shit with the fiddle,' in truth, she was not that confident. This was not her house, and she had little idea of what she was up against. The sobbing noises were thinner up here though.

"Whatcha think? We have a chance against this thing?"

Gabby nodded and glanced up. "Yes, but we need to move fast. The music is carrying runes. It can uncreate whatever it wishes." The Dead God held its chin, so like Sarah's own, between thumb and forefinger and gazed thoughtfully at Sarah. "I'd judge we have just enough time for one more language lesson on the way."

With her head shaking, Sarah stepped further into the deepening dark. Maybe they could do some alchemical transmutation exercises while she was fighting, too.

"You see, in Metzoferran, the phrases indicating creation and destruction are the same." Gabby shifted into lecture mode, as if Sarah were trotting down the lane on her favorite mare with nothing in the world trying to murder her. "Typically, it would require a thousand years of study to master the slightest grasp of the subject."

This hallway, unlike those below, was twenty feet wide with only two doors to a side. The second on the right was open, and gouts of darkness flowed out of it, long fingerlike tendrils pulling it across floors and walls and staining the stone it found as it went.

"Like all runecrafters, this one is using a derivation of Metzoferran similar to the language of the gods I have been teaching you. Unlike the others you've faced, he plays the runes into his music, allowing him speed and precision no other runecrafter can hope to match."

Even with the extra power she had absorbed from the rune engine, Sarah could not see through the dark, though she could navigate the hall easily enough.

"Now most would be entirely unable to craft runic rings this fast. The process is complex and interdependent by nature. Unfortunately, our fiddler seems to be something of a savant. Quite brilliant, actually." Gabby grinned, though it faded in the face of Sarah's flat glare. "Well, he is. At any rate, he seems to be operating by instinct without any particular understanding of why the things he does actually work. I believe we can use that to defeat him."

"I'm feeling pretty good about ramming him through the wall with a tornado and scattering the bits across the rest of Arlea." Sarah hopped past the first pair of doors, clinging to the right wall.

"The darkness protects him. It's likely you wouldn't find him in it. You'd have just as much chance of killing Raven or the two others. Thrice, really, given there're three of them and only one fiddler."

Sarah could no longer see at all. She kept one hand on the wall beside her and, when she got to the open doorway, stepped inside. The fiddling changed tone. Ominous laughter was replaced by the promise of imminent violence. Sarah flinched away, though there was nothing to flinch away from.

"He's merely toying with you." Gabby's voice was calm, conversational. "Manipulating your emotions by communicating his own directly into your limbic system. Quite clever."

"Are you helping?" Sarah pushed her back against the wall and swung her blade in front of her. The shaking blade remained hidden from view. She had never been so scared.

"Oh, right. Forgive me. I already said he was brilliant. What I'm telling you now is that you are not feeling your own fear, but his. Truth be told, we're fortunate he's cruel. If he wasn't so intent on making you suffer first, he could have simply removed you from reality."

Sarah ignored the part about being erased from the world and concentrated instead on the idea that the fiddler was more afraid of her than she was of him. Huh, that really *did* help. She stopped swinging the sword for a moment and strained to see through the murk. Centering on the music was fruitless. It surrounded her, trying to get its claws into her from every side.

Gabby cleared its throat. "Stop trying to see with your eyes. Perhaps you should just close them altogether. See as I showed you before. Look for the fiddler's *language*. Remember, he doesn't understand what he's doing, why it works, but you can see all of it."

She shut her eyes against the black. Her heart still raced, and cold sweat broke out on her arms. With a deep breath, Sarah pulled against the edges of her ballooning fear. The idea that she had a means of perceiving that no sorcerer anywhere possessed unnerved her. Would it work again? Or would her power desert her—like the music told her—now that she understood she was not special enough to have it?

"The worst part about all of this," Sarah said to Gabby, forcing herself to smile with some false bravado, "is that this magic fiddler can't see my wonderful new hat."

"What's that? Oh. Yes, quite."

Then she saw him.

Not him exactly, but hundreds of swirling rings of brightly glowing golden runes emanating from a central point. She might be able to cross the twenty feet to him and cut him down before he was able to unmake her, but she had no way of knowing that, and she still didn't know where Raven, Catlia, or Romi were.

So, she tried something else.

Thanks to Gabby's lessons, Sarah could read the runes blowing through the air, carried by the deadly music. She read the fear—the darkness—and understood what it meant and how it moved.

And she changed it.

With a finger, Sarah rewrote a single rune on one of the spinning rings, whisking it back to its master with a *snap*.

The music hitched and stuttered. There was a small sound as if someone stifled an angry cry. The twirling tune returned with savage force. It smashed against her, breakers of sound and magic wearing away her ties with reality.

But Sarah was not unmade. The music corkscrewed at her in flaming letters, violent and hot. It spun a madcap dervish of void at the very reality of her. But Sarah rewrote it as it battered her, turning the insane weapon harmless. She gained ground, writing faster than the fiddle played, and she heard the desperate and muffled whimpers of her attacker. After all, she only needed to change a single rune to make an entire ring useless.

She felt pity for him. Not that she slowed down any.

The darkness lifted. Behind a dark-haired man who fiddled furiously, very average except for the burn scars on his face and neck, Raven, Romi, and another woman lay unconscious or dead on the ground.

No longer bothering to rewrite his runes, Sarah simply pulled them apart and sent glittering shards of letters flying through the air. She reached the fiddle itself, and when she pulled at the magic flowing through it, the instrument tore to pieces in his hands with a sound like the cracking of a castle wall falling on a dozen tundra cats. The Dovenhouse lurched, and a fissure appeared in the floor beneath them. The fiddler fell sideways.

The silence was stupefying in all the most wonderful ways.

"Good show." Gabby beamed, very pleased with itself, as if *it* had done all the heavy lifting here. "Quite good. Much easier than I'd thought it would be."

As Sarah ran to Raven's side, she cut her eyes at Gabby and decided to let *that* one pass by unanswered.

"However, we need to move immediately." Gabby clapped its hands and rubbed them together. It seemed so *human*. "Carry the fight to Finnagel now before he can prepare himself for you."

That assumed Keane and Megan's illusions held and that Finnagel had not *already* prepared. And *that* assumed that he would even require preparation to crush her.

Sarah checked the women. All were breathing; none were waking. She lifted Raven over one shoulder and dragged Romi and Catlia by the backs of their shirt collars in her other hand. Thusly burdened, Sarah picked her way out across the crumbling marble. It occurred to her to wonder why the gaffarmord-controlled fiddler left the three women unharmed. She shook her head and pushed away the answers that rose up in her mind.

The fiddler pressed himself into the corner of the room, watching her with round frightened eyes. She wanted to take him with her, but there were more immediate problems to deal with.

"Fight Finn? No way. I could handle a kid with a violin, but Finn's like a thousand years old and knows everything about sorcery there is to know." Sarah shook her head as she hopped over a widening crack in the hallway floor. "He'd paste me in a second. Or even worse, he *wouldn't*, and then I'd be his slave or something for the next few forevers."

"Finnagel is an accomplished sorcerer, as you say." One side of Gabby's mouth quirked up in a crooked smile, just as Sarah's so often did. "But sorcery is only one-half of the equation. You now hold both of those halves."

It sounded stupid to try and take on Finnagel. But Sarah had taken on enemies just as frightening with less behind her before. She hadn't gotten the nickname Hill Fury because she got angry when her fish came back overcooked at the Jolly Chicken.

Most tavern cooks were dramatically underpaid. They didn't deserve that kind of abuse.

At the end though, an encounter with the old Egren bastard was inevitable. Finnagel had placed her on this path to kill or capture runecrafters who did not deserve it. He revived the Temple of the Sky to control the wealthy and powerful of Andos. He would not stop until he controlled everything. Everyone. How many times had Finnagel told Sarah that humans were nothing more than tools?

If not for Finnagel, Captain Falt would still be alive. As would Glauth, to say nothing of the dozens of others who were caught in the way.

Sarah's wide lips thinned, and her eyes narrowed.

If Gabby thought now was the time to carry the attack to Finnagel, catch him by surprise before he could prepare, then by Al-Dagos's eyes, she would do it.

A rumble threatened to unbalance Sarah and her three burdens, and the wall fell off the entire top story of the building. The crash flung her into the air, and she bent backward, landing without dropping anyone's heads onto the marble floor.

Sarah went left into a room filled with metal beds, manacles, and the smell of old blood. The front wall lay three stories below, cratered in the yard. To the right of it, Sabni helped Mahu walk away, and Morholt dragged Ameli.

Of Reinar, there was no sign.

"Wake up," Raven said. She squirmed in Sarah's grip and shook Romi and Catlia. Romi lifted her head, but Catlia remained stubbornly unconscious.

"Down you go." Sarah used Blow Out the Candle to create a strong and precise enough wind to lift Raven, Catlia, and Romi up and ferry them safely to the ground. Eyes wide, Raven and Romi clung to the limp Catlia.

"We must go. There isn't an instant to waste." Gabby's jaw was tight, its lips pursed.

Sarah waved down to Morholt. "Fine, you old hen. What do I do?" If there was even a chance of taking down Finnagel, Sarah had to take it, no matter the risk. She only hoped that if she failed, he wouldn't take it out on Keane or Megan. Keane had responded to none of her attempts to contact him and was undoubtedly back under Finnagel's control by now.

Of course, she knew the old sorcerer planned to kill Keane already, so she probably was not making things any worse.

"Create a tiny portal high in the sky above Treaty Hill, as close to the Forest Castle as you can make it. We're taking this fight to his doorstep."

"All right." Sarah visualized the castle but stopped herself. "No, I've got a better idea. We're going to Tyrrane. When was the last time you saw the capital?"

Gabby smiled and stepped close. "Much better. Now repeat after me..."

38

STREET FIGHT

SARAH

No matter how much Sarah learned, there was always a thousand times as much she did not understand. She did not even begin to comprehend what Gabby had asked her to do to her tiny portal spell to land her here on the dark cobble-stoned streets of Dismon, but here she was regardless.

Solid business fronts of dark timber, gray stone, and whitewashed plaster lined both sides of the broad street under a turbulent gray sky. In the distance, the Fell Citadel menaced the city, foreboding and judgmental.

Black-capped citizens moved fast and efficiently to their many destinations, and Sarah was a stone in the cogs of their machinery. At first, they bustled past, giving her nothing more than rude glances—until someone recognized her.

"It's the Hill Fury. Flee! She's here to murder us all!"

"That's unfortunate." Gabby made a tutting sound. "I imagine we have a limited amount of time now before the troops arrive. Ah, well. We never thought this was going to be easy, did we?"

"I was hoping I might live through it." Sarah drew her sword. "What now?"

"You won't need that." Gabby glanced meaningfully down at Sarah's unsheathed blade.

Sarah did not move.

"Very well. Do as you like. What do *I* know? I only created the universe." It looked up and shook its head. "Use the rune engine's tunnel to power a communication spell with Finnagel. Be prepared for anything."

Sarah had never felt less prepared in all her life. Power coursed through her, suffusing her being. But could any amount of raw power be enough to kill the sorcerer of Greenshade?

The spell made mental contact. She could feel Finnagel but saw no more than a gray mist.

"What? Ah, Sarah my dear." Finnagel was not visible, but his presence was overpowering. "It has taken me considerable effort to track you, and here I should've simply waited for you to contact me. I understand you have been unforgivably headstrong."

Sarah gasped as Finnagel pulled at the spell, forcing them into closer alignment. She could now see him clearly, as through a darkened channel. She could smell the high breezes and musty stone of the Forest Castle, and she could feel her own fear.

"You intend to kill *me*?" Finnagel glanced at the blade in Sarah's hand. "With that?" He reached into the passageway between then and motioned in Ghost Hand, taking the spell from her. The darkness inside the channel began to spin. It grew teeth and hungry razored talons.

"You know, I've had your Keane and a hundred of the most elite King's Swords available drilling in the courtyard since your last visit. I thought it'd be entertaining to watch them bring you to heel. But no, I should've realized this is all too personal to you to let anyone else come between us. Well, come ahead then, girl. You are not the first apprentice I've been forced to slaughter. I doubt you'll be the last."

In a twinkling, Finnagel's hand was on her hauberk, dragging her into the toothy maw. She redirected the power of the engine down through her feet and cemented herself to the cobblestones.

"The phrase for a 'place of power' in Metzoferran is *pahn-hu*.

Similar to rigid tide but without the ebb and flow connotations." Gabby could *not* think this was an appropriate time for another lesson. "Pull him through."

Sarah let the rune engine's magic flare, and hot and cold pins prickled across her muscles. She gripped the Darrish sorcerer's hand and watched surprise break across his face when *she* yanked *him* through the tunnel and threw him to the street behind her.

"Reduced to a word, the sorcerer's place of power, or *pahn-hu*, shares certain traits with other tools and phenomena a certain kind of magical practitioner uses all the time."

Sarah blew a strand of hair out of her face and cut her eyes at Gabby. "Not the time."

It smiled at her, showing straight white teeth that made the comfortably worn linens it wore look dingy. "There's never a bad time for learning."

"Clever." Finnagel hopped to his feet. Short and dark, his graying black hair blew over his powerful shoulders. "I didn't think you had the ability to do something like this. Here in the house of Angrim himself, with neither of us able to use sorcery, you doubtlessly thought we would be on more even ground." He narrowed his gaze. "But you *are* using sorcery. How are you doing that?"

By way of answer, Sarah aimed a tornado blast of wind at Finnagel's chest and created a tiny portal both in front of herself and directly behind him. She jabbed her sword through in a straight clean lunge. If she failed to take him down before he figured out how she was doing what she was doing and created a counter to her, she would be killed—as would Keane, probably Megan, and however many more tens or hundreds of thousands that stood between Finnagel and his subjugation of everything he saw.

Finnagel's hand came up in front of him, directing the wind around him. At the same time, he twisted, ducked, and jammed a finger beneath the biceps of her attacking arm, which stuck through the tiny portal behind him. The gold-colored kaftan he wore snapped with the speed of his motion.

A shock ran down Sarah's limb, and she dropped her sword into

Finnagel's waiting hand. She leaped backward and yanked her hand out of the portal just in time to avoid his swinging cut.

She drew a dagger.

"Consider a *pahn-hu fendreeth*. Or a *gelran pahn-hu ohnashi*. Do you see?" Gabby tutted. "Mind the sword. It won't do you any good to learn all the Metzoferran in the world if you let him cut your head off."

"It's not too late to reconsider." Finnagel waved several swipes at Sarah's middle, which she barely avoided. Finnagel was smaller than she was but faster and stronger. His extreme experience worked to negate her advantages here, and if she did not take care of this fast, the Ebon Host would be sure to take care of her when they arrived. Finnagel lowered the sword. "What is this about? The dominance moths on your pet royals? I did that for your benefit. If they can't get into trouble, I don't have to kill them."

"That's part of it." Sarah circled right. Finnagel was too crafty. What was she doing? "The runecrafters haven't done anything wrong. They don't deserve to be killed."

Her foot wobbled on a loose cobblestone. She stopped.

"How many times must I explain this to you?" Finnagel frowned, gray anger gathering on his face. "They are chattel. Fleeting. You are too young to understand. I'd intended for Angrim to be killed after you'd had some perspective behind you, but things moved faster than I'd expected."

With the toe of her boot, Sarah pried the heavy stone up. She got her foot under it and kicked, catching the flying cobble in a stream of tornado force wind that sent it at Finnagel's head.

He sidestepped the wind and—impossibly—reached out to catch the cobblestone missile.

"You're never going to die, Sarah, unless you make me kill you now. They *all* will, no matter what you do. Saving one human today preserves his life for the merest eyeblink of time." Finnagel kept the sword down, but Sarah knew it could be up long before she could cross the fifteen feet that separated them.

He dropped the stone to the street.

"You don't even think of them as people." Under different circumstances, Sarah might feel pity for Finnagel. How lonely must he be? "How could you think I'd let you dominate them all?"

"Think of the exercise like sewing a bag." Gabby stood over Finnagel's shoulder. "Pulling the metaphorical drawstring, as it were. Am I making myself clear?"

"Gabby, *please*." Sarah did not take her eyes off Finnagel. "Just shut up until this is over."

One of Finnagel's brows shot up. "Gabby? Who are you?" The sorcerer's mouth fell open. "He's here. He's talking to you. The Dead God is here." Finnagel twirled a finger, and a bright burning line constricted around Sarah's throat.

"I have experience using sorcery in the places of power of others." Finnagel walked to Sarah and plucked the dagger out of her hand as she fell to her knees. Great. Now he had *both* her blades. "I might have no more power than I brought in with me and be unable to pull more, but I know how to make the slightest bit of sorcery utterly lethal. Please consider what that means."

Blood ran down Sarah's fingers where she tried to pull against the hot wire around her neck. She could not breathe. She could barely think. Finnagel had died ten thousand times during the occupation of Treaty Hill, and each of those made him more powerful. This was madness.

"I know this isn't yet second nature to you," Gabby said, "but I really think you should be able to carry tactics from one battle to the next."

Wait. She didn't have to do it this way. She was being stupid.

White light spilled out of Sarah's eyes, and her head snapped up to glare at Finnagel. The fiery garrote burned away. He could not learn. He did not care. He was after a tool, not an apprentice, not a human being. She had known for *years* what kind of thing Finnagel was, and she had simply been too afraid and too powerless to do anything about it. He could not be allowed to run Greenshade. He could not be allowed to rule the world.

"At least Angrim is an honest evil." This time, the wind alone that

Sarah whipped up tore dozens of heavy cobblestones out of the street and flew them at the old sorcerer. There would be no catching these.

Somehow, he got beneath them, rolled forward, and stabbed Sarah in the foot with her dagger. She grunted and showed her teeth —and redirected her winds to include him.

"Now you're just being ridiculous." Gabby folded its arms over its chest. "I can't make myself any plainer. Sometimes I wonder why I bother."

Finnagel let go of Sarah's sword and gripped her dagger with both hands. His kaftan whipped like a torn sail in the furious wind. Jarring pain robbed her leg of strength, but she mastered it. It was only pain —pain, she knew well.

Sarah punched down at the back of Finnagel's head, but he let go of the dagger and grabbed her arm.

"And just what is this?" Finnagel's fingers found the rune engine.

His eyes flared with stolen yellow light.

"Oh, ho, *ho*. Entertainment after all." He let go and flew backward, arms creating exclamations in Ghost Hand while he shouted a spell in Ancient Egren. Behind him, a scene painted itself across the broad street, showing the main courtyard of the Forest Castle. A hundred men in green-on-yellow tabards stood at attention, longbows ready for violence.

At their head, Keane called the charge.

Just on the Greenshade side of the huge portal, Finnagel floated in the air, unaffected by Angrim's place of power. His deaths swelled his sorcery stronger than ever before, far stronger.

In black plate with one yellow pauldron and one green, Keane ran for Sarah, limp vanished, sword outstretched, and an inhuman howl on his lips.

And a dominance moth curled tightly around the top of his head.

Keane came in hard and fast, crackling with energy from Finnagel. Sarah got inside his swing and elbowed him in the face.

He did not notice.

His blade came down against a plaster storefront, and it exploded outward, covering them in dust and bits of shattered sticks. If she had any doubts about Keane being Finnagel's creature before, they were gone now.

The next blow destroyed what was left of the downstairs front wall, and Keane shoved Sarah inside the building, rushing along behind her with his sword poised to run her through. She had nothing to defend herself that might not kill him. The thought bubbled up that she might die here.

Behind Keane, the upstairs of the building fell in and blocked any hope of escape.

Sarah smelled cheese. They were in a cheese shop. Destroyed counters stood at crazy angles, covered in debris. Her stabbed foot throbbed.

Keane winked.

"You *bastard*." She punched him in the armored shoulder, denting the green pauldron but not affecting Keane.

"Please don't do that." Keane's grin warmed every part of her. "That evil sack of wet shits filled me up with magic nut butter, but it doesn't keep me from getting injured; it just keeps the injuries from affecting me until the spell ends. When it does, that arm you just punched is gonna fall off."

"Oh, Keane." Sarah grabbed Keane and hugged him tight—but not tight enough to drive his ribs into his lungs once Finnagel's spell faded. "Thank the wisdom of Al-Dagos, you were able to keep Morholt's illusions intact. I was so worried when you stopped answering my communications."

Outside there were shouts and screams. Sarah guessed that the first of the Ebon Host had arrived and walked right into hell.

"Couldn't take the chance." Keane shook his head. "After your visit, Finn watched Megan and me like a hawk that thought someone was gonna steal his favorite pile of fish heads." His grin turned shrewd. "Of course, if I'd known you were gonna take him on directly all by yourself, I'd have just jumped off a parapet. That's right. Don't look so shocked. I know what a parapet is."

"Not totally alone." Sarah waved at the empty air. "Some god's ghost has been giving me pointers, but it's gone now." She stood straighter. "Hang on. That makes sense. It *is* like sewing a bag."

"Sure." Keane took a step away from Sarah and nodded. "Why didn't you just say that before?"

She gave him a flat stare. "I need to get Finn back on this side of that portal he created. Can you help with that?"

"Yeah." Keane nodded. "I think I can help with that."

Sarah erupted from the destroyed storefront with Keane hot on her heels. To their right, soldiers of the Ebon Host died in the streets, riddled with green- and yellow-fletched arrows, while to their left, a hundred handpicked King's Swords waited for their next targets. The instant Sarah came to her feet, they drew.

Keane bowled into her, his sword clattering against the stones as she spun away. He rose and reared back to deliver a death blow.

Behind him, a hundred archers released their deadly bowstrings.

Keane flew straight up, buoyed by rushing winds.

The arrows hit a hurricane and flew back the way they'd come. Sarah howled with the effort of controlling two discrete spells at once, and the bowmen fell backward, some rolling through the portal into Greenshade.

Keane dropped into the screaming gale and shot away like an arrow himself.

Finnagel sliced the wind with a hand, shunting arrows off to either side. Keane hit him like a stone from a trebuchet, and the pair went clattering to the grass of the Forest Castle courtyard.

Finnagel disentangled himself from Keane and his armor and stood. He reached down and lifted Keane off the grass. He shouted at Keane and gesticulated angrily.

Keane drove his sword through Finnagel's middle with both magically enhanced hands.

For the breadth of two heartbeats, there was silence on the violence-strewn streets of Dismon as well as the bright courtyard of the Forest Castle.

In the sunlight on the other side of the portal, Sarah saw Keane grab the now-impaled Finnagel and run back toward her, deliberately kicking the sorcerer with every steel-shod step.

"You bastard. You *insect*." Finnagel was having a hard time expressing his outrage while being repeatedly kicked in the face. "*I control you!*"

Sarah laughed at that. In all her life, she had never known anyone as difficult to control as Keane. She couldn't wait to tell Megan.

And then Sarah closed her eyes.

"Well, finally," Gabby said.

A white light intruded on the dark behind Sarah's eyelids. She recognized the symbols in Ancient Egren that formed her Blow Out the Candle spell as well as the alterations she had made to them in Ghost Hand. This stanza moved the air, and that one directed it. They glowed with brain-searing intensity due to the inordinate amount of energy being channeled by the rune engine on her wrist.

A short distance away, she saw the portal Finnagel had created with the stolen bit of power when he touched the engine. It took her breath away.

The doorway to the courtyard of the Forest Castle was lit—no, it was *suspended*—by thousands of points of golden light, each one an expression in one of the three primary languages of magic. The structure of it not only ran the spell but also supported itself. And Finnagel had made it in *seconds*.

Sorcerous energies poured into Finnagel through the portal as he gathered strength for his next spell. Keane was visible to her only by the tiny ring of runes Morholt had placed on him to keep the illusion of the dominance moth alive. Finnagel must have already taken the extra strength and endurance back from him.

Sarah reached out with her mind and picked apart the complicated edifice that made the portal, rearranging it into a crude barrier that Finnagel destroyed with a spell meant for her.

"That certainly seems to have taken the wind out of his sails." Gabby sounded amused. "The portal is gone, and he just expended all of his strength trying to kill you. He's coming back. I think he wants the rune engine. *Ouch*. The king of Greenshade just boxed his sorcerer's ears. Finnagel does *not* look good. There's also still a sword through him."

Good. If Keane could keep Finnagel busy without either of them killing the other—

"No, I think I spoke too soon. Finnagel is definitely going to murder the king."

Sarah reached into the black fabric that made up Angrim's place of power and pulled it tight. She reinforced it with tunneled power, and in so doing, created a tiny bubble of reality shut off from everything.

Even from the rune engine's source.

Sarah opened her eyes.

Most of the archers fled back through Finnagel's portal before Sarah snuffed it out, and more lay unconscious in the street. But eight men remained and tried to sink their arrows into Finnagel, who stood over a bloody and battered Keane. They followed their king, not the man trying to kill him.

The sorcerer hooked a finger and eight bowstrings twanged apart.

As Sarah stalked toward her former mentor, she smiled her crooked half smile and shook her head. With almost no power left, cut off from everything and in the most rigid magical environment possible, he still defended himself effectively. She limped left and picked up one of the King's Swords' blades.

How were they *still* using these old round-gripped swords?

Finnagel noticed her. He squeezed his eyes shut and showed his teeth as he pulled Keane's blade from his own guts.

Blood spattered on the dark cobbles. In the upstairs home of a narrow bakery across the street, a round-eyed Tyrranean woman yanked her threadbare curtains closed.

"You should hurry this bit along." Gabby pointed up the street toward the Fell Citadel. "Angrim's response is on the way."

"You can't beat me, Sarah." Finnagel leaned sideways and spat in the street. "Even here, you are no match. And if you were, the best you could hope for would be to send me back to the Forest Castle."

The sorcerer flicked Keane's sword up to push aside Sarah's first attack. She hopped backward to avoid his return cut and almost fell over when the dagger wound in her foot flared.

"I'll have you back by my side, Sarah. Willing and compliant. Don't forget, when I awaken back home, the two royal brats will need a new father. Should I bring them sweets or stuff them in a sack and drop them in the canal?"

"Take care." Gabby nodded in Finnagel's direction. "He's goading you."

Sarah came in hard, trailing blood, and beat back Finnagel's attacks to force him off-balance. He spun and drove a rock-hard fist into her ribcage. Sarah cried out and dropped below Finnagel's follow-up swing, banging her knees on the cobblestones.

The only thing that filled Sarah with more loathing than being forced to serve Finnagel was the idea of him left alone with Volker and Shayla. The old sorcerer did not care for anyone other than himself or anything other than enslaving her. He killed his last apprentice's wife just to get the man's attention. Even his crusade against the demon runecrafters was only because he did not want mere humans to have magic.

How could she have taken so long to see his true monstrousness?

Her world narrowed to just her and Finnagel—and she intended to narrow it a bit more.

"I am going to kill you, old man." Sarah swung her borrowed blade in a long arc that forced Finnagel back a step. She had better reach, so she would use it. "But you're wrong about one thing. You're not just cut off from the magic; you're cut off from everything—including your own place of power. I pulled up the edges of Angim's house and sewed you into them. You die here, you're just dead."

"You can't do sorcery like that." Finnagel's eyes were wide, and his gaze darted left and right. The wound in his stomach bled freely, and the normal rich darkness of his face turned gray. No one can do sorcery like that."

"I don't think it *is* sorcery, strictly speaking." She raised an eyebrow at Gabby. "What kind of magic is this?"

"God magic," Gabby replied.

"How 'bout that?" Sarah poked a sword point at Finnagel's shoulder, which he was not fast enough to defend. "Gabby says it's god magic. Maybe it is. It seems like once you know Metzoferran, you don't need all those other languages the sorcerers made up. And runecrafting? The thing you've been trying to stamp out? That's the other half of it." She held up her arm to show him the rune engine. "This thing is amazing."

"Sarah, I know you don't want to accept this, but I know you better than you do. I'm older. I've seen the patterns." Finnagel put his blade on the ground and opened his hands to her. "Harden Grayspring abused your trust in order to keep you by his side. But you rid yourself of him when you came to me. Now you're repeating this paradigm because you think my motives are selfish. You can't see it yet because you are too young, but I am only trying to make you grow into what you should be."

He smiled, and for an instant, Sarah saw the face of the man she met all those years ago on the steps of the Forest Castle—warm creases in the dark folds of his skin where mischief twinkled and hidden secrets danced. But then he spoke, and the illusion vanished.

"My many deaths have burned the weakness out of me." He ran a knotty hand down the front of his dirty kaftan. "The humanity is gone. I am as close to divine as any creature born of woman has ever been. Follow me. This will be yours, too."

In the distance, the sound of hundreds of troops running down the cobbles rattled between buildings as well as something else, something larger.

"I've been letting you talk because we have history, but you're running out of time." Truthfully, she only let him talk because she had as yet been unable to kill him, but there was no need to admit that. Sarah rested the blade of her sword over her shoulder. "Is there a point?" She hoped there was not. If there was, that meant she was far stupider than she liked to believe.

Gabby strode around the pair, stopping when it got behind Finnagel.

"Harden wasn't your father, Sarah." Finnagel winced and put a hand over his stomach wound. "Neither am I, and neither is the Dead God. The difference is to them you are just a tool to be used for their own ends. I only want you to grow. Release us, and we'll go back to Treaty Hill. I won't go easy on you, but you and I will eventually stand over all of Andos as new gods. We will—"

Gabby arched an eyebrow. "Well, *that's* unfair. Also, I believe he intends to throw that knife behind his back into your throat."

"I'm sorry, Finn. I really am." Sarah swung with all her sorcerous might to slice through muscle and crack through bone. Finnagel's head spun a wheel of blood before it fell twenty feet from the rest of his corpse. The knife bounced on the stones.

"Nice job. Of course, he was already mostly dead from when *I* killed him." Keane limped over and picked up his sword from next to Finnagel's body.

"*You* killed him?" Sarah's mouth hung open. "You slept through most of it. Like when I tied together a whole city so *that* son of a bitch wouldn't just come back to life again?" The size of what Sarah had done hit her. She had killed an immortal. Permanently. Twice now. She almost forgot about Angrim's apprentice Valafar at the gates of the Forest Castle.

"Fine." Keane held up his hands. "All I'm saying is that I murdered him first."

"Touching as this is, you really should be going." Gabby stared up the street at the oncoming Host.

"Before it is entirely too late."

39

IF YOU CAN'T SAY SOMETHING NICE, JUST LEAVE THE BALL GAG WHERE IT IS

MORHOLT

Raven, are you good?" Out of the terrifying Dovenhouse, Morholt's senses returned to him. Along with his wits came concern for his sister. They were still in the broad grassy yard between the horrible marble building and the wood, but Morholt's fear of discovery had left him. He might never be afraid again.

"I'm fine." Raven shrugged Catlia's unconscious arm further up on her own shoulder. "I think Catlia's been eating pretty healthy though."

Across the vegetable field, a war horn blew, and soldiers of Tyrrane's Ebon Host came galloping through astride barded chargers, spears raised, sending pigs of all sizes squealing into the trees.

"Ah, toad dicks," Morholt whispered.

For just a single adrenalized instant, Morholt froze. Behind him, he heard temple knights sound the attack, and in front, archers of the Ebon Host set up in the vegetable field behind galloping cavalry. Caught in the open yard between, carrying their wounded, the Free Hand limped toward the trees.

A sandwich shuffling off the dinnerplate of a ravening four-armed lord, with equal chances of escape.

Morholt's vision swam with spinning rings. He inhaled deep and attempted to ignore the shouts of soldiers come to kill him. Without the rune engine, trying to control this many spells at once would most likely result in a massive headache, a complete loss of control, and their subsequent deaths.

"You can't get a blowjob without risking your dick being bitten off," Morholt said through gritted teeth.

"What?" Romi glanced at him over her shoulder.

And they all vanished.

"Turn." Raven's voice was a harsh hiss. "Go right." The group crossed in front of the Dovenhouse, away from the garden and out of the onrushing vise of men, steel, and horses.

All of Morholt's concentration bent to his spells. Blazing rings spun behind closed eyelids, and he dragged Ameli's soft body in the direction of Raven's voice.

A shout from the knights rose above the din. "Watch the grass. You can see their steps. We will kill them for Prolocutor Vancess."

Raven spat. "Shitting temple fucks. Romi, you got Catlia? I'm going to give those assholes something else to think about instead of following. *LOOK OUT!*"

Arrows whistled through the air and thumped into the ground around them. Louder were those that banged into the armor and shields of the temple knights, now less than thirty feet away. The edges of Morholt's concentration slipped, and Ameli faded into view. He squeezed his eyes shut and tried to cover her again, but he failed, and Raven's invisibility slid away too.

The Ebon Host cavalry crashed into the knights, and the cacophony shattered what was left of Morholt's spells. He opened his eyes, but all he could see were blurred images of his friends and a distant tree line. His feet dragged, and hot sweat ran into his vision.

Dammit. This made no kind of sense. Why were the *Tyrraneans* here? And although he had fewer problems with this part of it, why were they fighting the temple knights? Oh. This must be about *Sarah*.

"There!" shouted a man behind them. "I see them. They're right —" The voice cut off with a loud crunch.

Catlia woke and screamed.

Over his shoulder, Morholt saw one of the Host dragged from his horse and killed just before the last of Vancess's temple knights fell to Host spears. The cavalry reoriented on the Free Hand. Behind them, the archers put away their bows for swords and came running across the field.

"Catlia, *no*." Romi tried to hold the frightened woman, but Catlia broke away. Instead of running in another direction, Catlia stopped, fists clenching and arms sweeping in wide circles. She faced the two dozen mounted soldiers and let out a ragged, keening wail.

The Host's charge rambled and went off in two dozen directions at once. Some of the riders smiled, some were frightened, but most simply appeared confused. Whatever their state, they had forgotten all about the Free Hand.

Raven rushed ahead and ran further right across the front of the Dovenhouse, out of sight of the soldiers on foot. The stained marble edifice lost its threat in the face of the oncoming army. But she ran past the door toward the close trees at the far corner. The last of the Hand made the tree line just as the first archers ran into their own milling and confused cavalry.

————

From their hiding place in the trees, Morholt and the rest of the Free Hand watched the Ebon Host search the Dovenhouse and fan out into the woods. The Free Hand were fearful of moving, lest they be spotted, and scared to stay where they were. For now, staying put had won out.

"Where did they all come from?" Romi stood on tiptoe to peer over a bush. "And why are they here?" She kept an eye on the soldiers while the Hand decided what to do.

"The sword strokers came from Tyrrane." Morholt massaged his temples. It had been a long time since he had done any runecrafting without the engine. He never should have tried to do so much on his own. "And as for why they're here, I couldn't say. They're probably after Man Hands." Damn everything to hell. He wanted to make a new future for himself and these people. Do some good in the world. Protect people, not kill them. And Sarah took that from him. He may not hate her anymore, but he sure as hell resented her.

"Who?" Romi asked.

"The Hill Fury." Morholt turned and nodded toward Ameli, who sat between Sabni and Mahu, her knees pulled tight against her chest. The two big men held her protectively. "This one going to be all right?"

"Don't talk about me like I'm not even here." Ameli glared up at Morholt through tear-swollen eyes. "Why don't you decide which of *your* exes dies and see how you feel? And don't say Selenna because we all know she doesn't count." Ameli could not yet walk on her own after her efforts saving Mahu's life. But Morholt thought that Sabni would act as her legs for the rest of her days if she required it. He might have to be Morholt's as well.

Sabni shrugged and offered Morholt a sympathetic smile, and Mahu hugged Ameli tighter.

"How about you, big brother?" Raven settled in the leaf clutter beside Morholt. "That was a real shitshow. I assume we're in for some whining about how you let everyone down and got two of us murdered and a lot of innocent people died all because you weren't good enough."

"Dammit, Raven." Morholt straightened and put his hands on his knees. "Reinar and Selenna are dead, and we'll be soon if we don't figure a way to limp out of here without anyone seeing us. Just give it a fucking minute, all right?" The truth was that even if he had wanted to, Morholt did not have the energy to consider his own failings. He made that rune engine more than fifteen years ago. No wonder he was so out of practice crafting without it.

A rare grin broke across Raven's features. She held up a hand. "See?"

Romi watched the soldiers. As long as the Host stayed away from their little area of woodland, they could afford to sit tight and wait for them to leave. The one thing they had in their favor was that the mounted troops were useless, not just because the horses would not run in the wood but because the riders were all having the reason they were here re-explained to them after Catlia's runecrafting.

"Whatever reason the Host chose to crash our party, we can be glad they've taken care of Vancess and his Shepherd knights for us." He directed a glare at his sister. "So maybe you can wrap all your bitching about *my* failings around a broom stick and shove—"

"Fine." Raven raised her hands. "You've saved all the best screws of your life that wanted to be saved—and one that apparently didn't. Do you have a plan now?"

"How *is* Catlia?" After erasing the Hand from the memories of the mounted Host, she remained sullen and fearful and refused to so much as raise her head. Morholt hoped this was because of the gaffarmord, though Catlia had always been a frightened woman. Just to be safe, he tied her hands together. She could not runecraft without making the rings with her arms, and Morholt did not want her getting scared and accidentally making him forget how to wipe his own ass.

"The same." Raven pulled out one of her knives and ran a thin finger along the edge of it. "Scared bird living in your asshole and hoping you never have to take a shit. Though I think we can add drugged out of her gourd to the list. Probably be back to just normal scared-as-fuck once that wears off." She sheathed the blade and drew another, repeating her actions. "You gonna answer my question, or should I beat it out of you?"

"I thought we could go home." Morholt smiled at his sister, love and sadness clouding his thoughts even more than the exhaustion. "Maybe kill our parents, reclaim the estate. That sort of thing."

Raven's eyes flew wide, and her huge grin lit their hiding place. She actually squeaked as she jumped forward to embrace Morholt.

"Oh, toad dicks. Get off of me. I wouldn't have told you if I'd known you'd go all teenager's-first-orgasm over it." Morholt pushed against Raven, though both laughed as quietly as they could. "Have some self-respect, woman. You're going to get us caught."

"I'm not trying to interrupt the family reunion plans, but maybe we need an idea for right now?" Romi crouched behind the bush she had been looking over. "Have you talked to April recently?"

Morholt thought about it for a moment and then opened his pack. He unwrapped April's card and held it up. His vision blurred, and he shook his head to clear it.

"Hey, Bean. Know any good jokes?"

Beady little eyes held him in black regard. "You're going to die."

"Unconventional, but it's better constructed than most of them." Morholt scratched his chin. "But it's not really—oh, what's the word —funny?"

"So, we're still doing this doom and gloom?" Romi sat down on Morholt's other side and looked over his shoulder at April. "Sweetie, we're not going to die. You're going to help us stay alive."

The heat of Romi's body, so close to his, sent a chill through Morholt. A hot chill? She already said she was not interested. He needed to get his thoughts in order.

"Maybe you could help us just not die *today*." Morholt wanted to goose this conversation along, but April was effectively a permanent little girl. Rushing her would only upset her further. "Why are there Ebon Host here?"

"I don't know." April reached out of view of the picture and pulled back a stool to sit on. "They will return to Dismon empty-handed soon whether they find you or not."

"Then they're not looking for us." Romi sat back and leaned on her hands.

Her distracting heat gone, Morholt refocused on the problem. "Maybe let's set smaller goals, all right?" He waited for April's nod and continued, "Great. The Host is all over. What direction do we go to avoid them?"

"Too late for that." April wrung her little hands. "I'm sorry."

Morholt did nothing for the space of an eyeblink before filling the air in his mind's eye with spinning wheels of glowing runes. But as he spun new rings, the first few fell apart behind them. He did not have the mental reserves left to hide the group.

To his right, a lanky soldier in the Host's black and gray poked his head between a pair of tree boles, led by a taut bow. His gaze traveled over Catlia's head, and the arrow tip hovered inches from her face. Behind him, another two men crept, arrows at the ready.

Mahu and Sabni burst from nearby hiding places, while Ameli ran the opposite direction. Morholt watched himself, Raven, and Romi flee left, while Catlia went after Ameli.

The two archers following ran left and right and yelled to their comrades who closed in on the fleeing mercenaries from all sides. The sound of fighting broke out, followed by screams.

The lead archer stared, confused, at the mercenaries still sitting in front of him.

"Who are you?" He looked up into the trees. "Where are we?" One of his hands reached up and caressed a tree bole. "Feels nice. Gaarhoo. Ha." The hand moved to his own purpling face, and he fell over backward, struggling against something unseen.

"Catlia." Morholt retained just enough presence of mind to piece together what he was seeing. "Did you just make that man forget who we were, how to talk, and how to breathe?"

"Yes." She lowered her head even further. Through the trees, the sounds of combat stopped.

"I thought you needed to use your hands to do your tricks."

"That was years ago," she answered without looking up. "I can do it all in my head now."

"Hang on." Raven's voice was an angry growl. "Are you telling me she could have fucked any of us in the brain at any time, and we wouldn't even have known it?" She frowned on one side of her face and studied Catlia. "Hey. Why *didn't* you fuck us all in the brains?"

"Because you were helping."

"Thank you for making a fake Free Hand for the Host to chase, Romi." Morholt breathed a deep, tired sigh. His reliance on the rune engine now made him the weakest runecrafter in the group. "This way they'll have dead bodies. No reason for them to keep looking for us. Why didn't you do that to begin with?"

"I use my runecrafting to farm olives, not dodge armies." She fixed Morholt with a meaningful gaze. "Some of us haven't really had to spend a lot of time figuring out how to best use our abilities to get our asses out of the slings we jumped into."

An idea occurred to him. "Hey, can you make a Sarah?"

Romi grinned and nodded, though she too looked worn out. "Yeah. I think I can do that."

A few seconds later, Sarah appeared in the front vestibule of the Dovenhouse and bolted east out of sight and across the small patch of farmland. Soon after, a soldier shouted, and chase was given.

"Amazing." Morholt watched as more and more Host poured out of the woods around the Dovenhouse and out of the cracked building itself. "Look at 'em go. We're free and clear gang. Every one of us."

"Not every one of us." Mahu spoke without reproach, but Ameli glared daggers at Morholt. "I'm going back for Reinar. We can bury him here in these woods. He liked the trees, didn't he, Ameli?"

Ameli did not answer but stood up and tottered back to the broken Dovenhouse. Mahu and Sabni followed her.

"Whoo. Creating people'll really take it out of a gal." Romi leaned back against a smooth-barked flowering tree with broad shiny leaves. "Why'dya think Sarah run off on us like that? You think she saw the Ebon Host rolling up and just ran for it?"

"I don't know her that well." Morholt thought about the various things he'd heard Harden and Eli—or the king and queen of Greenshade—say about Sarah. "Doesn't seem like her style, though."

"I know why the Hill Fury left. I was there when it happened." Raven watched the other three disappear around the corner of the Dovenhouse to get Reinar. "Soon as she saw the Tyrraneans, she told me, 'The Ebon Host is here to murder all of you stupid fuckers. I'd stay and get murdered too, but the fur on my ass has grown back, and I need a trim before I go home, so all of Greenshade can stick its nose up my giant clean-shaven ass.'"

"Lady has priorities." Romi winked at Raven, who smirked back at her.

April cleared her tiny throat. Morholt had forgotten he still held her card in his hand. "Well, now you can go southwest, I guess, but you'll still die later. There's hot pox in Sedria."

"Thanks, Bean." Morholt smiled down at his painted friend. "You just saved our lives."

In the distance, well beyond the Dovenhouse, a cheer went up from the Host. They had captured, or even killed, the false Sarah.

"For now." April frowned, angry and sad.

"I'm not so sure." Romi poked her head over the top of the card. "Just a minute ago, you said the Ebon Host was going to return empty-handed whether they found us or not. Didn't that mean they were after Sarah?"

"I don't know." April's tongue darted out of the side of her mouth and licked her eyelid.

"But are they returning empty-handed now?"

The little imp screwed up her snouted face and squeezed her beady eyes shut. All at once, she popped open. "*No.* They're going back to Dismon with the Hill Fury's corpse. The future *changed.*"

Romi raised her head to look straight into Morholt's eyes and grabbed him by the shoulder. "See? We didn't get killed here. We're responsible for our own outcomes. Take your future into your own hands, and you'll be fine."

"Oh no," April said from the card below them, "you're still all gonna die. Just not 'til tomorrow. Maybe the next day."

40

DOING GOD MAGIC BEFORE IT WAS COOL

SARAH

S arah, Keane, and the eight Swords hid behind carts, porch support beams, building corners, and one sedate-looking pony and worried over the contingent of Ebon Host that filled the street a hundred feet away. These Host all held strung bows, arrows nocked but not pulled.

Using Blow Out the Candle would have sent the soldiers bowling back up the broad street had Sarah not hobbled herself by reinforcing Angrim's place of power. On the other hand, she had also effectively cut off Angrim's magic too, and she assumed the ancient and cautious beast would not dare to venture out of his lair.

So, there was that.

The King's Swords had both retrieved and restrung their bows, and though Sarah figured that could only get them into trouble now, she could not bring herself to ask them to put the weapons away.

A cold breeze blew up the cobbled thoroughfare, ruffling the hair of the corpses littering it. Behind the line of black-and-gray clad Host, several children cried for their mothers.

Gabby stood in the center of the street, head cocked to one side as it stared past the soldiers.

"They're just standing there, not killing me, and making me

nervous." Keane peeked around the rump of the pony, who chewed unconcerned on an apple it stole from a costermonger's cart. "It's like when you fall off a boat into sharky water, and you know they're down there looking at your tasty brown legs, but you can't see them, and you're just treading water thinking your only defense is pooping your brains out to drive them off, but you don't because then you'd just be swimming in a cloud of your own turds, and, for all you know, sharks *like* eating terrified king poop, but either way, is it even worth it?"

"To be clear," Sarah asked, "were you planning on pooping on the Ebon Host?"

"No." Keane ducked back down behind the larcenous pony. "Not anymore."

"Sarah"—Gabby pointed to her while continuing to gaze up the wide cobbled road—"it's time to run now. The thing that's coming, it's an abomination, and trust me when I tell you I know what I'm talking about. You can't fight it. Not yet."

"Time to run, everyone." Sarah glanced at the Swords, who nodded back to her.

"How was it *not* time to fucking run before?" Keane sheathed his sword. "And where should we run *to*? Do you think we can hit that alley before one of those hundred and fifty bowmen gets lucky and murders us?" He raised his head over the pony's back. "What's that noise?"

A clattering thunder grew louder, and from behind the Tyrranean soldiers came four huge oxen pulling a heavy wagon reinforced with iron plates. Big metal-wrapped wheels crunched against the cobblestones, and a dozen more soldiers dressed all in black trotted to either side. They had no gray on their tabards and bulkier armor than ordinary Ebon Host.

The rest of the Host lowered their bows and stood aside to allow the wagon to rattle through the center of the street.

A thin woman stood in the back of the open wagon, nine feet tall, blue-purple skin, and a very long-bladed spear in her hand. Lightning danced in her eyes, and a long braid of thick red hair blazed over her shoulder. She wore a sleeveless gown of burgundy velvet with a high slit up one side.

What was this creature? The goddess Magda showed Sarah a vision of Angrim years ago, and this was not him.

Keane glanced at Sarah over his shoulder. "If she asks, I'm telling her you killed Finnagel."

Gabby spun to shout at Sarah. "Go now while the soldiers are letting her through."

"*Go.*" Sarah sprinted back down the street, away from the Host. The Swords followed, and Keane ran behind as fast as he could limp.

Behind, soldiers shouted and bowstrings twanged. Sarah stopped at the corner and urged the others to greater speed. Two of the Swords dropped immediately, and Keane dove behind a thick wooden timber that jutted from the front of a big chandlery building. The pony suffered a grazing wound on its cheek and became considerably less sedate, bolting for the far side of the street and screaming bloody murder.

The instant the arrows stopped cracking against the cobbles, Keane took off for the alley, running past Sarah even as the sky once again filled with feathered death. In the alley and out of the most immediate danger, one of the Swords went down against the walls, his yellow tabard with the diagonal green stripe and green castle turning crimson. Two more bled from serious wounds but remained on their feet.

The alley was spacious and clean but not so wide that the gigantic wagon would fit into it. Stalls and carts of goods lined the north side of it, their owners now run off in sensible terror.

The voice of a cultured young woman riding on thunderstorms gripped Sarah by the teeth and vibrated her skull. "Sarah, mercenary, Hill Fury, and Pilgrim Handmaiden. *Button.*"

"Button?" Keane's brow went up.

"That was Magda's name for me." Sarah leaned down and lifted the worst-wounded Sword over her shoulder. He groaned once and lost consciousness. "Let's go."

"Turn right at the end of the alley. Mind the pickle barrel." Gabby ran alongside Sarah, its footfalls silent as ever.

"I am Jasmayre, Monarch of Tyrrane, Steward to the Son of the Serpent, and Daughter to the failed King Brannok Swifthart the Second. I am willing to fight you if you are willing to die."

The cacophony of clattering wagon wheels filled the world. It bounced between the buildings and made it impossible to know what direction it came from. Arrows greeted them as they emerged from the market alley, but they were fired in haste by far fewer Host. None connected with their targets. This street, far from the wide avenue full of flat-faced shops and businesses they'd just fled, was narrow and crowded in with tall tenement buildings that closed in over it and blocked the sun.

It was still wide enough for Jasmayre's wagon, though.

"Across the street. Over here. *Faster.*" Gabby gestured from a thin shadowy passage between a square stone tower and a grim-looking tavern. To Sarah's left, the Fell Citadel glowered down on them, an angry mountain atop a hillside filled with swords and arrows. Much closer, Jasmayre and her oxen crackled across the cobbles of a side street and turned toward them.

"You killed Omah Finnagel, Sorcerer of Greenshade." Jasmayre's steel-hafted spear tore the air it cut through, and she spoke with hurricanes and thunder. "I suppose I should express my gratitude. As a girl, I was threatened with tales of the monster Finnagel who would snatch up Tyrranean babies and stew them in his rusted iron pot."

"Oldam's pebbly pee-pee, lady." Keane stumped along at top speed as he shouted. "Have you *seen* you? Finnagel was only an itty-bitty little monster in comparison."

Jasmayre glanced at Keane, and her body flared. Dark rings of black runes crawled across every inch of her, rings within rings of unimaginable complexity and power, only to vanish again in the blue sea of her skin. This magic was entirely self-contained. It required no connection to the outside world.

It was hardly fair.

Despite herself, Sarah shivered. Pain lanced her foot against the additional weight of the Sword on her shoulder as she raced across this much narrower—and darker—city road. Alarmed, she realized the man she carried no longer breathed.

She let him down in front of her. *I'm sorry.*

Gabby stopped in the middle of the road and yelled to Sarah, who now waited at the lightless footpath's entrance for Keane and the remaining Swords. "When you get past the tower, turn right and run until you hit the river. There are boats there. Don't stop."

Everyone reached the light-starved path between the two lengthy buildings, and the small band resumed their flight. It was skinny enough that they had to run with their shoulders at an angle, and a pile of crates in the middle halted their sprint for precious seconds.

Behind them, the huge wagon clattered past on the tenement street.

"I don't mean to sound alarmist," Gabby said, though Sarah could not even see where the Dead God's voice came from, "but I believe Princess Jasmayre intends to make the block and cut you off. A bit of hurry would not go awry."

"Can we go back?" Sarah nearly tripped over something metal and rusted in the dark that bit into her already torn foot. Lights danced in front of her eyes.

"Afraid not. The soldiers are already entering the pathway behind you."

Ahead, black-capped citizens of Dismon screamed and ran for cover from the all-encompassing clamor of iron-shod wheels on stone. Just as Sarah reached the path's far end, the huge wagon rattled to a stop in front of them, and the point of Jasmayre's enormous steel spear forced them all to halt. Gabby's assessment had proven entirely true.

"King in Greenshade. Do you bring peace or war to Tyrrane?"

"I'm gonna say peace?" Keane held out his hands, palms up. "That certainly seems safest."

"Are you not the War King?" Jasmayre's mouth hinted at a secret smile, promising storms. "Do you not even now gather troops from your allies to march on Dismon?"

"I think there's been a misunderstanding." Sarah spoke over whatever Keane had been about to say. "The king has been under the sway of Finnagel. He put a dominance moth on him. All that war-king business was Finnagel's doing."

Improbably, the illusion of the moth remained on Keane's head. With a mental flick, Sarah dismantled it.

"I might be inclined to believe you, Sarah." Jasmayre's smile became a bitter frown. "But your king is a liar and a murderer. He has killed three of my brothers. He may not leave here alive."

The side of the wagon covered the end of the pathway. Behind them, the Host grew closer. Sarah had caused this confrontation when she challenged Finnagel. It was at Gabby's behest, but she went along with it. This was her fault, and she would be the one to fix it.

Sarah slid one foot behind her to jump up into the wagon. The boot squelched and pushed blood out between the stitches. She believed Gabby's opinion that she would not survive a direct battle with this woman, but maybe she could buy Keane and the others time enough to get away.

Her legs tensed.

Gabby appeared in the wagon beside Jasmayre and caused the giantess to leap back, a hiss in her throat and her spear held low and ready.

She saw Gabby?

Not waiting for a group decision, Keane rolled under the wagon and came up running on the other side. The Swords followed. Sarah wanted to go with them, but Gabby gave her an opportunity here, one she could not allow to pass her by. So instead, she closed her eyes.

The blanket Sarah pulled down against the sources of magical power still held firm, but this perception Gabby taught her was passive. She did not need magic to use it.

Whirling black circles surrounded Jasmayre. Circles *made* of circles. *Thousands* of them. Complex, interconnected, and solid. If Sarah had a year to pick it apart, she *might* be able to do it.

Wait. What was *that*?

She opened her eyes, the mental vision laid atop her actual sight.

On the other side of the wagon, Keane and the Swords ran south toward the Blackwood River, and the people of Tyrrane screamed and bolted for cover. Behind her, she heard the Host enter the darkened path.

But in Sarah's inner gaze, she saw a hot red splinter shoved deep into the construct of Jasmayre's mind, and she knew exactly what it was. To her immense relief, Sarah could clearly see that the sliver of Angrim had no access to outside magic here. He would not even be able to witness these events or control Jasmayre. Manipulating the ability of sorcerers and runecrafters to power their spells would prove to be an incredibly valuable weapon against him in the future.

Should she survive today.

A piece of the demon inhabited and dominated Jasmayre. Now Sarah knew why Angrim had turned her into this creature—so her body could withstand the violence of his presence.

The spear flashed forward and pierced Gabby. Though the Dead God's form provided no resistance to the huge blade, Jasmayre's lunge tore Gabby open as surely as if it were made of smoke.

Did Sarah just watch Gabby die? Could Gabby be killed? Wasn't it already the Dead God? *The* Dead God?

Sarah swallowed her feelings. They would not help her now. She dove under the wagon rather than onto it and came up on the other side ready to break into a full sprint when the butt of a steel spear jabbed her in the back of the neck. She went down on the stones and bashed the side of her face against them.

Far away down the slope of the grand wide thoroughfare, she saw the Blackwood, merchant boats crawling past along its frothy surface.

Sarah rolled over and pulled herself to her feet. She could hear Keane yelling at her, but with everything spinning, she could not pin him down.

Arrows flew past her from the front and thudded into flesh behind. Jasmayre growled. Sarah was certain the giant woman would have crushed the King's Swords had she not been as cut off from sorcery as Sarah was.

A small cry escaped Sarah every time her knife-stabbed foot

struck the street, and her head pounded behind her eyes, but she still managed to run. A loud crack sounded behind her as of immense feet crashing down on the cobblestoned street, lending her speed and fear in equal measure.

Loudly thudding footsteps pounded the stones at Sarah's back. Keane screamed ahead.

Sarah ran faster. Jasmayre had already killed Gabby. If she killed Sarah, Keane would be but instants behind. The giant woman's bounding steps shook the ground. Sarah ran faster still.

Just not fast enough.

As easy as lifting a child's doll, Jasmayre's long-fingered hand closed around Sarah's wrist and lifted her up off the cobbles with a jerk. Wrist bones ground together. Sarah gasped and squeezed her eyes shut, her teeth clenched in a vise that could crush stone.

Caught between Sarah's cracking wrist and Jasmayre's relentless grip, the rune engine popped and died, the last of its energy steaming away in yellow smoke. Sarah, half blind with pain, tried to stab at Jasmayre with her sword arm, but the giantess caught it easily and held Sarah up in front of her by the arms.

"*Button. Finally mine. So delicate. With no place of power to call home.*" The voice changed. The storm was gone, replaced by scraping rock. Angrim had managed to pierce the blanket, if only barely, and asserted himself at last.

"*When I pluck your wings, you will not fly away, little Button. You will only die. WHAT—?*"

Jasmayre went off-kilter and stumbled to one side. With one hand she reached for something behind her, and Keane went the other way.

Just before Sarah closed her eyes, she saw Keane's sword sticking out of Jasmayre's right buttock. Three yellow-fletched arrows thumped into Jasmayre's side.

Perfect timing.

The runecrafting around Jasmayre was too well created. Sarah would be killed a thousand times over before she could unravel it. But she *could* touch Jasmayre, if only slightly.

In her mind, Sarah reached out to Jasmayre, who reacted with a lightning-fast assault, buffeting Sarah back. But this was Sarah's trap. She *saw* the battle, while Jasmayre only flailed in reaction.

Sarah clutched at Jasmayre's fist—she clutched at Jasmayre's imaginary fist with her own imaginary hands—and tore at it. Without the rune engine, this one act took almost all the strength she had. While Jasmayre howled, both in the street and in their minds, Sarah spun Jasmayre's fist into a spike and stabbed it with all of her strength into the bright red splinter of Angrim.

Sarah was pitched to the street.

"I am not yours!" It was Jasmayre's voice with no thunder and no scraping rock. "I hate you. I will *always* hate you." And to Sarah, "Flee. Go now. You will not have another chance. *I command it.*"

Sarah held her throbbing wrist as she and Keane ran south toward the Blackwood River, the three remaining King's Swords ahead of them. She spied wild-eyed horses tied off in front of a dreary tavern and angled right.

Once Keane was mounted, they rode hard south, but they had not gotten far enough for Sarah not to hear Angrim's reply to Jasmayre.

"You are what I have made you, Queen of Tyrrane. I will make you love me."

41

OLIVES MAKE THE HEART GROW FONDER

MORHOLT

Romi's ranch house looked south over a small meadow into woodland. Her orchards north and east rolled up and down over the low countryside hills. A pair of burly Morholts played a game of draughts on the long porch, stopping briefly to watch Catlia run inside. Romi volunteered to teach her how to farm as a means to help pull the frightened woman up from her fears.

Nearby, their horses grazed, happy to be standing still in the rich green grass, the golden afternoon light giving them a last kiss before retiring for the night.

Although the journey here was long, Morholt, Raven, and Romi all found themselves stopped in the long grass in front of the house. Beside it was a rusting heap with blades and edges that Morholt assumed must have been some kind of farming equipment but would not have been surprised to discover in the dungeons of some horrible bastard's castle. He wanted to go inside, but he couldn't bring himself to do it. The trip, the danger, the breathless rescues—so many feelings churned inside him. If he went inside her home, he might never leave.

And he had to leave. He made a promise to Raven, and he would not let her down. Also, Romi let him know without doubt that she did not want him around. With Finnagel and Prolocutor Vancess dead, even the Temple of the Sky did not seem like so much of a threat anymore.

"Oh, stop." Raven flicked her fingers at her brother. "If I'd wanted to stare at sad assholes, I'd have gone to Norrik and watched the sheep."

"What?" Romi's brows went up.

"She's saying that Norrikmen fuck their sheep, and it makes the sheep's assholes sad," Morholt spoke without any emotion in his voice. He just did not trust himself to open that floodgate. This was *so* much harder than he had thought it would be.

"Oh." Romi smiled. "That's funny."

Raven rolled her eyes. "Especially when you explain it like you're dissecting a puppy."

"I..." Romi put one weathered hand on Morholt's chest. "That is... thank you." She flattened her hand against his breast and stroked him ever so slightly.

Morholt turned his head away. He felt as if he would explode, or wail, or fall into tiny pieces. This was too much.

"I appreciate everything you've done for me. All of it. Both of you." She removed the hand, and Morholt started breathing again. "More than you'll ever know. Holt, you gave me a life here. I'd have been some farmhand's wife if not for the gifts you taught me. Then you gave me that life back when a bunch of evil bastards tried to take it from me."

"He'd have done the same for anyone he thought might fuck him again." A grin spread across Raven's thin face.

Unable to stop himself, Morholt chuckled. "That's probably true."

"Hmph." Romi's hands went to her hips. "I'm trying to tell you I still love you, jackass."

Raven's grin vanished. Her eyes slitted, and her jaw clenched.

"You mean you want to give it another go?" Morholt could not believe what he was hearing. She *just* told him the exact opposite.

Romi cut her eyes at Raven and moved several steps away. "No.

I'm sorry, Holt. Like I said, we both know what the end of *that* road looks like. Also, I don't want to get murdered in my sleep." She nodded to Raven, who only lifted her jaw in return. "I just don't have much to give you in return for everything you've done. I wanted you to know you had my love. For what it's worth."

Morholt's hand went to Raven's shoulder to keep him upright. "You could come with us. We'd be able to use your skills where we're going."

"I'm not going to do that." Romi pulled in a deep breath and let it out. "It'd be the same thing. We've already *made* that mistake."

"So you keep saying." He felt gutted, hollow.

"I love both of us too much to let that happen again." Romi cast a glance over her shoulder at the porch. "Love and heartsick is still better than hate and resentment. Would you hang on for a second?" She walked away from them toward the house.

"She's right, Holt." Raven did not meet Morholt's gaze. "I love you guys, but I hate you guys together. Everything's great now, but it wouldn't last. You want to be in the middle of fighting our parent's army of attack-fucks when *that* shit pie explodes in our faces? You do *not*."

"Raven, I can't *breathe*."

"I know it feels bad now. But you'll get over it. Trust me, I know how losing someone feels." She patted his hand and smiled at him, not unkindly. "You're going to have plenty to think about. We have to get back to the Undergates, all the way across the Infernal Kingdoms to Savach, sneak through *there* to the estate, and *then* figure out how to kill Mom and Dad. Your dinner plate's already full of dicks."

Morholt resented Raven for his promise to take her home. He resented her for Romi's refusal to be his wife once more. Most of all, he resented her for being right.

"When it's all over with back home, assuming we're still on the drinking and screwing side of the dirt, you'll come back. Bring flowers. Try not to be such a selfish prick, and see if she'll have you." Raven brushed off Morholt's grip on her shoulder and clapped him on the arm. "I don't want you to be miserable, brother, but your relationship brain isn't done cooking yet. You aren't ready for her. And I *know* you don't want to be the one who makes *her* miserable."

"What if I come back and she's already found someone else?"

"Then you kill that guy and step in a month later when she's all needy." Raven smiled sweetly and fluttered her eyelashes. "You'll be her hero."

He shook his head. "You're a monster. If I didn't *have* to love you just because you're my sister, I'd probably set you on fire."

"Glad I never told you about you being adopted."

Romi returned bearing a large glass jar full of green olives bobbing in brine. "This is kinda stupid, but I thought you might like something to keep ahold of for a while. From me. The cork is painted. I mean I painted it. It's supposed to be an olive tree. You could hold onto it as a keepsake after you finish the olives if you wanted to."

The glass jar was heavy, but Fog, the gray brindle Morholt stole back in Sheaf, would not mind overmuch. "Yeah, I'd like that." He glanced at the ranch house. "Do you really think that Catlia is going to be all right here?"

"Dunno," Romi replied. "But farming helped me, I don't see why it can't help her. I'm honestly more worried about that Ameli girl. Those boys're gonna have their hands full with her."

After burying Reinar at the Dovenhouse, Ameli sank into a depression that looked from the outside both bottomless and isolating. When she killed a boy in the streets outside Sejent for winking at her, Sabni and Mahu decided to take her under their wing and shepherd her recovery. They not only keenly felt their debt to her, they also felt responsible for Reinar's passing and Ameli's sadness.

Of course, it was not their fault. It was Morholt's. A hollow stab of guilt gutted him yet again, as it cut him when he had been forced to make the decision to save Mahu over Reinar, and every time he thought of it since then. That invisible blade did not slice just him but also the fellowship he worked so hard to maintain amongst the other mercenaries.

The Free Hand was gone. It had never become what Morholt wanted for it anyway.

"Ameli and Mahu are tight," Raven said, "and it's not possible to stay sad around Sabni for long. Angry, maybe. Desperate for quiet. But not sad."

Morholt sighed. In the end, Reinar and Ameli were just another thing to feel bad about even though the big Mirrikman had been looking for an opportunity to go out in some great orgasm of stupidity, squirting bravery all over everybody as he died.

Asshole.

"Well, this is about all of this shit I can stand." Morholt gathered Romi to him in his non-olive-bearing arm. "Take care of yourself. If I'm not dead, I'll be back inside of two years. Make that three. Can you wait that long?"

Romi grinned broadly and wiped away a tear. "I'm not waiting for you, dumbass. There's lotsa gentlemen around these parts'd be happy to make my intimate acquaintance. I'm not some temple postulant."

Raven elbowed Morholt in the ribs. "No worries. Holt here can stand the pressure. He's a hero that way."

The three hugged and moved to the horses, where Morholt secured the jar of olives.

"I have a theory about Sarah." Raven raised a finger into the air.

Morholt and Romi exchanged a look. Raven had been theorizing since the Dovenhouse all the reasons Sarah might have abandoned them the way she did. Those reasons were rarely charitable.

"I think she fucked a dog and had to run home to nurse her puppies. It's really the only explanation. Come on, it's sweet that she's so motherly, right? *And* it explains why she's such a bitch." Raven shrugged at Romi's scowl.

The three made their final goodbyes, and Raven and Morholt rode west. The setting sun hung low and orange in the sky ahead of them. Though it broke what was left of his heart to do it, Morholt twisted around in the saddle and waved goodbye to Romi, who had not yet moved from her spot in the grass.

She waved back.

"You know, I think I'm going to miss knowing how all this is going to turn out. With Sarah and the king and the temple and Tyrrane and all that mess." Morholt lowered Fog's reins once they reached the narrow track through the woods and nudged him ahead with a squeeze of his knees.

"That's not our story anymore." Raven leaned forward and scratched Nightwind behind the ears. The horse made an appreciative groan deep in its chest. "Our story is ahead of us. Forward. All these Andos fuckers're trying to hold us back."

"I'm not sure going back to Mom and Dad's house is really a step forward."

"That's not their house," Raven said, her teeth glinting in what dying light made its way through the leaves. "It's mine."

"Scary." Morholt smiled sideways at his sister. "Although I'm the oldest. Technically, it'll be *my* house."

"Try me, fuckstick. I am *literally* an expert in making accidents happen to people." She pulled at the armpit of her dark leathers. "Would you like your rooms to be where we let the dogs shit or the servants? I could go either way."

"If I'm dead of accidental face stabs, I doubt I'll care. I am going to insist on a nice funeral though."

Raven flicked black hair out of her eyes. No matter how short she cut it, there always seemed to be enough to hang in her face. "I'm not spending *my* money on *your* funeral. Get your own."

"That's it, I'm going back. I'll take my chances with the suicidal Greenshaders." Morholt grinned openly now and did not turn Fog around.

"Hey, that reminds me. For the past forever since we got here—what, twenty years or something?—you've been teaching your sex bunnies to runecraft. And not once did you make any of them an engine. It's what broke up you and Selenna, and you barely survived what it did to you and Glauth. Then Sarah tries to straight up murder you, and you give her the thing right off your own arm. And what does she do? She promptly fucks the fuck off with it." One brow went up on Raven's face. "I kinda think you're an idiot."

Morholt laughed.

"You know, I kinda think you're right." The conversation paused while Morholt thought about where on the island of Kos he could open a door to the Undergates and when he might create a new rune engine. He'd have to get it done before they finished crossing the demonlands. Things would get a lot more dangerous once they entered the human country of Savach. But he would make a better one this time anyway. He had plenty of ideas about it.

Raven drew a curved dagger and sighted along the edge. "Fuck a donkey. It's nicked." She sheathed the dagger while she rubbed oil onto a whetstone and pulled it out again. "I bet I know the very asshole whose ribs I caught it on. That pisses me off. I ought to go back and kill him some more."

"He's just lucky he didn't scratch the grip. I can't imagine how upset you'd be if he'd spoiled your date night."

The dagger flipped up into the air and Raven caught it by the steel. She considered the pommel for a second and then flipped it again, pointing the talon-shaped blade at Morholt's head.

"You can have a date night too. Just hop off that horse and bend over."

"With my *sister's* knives? Yuck. No thanks. I'll stab myself in the butthole with a respectable stranger-lady's knife, thank you very much." They rode in silence for a few hundred feet before Morholt spoke again. "Just promise me that no matter what else happens, you won't let me teach any more women how to runecraft unless we've been having sex at least a month."

"Done," Raven replied with a wry smile.

42

EVERYTHING IS TURNING UP ANGRIM
JASMAYRE

Lightning battered the countryside all around Dismon. Advancing like black and gray clouds, a sky bound Ebon Host on the march to war against sunlight and hope bore down on the city.

From her vantage far above the bleak and utilitarian capital, Jasmayre watched the citizens clutch their black felt caps and run for shelter. It had been a month of raving and madness for her since her battle in the streets with the Hill Fury, and while Jasmayre still did not understand what Angrim's precious button had done to her, she was no longer hobbled by it.

And her master's strength burned the Fury's effect on his place of power away as so much chaff caught in an open field.

A peal of thunder hit Jasmayre, rolling over her as a wave in the water might a stalk of river grass. The Fell Citadel squatted a hundred yards below her bare feet, an ugly canker on the head of an unappealing city.

She missed her father.

Rain fell as the tears came. She had not mourned her king, not while her soul and body healed the things Angrim had done to her. A sob escaped her traitorous throat, drowned by the sounds of rain and thunder. So much loss. After so many years of inattention, she had finally earned a place by her father's side only to have it stolen away alongside her very humanity.

What was she now? An orphan. A monster. Stripped of all meaning and love. Chattel for the angry godling that lived in the bowels of the mountain.

"What am I?"

"You are a queen."

Jasmayre spun, startled to find Angrim floating beside her. His cowl was back, and rain pattered off his hairless white head. One thin arm stretched out to her to take her hand.

He was so beautiful.

Her hand in his, the disease and filth tactile beneath smooth white skin, she allowed herself to be pulled into his embrace. The horror of worlds lay there, yet she drew his arms around her and smiled.

"We are remade, Queen of Tyrrane. This place of motes and the so-called gods that think to watch over it. We shall ascend past them all. We will be limitless."

"How?" Jasmayre wondered that her voice had returned to normal though her body remained nine feet tall and the shade of a day-old bruise. She felt she needed to know what Angrim's plans were. Would she follow him, or would she batter herself to death against the rocky cliffs of his will as her father had? "What will we do?"

"It is not time for you to know, Queen of Tyrrane. I do not explain myself to my hand when I reach for a throat to crush. Your purpose is my bidding. Nothing more."

"I am sorry, my lord. I will not ask you again. And for the button. Sarah. I... failed you. I let her escape."

"You let her escape because I willed it so. The sorceress contains a power I do not understand. She must be allowed to roam. Exercise her abilities. I will watch and learn her secrets. And then I will smite her down with them."

Jasmayre's skin crawled—and thrilled—at his touch. Millennia of corruption and hate pulled her ever tighter against him. There was no warmth in that pale hard body, only despair.

Why then was he so captivating?

"The Alir and the P'tak hide in their mountains and the multitudes of the Untamed in their paradises so far from here. By the time they understand, it will be too late. They hide from the Dead God. I strike at the Dead God. It will fall alongside all the others. We are unassailable. We cannot be defeated."

As everyone else had fallen. As her king fell.

Angrim's beauty and his decay entwined her, held her fast— enraptured—like a burned and wingless moth still crawling toward the flame.

A release in her brain flooded her with pleasure and strength. New abilities whispered themselves into her ears. This occurred with increasing frequency and... intensity.

What am I? What am I becoming?

But Jasmayre knew what she would be as she floated in the storm, wrapped in those perfect gleaming arms of violence and depravity— the same arms that broke her father like a fox biting down on a hen's egg.

She would be what her *father* would have wanted her to be.

She would be vengeance.

43

ARE YOU TRYING TO TELL ME THIS ISN'T THE END?

SARAH

The swelling in Sarah's wrist receded daily which meant the splints needed to be tightened every morning. But the pain also faded, and now her right wrist made an exciting new clicking sound when she twirled it.

When the damn splints weren't on it. The castle surgeon became *very* irate when she tried to demonstrate the noise.

Volker and Shayla ran in circles around the Red Room and ignored their father's pleas for quiet. Volker stabbed at the white and gold figures in the tapestries with a wooden play sword, slaying them in the name of the kingdom while Shayla directed him which ones to kill for the best loot. Megan stared at the map table brought in from the war room and scowled.

"I don't see any way to avoid it." She leaned forward on the table and brown curls fell from her shoulders. "If we don't move ahead with Finnagel's plan to invade Tyrrane, we're done for. Jason Swifthart has married Tove the Mountain, and it looks like all of Norrik is going to fall in line. We have a month, maybe two, before we're overrun with Northmen."

"What about Coldspine?" Keane grunted as he spoke, trying to pull Volker away from the tapestries. Not one to go peacefully, the prince threw his miniature sword to his sister, who slayed the king in his own name. "*Ouch*. Don't we have our own Northmen to throw at them?"

"I was counting Coldspine. Children, don't slay your father. This would certainly be easier if we could get Egren or Verran in the fight. I think they're just hoping all the Andosh countries tear themselves to bits so they can move in and finish the job."

Sarah leaned back in her plush chair and closed her eyes. This was bliss. Back with her friends, the sounds of kids run amok, and a warm breeze fluting in through high and narrow windows. The dull red paint on the three interior walls was not the red of combat; it was the comforting red you saw behind closed eyelids, and the bright paintings and tapestries that festooned the walls turned the space light, busy, and intimate.

"Hello, Sarah."

She jerked up out of her doze to find Gabby on a stool next to her. Its calm smile spoke of reassurance and optimism. Or maybe that was her own relief at its not being murdered on the end of Jasmayre's spear.

"Hey there. I kinda thought you'd been killed. Again." Sarah was not sure what the rules were for gods. Especially if they were already dead.

Keane and Megan exchanged looks. "Sorcerer thing," Keane said. The children played on.

"Not quite, though I admit to having been taken aback a bit." Gabby smoothed the front of its worn linen tunic. "I was not expecting to be perceived, much less discorporated. I was looking for a weak spot. Instead, she seemed to have found mine."

"I think you've made a few more waves up here in our world than you realized." Sarah smiled crookedly at it. "They were ready for you, thank the wisdom. If Jasmayre hadn't seen you and attacked, I'm not sure I'd have gotten away."

"Should've run when I ran." Keane lifted a laughing Volker over his head while Shayla chopped at his knees.

"Thank you, My King." Sarah stuck her tongue out at Keane.

Shayla giggled and stuck her tongue out at him too. "Although I'd like to point out that if I'd behaved as well as the crown from the first, we'd all be wearing bugs for hats and doing Finn's bidding. Instead, we're playing with the kids and relaxing in comfy chairs and *that* bastard is dead."

Keane put Volker down and rubbed his hip. "No one likes a showoff."

"Yes, well, that was something I wanted to talk to you about. You no longer have a mentor at all now that Finnagel is dead for real." Gabby nodded along to emphasize its points. "But Sarah, you *need* a teacher. Sorcery is about power, and runecrafting is about control. But they are two halves of a single thing, and that thing is what makes the gods what they are. I can teach you all of that. I can teach you everything. I can make you *the* new god."

Sarah looked around her. Everything she had ever wanted was in this room. There was only one more thing to set right. It was a conversation she had been putting off, but it needed to happen. "I think it's time I stopped living under the wing of powerful people who are just looking for tools to push their own agendas."

"That's not fair."

"I'm not saying you haven't been good to me. You have. I wouldn't even be alive if not for the things you've taught me. I have an ability that no other sorcerer *or* runecrafter has. But Harden was good to me in the beginning. So was Finnagel. I don't want to be the woman who keeps making the same mistakes over and over."

Gabby cocked its head to one side. It was its only mannerism she could think of that had not been lifted from her.

"But you're not. Surely you must see that. I've never lied to you."

The sounds of play and plans quieted. Sarah became intensely aware that everyone was staring at her. But this was her family. They understood.

"No." Sarah pressed her lips together and sat up in the chair. "You haven't. But this isn't about you. It's about me growing up and standing on my own two feet. I can't do that as long as I'm in the shadow of some great man or another. That's my pattern. It's self-destructive, and I'm not going to do it anymore."

"Hey." Keane crossed his arms. "Standing right here."

Megan tutted at him. "She obviously wasn't talking about you, dear."

"You can't do this alone." Gabby leaned forward, hands clasped in worry. "Angrim has millennia of experience. He has already shown himself capable of things even I had no idea were possible. How do you intend to stand against that? I'm all for your personal journey, but don't you think the stakes are a bit high here?"

"I do." Sarah nodded. "And that's the other half of my thinking. If I have to make decisions that affect the lives of everyone around me, I need to know those decisions are being made free of the influence of agendas I don't fully understand. And before you argue, *you* are the very definition of a thing I do not fully understand."

At Gabby's defeated expression, Sarah continued, "I'm not saying I don't want you around or that I don't want to learn from you. I'm only saying that I'm not following your orders anymore. I'll decide when it's time to attack the all-powerful sorcerers. I let you throw me into a situation that almost got me killed."

"Still right here." Keane raised a hand. "Almost killed too."

"That can't happen again." Sarah pushed herself further back in the chair. "If you have a plan you want to let me in on, I'm all ears. Otherwise, I'm driving this carriage. You're just a road sign." At Gabby's bleak expression, Sarah leaned forward to explain.

"Relax. We're friends. You are *nothing* like Harden and Finnagel. I'm not judging you for having your own goals, even if they're not mine. All I'm saying is that rather than you leading me into the unknown, for this to work, I need you beside me lighting the way."

"That may not be enough." Gabby gave a small sigh. "If I'd taken the time to teach you everything you truly needed to know for our experience in Dismon, we'd have been several years too late, and you'd either be dead or in Finnagel's thrall."

"It'll be enough." And she knew it would be. "Have a little faith in me."

Gabby sighed and slapped its hands down on its thighs. "I suppose you're right. Life is for the living and all that. You know I have an end goal in mind: annihilate the Alir and the P'tak and take back the life they stole from me. But I also want us to be friends."

It smiled, though sadness stayed in its eyes. "I do have faith in you, Sarah. Quite a bit, really. You are unique in your world's age and still fragile. Remember that. Call if you need me. I'll be listening." And so saying, Gabby faded from Sarah's view.

"Why is Aunt Sarah's friend avisible?" Shayla asked, pulling on Megan's skirts.

Megan's brows came together. "I'm beginning to wonder just how much time Aunt Sarah's invisible friend spends wandering around the king and queen's private chambers."

"He's not watching when I jerk—*work*—on the royal... uh... things? *Paper*work. I'm talking about paperwork. Don't you kids have someplace to be?"

"We love you, Daddy," Volker said.

"We love you, Daddy," Shayla said.

Sarah smiled, then grinned, then laughed. Gabby had not been wrong. Sarah had always needed help and always would. And that was just fine.

She had faith in her friends.

KEVIN PETTWAY'S NEWSLETTER

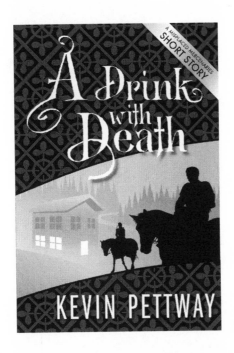

Join Kevin's newsletter and download this free adventure.

ACKNOWLEDGMENTS

Book four. Not so long ago that did not seem like an attainable goal, and as I sit and write this I am taking a break from book five, the finale of Keane and Sarah's saga.

How the hell did this happen?

Unsurprisingly, as with most of the miracles in my life, it starts with Lena. She gave me the space to find the thing I was passionate about and the shove in the ass not to run away from it once I had. A dear friend of mine tells me frequently that everyone needs a Lena, and it's true. Someone who believes in you so fervently that you begin to believe in yourself too. The experience is the very definition of life changing.

But this Lena is mine. Go get your own.

I can not discuss acknowledgements without bringing up Kelly Colby and her company Cursed Dragon Ship Publishing, as well as her husband Kevin. (I still believe that Kelly chose me as her first author to avoid embarrassing name slips.) At a recent convention I sat on an author panel and found myself explaining to the other writers how it was possible to be both partners and friends with your publisher, and how special that relationship truly was.

I think until that moment I did not understand the truth of that.

A lot of this job is just you, a chair, and a keyboard, and I think the popular conception of it is that's all you need. But it is not. The chair and the keyboard bring into focus just how much every other human being (and a few dog beings too) lift you up and make you able to do the work of bringing a bit of laughter and joy into people's lives. I'd like to acknowledge you here. From my loved ones and closest friends to the people who have touched my life in the most tangential fashion and everyone in between. I have seen you, and I appreciate you.

Finally, and most importantly, I would like to acknowledge the real you. The you who is reading this right now. It is possible I might have written a book without my Lena, though it certainly is not likely. It is possible I might have written a book without Kelly, though it would not have been close to as good. And while it is possible I might have written a book without you, the reader, there would not have been a point. You provide the purpose to my passion, and my career.

And I thank you more than I can say for it.

ABOUT THE AUTHOR

Years ago Kevin Pettway looked around and decided that while there was plenty of amazing fantasy produced today, there was a definite theme to it, and the Red Wedding just wasn't funny enough. Resolving to address this critical oversight, he has produced the Misplaced Mercenaries series of books, which puts the laughter back in slaughter.

Kevin Pettway has shaken the hands of several prominent authors whose names you might know, and has never had a restraining order filed against him—as of date of publication. Chief among his other accomplishments are taking first place in the Best Writer in His Own Household awards the last three years running. (Now that the funny dog has died.)

Kevin lives in Florida by the river in a house he always dreamt of, with a woman who is too good for him, and a pair of dogs who love him even when he forgets to feed them. (Unrelated to the funny dog incident.) Now he wants to be a writer because it is one of the few professions that will overlook his cursing with profusion and gusto in public.

You can find Kevin on FaceBook, Instagram, or his own website at www.kevinpettway.com. To file a restraining order against him, please call your local sheriff's department.

facebook.com/kevinpettwayauthor

instagram.com/kevinpettwayauthor

MISPLACED MERCENARIES
BY KEVIN PETTWAY